# HER DE
# OWED

## BOX SET COLLECTION
## BOOKS 1-3

# EMMA JAMES

**HER DEBT OWED BOX SET**
Copyright © 2021 by Emma James

Published by Emma James.

All rights reserved. No part of this book may be reproduced or transmitted in any form or by any means, electronic or mechanical, including photocopying, recording, or by any information storage and retrieval system, without permission in writing. Except in the case of brief quotations embodied in critical articles or reviews. For permission requests, email the author at authoremmajames@bigpond.com

This is a work of fiction. Names, characters, places are incidents are the product of the author's imagination or are used fictitiously, and any resemblance to any actual persons, living or dead, events, or locales is entirely coincidental.

This book is licensed for your personal enjoyment only. This may not be re-sold or given away to other people. If you would like to share this book with another person, please purchase an additional copy of each person you share it with. If you are reading this book and did not purchase it, or it was not purchased for your use only, then you should return it to the seller and purchase your own copy. Thank you for respecting the author's work.

Cover Design: Najla Qamber
        www.najlaqamberdesigns.com
Editing: Hot Tree Editing
        www.hottreeediting.com
Formatting: Cover Story Book Designs
        www.coverstorybookdesigns.com

# PRAISE FOR HER DEBT OWED

I'm just not sure if I can express how much I loved this book. I was concerned going into this read that I would have trouble separating this type of writing from Emma's previous work (which I also loved) but it wasn't even a problem. The story-line was clear and there were times I was right on the edge of my seat. I find with a lot of stories, after a few chapters I can kind of piece together a rough idea of what is going to happen .... not in this case. I read the entire thing in one sitting I just couldn't stop and put it down!!

**Jessica Cullen**

Emma James has created a darkly wonderful piece of art. Gritty, poignant and beautiful, I couldn't put it down!

**Author Cherry Shephard**

WOW... I'm not one for a dark read but holy S$%t, this story had me hooked from start to finish.... the stress of the unknown, wanting Whisper who has never had anything good to get some peace.

**Raelene Barns**

Emma you have turned me into an addict once again! Your books are amazing and this one is no different!

Dark, edgy, sexy and exciting is what this book is! Whisper is an amazing character who is working through everything she has been through along with learning things about herself that she never thought possible! Then comes Edge! He's built, sexy as sin and a biker that holds no bar!

**Book Boyfriend Hangover Maria York**

Wow!!!! Great book.... With a twisted line up on characters and story.

**Nicole Feichtl**

I honestly had no emotional control reading this story. None at all. And damn it if I don't prefer dark stories - it's my thing. With Wrenched, your emotions get hijacked, are never returned and you can't help but feel like you won't be the same person once you finish with the story... the pacing of the story and the characters specific perspectives were amazingly well crafted.

**Jelena Bosh**

OMG Shhhhhhhhsh it got hot and steamy - by the end I wanted more.

**Selena**

5 HUGE THRILLING DARK STARS!! You're not going to want to put this one down!!! Give yourself a few hours, this is DEFINITELY a one sitting read!!!
**Mommy's Naughty Playground, Missy Harton**

WOW! This is not your normal MC read! Wrenched is dark, twisted and utterly fantastic. Right from the first I was hooked and could not put this book down.
**United Indie Book Blog, Raychel Shannon-Faulkner**

I am going to start my review by saying GET.THIS.BOOK.NOW. Pre-order or one-click, whatever you have to do to get this book on your reading device ASAP. Wrenched is a complex, dark tale, written from multiple POV. This is a writing style Ms James seems to have mastered. I enjoyed the depth of story created by being able to get different perspectives.
**Tina Louise**

This is very easy to get into, enjoying the author's easy flow writing style, her use of words, how straight away you start inhaling what's written.
**Kitty Kats Crazy About Books, Kat Fenton**

A read where the darkness pulled me in with a crack of light, but still in the dark.
**Rebecca Paterson**

Emma has taken on a dark romance and has blown me away with this story. Her characters had me reeled in the story is full of suspense and has you guessing what's happening next.

**Debb Lynn**

I really enjoyed the story and as always the author's descriptions keep you completely enthralled with the plot. Such extremes in the character's personalities it was fascinating to see how she brought it all together.

**Book Boyfriends Rock, Karen Lee**

I was given an Arc of Wrenched by Emma James and holy hell I'm I glad to have been given this opportunity to read it. This book hooked me from the first page it is dark intense and not for the faint hearted.

**Tracey Supple**

Emma James wrote with such detail and depth that you simply couldn't be anything other than drawn to every page turned. An absolutely captivating, hard core, highly emotional read that has so many twists which you will never see coming.

**BFDU, Bloggers From Down Under**

HOLY HOT HELL'S BASTARD!!!!

**Sam Shemeld**

Beta read. This has just started another addiction for another series of books. Awesome plot and brilliant characters. I loved it xxx

**Hot Tree Editing, Andrea**

HOLY SHHHH....CRAP.

Honestly that was an intense read and I can say without bias because I'm not much of a reader of dark romance that I still enjoyed the action and tense moments in the book.

**Janet**

Awesome storyline, awesome writing and a bit scary and freaky, but so worth the read. I cannot wait for the next book to come out! Emma James you ROCK!

**Flavs is Mrs David Gandy**

Emma has given so much detail in so few words, and she has you hanging on each word right to the very end. Trust me, you will never guess where the story goes, as there are curve balls throughout.

**Kasey Crees**

Holy hotness I'm unsure where to start. Wrenched will take you on a roller coaster ride , you'll be covering your eyes not wanting to read on yet opening your fingers to peer to find out more .

**Page Flipperz, Katrina**

I'm in love with Emma's writing style. I enjoy the many different POV she uses in her books. Although it's a dark read, which usually takes me a couple of chapters to get in to, it draws you in from page one. There's so much happening, you can feel it at every page turning. I could just imagine how Whisper's first chapter played out. So detailed in her writing.

**Jolene Hendriks**

This story was everything I love in a book: hot, dark, violent, suspenseful, and packed with twists and turns. I loved the complexity of the story, and the way the characters were unknowingly interconnected with each other. Whisper and Edge are two people that come from different worlds and are thrown together due to circumstance.

**Samantha Baker**

Emma James has written a dark, gritty romance that keeps you guessing through out the book. My heart was racing with the suspense! I can't wait for the sequel, Warped, to be released!

**Laura Colson**

OH. MY. GOD. Mind officially blown. My body is full of goose bumps, my insides are twisting and my mind is yelling at the book. This, is my body's response to this tale.

**Kasey Crees**

I am blown away by this book by Emma James. She is one of those authors who can do multiple POVs and do it well.

**Jaime**

Wrenched is brilliantly written, dark, shocking, gritty, intense, raw, twisted, thought provoking, addictive... it is everything. It's edgy and will have you hanging on the edge of your seat. Emma James has created an amazing story that grabs you in the prologue and has you turning the pages to see how the story develops. You are captivated, intrigued, consumed, and mystified.

**Cheryl Graham Petit**

Emma James is a new author to me and I loved her spin on the genre. From the first chapter I was hooked and by the last page I was shocked.

**Jezabell Girl & friends, Luc**

I absolutely loved this story I got so sucked in I finished in 3hrs. You will love this read! I kept going NO Way, wait what??? OMG run lol!

**Kristina Ehrler**

I'm usually not a fan of cliffhangers, but this one was intriguing and sucked me in. I want the next book and I want it now!

**Suzy**

Hot Damn!!!! Wrenched is such a refreshing change from the books I have read of late and I cannot rave enough about it. This may have an MC character in it but it is not an 'MC' book, but the aspects add that level or danger all the same. Emma James has a distinct style of writing and it is an incredible gift. She allows us access to numerous characters as she builds her story, both of which speak volumes of how much she puts into her work. Not only that, she also has a way of introducing plot twists that you cannot see coming. That is another gift and why I will be a fan of her for a long time to come.

**Sarez Tomoan**

Once again Emma has done it. She has drawn me into a book that I couldn't put down. Wrenched is a story of revenge but not the type we are all use too. I'm not one to often read dark romance but I loved this one.

**Two Peas In A Pod, Donna Miller**

This book is a dark read but I simply couldn't put this book down or recommend enough.

**Cally Boyd**

Ok this book is not for the faint hearted if you're looking for a typical MC love story this isn't it.

**Adriana**

Omg this book is totally awesome love each and every character. Once again Emma you've done it again, very well written love the story so much, can't wait to get the next part.

**Mischelly Velasquez**

I'm into MC books, rough, raw and biker men that are sexy as hell! This book was a bit atypical from my normal MC books that I read, it has some major suspense and very dark moments. It definitely kept me on the edge of my seat biting my nails, and turning pages as fast as my fingers would go.

**Jen**

Emma, Emma, Emma what have you done, I'll tell you what you've done. You have just got yourself a new life long fan. This story is dark, twisted and hot I'm going to take a while to forgive you for what you have done to me it's going to be a very long wait till the next book and I may or may not hound you about it.

**Chrissy Van Der Laan**

What could I write that would do this AMAZING dark addition to the Hell's Bastard justice. This book begins where Wrenched ended and like the first book it had me hooked from the start. So dark, so sinister, so good.

**Raelene Barns**

Absolutely awesome book!!

**Cassie Hess-Dean**

6 STARS. INTENSE...DARK...UNPREDICTABLE... CONSUMING... IT IS UNDENIABLY WARPED !

I could not put this book down. The plot is extremely complex and the web became more tangled. New characters were introduced and it was impossible to determine where this story would go next. I was on the edge of my seat and biting my nails. The intensity level was through the roof. It added more kinks to the overall story and made it become more intensified. I can't wait to see what comes next. Warped was the perfect title and brilliant addition to the Hell's Bastard series by Emma James.

**Smut Book Junkies Book Reviews - Michel**

ABSOLUTELY AMAZING. A THRILLING, SUSPENSEFUL READ.

Oh Emma James, you tore apart my heart in WRENCHED and now you have blown apart my mind with WARPED. Never have I read a series that has had the ability to twist and turn my heart and mind in all directions...

**Reading Is Our Satisfaction - Maria Alexander**

AMAZING!! James brings these characters to life with her incredible imagery. Creating bonds and presenting a united front in this death defying ride of Warped and inconceivable actions. This riveting second installment in the Hell's Bastard Series is crippled with violence, inner turmoil, and an epic demonic under world.

**Missy Harton**

Warped. Man, what a crazy ride this book is. I enjoy all of the authors work, but Warped really blew me away. This book had me on the edge of my seat the entire time. I was just wanting to get through it as quickly as possible because I need to see what happens, but also wanted to savor it and make it last longer. It was so good. Emma really created a wonderfully twisted world that I can't get enough of! I am eager for more.

**Jen In Bookland**

Emma James you've just simply blown me away with another brilliant story. I was so excited to dive back into this crazy, dark world Emma has created and she didn't leave an ounce for disappointment in Warped. From start to finish I was on pins and needles, with on going twists and turns you're always left speechless and wanting more. I was utterly & completely hooked. Amazing character development (LOVE Edge!), emotions running high... my head is still reeling from it all.

**Sassy Book Lovers - Stacey**

Wrenched was not what I expected when I first received this book. Its very dark but utterly amazing. The characters show strength; a depth that most would never be able to achieve.

**Cherie Hocking**

OMFG!!!! Could this series get any better? I absolutely loved the complexity of the first book, Warped does not disappoint at all! And the characters... Again, it's an Addiction you just can't stop yourself from taking part in. Another MUST READ from Author Emma James!!!!

**She's A Lip Biter - Cherie**

A new Hell's Bastard is described so perfectly it brings a shudder to the reader. The description of the characters, settings and happenings are superb... Emma James once again takes you on a heart stopping ride and right up to the last sentence the reader is captivated and intrigued by the story.

**Robyn Corcoran**

Warped is the follow up to Wrenched and doesn't disappoint, Emma has dug deep with this series and I look forward to the next installment of Hell's Bastard series. This book has you hooked from the start and all too soon you're left wondering what's going to happen next.

**Debb Lynn**

Warped will Keep you on the Edge of your seat, whispering to yourself OMG ! Eager to flip each page and find out more. A gripping edge of your seat suspense. With Relentless tension, dramatic, intense and certainly compelling story line. Brilliantly written, absorbing and well delivered.

**Page Flipperz – Katrina Whittaker**

5 stars and nothing less!! Wrenched was amazing but Warped was addictive!! Emma, you have done it again! I need more of Miss Catherine, Edge, Whisper and the crew. I cannot wait to see what Contorted brings to the table with this series getting better and better!!!!!

**Jessica Cullen**

Warped started right where Wrenched left off. This novel is again another well written story filled with lots of emotion and it will have you hooked on each word. Emma James did a great job of giving the reader hope on one page and then dashing that hope on the next page. You will not be able to put it down as there are lots of twists and turns which will blow your mind.

**K Ramjohn**

These characters come to life and you are sucked into the pages. You are left feeling every emotion...frustration, anger, terror, excitement, and sadness. I need more of this series because I just love Edge and Whisper. Miss Catherine. Boxer. Lincoln. Heck, everyone even the bad guys because you want to be in the book kicking butt.

**Jaime Lynn**

WARPED is full of suspense and twists. Just as you think you know something boom something else happens.

**Two Peas In A Pod – Donna Miller**

OMG! What more is there to say? Mrs Emma James books never disappoint me. She takes her time with each character so u feel like u know them personally. She takes your mind to a new level and I promise it's a level that won't disappoint you.

**Kayla Lebouef**

It's the kind of read that has you on the edge of your seat waiting to see how everyone comes out and how much damage they are going to have when it's all over. There are some twists that I never saw coming which makes it a great read. I loved this one and can't wait to read the next one.

**Amazeballs Book Addicts**

Bloody hell!!!! There was a reason why I was stalling to finish it. Gaaaaaahh! Emma you're such an evil genius! Now I need to wait till the next one comes out! I'm stuck in the rabbit hole and never to be found not until I know what will happen next! It's so fucked up and twisted. I had goosebumps and chills while reading this. And the urge to slam my e-reader from the motherfucker bad guys!

**Caryl Casanova**

Oh my word, if you haven't read the previous book then you shouldn't read this book. It follows on exactly where Wrenched left off. I love the characters in this book, especially Miss Catherine. What a bad ass old lady with her talking bones...lol

**Flavs is Mrs David Gandy**

Emma James has woven an intricate Web of lies and deceit with a number of complex players caught within it. There is so many layers to this story and I feel as though we are still barely through the surface. It was suspenseful, intriguing and an absolute page turner.

**Sarez Tomoan**

What I love most about this series is the unpredictability. There are twists, turns and when one question is answered more are presented. I am an avid reader, and in most instances I can tell you how the story will end. Hells Bastards has me thinking, guessing and re-evaluating constantly.

**Tina Louise**

Warped had me on the Edge (pardon the pun lol) from the beginning to the end. Contorted cannot come out soon enough!

**Shell Giallo**

Hmm… How to describe the way I'm feeling after reading Warped… It's like being in a damn good action film! I bit all my nails (again) Emma!!! I can feel it in dem bones of mine that November ( "Contorted") will not come soon enough for me.

**Jolene Hendriks**

# BY EMMA JAMES

## Men of Ocean Beach Series
Retro (A Little Faith)
Keanu (Hope Is Lost)
Levi (Joy is Found)
Harley (Will to Protect) (*Coming 2022*)

## Standalones
Bearing the Rock Star (Paranormal novella)
Fangs for the Memories
King's Gambit

Cocky Caveman
(Tucker Royal & Ophelia from Men of Ocean Beach)
*A Cocky Hero Club World –*
*Vi Keeland & Penelope Ward (Coming 2022)*

Witnessed
*A Salvation Society World –*
*Corinne Michaels (Coming 2022)*

Pit Stop
*KB Worlds –*
*K Bromberg (Coming 2022)*

## Her Debt Owed Series
## (formerly Hell's Bastard Series)

Wrenched
Warped
Contorted
Entwined
The Enforcer's Revenge
Venerated

## Her Debt Owed Spin-off Duet

Hitched (The Wedding)
Destined (Coming 2022)

# PREFACE

This story is a dark romance, it contains uncomfortable situations. It's twisted and sexy and it's a rollercoaster of a ride. All is not dark, there is light.

Please note there is a cliffhanger ending. Dark romances rarely come without one, it is part of their makeup. Answers will always come as the storyline advances over the series.
There are five books in this series.

If you would like to join Emma James' Sisterhood closed group where you can meet other readers and be a part of exclusive news you can do so at www.facebook.com/groups/763744350386831.

Join Emma's newsletter subscription at http://goo.gl/27pFQj so you can be the first to know of upcoming releases and other information. Newsletters will be sent every couple months.

This is for all the twisted and dark romance readers.

You rock my world.

# EDGE

## An Eye For An Eye

### February 28th

I'm Dallas 'Edge' Masson, the Soulless Bastards MC's enforcer. I'm a killer, and I'm fucking good at it. I make no bones about that. If you are on my radar, or the Soulless Bastards', then you'd better start praying.

Don't get me wrong—I'm not hard to get along with. I'm a fair man. I can be an asshole; I can be wrong. I can also be the guy who'll be your friend for life and never turn on you.

And I can be your fucking savior.

But if you fuck me, my brothers, or what's ours over, and it's deemed your shit's worth an eye for an eye, then you're going on our retribution list. You better start running and hope never to be found, because I'll be coming for you and I'll be your judge, jury, and executioner.

There is a whole set of different rules in my world. We live differently. We all understand this. We're not civilians, so their rules don't apply to us.

The Soulless Bastards and the Lion's Den have an alliance. Something big went down last year and we covered each other's ass, or else we both would have lost a lot of men. Now we've got one another's backs if called upon.

Drill and I have just finished up a job, which affected both clubs, so it was settled that a member from the Lion's Den MC would assist me in what started out as a shakedown for information, but escalated into two dead bodies we needed to dispose of.

The two dickwads, whose souls we evicted off the planet earlier, weren't going to give up the information we needed. Whoever had these two nomad bikers on their payroll, chose them because they were dispensable.

Nomad one and two didn't belong to a club. They were on their own, making their own decisions, with no protection—a very dangerous place to be in our world. They were responsible for their own actions and lives.

These two hung on to their information like a safe that could not be cracked, which only made me amp up my ingenuity because I can normally make the person on my shit list sing loudly, and pretty quickly, but tonight dragged on and on.

A girl from each of our clubs went missing.

Poof!

Gone.

Completely vanished without a trace, we're talking a beam-me-up-Scotty type of vanishing.

These nomads were our first real lead.

The girls had been missing for nearly two weeks now. It wasn't until Ruby had up and vanished seventy-two hours after Santana, that we started to think maybe the girls were in danger. Santana had been talking about leaving and going back to college, according to word from the Lion's Den just before she vanished, so alarms weren't raised. Ruby, though…she enjoyed stripping. She was good at it, and she made good money. Two girls disappearing without a word from two different clubs, so close in time, had us sitting up and taking notice.

Each girl was under the protection of her respective club, and we look after our own, so we started digging for information. We were all on alert with our remaining girls and taking precautions to keep them safe, but we just couldn't get a lead on where Ruby and Santana had disappeared to. It was a fucking enigma.

We had received an anonymous tip earlier in the day, and it was all we had to go on, so we had to check it out.

Drill and I had been holed up inside the nomads' isolated, beat up, old house in Socorro, about an hour's drive from our club, waiting for them to come back. We gave them quite the welcome home reception. We'd left the bikes hidden and legged it a short distance.

They certainly weren't expecting us, with their oh-fuck-me-this-ain't-gonna-end-well, surprised looks on their faces as we took each down, knocking them out cold so we could truss them up, and be ready to get some answers.

We got lucky. We'd already done a thorough sweep of the shit box and found both the girls' handbags hidden in a false floor inside a cabinet—pretty damning evidence—which raised the stakes from shakedown to dead-men-walking, and it didn't look good for the girls still being alive.

An eye for an eye.

Time for *No Mercy*, my aptly named little black bag of tricks, to come out, and I started working my artistry on them. I had plenty of ideas up my sleeve. I don't need a big bag because it's often the small things, placed in the right places, which can inflict the most damage.

I have no problem using a melon baller to gouge out your eyeball. Why lug around a hammer, when I could be so much more imaginative with a corkscrew or a pair of chopsticks shoved into the right cavity?

I'm a creative son of a bastard.

It became clear that no matter what I did to them, they weren't gonna run their mouths. It was either because they were too scared to admit to *us* what went down, or they were more frightened of a higher entity. I should've just been done with them and let Drill shoot them, but I couldn't stop.

They were two of the most insane bikers I've ever come across. They had to have been, to let me go through sliding razor blades under their fingernails and tying a wire garrotte around their balls, tightening it until they were sliced clean off their bodies. But still, those fuckers never sang, and that takes balls—pun intended.

Torture is a bitch made up of a whole lot of karma.

We gave them the opportunity to sing for their souls. Theirs would have been quick and painless deaths—a bullet between the eyes...done and dusted—but they chose to fuck around because they sure as hell were hiding something pretty big.

As far as both clubs knew, we hadn't pissed anybody off that would warrant our girls being taken, and we can't have any fucker coming along and stealing our girls without deadly repercussions.

You don't cross the Soulless Bastards MC and get a slap on the wrist.

Fuck with us.

Pay in full.

The last words one of them croaked, with a fucked up grin on his face, while he spat blood at my feet were, '*Warped fucker.*'

Well, my methods might be a little warped, but usually they got the job done. My ego is dented just a little, but I'll get over it. I could have just put them down like dogs in the end, but I had a perfect record for getting people to talk. I honestly thought they would spill in the end; they had nothing to lose and they were dead anyway. You play in our world, be prepared to pay the ferryman.

Now their bodies are buried deep in the forest...minus their balls and a few other things, and both clubs are still none the wiser. God knows what's been done to Ruby and Santana. They were only twenty-one years old, just trying to get by in life.

Chances are the girls are both dead because it seems like they've just disappeared off the face of the earth. It's been two weeks, and their handbags with their money and ID were with the nomads, which means they'd probably disposed of the girls' bodies when they were done with them and were too dumb to get rid of their handbags. Hell, maybe they liked to keep tokens of their crimes.

We have nothing more to go on at the moment but assumptions, and they are not enough. We will keep searching for answers. Some fucker will pay for this. I did my best and, this time, I'd failed, and it's a jagged pill to swallow.

Drill and I are gonna go get cleaned up, and then we are gonna pay Cyn a visit on the way home because torture and interrogation are both mentally and physically demanding. I have to replace what just went down with an after-job hard fuck. You can't go through what we did and then just have a quiet beer or catch a few z's. That shit has to be worked out of our systems.

# Whisper

## In A Bind

The first thing I noticed when I came back to myself was the searing pain in my wrists and arms. My flesh felt raw, my shoulders were still locked straight above my head, and I was in complete darkness, still hanging far enough off the ground to cause me immense pain.

I was used to having my face slapped around to help speed up my come back from the spaced-out land I had to endure, and then cut down like a side of beef to fall naked onto the hard wooden floor. My hands would then be sliced free and my sight returned while the drug he used to take my mind to another place left my system and I could eventually have the strength to get up.

But this time, I was still bound, hanging, and unable to see.

Something was wrong.

I am far more alert. I can't hear his breathing; the house is deathly quiet. He's normally close by, observing me, waiting for me to resurface from the inky black depths of my mind.

"Master William?" I whisper, but the house doesn't breathe a word. "Master William?" I whisper with more volume as a shiver vibrates through my body.

*Nothing.*

I lift my head slowly. My neck is stiff and it hurts to move it, another sign I've been hanging like a dead weight for too long. My shoulders protest the small movement as I hesitate a little longer.

"Master William!" I raise my voice as loud as I dare, risking being punished for my insolence.

Still, no response.

*Why am I still bound?*

I need to be able to see. "Master William, I would like to remove my face mask, please, Sir."

I wait. The silence is deafening.

I receive no orders to keep it on, so I start rubbing my face against my shoulder, trying to remove the thick, black eye mask he puts on me. I rub harder, working to nudge it above my eyes, while the movement has me bouncing against the staircase, pain attacking my body.

I can finally move the mask enough to see, while

my eyes start blinking, trying to adjust to the late afternoon light streaming through the windows.

*Where has the bastard gone?*

"Master William!" I yell out as loud as I have dared to speak. I've never heard myself talk this loudly before.

*Ever.*

I spend so much time in my head shouting, but never out loud.

I wait.

Another shiver wracks my body. I fear being left here, more than the punishment that will come later for speaking out, but still, the walls are silent.

I focus on myself and notice my dress hasn't been cut from my body. I'm fully clothed.

*He hasn't touched me yet.*

I can't even rejoice in this knowledge because I'm afraid of what this all means for me today. I don't understand. Master William *never* deviates from his pattern.

I twist my body so I can see to my right, biting down on my bottom lip as pain assaults my shoulders while I wrench them, trying to take in my predicament.

Then, I see him.

He's lying in a tumbled heap at the bottom of the staircase, which I hang from the side of.

*Is he dead?*

*Please, if there is a God, please make him be dead.*

What if he is dead? What does this mean for me?

Reality hits me like a thunderbolt because he hasn't responded to my calls, I'm hanging bound by my wrists, and nobody knows I exist.

*Nobody is coming to save me.*

I shut my eyes and let my head slump forward as I try to calm myself so I can think clearly about the unbelievable situation I find myself in. The pain's getting unbearable, and I can take a *lot* of pain.

I dare another look at the body, and it's still unmoving and as still as the walls holding up this house, while I'm trussed up like a pig.

*I have to get myself down from here.*

I look up as high as I can. Even though my head bangs against the side of the staircase, it's protected by the thick Rapunzel braid he's roped my hair into, the same as always. It's not that far to get to the banister.

I take note of what I can use to rescue myself, then I tick off the list of things I need to do in my mind to get out of this predicament.

First thing I have to do is get myself facing the side of the staircase, then I can use my feet to push up on the brass doorknob that opens the always locked storage room underneath it, which is currently pushing into my lower back.

Today, this doorknob might save my life. I try not to panic, afraid he will wake up at any moment. Hurrying will only lead to mistakes.

I take a deep breath and center myself.

*Inhale.*

*Exhale.*

*I can do this.*

I test my legs first by giving them a shake. I have mobility, so I swing my lower body and twist as hard as I can. I flip around, pain hitting my belly where the brass knob's now pushing into it, while this sudden movement awakens a new pain in my wrists from the rope rubbing my flesh.

I'm panting from the strain on my body. My neck's now tucked in tight as I clear my mind and concentrate on grabbing a hold of the rope with what little movement my fingers have. I wriggle them a little and grasp the rope as best I can, visualizing what I need to do.

I take another deep breath because this is really going to hurt like a bitch, and I lift both legs up as high as I can, using what core strength I can find. My bare feet hit out at the brass knob as I get traction with one foot and push up with all my strength, grunting as I claw with my fingers up the rope at the same time.

Every part of my body is working together as a team to get to the goal of me standing on the brass doorknob, while busy fingers are creeping up the rope like spiders to take some of my weight and help my legs out.

I manage to take in nervous, quick glances at the body, for fear of seeing it move as I work to raise myself up. I'm making barely audible grunts from the exertion as sweat dribbles down my face. I rub my head again on the side of my arm in annoyance of the face mask, dislodging it and giving my head a little shake when it finally falls away.

I forget any pain and keep clawing my way a little closer to freedom as I push up with my feet. My thighs are burning from the awkward angle until I'm standing with one foot on the knob and I have both hands holding onto the bottom of one of the railing's carved wooden posts.

I rest my head for a few seconds from the strain on my body and roll my shoulders, trying to loosen them up a little. At least my arms are no longer pulled tight above my head. There's a small relief in my joints, but I have a long way to go still to get out of this mess I'm in.

Master William still hasn't moved.

I reach up as high as I can, with my hands locked around the banister post, the sculpted wood giving me something firm to grip onto. I swing my other leg up until it hits the bottom of one of the lower stairs, the sole of my bare foot sliding in between the posts. I use that leg to bend and hoist me a little higher, and my hands work together, clawing their way up the post they are latched onto. My other foot pushes off the brass knob with as much spring as I can muster, so my knee can leverage against the side of the staircase and I can try to push off with it. Any part of my body I can use to gain height is worth a shot.

I'm now at an awkward angle as I tell my brain to get with the program and move what needs to be moved to get the job done. Arms, legs, and fingers are battling for the end result. I grapple my way farther up the banister post until I can get my knee onto the step between two posts. I move the rest of my body over to be in line with it, and pull myself up until I'm standing.

*Holy shit. I did it.*

I hang over the railing, panting, trying to catch my breath for several heartbeats, and then I swing my tired body over, landing on the hard, jutting steps in a clumsy heap, forcing an, *"Oomph!"* out of me. Bruises will be inevitable.

I lay in an awkward mess with my limbs hurting, and notice the rope wrapped tightly around my wrists has turned a dirty red. It's a small price to pay to no longer be hanging there.

I give myself a couple minutes to recharge until I have enough strength to get up and start working the knot, which holds me prisoner. My fingers are sore from gripping the rope, but they know their job is not quite done. They continue to work together, pulling and loosening where they can to get the knot undone. Master William has a padded piece of suede wrapped under the rope, so it didn't damage his precious railing.

Without my weight pulling it tight, it only takes a few moments to slacken the knot and get the rope off the rail. I drop it onto the steps, where it will just have to drag along behind me.

*Victory!*

There's no time to celebrate. If he's still alive, this is my opportunity to kill the bastard while he's knocked out.

*But can I do that?*

*Am I a killer?*

I already know the answer to that.

I need something sharp to cut the rope binding my wrists, then I will be free to make the next decision.

I get to the bottom of the stairs and freeze.

I'm afraid to move past him in case this is some cruel joke and he's testing me, so I sit down on the bottom step, his splayed body just a couple feet away from me, and hope this whole scene is not set up to catch me out and see if I'll run.

He's wearing that horrible midnight black, satin shirt without buttons with the hood attached. It's the one he always wears when he comes for me, paired with the loose black pants. The hood's always up, but it has folded back from the fall, revealing the back of his head.

"Master William," I whisper. "Can you hear me?"

I wait a beat.

He appears lifeless and I'm frozen on the bottom step, nervous he's going to jump up and attack me, making sure to beat the shit out of me.

So I wait another couple moments.

"Master William!" My voice carries throughout the silent house on a determined echo.

*Nothing.*

He's lying on his stomach. I feel braver and stand up, giving him a good solid kick to his leg to wake him...but he doesn't.

I watch his back as I inhale and exhale slowly, waiting to see if it rises and falls with my breathing. I'm counting in my head slowly, *One thousand...two thousand...three thousand... four thousand.*

There's no movement.

I have to know, so I take the plunge, leaning down

to fist a handful of his hair between my bound wrists and lift his head. I cock my head to the side so I can see him properly. His eyes are staring vacantly back at me. His nose has bled; it looks bent out of shape, and that's when I realize how wobbly his head feels. I give it a little wriggle. It feels loosey-goosey on his shoulders, and his facial expression is frozen in place.

I think his neck is no longer properly attached to his spine, and I can smell the strong scent of alcohol coming off him. I place his head back down the way I found it, careful not to have caught any loose hairs between my fingers.

I flop back down on the bottom step, placing my bound wrists on my knees. This is a lot to take in.

Master William.

Is.

Dead.

I've waited for this day for an entire lifetime. I honestly didn't think it would arrive during *my* lifetime, and here it is.

I. Am. Free.

*But am I?*

I feel so disconnected from the scene in front of me.

My mind doesn't feel free. Maybe it's the drugs still leaving my system, but I don't feel excited. I don't know how to explain how I feel, other than I've spent my life without any freedom, any happiness, a social life, a caring, nurturing family, or any friends. I've lived from day to day without an opinion. My mind has witnessed cold-blooded murder and lived with the constant threat of violence. I've had things done to me without my consent. Those things I won't label. My life has been constantly monitored.

My mind has been abused.

I should be excited about his death. I should be smiling, laughing hysterically over how I won.

I fucking *won!*

I survived Master William.

But my happiness had flat-lined years ago.

I don't know how to be happy. My life has never been happy. I can't switch happy on. I don't know where my life goes from here.

I could still have heartache waiting for me around the corner. What happens if something worse than Master William is out there lurking in the shadows?

I shake my head to stop these negative thoughts.

I'm free.

I'm *fucking* free.

I get this sudden urgent crushing feeling to be out of these binds immediately. It's all-consuming and intense, and I react by starting to pull at my wrists...*hard*. It isn't doing anything other than hurting me more, and yet this feeling won't let go of me, which makes no sense. I start yanking and twisting my arms about, trying to get out of these binds like a crazy person.

All I'm doing is crying out in pain, but I can't seem to purge myself of this feeling. I yank my feet up and push with my bare toes, trying to will the rope to push over my wrists and release me, while my small grunts fill the ever-present silence.

I feel too anxious to be rational. I'm determined to damage my wrists even more, and that's when out of the corner of my crazed eyes I see the knife laying on the floor.

*He always cuts my dress off, but he never got around to doing it this time.*

The realization dawns on me and I stop wrestling with myself, doing some weird worm wriggle over to where the knife lays, and I pick it up clumsily in my fingers and collapse back on my haunches.

I'm normally a very contained person, showing no outward signs of distress because it's all hidden on the inside.

I'm robotic. I'm on remote control because I have to be.

Now, I don't. Now I can shout and scream and swear at the fucking bastard, who can no longer touch me. He can't lay a finger on me. There's this wildness inside me wanting to escape, a black fog of rage taking over me.

I stand up, take a step closer to him, and stomp down hard using my bare foot on his head. I put as much strength as I can into it. I stomp with my heel until I'm breathing heavily with rage and a guttural wounded animalistic noise is leeching out of me. I want to fuck him up. I want to hear the crunch of his skull as I smash the bones under my feet.

I know he can't fight back, but wasn't that what he did to me? He was a bastard coward. I want to smash his evil brain until his eyes pop out of their sockets. I want to...

A sharp sting forces me to look down, and that's when I realize my fingers have clenched around the knife blade and not the handle. Blood is oozing out like a flowing creek, and I was making that horrible noise. The pain brings me to my senses and I quickly let go of the knife. I realize I have been lost in my own dark, manic, fictional thoughts, and I hadn't touched Master William at all.

My mind was playing tricks on me.

I move my body so I can use my feet to sandwich the handle between them, making sure the blade's facing up, and I start rubbing the rope binding my wrists over it vigorously. I wince at the pain in my limbs, but I keep going, watching as each piece frays away until my hands spring free. I'm dripping blood everywhere, but who's here to punish me?

There's a bloody, raw mess waiting for me underneath my bindings, but my mind has switched off. I'm an outsider looking in. It's always easier to put things into boxes as quickly as possible and seal them up.

The pain will come back in full force, eventually. It always does, but for now, I'm thankful to become the robot girl.

I cut strips off the bottom of my dress with the knife and do my best to tie them around each wrist, using my teeth to secure the knots. The cuts on my hands need to stop bleeding; they are making a mess. I hack off some more strips and bind my fingers and palms roughly. It's enough to hold the wounds together until...

*Until...I don't know.*

I walk over to the far wall and slide down it until I'm sitting with my knees bent. I look around me and try to piece together what happened. Master William must have tripped and fallen in a drunken state; it's the only explanation.

I look over at the window. The sun has almost closed up shop for the day. I so could do with a friend right now, somebody to share this burden with. I was happy he was dead, but I did not know how to rejoice.

*Because I am so alone.*

It can't be this simple, his death.

It can't be this simple, my freedom.

Do I bury him out back?

Do I leave him here and just walk away?

Nobody will come visiting the house to check up on Master William. Nobody ever visited. He can just rot away and I'll be long gone. I look up to where I know a camera is hidden, recording my every move. My innocence will be sitting on that tape. I didn't kill him. I couldn't have. I could just disappear.

But how would I live?

There are too many questions I can't answer, but I can't stay in this house with a dead body any longer—I know that for sure—so I haul my ass up and make myself climb the stairs to my room.

I strip out of the dress, which symbolizes so much I want to forget, and hurriedly change into my jeans, a simple sweater, and put on my black Converse.

I make my way around to my bathroom and up-end the little bin, dumping the contents onto the floor, and take the plastic bag and quickly walk back around to my bedroom. I pick up my copy of *Wind In The Willows* off my bedside table, placing it carefully inside the plastic bag. I look over at my bed and see Jenny, my ragdoll, sitting there. I can't abandon her because she's my only friend. I remove my pillowcase and put her inside it. I look around my room for anything else that means something to me, but there isn't anything that's worth more to me than these two things.

Now I need to find some money, and the only place it could possibly be found is Master William's wing of the house. I have to hope he has left his main door unlocked.

If it's locked, the key will no doubt be on his body. My stomach lurches at the thought of feeling around in his pockets for it. I grab the pillowcase and the plastic bag, then take a chance and head around to his wing.

It's open. Of course it is. He would have felt secure leaving it open, knowing I was bound to the banister. I scurry through to the library. It's been a few years since I have been in here; things have changed. It takes me a few moments to find the clearly labeled hard drive and I place it inside the plastic bag, as well.

I run around to his bedroom and look for any money. There are a few bills and some change sitting on his bedside table. I grab them and stuff them inside the plastic bag, throwing it into the pillowcase.

I'm not dressed warm enough for the night, so I

reconsider, grab a jacket out of his closet, and put it on. It envelopes my body and is far too baggy on me, but it will do. There's a big pocket on the inside, so I stuff the pillowcase holding my few things inside it and zip up the jacket.

I take a moment to look around and can't think what else would be important enough to take with me. I command my feet to walk back down the stairs and out the back door.

I have never been able to use the front door, and I didn't want to now. My mind was geared to what I was allowed to do, and that was what was going to get me out of this house. Rules are important at this moment, or else I fear I would stay here purely because I'm petrified of the outside world and the unknown.

I start walking down the back of the property, away from the big majestic oak tree with its twisted and gnarled old branches, which curl toward the house as if in worship. It's a beautiful tree in its own way, but I always thought it also possessed the power to change into something creepy at night, with the moonlight silhouetting its dark, twisted branches.

I keep on walking, never looking back, until I eventually come to a fence line, climb over it and onto a dirt road.

And then I keep right on walking without a clue of what the night will hold for me. I don't even want to think beyond this point in time for what my future holds because that is too frightening. Fear could so easily devour my courage.

I try to calm my wayward thoughts by hoping there are people right now in this moment who are enjoying themselves and are safe and cared for because I have to believe it exists.

# Miss Catherine

## Dem Bones

I **had felt it in my bones that somethin' was goin'** to be comin'. I didn't know when, but dem bones of mine never lied to me. They always gave me a warnin', a feelin' in dem that left me to work the rest out for myself. I hadn't had such a strong feelin' seepin' into them in a long time.

There was nothin' much to be done but sit here in front of my comforting fire in my cozy livin' room with my crochet until I be called upon.

# EDGE

## Three's Company

Cyn, the long haired, raven beauty with the mile-long legs and lips that were made for sucking my cock, greets us at the door in a little black silk robe, which doesn't quite cover her bare ass as we follow her inside.

I met her at a bar a couple years back. I was intrigued to know more about her, and she was a hell-of-a-good-fuck. She went and fell for the wrong guy, and her dreams got swept away. A daughter was born out of that short-lived relationship.

*Short-lived* being the operative words.

Every kid should have the chance at having a parent who would be there for them. We have an agreement; I pay her enough to get her through the month for exclusive sex when I require it, and the rest of the time, she's there for her little girl.

This is purely a business arrangement. I keep her

fed and safe from the dangers of other men, but I do have a fondness for her. I want her to be a mom to her daughter foremost, and then she's available to me when I want to fuck hard and rough, so this arrangement works for both of us.

Until she tells me otherwise, or I end our agreement, she's mine. Cyn knows she only has to tell me and I'll walk away.

Simple as that.

I have no deep connections.

Drill and I are now both naked as the day we were born, our dicks hard and hungry, ready to grunt and sweat out the killings.

I call Cyn over, yanking the sash on her robe undone as she turns her back to me, letting it glide over her naked body and fall into a puddle at her feet, exposing her round ass and the glint of the fake jewel I can see nestled there. My dick went crazy at the sight of it. Cyn really makes it worth keeping her around.

"Fuck, Cyn," Drill growls out as he moves straight to the round table, which has everything we will need.

There's always a price to my soul for taking another's life. I know that, and one day I'll pay for it because karma will be coming for me, but for now, I'm gonna spend a few hours in fucking Heaven.

I look down at Cyn. She's eager to get this fuck party started, and I'm happy to oblige. She's grabbed a hold of the back of the couch on either side of my hips for support, and I'm already on board, working off my adrenaline by pumping into her luscious mouth like a steam train. You can almost hear my dick singing out loud, *'Choo-choo!'* the way she's sucking me off.

Drill's suited up, because he isn't wasting any time, and he comes prowling over like a lion, fierce and ready to be the king of her jungle.

She senses he's behind her and spreads her long gazelle-like legs wide, baring herself and preparing for him to penetrate her, but she hasn't missed a beat sucking me off.

Drill's stroking his dark red beard, eyeing up the jewel that's tempting him already. It's flashing at him like a neon calling card. He knows she would have gotten herself drenched the minute she'd inserted it, so he grabs hold of her hips and starts thrusting inside her saturated pussy while Cyn voices her pleasure deep in her throat. The vibration only adds to my dick's excitement.

We're all lost in our own thoughts and sexual sensations with Cyn, getting the bonus pleasure of that jewel in her ass being pounded every time Drill thrusts inside her, when he suddenly pulls out, heads back over to the table, and lubes up. He can't wait and she knows it too.

He struts back over and rubs his thumb slowly over his bottom lip as he eyes up that sex toy. He knows he's keeping Cyn waiting impatiently because she's rolling her hips, trying to find him. He grunts at her little aggravated display then gives her a hard spank on her ass for her impatience as she moans for more, so he slaps her again, hard, leaving a matching red handprint.

He can't wait any longer, giving the jewel a little tug and drops it to the floor while receiving an expectant deep fuck-me noise of desire from Cyn. Her ass is wiggling about in need, so he massages her wet pussy from behind, thumbing her juices over her rim as her teeth graze along my erection, making me hiss in a breath. Then he pushes two lubed up fingers, one at a time, inside her, stretching her for him.

She's pushing back hard on his fingers in pulses while still bobbing her head on my cock. She's ready for him. A quick lick of his lips and Drill enters her on a heavy sigh as he lets his head drop back. She can't help gasping out loud through a mouthful of my cock because Drill's a big boy. She stops sucking long enough to take him all the way in, then he starts thrusting and grunting like a caveman.

He's pounding her so hard I think she's gonna swallow my dick.

*Fuck, these two are hot together. I'm feeling like a third wheel tonight.*

My eyes are about to go all *hallelujah* on me and roll back into my head, because Cyn knows how to work a cock over like she was born to do it. I white knuckle the back of the couch as my own arousal floods through my veins.

My eyes can't stay levelled out anymore, and they go all vertical on me as I let my head drop backwards and my mouth drops open, letting out a deep growl of warning. "Drill, slow it down. I need my cock." Without having to look, I know Drill's grass green eyes will be trained on me, full of expectations. His mind will be visualizing it's me that he's pumping into like a demon, and I just shake my head from side to side.

Drill wants to fuck me, and he wants me to know it too. He has his own set of neon signs flashing in each eyeball, inviting me into the mother of all threesomes. His eyes don't lie, but I'm not going there.

I'll sandwich a female between us, but that's the closest we are gonna get to our dicks touching. A bit of skin and our balls slapping and sliding across each other from the positions we get Cyn in, but no closer. He knows not to cross that line with me.

I get back to concentrating on where I am, letting the thrill of the kill leave my body as my release shoots into her mouth, hitting way down the back of her throat while she tries to keep up, gulping it down expertly as my eyes roll back into my head and my body reacts with a little shaky leg action.

*Christ, she's good at that.*

I slowly slide out of her mouth so she doesn't choke while her tongue glides all over my dick in appreciation, lapping it all up. Only God knows how she gets the whole thing in there so deep, but she does.

I take a couple steps to the side and I let her finish off with Drill. Leaning against the couch, I watch these two go at it with a whole lot of appreciation for voyeurism. My long, thick penis must think so too, since it decides to stand right back up, commanding attention, still slick with Cyn's saliva.

Drill's hammering her and she takes every pound with a hum while her full and firm breasts jiggle about excitedly. She straightens up a little so he can touch her, spreading her long, lithe legs in those *fuck me* red heels she wears, which stretch her legs even longer, inviting more from his touch as she pushes her tight ass further into him. He takes the hint, wrapping an arm around her, sliding a finger over her sensitive bud, back and forth until she is writhing against him. Then he slides it inside her. Her head falls back against his shoulder as he keeps pounding her, and she winds a hand around the back of his neck, bringing him closer by his army issue cut hair so he can suck on her ear. She loves her earlobe being sucked on and gasps at the little bites he gives her, then whimpers when he takes it inside his mouth as his beard sandpapers her shoulder.

I could go again watching these two, so I palm my rock-hard erection and start moving my hand up and down its length, catching Drill's eyes reverting back to me, with that neon sign ring-a-ding-dinging. I meet his intense gaze. I didn't say I don't like the look in his eyes. I like the appreciation he has for me and my body. We're both big, strong, muscled men sporting a lot of tattoos. We work hard at it.

"Fuck, Edge," he grunts out. He's upped his game, his hands and fingers sliding all over Cyn's body while he watches me. I'm particularly horny tonight; it's been a while since I've shared a female and gotten to watch a couple go at it hard.

Drill's as tough as he is good-looking. The fucker knows it too. That's why I agreed to bring him along to watch my back tonight. They see the pretty eyes and don't think he's as dangerous as me, but he'll have you handcuffed and incapacitated before you know what's hit you.

Cyn has eyes for Drill. I saw the way she looked at him when he followed me through the door. The thing is he's too busy on the business end of her ass to notice. His sexual appetite is more diverse than mine. He didn't get the road name Drill for shits and giggles. He knows how to work a woman over, as well as a man.

I've brought him along as my guest a couple times now, and he can't see what's in front of him. He's an all-out intelligent guy, whose IQ is off the charts, but he's blind to Cyn's desire for him.

The faster I pump my hand, the more excited Drill's eyes get. He's sweating from thrusting and Cyn is delirious with ecstasy. "Drill...God...." Her scent is invading both our senses. She likes to be ridden rough until she can hardly walk, and she smells so fucking good.

I walk up to Cyn and grab her jaw roughly with my hand, pulling her mouth to mine, biting down on her tongue, tasting myself as I draw blood. I release her tongue while palming her breasts, spitting on one and rubbing my thumb over the hardened nipple, while dipping my head to bite down on it, which leaves her arching into me as I slowly let it pop out of my mouth.

I'm still fisting my dick, and I'm close as I thrust two fingers inside her wet pussy, pulsing them in and out, her body consumed by the avalanche of sensations Drill and I are assaulting her body with.

I move away again, eliciting a small whimper of disapproval from Cyn, so I can watch these two some more. The show is half the turn-on for me.

When you share, you can only move so much. When one of us gets off first, the other then gets the green light to move with more freedom. I make sure Drill gets off second. It's a quiet agreement we have.

"Fuck, Cyn, you need to come. I'm about to blow," he growls into her neck. If Drill pounds her any harder, she's gonna break. Skin's slapping between them, tits are bouncing, and she's making all the right noises you'd expect from a female you're nailing hard, while my hand's just about strangling my cock.

*Fuck, these two are such a turn-on to watch.*

I grit my teeth and work myself faster, then slide back over in front of Cyn when I know I'm close to lift off. I spread my legs and she lets go of Drill to grip my shoulders while I shoot over her stomach and breasts on a loud shout, while Drill swipes a hand over her stomach, rubbing my cum all over her. Then he slides two fingers dripping with me into her mouth so she can suck on them before she

cries out at the same time as he explodes on a roar.
*Christ, I needed that. I think we all did.*
*And the night is still young.*

# Whisper

## Boxes Of Memories

I walk in the direction my feet take me of their own accord, the decision out of my hands, having no idea where I'm headed.

I now realize I am indeed a *coo yon,* a stupid person. Master William had called me a *coo yon* more times than I could count, and now I agree with him.

*What am I doing? What is my plan?*

But, I keep on walking, knowing I have freedom, yet I don't know how I'm going to cope now that it has been granted.

The only two people I have ever known, or been able to remember, aren't my parents. They were not my family because one was my abductor and one my mistress.

I made the mistake of calling her mother once and was beaten severely for it by Master William.

Mistress had explained I was wrenched from my home as an infant, stolen to be used one day for Master William's needs. I never, *ever* referred to *him* as my father. I learned they were just people in my life and I did what I was told without question.

I was a quick study. Mistress told me I was gifted, so I made her job a lot easier. I, of course, was only taught what Master William would allow because there was a bigger picture I was yet too young to understand.

When I was little, I was granted television time, watching children's programs only. I learned from these programs that I lived a vastly different life from what most children did. I hadn't understood that my life excelled at being different until I started getting older.

I loved reading, and I had one toy, my small ragdoll, Jenny. She was dressed in her little white apron over her little black and white checkered dress, with her bright red shoes and a bright red bow in her dark, curly hair. I cuddled her at night. I never wanted my mistress or Master William to see me loving something. I did it in the safety of my room and under the covers.

I was told when it was my birthday. I was given necessities for my existence and growth during the year; a birthday meant turning a year older and nothing more. I didn't know I should be praised for getting older, sung to and given gifts and a cake. We didn't celebrate Christmas or any other holidays. My life was on repeat, every day of the year.

The woman who raised me from an infant to a teenager is now long gone. Master William slit her throat in front of me when I was just thirteen years old. I clearly remember the gurgling noise she made as she fought to keep breathing, her eyes widening in surprise and recognition as all that red drained out of her. It was so quick.

I was to be the last person she saw before she died. Her eyes had searched my horrified face out where I had been quietly reading on the couch. He let go of her body when she had taken her last breath, and she slumped to the floor in an undignified heap with a disgusting squelching sound.

I think it took a few moments for my mind to play catch up with what had happened in front of me. He had snuck up behind her and slid the sharp metal across her neck, making a clean gash, which opened up as she threw her neck back in surprise, red soaking into her crisp white blouse, a look of triumph on his evil face.

I think, to a certain extent, I checked out the day she bled out in front of me. Master William chained me up while he got rid of her body, then made me clean up what had been left behind. It was a thick and sticky mess that smelled of fear and metal.

Blood is not easy to clean up, and it had sprayed everywhere. You have to scrub and scrub to get every last spot clean. I wanted to vomit, but I knew I would be punished, so I had to go to another place inside my head to get through it.

I knew this was all a game to him. He wanted me to have a front row seat and be a witness to what he'd done. He didn't have to do it in front of me, but that was all part of his twisted, evil mind. It was also a warning to me he highlighted in dramatic style.

My youth was starting to slip away and I was becoming a teenager. He took her life knowing I was old enough to take care of myself, to obey and fear him into total submission.

*She* was expendable.

*She* made the mistake of thinking she wasn't. My mistress lived in a fantasy world filled with his evil, but thought she was his partner, his equal. Even at a young age, I could see the tight rope she walked so carelessly.

She had an expiration date.

He was so calm when he took her life, and that was when I knew I was on borrowed time, because any time he pleased, I knew my life would be taken in just as gruesome a manner. I did not doubt that for a minute.

Was *she* my friend?

Well, you learn to make do with what you have. She was all I knew in a female. She was very guarded with me, and she kept her walls up emotionally, but she didn't physically hurt me. I didn't fear her like I feared Master William. I didn't even know her name. She was simply Mistress to me.

I wasn't capable of mourning her death because my emotions were too broken, but I think in a twisted way I did miss her female presence in the house, although I couldn't understand why she would want to live with a man like Master William voluntarily.

Every now and then, something will trigger a particularly bad memory and I have had to break off another piece of tape and tightly reseal the box. Mistress' death is one of those memories.

It's the way I survived in my world.

He was sick and twisted, prone to outbursts of great violence for no good reason. Sometimes I was on the receiving end, and other times I witnessed my mistress receiving punishment.

He had no soul, no conscience. He was Hell's bastard. He was spontaneous with his actions, which made him dangerous and unpredictable.

I was beaten black and blue when I failed at any

task set before me. To be the best would mean no time in the slave cabin behind the main house, chained to that filthy floor, where I would be beaten and kicked, only enough to break me a little more each time.

When my mistress was alive, she was good at fixing broken bones. I was very careful not to be given a broken bone when she was *gone*. It was enough to kill the last bit of my soul, which had been fighting back. I didn't want to be in pain and mended, only to be in pain again.

So I gave myself over and became submissive to everything he asked of me. Sometimes I slipped up by not doing something right. I tried real hard to be flawless, but sometimes I was unable to be the kind of perfect he needed.

As I grew older, things changed. When I turned fourteen, I started to bleed. I didn't know what was happening to me. I thought I was dying. It crossed my mind that I was excited my life was coming to an end. I feared it, but it also meant the end was near and on my terms.

Master William threw a book at me in disgust along with a bag of female hygiene products, while I lay on my bed after I'd told him I needed help.

I did as I was ordered. I read the book. I then understood I wasn't dying. I felt disappointment at having to endure more time with this man.

From then on, I was given access to a computer, but only while he supervised me. I could never surf any sites unless he approved of them, unless he watched my every move with that mouse.

I began to understand there was a world outside my existence that I was missing out on.

A *big* world.

I was allowed to shop online and choose nice, pretty things. I could buy personal items for myself as a reward for turning old enough to bleed.

I was granted movie time. I loved superhero movies. What I would have given to have had some of their powers, been the one being saved. Although my life was not nurturing or loving, I was also allowed to watch chick flicks about finding that elusive love. I chose *Pretty Woman* because of the title, *Sleepless in Seattle, How To Lose a Guy in 10 Days, The Holiday, The Notebook, The Lucky One, Valentine's Day*...I devoured them. I saw how people communicated and loved each other. I learned what heartache did to people. YouTube videos on how to style my hair were welcomed. I had no idea at the time it was all a pay-off for what was to come. You see, I was making myself prettier for him without even knowing it. I was making myself knowledgeable about men and women. I just needed to age, as

I was not yet what he wanted. I was being groomed.

My life became like a piece of wood that somebody had taken a knife to and whittled into a shape, which could only be changed with more whittling.

It couldn't be bent. It did what the whittler pleased.

The wood couldn't stop what was being done to it, but nevertheless a shape was formed, which was pleasing to the whittler.

I was carved and shaped. I hurt and bled when beaten. I was bruised and felt pain for days. That's where the piece of wood and I were different, because wood feels nothing.

Another thing I learned over the years was he liked to film me. Cameras were set up all around the plantation home. I would catch their winking red lights out of the corner of my eye when I'd worked out where they were all hidden. When I had free time, I would take a book into a room and sit and pretend I was reading as I looked through my thick curtain of hair for where the camera could be. It became a game. Mistress told me he filmed many rooms I frequented, for security reasons.

I soon switched off and forgot about the cameras, as I didn't fully understand what they meant. I grew bored of them watching me, and there was nothing

I could do about them.

When I was older, I discovered his library by a pure lapse of Master William's mind. He always kept one door locked, which led to his end of the house and his rooms. Because of this one powerful door, which shut me off from his privacy, he didn't have to lock each and every room within.

He got drunk on my birthday every year, and when Mistress was alive, he could afford to be more careless. But now she was dead and he'd made a big mistake. It was my first birthday after he'd slaughtered her, and he obviously wasn't thinking when he started hitting the bottle. He never drank at home any other day of the year.

I was on my way to my room to save myself from the punishment which would come when he woke up and realized what he had done, but then I saw the door was wide open. It was a temptation calling out to me, too hard to resist.

I knew he was blind drunk, out cold on the couch downstairs, and I was old enough to smell an adventure and be a teenaged rebel. That open door beckoned to me. I was curious.

He didn't have cameras in his wing of the house, so I was free to enter the library without fear of being filmed. I knew I had at least six hours before he would regain consciousness.

The library, I discovered, housed all the footage he had taken of me over the years. Everything was labeled and dated. He must have spent hours editing so he had the most memorable moments of each month of my life recorded.

*The fucking perv.*

It was proof of my existence. These were his personal tapes to view as he pleased.

I spent three hours watching as much of my childhood as I could, for I knew he would not make the same mistake twice. I watched the pain of the little girl growing up before my eyes, as I fast forwarded through year after year. I felt so sad for what that little girl had been forced to become.

I was too scared to stay there any longer because I was breaking the rules. Very costly rules if I was caught.

Sadly, I couldn't stop the inevitable. I was led into a false numbness, which had protected me from thinking about what worse things could be done to me to degrade and humiliate me for his pleasure.

Master William liked routine, but things escalated when I turned eighteen. I had been made to watch porn for hours and hours on my eighteenth birthday.

That was the day I was introduced to his satin, midnight black, hooded shirt and pants — his uniform.

Master William had me sit between his legs with my back against his chest while I viewed what he put on for me. All I wanted to do was shut my eyes and think about one of those romance movies I had watched, but he would know if I wasn't paying attention and I would be punished for my insolence.

I *always* did as I was told. It was the smartest move. I was granted reasonably safe passage if I did what I was asked of me the first time.

On this birthday, I was expected to learn from these women, who had sex in the back of taxis and on couches, on kitchen floors and counter tops, while their bodies got sweaty and their makeup ran down their faces, making them look like racoons. Some got slapped about and appeared to enjoy it, while others liked their throats clenched as they struggled for air, their eyes bulging, while the man pumped and grunted inside them in front of the camera.

I watched, not understanding what was going to come next.

I heard his breathing change and felt his hardness poking into my lower back. I did not flinch or show my discomfort. It was better to play ignorant and not invite the devil in. I remained outwardly calm, while I was so fearful on the inside, my heart pounding heavily against my chest. It wanted to escape from this man too.

Master William had requested I wear the new low cut white maxi dress he'd recently purchased for me. I still didn't understand what was expected of me while I watched the porn, and felt nothing but fear as I tried to ignore his hardness pushing through his loose black pants into my back.

I had been obediently watching, when one hand snaked around and latched onto my throat, squeezing my neck tight. My immediate reaction was to panic and start bucking against his chest.

That little box I had *her* murder tucked away in burst open like a jack-in-the-box, and I thought I was going to have my throat slit too. I cried out pathetically, knowing nobody would hear me on his property. He lived on a lot of land, and there was not a single neighbor close by. I was only ever allowed a short distance from the house, and I didn't mind. I didn't like venturing too far, but I welcomed the sunshine and the rain.

I wanted sunshine and rain now so badly.

My heart skipped a beat and I gasped when his other hand slid down between my legs and moved up slowly. The sounds coming from the porn were drowned out by my heartbeat pounding frantically inside my head.

*What is he doing?*

His growl in my ear was deeply low and menacing. "Your time is running out, Whisper. I've been patient, more patient than should be asked and expected of any man, who has you tempting him every day. Who knew you were going to turn into such a beauty? I cocooned you for all these years, and you turned into a beautiful butterfly." His unshaven face was scratching my skin. I could smell his stale breath from the cigars he liked to smoke. I tried never to look at him if I could help it. It was better for me to think of him as a faceless man, rather than the attractive man he was, even in his late forties.

*He shouldn't be attractive.*

*He is so ugly on the inside.*

*He is a contradiction.*

*He is a Venus flytrap.*

When my mistress was alive, I knew he went out, and now I understand more fully why he went out. I remember hearing her talking to him. She was jealous about what he had been doing, even though he did it to her as well.

When he'd killed her, he started cuffing and chaining me to a floor-to-ceiling thick pole that was inside a deep storage closet whenever he went out. I waited in the dark until he returned and released me, the heavy chain weighing my torso to the pole. I would dream of more for my life when I was inside that closet. It was the only way to make it through. I would go to my happy place of movies and let them play out in my mind until he came for me. I was no longer in a closet, though. I was in a big room watching a big screen TV and laying on a soft comfortable couch with a warm blanket. I always saved the comedies for that place.

I feared then he wanted to do *it* to me. I understood then what their conversations were about.

As I walk aimlessly, I let my mind wander back to that wretched night.

••••

*His hand had stalled.*

*"Watch the television. Watch what I will do to you. I have kept you whole. You have no idea how much I want to take you now." He bites my shoulder hard and takes his time letting go.*

*I'm frozen with fright.*

*I'm screaming on the inside.*

*"Today, you just watch." The remote clicks by my ear and the movie speeds up to a scene he's obviously all too familiar with and he hits play.*

*The guy has the girl in front of him. She's naked while he's standing behind her clothed and cupping her chin in his hand. One finger's moving up and down her slit, while her head rolls back onto his shoulder as she closes her eyes and moans. He pushes it in further, and she cries out in pleasure as the camera zooms in to show his glistening finger as he pumps it in and out of her. She tries to stand still, but her body betrays her and her hips move, greedy for more.*

*He stops, and she whimpers as though she wants him to continue. He slides his finger all the way out and glides it up her body and over her erect nipple, making his way to her mouth and slipping it inside as she opens wide for him. She moans again as her tongue flicks out, licking as much of it as she can, then sucking on it so deeply, dimples formed in her cheeks.*

The video is paused.

He taps me on the head with the remote control. "When this happens," he points to the screen, "I want you wet for me, Whisper. Do you understand?" His thighs tighten on either side of me when he talks to me.

I can't pull away from him. I'm caught in the Venus flytrap.

His fingers creep their way under my dress to make a point. He rips at the side of my panties, painfully tugging until I hear the cheap seams give and tear.

I now understand from all the movies I have been allowed to watch in the past, and the porn today, that *he wanted me to wear white because I'm a virgin. He methodically plans everything, and I'm too naive to know what's coming for me.*

I am trapped.

*My heartbeat has accelerated to dangerous levels, and I know the camera trained on me for his sick pleasure later will be capturing my anxiety and my undoing.*

But he said it wasn't happening today. He's just trying to torture my mind.

*He rocks us from side to side so he can pull my underwear roughly from my body as his excitement builds.*

I'm a block of wood. I don't feel.

He said it wouldn't happen today.

*He licks the side of my cheek slowly as his hand cups my breast hard. I squeak out in protest, while his other hand at my throat tightens more. He could break my neck if he chose to.*

*He's a strong man; he spends time on himself. I'm lean and tall; I would weigh nothing to him. He is also much taller. My neck is long, and it would snap with a twist. It would bleed out if sliced open. I could be defeated so easily, and he knows it.*

"Whisper, when the time comes, you will be sopping wet for me." His hand is painfully tight wrapped around my throat, and I think he has finally lost his *mind and I will be suffocated.*

"Stop...please," I rasp out.

*I thrash my body out of sheer uncontrollable terror, and he responds by squeezing his hand even tighter. I'm gasping for a small bit of air to inhale.*

*This excites him more. He wants to see how far he can go. I'm being choked to death. If I live, I will bear the bruised fingerprints on my neck for days.*

*I try to thrash about, or my mind wants to thrash, but I can't even feel his hand anymore. I'm starting to see spots. I have been mindlessly clawing at his hand on my throat, but now they have given up the fight and fallen limply to my side.*

*He's crushing my windpipe. My soul feels like it's leaving me. I have nothing left in me.*

*I have stilled.*

"Fuck! Whisper! I haven't waited patiently all these years for you to take the easy way out. You do not have permission to die today. You will die on my terms!" *I faintly hear him shouting abusively at me.*

*I'm in a tunnel.*

*I'm no longer able to keep my eyes open.*

*His fingers have released my throat and he's shaking me.*

*I am a blob of jelly.*

*My body and mind can take no more today.*

*I wake up later in my bedroom with a sore throat*

*and having a hard time swallowing. I check myself over. My panties are gone and the dress is in place. I'm trying to feel for any changes to my body.*

*"You're finally awake." He's walked in on me while I was assessing myself.*

*I wait for him to brag.*

*I won't look at him. My eyes are downcast. He's faceless to me; it's a coping mechanism. I won't think about what he could have done to me. I can't change it.*

*He tells me nothing. He waits because I know he wants me to ask.*

*I won't give him the satisfaction.*

••••

From my eighteenth birthday onwards, he came for me twice a month. He knew my cycle, and I was left to fret when those two times would be. The only peace of mind I had, was knowing he wouldn't come for me when my period was due. He granted me ten days of peace, but when he did come for me, I would have to wear an identical white dress every time, and I would be drugged, blindfolded, and bound by my hands to the banister of the staircase. He always liked to remind me of the punishment ahead of me, but he never told me what he did to me.

I never remembered.

I didn't want to remember.

I just put it all back into a box and sealed it down tight. I knew it was a game and I didn't want to play. I could at least keep that for myself and show no outward signs of anguish.

It was a form of torture not knowing, a hideous mind game, which he played for his own amusement. I found no physical form of sexual assault, but that didn't mean it didn't happen.

He would play with my mind by leaving sex toys on the floor and empty condom wrappers to be discovered when I came to my senses, my mind still foggy, while he sat in a high-backed chair he positioned facing me. He would be dressed in the same outfit, his face shadowed by the fabric of the hood, laughing while I slowly moved, trying to get my body back under my control.

He was mocking me.

He would grant me permission to go to my room, knowing I couldn't stand properly and I was bared to him. I didn't care. I would pull myself up, feeling as wobbly as a newborn calf, hold my shredded dress to cover some of my body, and make my way back to the sanctuary of my room.

I had long lost the emotion of embarrassment for my nakedness displayed in front of him. I was a cardboard cutout of a person.

He took to handcuffing me to my bed every night from the time I turned eighteen. It crossed his mind I might entertain the thought of fleeing; he really didn't get that my mind was too broken. I was a pet who lived in an invisible cage. I had mental boundaries I was too scared to breach.

Cameras were my constant spies, always ready to confess all my sins for breaching the rules. Master William did grant me the privacy of my bathroom and bedroom, which I was grateful for. Small mercies I devoured.

My days were kept busy. I did what I was told. I was the cook and did the washing. I kept the house tidy, not that there would dare to be anything out of place. Gardening was a true joy of mine.

My life was on a timetable, which was monitored each and every day.

I was waiting for a superhero to save me, but my mind wouldn't entertain the thought of leaving by my own will. It was trained too well. I was a hostage to my own fears. This is where I had lived all these years.

How was I ever going to get freedom? I craved it so much, yet what would I do with it? Where was I going to go, anyway? I had no money or transportation. Those thoughts were always on a hamster wheel, going round and round.

Never an end in sight or a solution.

Master William always promised me he would find me if I ever left him, and I wholly believed he would because he would be quicker than me, he had money, and he had transportation. He'd hunt me down and execute me for escaping, and I totally believed he would follow through with his threats.

I only knew I was in Louisiana, somewhere, because I had overheard my mistress and Master William talking one day. I held onto that valuable information, even though it did me no favors.

I was too young to understand what a Louisiana was. It wasn't until I had been able to use the computer, looked at a world map, and studied the vast planet that was laid flat before me that I understood what it was. He had no idea I even knew the state I lived in, so he wasn't worried about me seeing a world map.

He wanted to show me how big the world was, how small and insignificant I was in relation to it, but I knew this one piece of information, which I kept tightly packaged up in one of the boxes in my mind.

*I live in Louisiana.*

I shake off the memories and seal them back down in their boxes again as I keep walking. The skies have opened up and rain has built from a slow patter into an angry downpour. It's dark and cold now; I'm shivering and drenched through to my skin. The jacket is too big on me, leaving room for the heavy bloated drops to run down my back.

I can handle rain.

I remind myself, *none of this is going to happen again.*

It will *never* happen again.

I was out here walking in the dark, and I only had a pillowcase stuffed inside a stolen jacket and nothing of worth to my name. I am officially a nomad.

I was purely moving, hoping on a wing and a prayer that my path would be crossed by someone kind. Miracles happened in movies, so why couldn't one happen to me? I can't think about what I had left behind dead on the floor, the bad memories. I can only walk, take this adventure, and see what will happen. I'm now free, and that's all that matters. Life could not be so cruel to me twice.

*Could it?*

But I keep right on marching. I have not seen another soul on this dirt road. All there is to keep me company is the sound of rain falling. My feet are getting muddy and soaked through, but I keep on going, huddled inside the jacket.

After what felt like well over an hour, I think I can see a light flickering in the distance. I squint through the harsh rain that's caking my eyelashes and hope to find shelter for the night.

Then a thought occurs to me and I let out a mad little laugh. I just remembered I turned twenty-one years old today.

*Happy birthday to me.*

# EDGE

## I Aim To Please

**I** **growl in masculine appreciation as I watch** Drill and Cyn. He has her coming for him all over his face. He's got his mouth latched onto her pussy and isn't letting go, and that beard of his is doing its thing. She's writhing all over his face while sucking his cock fiercely in a classic 69 position, and I can't stand around just watching anymore.

We won't be going anywhere tonight because it's all about carnal, lustful gratification.

And I aim to please.

# Miss Catherine

## Skinny Mullet

**T**he rain has not ceased its downpour for the past hour, and I was just waitin' on what was gonna be crossin' my path this cold, rainy evenin'.

And then it happens.

A knock comes at my door. It's a quiet, scared knock.

Whoever be waitin' on me on the other side of this door on my front porch needs my help. I pull myself up out of my comfortable old chair, layin' my crochet down and tightenin' my shawl around my old shoulders as I make my way over to it.

I am not afraid, but I can smell the fear this person be feelin'. This person don't know if I be friend or foe, but dem legs of theirs brought dem to me. They knew Miss Catherine was good.

I turn the key in the lock and tug on my worn, old, brass doorknob. The door swings open with a tired old sigh and there she be, shiverin' and shakin', soaked to dem bones, and she is such a *skinny mullet,* barely an adult.

Sad, wary eyes are lookin' back at me while dem teeth of hers are chatterin', and her body is rattlin' from the rain and cold night air. I don't doubt if she had anybody else to turn to this evenin', she would have. This child is all alone and she be knowin' it, and she be takin' a chance on me.

I don't be takin' this lightly. I once had to put a little faith in a stranger to help me out, too.

"*Mais,* child, you look like you be needin' shelter for the night. Have you been travelin' alone by foot on this cold, wet night?"

She nods her head at me while she be assessin' me. I can see she is poised to run if she be fearin' who opened the door to her.

"You certainly don't be lookin' like you are from around these parts. I lived here long enough to be knowin' that." I give her a little longer to judge me. "Come on in out of the weather, if you be choosin' to take a chance on me, and tell Miss Catherine all about your troubles." I hold my old arm out wide, givin' her the choice.

"There be no one else here but me, and you need not be fearin' an old lady. Dem legs brought you here because they knew to bring you to safety." She watches me for a moment longer, still judgin' me, and I can see when she be makin' the decision to grab hold of the wrinkly old hand I have held out in front of her, the bones all twisted up on my fingers from painful arthritis. A strong wind could be blowin' me over like a tumbleweed. I'm no physical threat, and she knows she gots nobody else to hear her words but Miss Catherine on this dark night, nobody else to bring her in out of the cold, unless she continues walkin' the night.

"S-s-sorry to tr-trouble y-you." The child is a quiverin' mess as I gently pull her over my threshold. I can see her wrapped hands, but I pay dem no mind. There be time enough after to be assessin' the damage.

"Hush now, child. Miss Catherine will get you warm, then we be talkin'. You be makin' no sense shakin' and drippin' puddles on my floors, and you can be takin' dem mud-ruined shoes off where you be standin', so I can clean dem up for you later on."

I usher her over to the warmth of the fire in her sodden socks and slide another log on for good measure. "You best be takin' those wet clothes off so your body can be warmin' up quicker. Your lips be goin' blue and I can feel you is ice cold."

She looks around my livin' area, searchin' for a man. "It's just you and me in my blessed home. I be livin' alone here; no man has *ever* lived under my roof. All I gots for conversation this evenin' is you." I give her a gentle smile. "Here, child, let me be helpin' you with dem clothes. They be stuck to you like a second skin, and dem hands of yours look like they be hurtin'." There is no way she should be usin' her hands until I can get an eye over dem.

I wait for her to give me a sign that she be willin' to accept my help, and then I make sure not to keep my eyes too long in one place on her body as I help her peel the layers away.

She does not fear me seein' her naked, and that concerns me—she's not bashful around a stranger. I'll put it down to bein' soakin' wet and needin' to be comfortable. I don't bat an eyelid when she turns her back on me and I see the scarrin' on her lower back before I can cover her bony body up from my pryin' eyes. The blanket is one of my finest. It's warm and thick, swallowing up her too thin frame so she can be afforded some privacy to take off her undergarments, while I hang her wet clothes up by the fire to dry.

I know what dem marks look like, and I can see purplin' bruises where she has had some recent trauma to her body.

I motion for her to sit on the couch while I go fix her a glass of warm milk, and she can be takin' in her surroundin's. I call out to her from my small kitchen. "You are safe in my home, child. Nothing bad will happen to you here under my roof. That be a promise I make to you."

I bring the warmed milk over. "Here, honeychile, this will take the blue out of those lips of yours." She takes the warmed milk and sips it timidly.

I settle into my old, comfy, worn sofa chair and wait patiently for her to finish her drink. I can see her mind churnin' away, questionin' my kindness, and so she should be. Her trust has been broken by someone. I can see that written all over her face, and I'm new folk who entered her life out of the blue, but I can see she be believin' what I tell her. She has good gut instinct. She has survived well usin' it.

I see a night of tales comin' before me, and I fear what she be tellin' me.

"As I have already stated, I'm Miss Catherine, and I am eighty-five years old. I have lived in this here home for fifty-two years. My life has not always been easy or without fear. Some memories don't disappear, but they do fade." I give her a soothin' smile. "What name would you be goin' by?"

"Whisper." The girl is so quiet.

"'Chile, I'm a little weak of hearin'. Can you say that a little louder, please?"

She looks over at me, huddled in the blanket, the

light from the fire flickerin' over her face. She be lookin' way too young for the life she's been dealt. I already know before she be tellin' me a thing that she has lived a life of great despair.

"Whisper," she says loud enough for me to hear this time.

"Nice to make your acquaintance on this rainy night, Miss Whisper. Do you be havin' a last name?"

"I don't know." She looks down into her empty glass. There be no tears comin'; there is only a deep sadness inside her that she don't be knowin' what to do with.

"*Mais*, Whisper, you only be needin' a first name. That's the important one." She attempts a weak smile at my effort to make her feel better. "I am here to listen now, and you can tell me only what you want to be tellin' me. I am a stranger, I know, but you can call me a friend from now on. It looks like you may be in short supply of them. You look like you are runnin' from some dark past, and the only way I can help you is if I know what you been dealin' with."

She sat lookin' into the orange flames until she is ready to begin, no doubt wonderin' where on earth she's goin' to be startin'.

I listen to her pour her stories out to me. When her voice gets quieter, I gently prompt her to speak up. She doesn't need to be afraid to speak up in my house.

The child is like a tap on a water tank that has been left turned on, and water pours on out until it be empty, and then she is all dried up.

She's probably sittin' there weighin' up why she chose my house and me to tell all her worries to. I know the answer to that: because she has never been able to talk so freely before. She never had anybody to be listenin' to her before. She had that one woman in her life, and I am the only other she has met face-to-face. That woman was a damaged shell who thought she be loved by this evil man, who made this child's life a nightmare. She didn't hurt Whisper, but she didn't save her either, and all that got her was dead.

I knew that William Dupré was no good, but even my bones couldn't tell me what was happenin' behind those closed doors. There was no way anybody could have known.

I was figurin' she would sleep better with a small bowl of my gumbo in her skinny frame, which I go and heat up while she quietly sits warmin' up and thinkin'. This is the first time she has *ever* left that plantation home. There is a lot she would be mullin' over. I am the first black woman she's ever met.

When I bring the steaming bowl over, she thanks

me in a timid voice, and I be pleased to see she eats nearly all of it while I sit patiently watchin' the flames cracklin' and hissin' in the fireplace as I be processin' what she told me. Her eyes were meetin' mine every now and then, and no doubt thinkin' on what the impact is goin' to be with what she said.

Long ago, I learned not to be shocked by what I be seein' or hearin'. Some human beings can be the salt of the earth, and some are dangerous creatures with evil poured into their veins and no hope for dem to ever be on the path of good. Some innocents would be crossin' their paths, and that be their fate in life.

Whisper be one of those.

She be chosen and she be plucked from her family, and there was no choice. It is what it is. Her past can't be changed, but it's what she be doin' with her future that will count.

When I see her eyes be droopin', I take the bowl from her bandaged hands before it slips onto the floor. "*Fais do-do,* honeychile," I murmur. "Go to sleep." I don't doubt she will sleep the next eight hours, and then I will have some answers for her, because Miss Catherine, she knows people who can help a *skinny mullet* who is very much *mal prise,* stuck in a bad situation.

She be so traumatized, her mind has not caught up to the day's events, and then she might want to be runnin'. I need her to be stayin', so she has a chance at a new life, a good life, one with choices. It sounds like the threat to her person is dead, good and gone, and she is no longer in danger.

My heart hurts for the girl; her mind be broken, turned to stone. She is not embarrassed about what left her lips because she don't understand that emotion. Submissiveness had been flogged into her, and humiliation had become her closest friend.

She is brave and in control of who she is more than she be realizin'. She has no experience with life to show her otherwise. She's a survivor and braver than she be ever givin' herself credit for.

The help of a strong sedative in the gumbo is what the skinny girl needs for now. We would work on the rest of her demons with a new day. She be safe now. Miss Catherine will see to that.

I need Boxer's help. He be knowin' what to do for her. When Boxer moved into town ten years ago, I made it my business to seek him out. It's rare in all my years of livin' in Connard that new folk be wantin' to be buyin' up a business and settlin' here. My bones be tellin' me he was one to look out for.

I owned a couple properties in town, one being the bar. I had made some money in stocks over the years and bought dem up cheap. I was always smart with money, and I didn't need much to get by on.

Amazin' what dem bones of mine be tellin' me, and where my gut instinct steered me. But that be one of my little secrets.

Boxer be needin' a reason to be livin' in Connard, so I sold half my share of the bar to him. I am now the silent partner. Folks be thinkin' I sold it all to him, but I am a smart one.

Boxer has become family to me, and family look after each other. Family are loyal and keep secrets.

There's an evil body waitin' to be taken care of, somethin' the child can't be doin' herself. She will be mine and Boxer's secret until we can resurrect her identity. I will make sure Boxer understands that. I might be an old woman, but I be knowin' things. He will need to be validatin' her story, because that be Boxer, but he will be doin' the honorable thing by this girl.

She didn't hesitate to do everythin' I asked of her without question tonight. This be a dangerous thing. Boxer must teach her to defend herself and be in control of her destiny from now on. She don't yet know it, but she be stayin' under our protection for as long as she be needin' us.

That is somethin' I am sure of.

What be layin' here before me is a broken child, a scared little rabbit, who is a danger to herself. She be an injured bird that needs to learn how to fly. The horrors that she been livin' down a ways from me for all her years, she needs to be leavin' dem behind in her mind and learnin' what a safe life is all about. But, even in this world, there are still dangers, and she needs to be trained. She has good gut instinct, but that can't fight an attack on her person.

I did not show the shock on my face from dem stories she told. That would not be helpin' her to release her inner demons to me.

I had helped to save souls in my younger days. I had worked for a shelter, among other jobs, and tried to help those who needed an ear to tell their hardship to, and feed dem and let dem know they weren't alone. I understood. This little one had slipped through the cracks. For that, I was deeply sorry. William had us all fooled.

I heard not a whisper of a child being raised in that home. I would have paid dearly to save this soul, had I known. But for now, this child, Whisper, be safe. She may have paid deeply for the sins of this vile man in blood and with her soul, but he be dead now.

Evil always loses out. That I be believin'.

Boxer is good at keepin' things hidden that need hidin' and cleanin' up evil, and then we can see how much damage has been done to the skinny mullet's mind. I can tell she be strong just from how she was when she be tellin' me of her life.

There were no tears. She be all dried up like a drought-ridden riverbed. I think a tear has not slid down those soft cheeks in almost a lifetime. She be hard on the surface, but Boxer will be able to help me see beneath and look for what needs fixin'. For now, sleep and warmth is what she needs. I be lookin' after her from now on. This is my place now to do because she gots nobody else.

Most are not smart enough to fear me, but this child should not. I am not what she needs to worry about...but what be comin' for her.

I fear there is still danger to her heart that be comin' for her over the horizon.

# BOXER

## The Gentleman

**M**y phone rang past midnight, waking me up. Miss Catherine was in need of my services, the services only the few I trusted know about.

They call me Boxer because I'm an ex-boxer, among other things. I was here playing a part in this small town, and Miss Catherine had received a visitor who needed both our help.

I arrived at Miss Catherine's to find a stunning female, who had a story of a lifetime, long asleep, knocked out by a strong sedative—the weapon of Miss Catherine's choice in case of any danger she needed to contain.

I gave her this sedative. It's something nobody will see coming. Given on an offer of food or drink, they're all welcoming things, that with a little sleight of hand, can incapacitate the danger until help arrives. This time, she used it solely for comfort, to ease the girl into a deep sleep.

She lay naked under the blanket, and I got the short run-down of events that led this girl to Miss Catherine's doorstep, while we both checked her over without uncovering her to my eyes. I didn't want to see what that bastard had no doubt touched without permission.

Her wrists were a shredded mess and her hands needed stitches, the cuts too deep to leave to heal on their own. She would have been in pain, but Miss Catherine said she was stoic, strong of body and mind…until it would come time for it to crack open.

*It always eventually does.*

Now, as I really look down at her for the first time since I arrived, I see she's beautiful. Her long, thick brown hair has dried from the heat of the fire. Miss Catherine had undone her braid while she slept. It is now in need of a good brushing. Her young face is haunted, even in her sleep. I doubt she has gotten a good night's rest in a long time. The best thing for her is a chemical induced sleep.

The stories she has told Miss Catherine painted a pretty damning picture. I agree to look into it for Miss Catherine. I just need to go over to the house and validate the girl's stories. I'll question her when she wakes in the morning, then make a visit to William's home.

I will need to be careful; it sounds like I'll be the only other male she has laid eyes on in person. That will be a frightening thing to a female who has only known one other male in her whole life, a son of a bitch who had abused her in more ways than one.

I'd seen William around town, but he seemed to be acting like a model citizen and he kept mostly to himself, but inside him was a dangerous monster, a master of deceit.

I trust in Miss Catherine's bones and what they are telling her, and they are telling her getting the police involved this early wouldn't bode well for the girl, nor would the public attention. Miss Catherine believes the media circus it will turn into would only damage her more.

I need a lot more information before I go turning to the local police, for my own peace of mind. The way it reads at the moment, she has been badly abused. This town is small, and none of us knew she had been living close by. William wanted her kept a secret for reasons this girl can't fathom. I've seen evil, and if William had abducted her, then there is more to her story than even she understands. I want to see the evidence of her stories for myself, then take it from there.

I send Miss Catherine off to bed after she gives me a warm blanket and makes me promise to wake her when the girl comes to. For now, I'm here to protect them. I throw another log on the fire and make myself comfortable in her chair to see the rest of the night out.

••••

SMASH!

My training has me jumping up out of the chair where I've nodded off, the blanket falling in a heap at my feet. I'm instantly alert, ready to protect the females in the house. I focus on where the girl had been asleep and realize she's now awake and must have knocked an antique vase off the sideboard, trying to snatch her clothes from the fireplace, where they had been hung on a rack. She obviously wants to get away from me.

The vase has shattered into pieces on the wooden floorboards. She gasps and freezes, more afraid now of having broken something that isn't hers. She has forgotten about me for a second, while her eyes are fixed on the damage. She's deciding what she should do.

"It's ok, love." I keep my voice light and hold my palms up as I sit back down in the chair to show her I'm not going to come after her. "My name's Boxer." She doesn't know whether to clean up the mess, hide the evidence, or move away from me.

She has her clothes in her hand held to her chest, trying to hide the fact that she's naked under the blanket, which is slipping off her shoulders, exposing her long legs beneath.

She's stunning, even in her messed up state of mind.

I can see she's losing her grip on the blanket as she tries to keep a hold of her clothing, which is adding an extra protective layer between her and me. Her hands must be stinging, since the pain will be kicking in now that she's awake. She loses her battle with the blanket and drops the clothes to the floor to save it from falling, and snatches it tighter around her small frame. I make sure to lower my eyes to the floor while she adjusts herself. I know she's watching me the entire time.

"Whisper, your body is safe around me. I will not touch you in a manner that will cause you distress, and you are free because nobody here will cage you or take away your rights." Her face reddens at my bluntness. "If you will allow me, and if you won't run, I'll slowly get up and go wake Miss Catherine. She made me promise to alert her when you woke up. I'm a trusted friend of hers, and that means I'm a good guy. She does not suffer fools."

She looks like a wild child, flighty and anxious. I carry on trying to give her a little peace of mind that

I'm here with good intentions. "She called me last night while you slept and we fixed your hands up. Your body was safe from my eyes. I stayed the entire time to protect you both, in case there was a threat we did not know about."

She looks down at her hands and wrists, which are trying to keep a grip on the blanket folds and notices the clean bandaging, and then looks back at me. "I cleaned your wounds and stitched your hands up while you slept." I point to the other room. "There are painkillers to help with the discomfort in the kitchen cupboard. Miss Catherine can give them to you when she comes down, if you'd like?" I've painted on the most nonthreatening, peaceful, friendly face I can muster, which is a little hard, considering I have a slightly crooked nose and I have a boxer's build.

"No drugs," she whispers to me. Her pupils are big black orbs filled with fear and confusion. I'm the only other male she has ever laid eyes on, and she simply doesn't know what my angle is. Her mind will be sending her mixed signals. She sounds like she needs me to command her and will do as I say, but I can't resort to doing that to her if I'm going to get her to trust me.

So I try my way. I reason with her and let her mind decide if I'm indeed a good guy. "They are just an over-the-counter tablet that *everybody* uses for pain relief, nothing more. They won't put you to sleep. "

"Do you have a computer?" she asks timidly.

"Well, yes, love, but not here. I have my phone? You can Google the name of the tablets. Is that what you want to do?"

She nods.

"Your name is Whisper, isn't it?"

She nods again.

"Whisper, you won't be able to hit the buttons with your hands bandaged. I tell you what—if you let me go get Miss Catherine, she will do it for you, and you can read all about Ibuprofen. Your hands must be causing you a lot of pain."

She gives me a little nod before she can stop herself. She doesn't want to show me she is hurting. I would bet a thousand bucks she'd never admitted to being in pain in front of William. I know from this small betrayal of her body that she already trusts me more than William, even if her mind doesn't quite want to accept it just yet.

"Miss Catherine drugged me last night. I can tell. That's the last time anybody does that to me." Her voice is determined and stronger.

*Ah, hell.* She's a smart girl.

"She wanted you to sleep, and nothing was done

to you other than taking care of your wounds. You wouldn't want to feel stitches being put in, love."

"I'm used to pain. I will not be drugged again." She ruins her confidence by looking down when she says those words to me.

*Fuck, and I need to be able to question her this morning. There goes the truth serum.*

"Nobody will do it to you ever again; you have my word. But we need to have a talk once you've had breakfast, and I need some straight answers to my questions. What you told Miss Catherine about the dead body, I want to be able to handle that for you, but I need to know details. Is that a deal?"

I wait for her while she works it all out in her head. *Is he a safe bet?* That's what she's asking herself. Can she trust me?

Then she surprises me with her response. "You sound different than Miss Catherine and Master William. Where are you from?"

*Master? What a fucking joke.*

"I'm British. You have my word I won't hurt you in any way, nor will Miss Catherine. She's a good sort. She did the right thing contacting me. Once we talk a little more, you will understand I'm trying to help you. I need to find out more about William, you, that house, and a few other important details. Miss Catherine believes you need to be protected, and I trust what Miss Catherine thinks."

She's staring at me all confused because she has forgotten about what her future holds.

I watch her as it all comes flooding back to her.

# Whisper

## Choices

**T**his British man before me is telling me I'm now safe. A *man* is telling me he won't let anybody hurt me again. He's different. I can feel it in my gut.

A calmness is radiating off Boxer, and when Miss Catherine opened her door last night to me, I felt a strong sense of goodness flowing from her. I had felt such relief that a man hadn't answered the door, and in his stead was this little, old, wrinkled, dark-skinned lady with sympathetic eyes and a kind voice.

The one thing Master William and Mistress taught me without any lessons, other than life lessons, was how to read a person's body language and sense a person's emotions.

When I woke up, my mind sent me mixed signals because I wanted to flee when I noticed a man sleeping in Miss Catherine's chair, it brought back bad memories of Master William. It was a natural reaction. My body was moving before I could tell it to calm down and, in my clumsiness, I shattered the vase.

He calls me 'love'. I don't understand why he uses that word, but I won't question him.

I know what being drugged feels like, and I'm not okay with what happened. I don't care for their reasons. I am angry at myself for letting that happen. This man in front of me tells me it will never happen again. It better not. I won't be treated that way *ever* again. I've lost one lifetime to a man who didn't care about my humanity, and I don't think I would survive going through it again.

*I couldn't be that unlucky, could I?*

I know the front door is so close I could open it and run, but this man, Boxer, would catch me before I even made it down the porch steps.

He's strong.

I have been cataloguing the first man I had ever met, other than Master William, while he talks to me, trying to pacify my urge to bolt. He wears a short-sleeved T-shirt pulled tight across his chest. I can see the shape of his muscles outlined by the fabric. He's an attractive older man with kind dark brown eyes. He looks a little younger than my master was, and he has short brown hair. I can see he has tattoos on the skin exposed to me.

He interrupts my thoughts. He's a clever man. "Don't think of running, Whisper. You need an identity and money to do that. There's a whole big world out there you have no experience living in. The police won't be getting involved until I have assessed William's home. Give me and Miss Catherine today for starters, and maybe tomorrow. I know there are recordings of your life and, no doubt, William's death, so I can see for myself what happened. Those recordings will be your saving grace, the proof of the past you've led. You need to rest and let your body recover for a couple days. I meant what I said; you're free to do what you want now, but the sensible thing would be to let me do my thing, and then we can talk about your future and help you move on, if that's what you decide."

I can't help shuffling nervously from side to side because I have a choice to either stay or leave, and I want so badly to have friends who care and can be trusted to help me.

But is it possible?

My mind is at war with myself because it wants me to run, but it doesn't know how we will survive. I've never had choices before.

"What is it you want to say?" He's watching me

with those kind eyes and uses a calming voice.

I want to speak up, beat my chest, and tell him I'm now in control of my life, but I know that's not true.

I have to let Boxer take charge for now.

One day, I will be in control, and nobody will change that.

# BOXER

## Trust Is Earned With Respect

**I** want to reassure her. I soften my voice and hope she believes what I'm telling her. "You have my word you are not a prisoner anymore, but you need friends, people you can rely on. You sound like you've lived a pretty shitty existence without friends, or a reason to trust in another human being. This is all going to be new for you."

She has no reason to trust me, especially since I'm a man. I have to keep reminding myself I'm the only other man she has met in her entire life and I'm asking her to believe my words when she has no good reason to.

Trust is earned with respect, and she hasn't known me long enough to respect me.

"We are now your friends. Friends don't hurt each other, not deliberately anyway. I know we will need to earn your trust, but if you can stay here today, rest, and let Miss Catherine look after you that would be great. You need to recuperate anyway. I know this will all be foreign to you, but I need some time. I will deal with William and the house. Can you do that for us?"

I need her to stay here for a couple days, and then we can hopefully convince her we are worth her respect. It's not a lot of time to win her over.

# Whisper

## Breakfast Bake Cajun Style

I can stay here today, and maybe tomorrow, and see what happens. Boxer knows the area. I do not. I'm a prisoner to my inexperience. I'm twenty-one and feel like a child. I'm very lost to a world I know nothing about living in by myself. I really have no choice but to stay here. I can't support myself, so I must do as I am told. I will not look at this as anything other than a means to an end for a new independent life for myself. A life filled with my own decisions.

I do feel safe around this man. Boxer doesn't make me feel like Master William did. I'm not frightened of him, and he trusts that I told Miss Catherine the truth.

It's hard to think; there's too much going on in my head. I need these people for the moment. I want support. I can't do this by myself. That much I know.

There's a dead body to answer for. I do not want to be judged for my master's death.

I don't want to be discovered.

I don't want strange people looking at the recordings.

"There's video footage I left back at the house that I don't want people to see. Master William said nobody knew about me." I can feel the panic starting to rise inside me, the sheer horror of anybody seeing those tapes of my existence and judging me, questioning me. "I don't want to be discovered. I want to stay a secret." My voice is stronger, trying to convey how important this is to me. I want to be heard by him.

"You have my word if I discover everything you have told Miss Catherine to be true, then I'm willing to think about keeping you a secret from the world and we can talk about the next step. Fair deal?"

He's giving me the right to answer for myself, but I really have no other choice. It's the only thing I can do.

I've never left William's home in my entire life, until now. I have no actual life experience except what I've seen in the movies or on the computer. I have no money, no way of supporting myself, no relatives that I know of, no friends—unless I lower my guard and let these two people in. I have no means of transportation other than my legs, and I'm so sore and mentally abused. I really don't want to accept help, but I have to. It's a frightening thing, spelling out to myself how alone I am, unable to feed or clothe myself or put a roof over my head without people asking questions I have no answers to. I had everything given to me at Master William's home, but it came at a great price.

Essentially, I'm an alien on my own planet. I've landed at Miss Catherine's house, and I can only rely on these people until I can do it myself.

They seem genuine and like they really want to help me, so I have to resign myself to the facts. If I run and Boxer doesn't help me, then I will be known to the world because the police will find the recordings and proof of my existence. Where would I hide? Somebody has to answer for what happened, and I don't want to be sat in front of people. I left all the footage for anybody to watch except the hard drive I took from the library, put inside my pillowcase, and brought with me. I will be hunted down because they will know I lived with him. I left a crime scene; the crime being committed against me. Master William drummed enough into my head to scare me out of ever running.

I need to let Boxer go, and hope he decides to keep me a secret. I have to give him time.

I nod my head.

He looks relieved. "I'm going to leave the room so you can get dressed." He slowly stands up, keeps his distance from me, and walks up the stairs to find Miss Catherine.

Boxer has shown me nothing but kindness and respect. Something I'm trying to understand. He doesn't know me. I could have killed my master.

I stop thinking and start getting dressed as best as I can. My jeans are the only difficulty, but I manage and grit my teeth through the pain. I don't want to be caught naked by Boxer.

My hair is no longer braided and, for the first time, I notice how long it is. Somebody took it out of the wet braid and it is now a shaggy mess. I'm used to being touched, but this seems caring rather than sinister. I suddenly have this determined feeling to cut it. The last time I had it cut I was still a little girl. I also don't want these clothes on because Master William bought them for me.

I'm dressed when Miss Catherine and Boxer come back downstairs, and I have the urge to do something. I do not know how to be around people, so I busy myself trying to pick up the pieces of the smashed vase, but find my hands are pretty useless.

Boxer comes over, crouches down beside me, and starts picking up the pieces. I stand up and face Miss

Catherine. "I'm so sorry. I didn't mean to break the vase. I..." I actually don't know what to say. I broke something that wasn't mine. I eye the door. It seems the only way I can escape what has happened. I don't know how to fix the vase, and I don't know how angry Miss Catherine will be with me.

A wave of doubt assaults my mind. *I shouldn't have come here. I don't know these people. I...*

Boxer stands up next to me, holding the bigger pieces of the vase. "Whisper, don't overthink it. We're not like the man who held you prisoner. That may or may not have been Miss Catherine's favourite vase, but it was an accident. You will not be punished for it. That's not how it happens in her home, nor mine. She may be upset that the vase is broken, but she will move on."

"'Chile, it was an antique, but a human is more important than material items." She comes over and pats my arm. "Boxer tells me you've agreed to be stayin' on a couple days. It would be my pleasure to have your company. Now, because you be trustin' that I be doin' right by you, I want to be extendin' the same to you."

She puts her hand into the pocket of her neat floral frock and pulls out a brass key.

"This be the only key I possess to the front door. If you like, it is now yours to hold onto until you decide to be leavin'. That way, you know you are free to be goin' on your way whenever you be wantin' to." She looks very pleased to be showing me this sign of good faith.

"Boxer, if you don't mind takin' dem pieces to the trash, and I'll be fixin' us all somethin' to eat." She puts a careful arm around my shoulders. "Come, honeychile, you can repay me by learnin' how to make a hearty Cajun breakfast bake." She looks me up and down. "I got me some work ahead, gettin' some meat on dem bones of yours."

I look at Boxer, who winks at me, then I do the only thing I know how to do, and that's take orders. My feet are moving before my brain tells me I should be saying no. But I must repay Miss Catherine.

Boxer's words follow me into the kitchen. "Whisper, this is what friends do. They make up for things by helping each other. Your life now comes with a full set of rights. You will be what Miss Catherine needs." I turn and give Boxer a worried look. I see the recognition in his eyes. "I meant somebody to fuss over. Miss Catherine has no family. She's kind, and she's loyal to those who earn her respect. You already have her respect. You are strong, and she is too. You have a lot in common." I give Boxer a confused look, because how could we have anything in common? While Miss Catherine busies herself getting things out of her icebox and pantry, Boxer leans in close to my ear and quietly says, "Love, she was once a slave too."

The shock on my face has Boxer laying a gentle hand on my arm to steady me. "I only told you so you know. She knows what it's like to be beaten as a child and survive to rise above it. She understands what having your rights taken away from you feels like. You may have different stories, but she gets it. You can rise above it too, and take back your life. We will both be here to help you in any way we can. Today is a new day."

Something inside me swells, and I feel like I want to cry for Miss Catherine. I swallow it down because I simply don't cry. I look away from Boxer and whisper, "Miss Catherine, I'm not sure what I can do with my hands bandaged up. I don't want to break anything else."

"You just stand and watch me, and that will be good enough, child." Miss Catherine is very gentle with me, and again it makes me want to cry, because I haven't been spoken to kindly, ever. It's a new emotion for me to accept and be comfortable with.

Master William always watched me make his meals, I think for fear I would try to poison him. He would eat an evening meal out a lot, and that's when I would be chained to the pole. I would miss that meal, or if he was feeling particularly generous, he would throw in some fruit.

I think he regretted killing my mistress so early because it meant he had to watch me more himself. He had less freedom because of me. Growing older meant I was not as naive, but fear always kept me under control. Fear is a powerful weapon when you know no different.

"Ladies, while you are doing that, I will just go make a couple calls."

I look worriedly at Boxer, afraid of what those calls will mean for me.

"Just some business, love, that I need to attend to." I'm still not sure of what Boxer means, but I decide to put a foot forward and place a little faith in him. "I'll be back in fifteen minutes," he states, and I hear the front door shut quietly as he leaves.

My hands hurt, but I didn't want to remind him of the painkillers. I turn my attention back to Miss Catherine, blocking the pain as best I can. I have cooked a lot of meals, but very simple foods. I listen while she explains what she's making, and I learn a new dish.

As I watch her breaking eggs and adding ingredients, I wonder what my place is going to be here for the next couple days, what chores I will need to do to repay Miss Catherine because I will gladly pitch in.

••••

Miss Catherine brings the breakfast bake straight from her oven over to the table, where Boxer sniffs the air appreciatively and thanks Miss Catherine before he has even tried a mouthful. He pulls a chair out for Miss Catherine then me, and waits for us to be seated. I whisper shyly, "Thank you, Boxer." My face feels inflamed from being treated this way. Miss Catherine takes it in her stride.

She gently squeezes the arm I have resting on the table. "Honeychile, that's the way gentlemen should behave around a lady. You don't see it happen that much these days, so when a man be doin' that for you, you be lettin' him."

The delicious smell from the breakfast bake fills my nose when Miss Catherine takes her first slice out of the pan and places it on Boxer's plate. My stomach actually does a little somersault of appreciation. I haven't had a hot breakfast, ever.

I watch both of them exchange subtle looks across her small round table as they make light conversation, all for my benefit, to keep me at ease. While they eat and talk amongst themselves, I eat in silence, because I don't know what to talk about. I didn't talk to Master William while we ate. I only spoke when spoken to, so I'd get lost inside my head with my own thoughts.

I mainly ate fruits and vegetables as part of my daily diet with Master William. It was all from the garden in the back-yard. I secretly really enjoyed watching everything grow. It gave me a little peace and satisfaction knowing I could help something meet its full potential. I could care for something and give it life.

Master William always bought meat, and we made do with the garden and fruit trees. We ate mainly chicken or pulled pork, and a little red meat when he was there for dinner or when I baked fresh bread for sandwiches. He wanted me thin and healthy. Doctors were never required. I never even caught a virus because I was so isolated.

The utensils and cutlery were always locked in the kitchen drawers when not in use. Anything sharp, or what could be used as a weapon, was never left unattended or unlocked without his supervision. As I got older, I wondered if it was to save Master William's own skin, or so I wouldn't do anything to myself.

I eat as much as I can of the Cajun breakfast bake while my bandaged hands are being a nuisance, but I manage to use a fork to break small pieces off. The food is rich, and my stomach is starting to rebel a little. I'm not used to all the eggs, greasy sausages, onions, or cheese. It's delicious, but I can't eat a lot in one sitting.

I had a lot of things drummed into me from an early age about keeping myself presentable. My teeth would be brushed three times a day, my hair always neat and tidy, and my clothes immaculate. Everything was orderly and precise.

Now, I don't know what I'm going to do after breakfast. I don't have to be orderly and precise, but at the same time, I have this urge to keep up appearances, but I am fully aware my current state is far from what would be deemed presentable.

My stomach is starting to cramp up and I need the bathroom.

"What is it, child?"

I feel too embarrassed to explain. I know my face is getting hotter. I can feel Boxer watching me. "Whisper, I'm gonna step out and organize a few things you might need. Miss Catherine will look after you. Don't feel shy about asking her anything. Remember what I told you earlier?"

That has me snapping my head up. Miss Catherine has been through her own troubles. I can do this. Boxer gives me another encouraging wink and excuses himself from the table. He thanks Miss Catherine, and even me, for the delicious breakfast and company, then lets himself out.

"Miss Catherine..." It's as though she reads my mind.

"Child, up the stairs and to your right will be what you be lookin' for. I will clean up. Off you go." My stomach is really cramping, so I thank her and go in search of the bathroom.

# BOXER

## Under The Cover Of Nightfall

**I made some calls outside while Miss Catherine** attended to Whisper and showed her around her home. The poor girl looked uncomfortable and I had to get out of there. I knew enough to know my presence was not required.

I called in a favor from a doctor friend of mine and organized some clean clothes for Whisper. I wanted her checked out, but that was something I would play by ear. I would let Miss Catherine handle it because Whisper was liable to accept it coming from her more than me. I was the gender that had let her down badly.

Before I could head over to William's place, I had to make plans and be intelligent about what I was getting myself involved in. This was not a paid job; this was personal. I had made it my business because Miss Catherine needed my help, and I wasn't about to let either of them down.

Next, I'd need to question Whisper myself. I knew how to interrogate a person.

I spent the morning carefully coaxing more information out of her without the use of a drug. That would have been the easier way for me to get straight answers, but I promised her she wouldn't be drugged again. It was important to keep that promise.

I know I was asking an awful lot of her to tell me, a man, what had happened to her, but it was either me or the police, and they wouldn't have been as kind as I was. I explained all this to her. I had to hear it all from her lips myself. I could do nothing until she told me as much as she could remember.

I gave her those two choices, and she chose me.

She was naturally guarded at first, her eyes returning to Miss Catherine when the questions become uncomfortable, but she answered everything I asked of her. It had been ingrained into her personality to answer when spoken to, and I used this to my advantage.

I tried to mask my anger, but it still slipped across my face. It was hard to put into words how a few hours of questioning did not even add up to the lifetime of abuse she had been dealt. The emotions and pain she would have gone through over those years would have been immense. I was hearing a very two dimensional version, but a three dimensional movie was playing in her head as she talked to me. That was the hardest part about questioning a victim. I was making her relive a lot of what she didn't want to remember. She radiated calm in the storm I could see flickering behind her eyes. She knew how to put on an appearance, but I could see what was really happening inside her head. But I had to know, in order to deal with her current situation.

I can always spot a liar, and she's not one. I wish she was making up a lot of what happened to her, but you can't fake her behavior. I know the questions to ask to get a person to open up to me. I know what body language to look for, and I can smell a story that stinks. The only thing that stunk was William, who is dead at the bottom of his staircase.

William Dupré's plantation home was a dressed-up cage of abuse no little girl should have lived in. She was stolen from her parents when she was around two years old. The timing was a little sketchy and something I was going to try to look into for her, if only to bring her some closure. The chances of finding her birth parents are low, but I promised myself I would try to find something that might lead me to them.

Because William was so organized and structured with her days, she had knowledge she didn't even know she possessed. I got as much of William Dupré's routine from her as I could. She knew he was due for his three week cleaning service to arrive in four days' time. I will make my final decision once I get to the house, but if the recordings are there, William's death has been captured, and everything else I heard from Whisper's lips is validated, then William would be staying where he was until they came, rotting away. I would have four days to remove all evidence of Whisper from the house.

I'll head over around nightfall with the men I have organized to help me out, and we will be prepared to pull a cover up job.

There was something more sinister going on here that was eating at me, and I knew I had to tread carefully. I needed to get in with my small team and get out without raising any suspicions.

But for now, I will spend the day in and around town as usual, just going about my business, letting the town see me, in case the shit hits the fan in the future.

I understand the importance of a healthy alibi; you never know when you are going to need one, so always plan ahead. This town is small, only around four hundred people, and they remember things. They remember details. They will notice something out of the ordinary if unknown cars start rolling in, looking all *Men in Black* badass.

I can't afford to be brought into this mess as an accessory. I know how to keep my hands clean, but I have to be smart about it.

What was William into? There's more to his story than keeping this girl as a house slave, a pet.

Where did she come from?

Who is missing her?

Those are questions I have no answers to, and I don't like the black holes they've left behind.

The man in me is feeling protective of her already, and wants to save her from further mental trauma.

Something smells wrong about all this. It stinks badly.

••••

It took me one night to make my decision, and two days to have the house cleared from top to bottom of all evidence of Whisper's existence. What my small team and I had discovered was a lifetime of mental and physical abuse.

I want to personally kill that fucker all over again…but slowly.

My mind was made up. It wasn't warranted to put

her through a media onslaught. She needed a new life as quick as possible, and I could do that for her. There would have been an investigation and too many difficult questions for Whisper to have to endure.

She'd been put through enough.

We entered from the back entrance of the home, where we knew Whisper had made her escape, leaving the door unlocked. This worked well for us. We wore head-to-toe black bodysuits, so we left nothing behind of our interference.

Whisper is now a ghost in this home.

We found the camera footage and watched his stupid death played out before our eyes, while she hung like a piece of meat waiting for him.

The. Sick. Motherfucker.

We watched the courageous, determined girl get herself out of her binds while we sat cheering her on, and we shared the moments where she quietly lost it. Her eyes glazed over as her fear started to take hold, but she still took those steps to leave the house and walk away from it.

We removed all her things from her room. She didn't have much in it. The things she had the most of were clothes. They were real nice outfits, and contained dozens of replicas of the long white dress she was forced to wear.

I doubted she would keep the clothes, but I boxed them up anyway. I didn't include the long white dresses; we would dispose of them. I added the few personal items of hers she had been granted, but I thought she could sort through it all, and I could dispose of what she didn't want to keep. If it were me, I would have chucked the lot and burned it, but I wasn't going to take those decisions away from her.

Whisper had none of the usual things you would find in a female's room. This fucker had decorated her room with a set of handcuffs attached to one corner of her brass bed to keep her locked down.

Every part of that big house was masculine and well organized. Even her bedroom was masculine, down to the bedding and wallpaper. It was a room for a boy, not a young woman. We stripped the bed and made it up with fresh bedding. It now looked like an unused spare room.

In the library, I removed all evidence of her life. We each watched some of the footage, which was enough to confirm her stories. It was a very sobering time watching what the little girl on through to her teenaged years, had gone through.

I could see from the hard drives and their dates there was one missing. He had done an immaculate job of keeping everything labeled. I knew it was safe because Miss Catherine knows where the other one is. She had found it inside the jacket Whisper had been wearing. She placed everything back inside the jacket as it was found after she had shown me the contents of the pillowcase. I should have taken a copy of the data on it, but I hadn't wanted to leave the two women alone at the time. I had no clue if there was another force gunning for the girl that night.

We had to let Whisper tell us she had it because this one would have the most damaging footage on it, and is the reason she took it.

There were twelve cameras all fairly well hidden around the house, and I took care of them all. We patched the surfaces to hide what had been taken out. Only if you scrutinized areas and bothered to look hard would you notice. He had placed them in well-hidden parts of his home.

Whisper thought she didn't have a camera in her room, but that cocksucker had one in the light hanging in the middle of her room. It was concealed well. He would have watched her in bed. I could not find that footage.

Who knows what this sick fuck was up to with Whisper?

We left no stone unturned when we went through his home. My team did their job well; we were all professionals. We removed anything that could lead to the life he was living with her.

We kept only what looked like it may suit a normal library, and everything else was removed. The pole in the closet was left. It could have been there for any number of reasons.

The library housed a lot of porn for his reading pleasure, and pornographic movies. I left them there. He looked like a man living alone with too much time on his hands.

As far as I could see, there was nothing else on any computer or downloaded anywhere that could incriminate Whisper in any way. He did a lot of the hard work for us himself. He was careful. He didn't want her to be discovered.

There was the possibility that William wasn't the only one who had access to this footage, but I had no way of knowing. I had to hope this was all there was.

Whisper said there was the woman he had killed. I saw no evidence of her existence, not how Whisper described her, anyway, in all the years she had lived with William. She had been killed eight years ago, and I had lived here for ten. Whisper said she never left the house, and there was no sign of a grave on the property, so William made that easy for us. We didn't need any of his past rearing its ugly head in the future. He would have been smart and disposed of the body off his property. He would never have let himself be caught for her death.

Nobody had missed this woman, even though she had been dead eight years, and nobody had traced her to William's home. He would have been careful and chosen her well for the task of raising Whisper.

She was a nobody.

A ghost who served William.

That was not my concern or business.

Whisper was my business.

The smell was getting worse, and the cleaning service was gonna get a rude shock, but this couldn't be helped. It will be a natural discovery. The cleaning service is from New Orleans. He was smart. He didn't contract anybody too close to home.

They would come to the door for their routine clean, and the smell will be enough to alert them to enquire more. The police would get involved, and it will look like the stupid accident it was. A man living alone had fallen by his own drunken stupidity to his death.

He must have gone on a bender, and that decision had set Whisper free. I feel bad for her because she had enough nightmares stashed in that young mind of hers. Now, the sight of another dead person has been added to it.

The thing with William is he didn't expect to die

before Whisper, but he still kept his files organized. His security was no match for my hacker. It was all very easy for us to retrieve and delete. He felt powerful in his role as her master, not believing for one minute she would outlive him.

The beatings, and the power that was taken away from her at such a young age, were hard to watch, but I had to make sure this girl was telling me the truth without a doubt.

She neglected to tell me she was locked up in the old slave cabin out back when the cleaners came to the house. She had been drugged and handcuffed to an old bed. I could hear William's voice as I watched some footage. I only ever saw the back of him. He would carry her in already totally out of it and handcuff her.

I fast forwarded three hours and he would be back, calling her name and telling her the cleaners had gone, and then he would carry her unresponsive body back into the main house.

It made my skin crawl to see the young Whisper like that.

All the hard drives will be locked away in my safe. They are hers to do with what she wishes.

We were on a tight schedule with time, so we watched as many as we could, but the others would have to be watched away from here. No wonder

Whisper took the last hard drive, so nobody would stumble across it. I can only imagine the nightmares it would contain.

My conscience is clear knowing I'll be doing everything in my power to show her how to protect herself from now on. I've watched only moments in time, but at least I know about what Whisper is dealing with by herself, and we are now here to help her if she allows us to.

William was living under the town's noses with his captive for nearly two decades. To have been able to uphold that secret is a pretty frightening thing.

Whisper's life had been wrenched from her, but at least now the twisted fuck is well and truly dead. I have no doubt he would have eventually killed her, and nobody would have been able to mourn her.

That would have been a real sad fucking thing.

Miss Catherine would have already pictured in her mind what the girl had gone through, because she has her own horror stories locked in her mind. She knew straight away listening to the girl that I would be helping out, because somebody needs to try to right the wrongs that were rained down upon her.

With the help of my team, one member being a computer hacker genius, we cleared any personal files we deemed 'too close to the subject' from his computer, and we got necessary information off his phone. William was a smart man; he had deleted all messages, assuming he had any, because he lead a fairly hermit existence. He covered his tracks well. If I hadn't observed the footage, I would never have believed the monster he was capable of being.

The time I spent doing this clean up job, Whisper stayed true to her word and didn't run. I need a bit more time because now I have to convince her that I can help her and give her a new life, but I need time to think this through.

The three of us have been up for nearly forty-eight hours straight, catching a couple hours sleep on rotation until we had the job completed. When we weren't at the house, we were at my bar in the back rooms, going through the files and hard drives we had taken. The files we retrieved had to be thoroughly examined to make sure nothing was going to come and bite us in the ass in the future with William's untimely death.

Who did the house go to in the event of his death? I need to find these things out before his death is on record. I had my accomplices help me scour the files, and that's when we found William's will.

Thank God there were no surprises. There is a son, who will get the lot. Whisper is free to stay a secret. I took a copy of the will for my records, always being on the over-precautionary side. It has saved my ass on more than one occasion.

I think finally our job here is done. The stink of William Dupré is getting to be too much, so it's time to leave and let everything play out naturally in a couple of days' time.

We breeze out like we breezed in, without leaving a stitch of evidence we had been there.

We are that fucking good.

# Whisper

## Gentle Giant

The past three days have really opened my eyes to the generosity and kindness of my new friends.

I asked Miss Catherine this morning to cut my hair shorter, because it was too long. She took a good foot off the bottom, and it was *still* too long, but I felt better for having that much cut off.

On the first day, in the afternoon, a big burly man a few years older than me introduced himself to Miss Catherine as Lincoln, and he was there on Boxer's orders. He had brought over clothes for me from one of Boxer's friends. He came to the door, but he did not come in.

I was a little overwhelmed this person was kind enough to share her jeans and shirts with me, and she didn't even know me. It was a really nice feeling getting out of the clothes I had worn from the house.

I was thin, and she was a little bigger than me, so the clothes were a little loose, but they felt like honest clothes.

Boxer had called Miss Catherine earlier that day to explain that Lincoln would be coming and going while he was working at Master William's house and that he was discreet and trustworthy. Lincoln was polite and very unassuming with his presence. I felt safer with him being around.

Boxer wasn't leaving us alone until he had everything sorted at Master William's house. He let Miss Catherine know not to be alarmed if she sensed somebody watching, because he had a man outside at all times keeping us safe until he knew there was no danger.

I did not leave the house to go outside. I stayed indoors, where I felt protected by the walls, and it was what I was used to.

The second day, I mainly slept on the couch. I think my body was exhausted from the life I had led, always keeping my guard up.

Miss Catherine tried to feed me a lot, and I accepted a little. I was still wary, and she knew I needed my space. I was still processing this kind woman and my freedom. She didn't raise her voice to me, and she didn't order me around. She was patient and quiet with me. I didn't know how to talk to people. Her actions spoke louder than words.

Miss Catherine tended to my hands and looked after me. My hands were healing, and I did end up taking some painkillers. They didn't knock me out, and I learned it was okay to take these pills and feel relief from the pain. I was so used to coping with pain and riding it out that I knew no different.

I kept my pillowcase with my personal things by my side, and nobody tried to take them away from me.

Today was day three. I haven't seen Boxer at all today. He would usually only drop by to check in on us for a short time, but he hasn't arrived yet. I feel like I need that contact with him, even if it's just for a short time. I know he has been working hard to erase me from the life I'd led. He had explained, to my great relief, that I would remain a secret.

I feel so much confusion that this man would do this for me, when he didn't know me.

Lincoln just arrived; I can hear him talking quietly with Miss Catherine. To my astonishment, I find I had been looking forward to seeing him, but Boxer still hasn't shown up. I'm worried about him.

I don't have long to dwell on my worries because Miss Catherine finds me where I'm sitting, watching the sun draw its shade down on another uneventful fear-free day through the back window. It's a favorite place for me to sit. She gently takes my hand with a knowing smile on her face and leads me to a spare room upstairs.

"'Chile, I hope you like it," she says, and I let out a little noise of surprise. "I had a little help, of course, from Boxer and Lincoln." She explains to me they had organized a few things to be brought over by Lincoln, who is already assembling what looks to be a big bed. He has all the parts laid out and is working away as Miss Catherine brings me into the room. I can tell she is very pleased with herself. "Now, I think it's settled that you will be stayin' with me until you are ready to be leavin', so it seemed right to give you your own privacy. This will be your very own room from now on, if it be pleasin' you."

The one thing I know for sure is I am okay with staying with Miss Catherine. "Thank you, it does." I feel shy and awkward about what everybody is doing for me, but I keep my mouth shut and don't fight it.

I realize now Miss Catherine has been letting me get my bearings, and she didn't want to put too much pressure on me to stay. She had been playing it very casual, and now she wants to make it a more permanent arrangement.

Lincoln was what Miss Catherine called a real gentle giant. He had been making sure not to come too close to me, and he would often give me a wink when he caught me watching him, just like Boxer does. Now, I'm standing here, staring at this man from the safety of the doorway, while he puts my new bed together for me. I feel a lump in my throat for the things everybody has been doing for me. If I could cry, I think I would have. I turn to thank Miss Catherine again, but she has quietly snuck off to leave me to it.

Lincoln likes to hum to himself while he does things for Miss Catherine, like chopping wood for the fire and now putting the bed together. I like hearing him being happy. He is indeed a gentle giant.

He gets up and goes out to his pickup truck and brings in more boxes, while I stand staring at my new room. The boxes he brings in are side tables, and he asks if I want to help him put one together.

And the next hour passes quickly as we set to work.

Lincoln sang songs softly to himself that I didn't know, while I watched what he did with his side table and I copied him with the other. He has a nice voice. It felt good to make something. He would encourage me when I had trouble with the screws, but he didn't once take over or touch me. I could use my hands a lot more now, and my wrists were getting better.

I stole glances at his handsome face. He really looked happy singing. He had a soft mop of blond hair that flopped over his eyes while he worked away. He would keep pushing it off his face until I took one of the hair ties out of my hair, which Boxer had brought over in a small box of my personal things and offered it to him. He smiled and took it from my outstretched hand, being careful not to touch me too much, and tied it up on top of his head. He looked real nice.

I noticed for the first time that this is the closest I have been to Lincoln, and he has the bluest, kindest eyes. He's only the third man I have ever met, and I don't feel fear around him. He puts me at ease with his body language.

Miss Catherine entered the room with an iced tea for both of us and then she discreetly left us alone again. I really like iced tea. I always made sure I tidied up after myself and brought any dishes back to the kitchen, cleaned them up, and put them away. I was used to making sure everything was always in its place.

I liked Miss Catherine, and I realized how much I didn't want to leave her because she is kind and generous. I felt like I would upset her if I chose to leave. I could see how much she enjoyed showing me things and having my company. I enjoyed her company too. I didn't feel lonely anymore. I could stay here a little longer until I had worked things out for myself.

Once the tables had been put together, Lincoln went back outside and came in with armfuls of bedding in packages. He didn't hesitate to make my bed up for me. He ignored my protests, and I simply stood in the corner and watched him. I didn't know what to say to a man doing things for me. He just kept on singing or humming as he made the space look like a female's room. The sheets were white and soft-looking, and the bed covering had pretty flowers on it. I had four fluffy pillows and one fancy smaller column-shaped pillow as decoration. The side tables had pretty lights sitting on top of them by the time Lincoln was finished.

Now, as a final touch, he turns one of the lamps on. He looks very pleased with himself when he is done, standing back and looking at his handiwork.

"Thank you," I whisper to Lincoln.

"You're welcome."

I'm curious. "Where is Boxer?" I whisper to him. I'm still learning I can talk freely if I want to. Old habits die hard.

Lincoln gives me a dimpled smile because it's the first time I've spoken more than one sentence to him in such a short time without him asking me a question.

"He had to run an overnight errand, but he will be back tomorrow." He then changes the topic. I don't miss what he just did. "I'm going to be staying indoors watching after you and Miss Catherine from now until he tells me otherwise. I need the couch to sleep on, so we needed to make you more comfortable. She picked out these things, and Boxer ordered them online for you."

I feel panicked that I can't pay them back and I start fidgeting, not sure how to fix how I'm feeling, so I blurt out, "I have no money to pay for it all." My heart starts speeding up and my eyes dart around at all the things in the room. It hadn't even crossed my mind when the room was being put together how much it would have all cost, because I was too busy listening to Lincoln. Now, it has all come crashing down on me. I feel overwhelmed.

"Hey, Whisper. What's all this about? You've gone from relaxed to looking like you are gonna bolt." Lincoln's holding my hand and rubbing his thumb slowly over it. My wandering mind starts to calm. It's the first time he's touched me, and I don't want to pull my hand away.

"I can't pay for all this. How am I going to pay for it? What will I have to do to pay for it all? I was happy to sleep on the couch. I didn't need all this." My free hand waves about the room.

"Hold on a minute. You don't think you have to repay them, do you?" Lincoln's trying to keep eye contact with me.

I know my eyes have gone wide in confusion, because I'm shocked by all their generosity. I have done nothing to earn any of these things.

I snatch my hand back from Lincoln's and stumble to my feet. "I have to speak to Miss Catherine." I go to leave, but his hand snakes around my waist loosely, holding me steady, but not imprisoning my body, and it's not intimate.

"Whoa there, Whisper. Where's the fire?" Once I've stilled, he lets me go and faces me. "Don't take this away from Miss Catherine and Boxer. They both felt you deserved a little happiness in the form of your own space, where you can come and go as you please. Miss Catherine had great fun picking out everything for this room. A simple thank you will be all that she will be requiring from you."

I look up into his kind face to make sure he means what he just said, and I see he does. I change the subject. "Why are we being watched?"

"This is just a precaution until Boxer knows what he's dealing with, when it comes to William Dupré. There are a lot of unknown facts at the moment. He

# WRENCHED

doesn't like surprises."

"Um, okay. I'm just going to go talk to Miss Catherine and thank her. Um...Lincoln, thank you too, for putting everything together for me. It really looks nice."

"Made my day to see you happy."

I can see he means those words. I head on down the stairs, taking the iced tea glasses with me, and find Miss Catherine in the kitchen, making dinner. When Miss Catherine showed me my new room, I wasn't sure how to respond. She doesn't know me and she is offering me a room under her roof. This is too much. I have the money I had taken from William in my back pocket, and I pull it out and put it on the kitchen table quietly. I had only taken forty-seven dollars and some coins from Master William's house, and I didn't know how I was going to use it. This seems like the right thing to do. Then I quietly walk over to the sink and place the glasses in it, ready to wash.

"You can leave those. I be cleanin' them up and you can go and enjoy that room of yours," she tells me. Her eyes seek out the money on the table, but she doesn't comment on it.

"Okay," I reply, my usual response when she suggests I do something. Then I take a couple steps back away from Miss Catherine while she watches me. I clear my throat because Miss Catherine likes me to speak up. "Thank you, Miss Catherine, for the room and everything in it. It's very nice." My face is heating up at the look she's giving me. She is so happy, and I can't repay her for being so kind. I don't know what else to do with myself, so I smile back awkwardly and then flee back up to my new room.

Lincoln has left, so I go find my pillowcase, pull out Jenny, and place her in the center of the bed. I open the drawer of the side table and place the hard drive inside, and then I put my copy of *The Wind in the Willows* on top of the bedside table.

When Lincoln had brought over my clothes and toiletries from the house, I had pulled out just a few basic things and kept them out of necessity, placing the rest by the front door for them to take away. I didn't want to wear anything that gave me a bad memory. The box with my remaining clothes had already been set on the floor of my new room.

Just as I'm about to undo it, Lincoln calls up to me from the bottom of the stairs in his deep voice, "Whisper, I have one more thing I need to bring up for you, and I'm going to need help doing it. Could you please come down and meet Joel?" He waits for me to reply, but I'm a little stunned at what else I could possibly need. "He's a friend of Boxer's too." As a way of explanation, he adds, "It's too large for me by myself."

I'm very curious as to what he couldn't bring up on his own. I walk down the stairs, and Miss Catherine is standing there, waiting for me with an even bigger smile on her face, if that's possible.

"Honeychile, I had this old French antique armoire in storage, and one of Boxer's men has been workin' on it for the past few days. I was hopin' you would like to use it in your new room. I did take the liberty of assumin' you might be stayin' with me. I hope you don't mind?"

My eyes almost bug out of my head at this enormous piece of beautifully carved furniture. It's painted in a creamy white, but a funny texture, with two doors which opened with a key. The wood, you can tell, has been carved by a loving hand.

Miss Catherine starts explaining the paint is called the distressed look, and very French, and then I notice the man standing by Lincoln. He has dark hair, and it's neatly cut short. He's tall, lean, and very strong looking, but not big and burly like Lincoln. He's watching me carefully through his black-framed glasses, which make him look a bit like Clark Kent.

"Hey, I'm Joel. Nice to meet you, Whisper." He's very handsome, and he gives me a little wave and a genuine smile.

I can't help but smile a little shyly back at him. I can see Lincoln grinning away next to him, and that makes me smile a little bigger. Miss Catherine has walked over to me and moved me aside, so the men can get the armoire up to my room.

"I love it, Miss Catherine, thank you." Again, I'm almost lost for words. I don't quite know what else to say to her.

"Hush now, child. You don't need to be sayin' anythin' to me. I know it's all a bit overwhelmin' for you. I just wanted you to be havin' some nice, feminine things for yourself. Every young lady needs her own room and a place to be storin' her clothes. The look on your face is enough." She pats me carefully on the arm. "You go up once they be finished and make use of that fine piece of furniture. That is all the thanks I'll be needin'."

I feel a tiny bit of excitement when I close myself in my new room, and I hope never to wake up from this fairy tale dream because this really can't be my reality.

How could my life be so wrong, and then feel so right in such a short time?

# Jonathan Boothe

## Clever Little Bitch

**W**illiam Dupré is dead.
Now, isn't this fucking interesting news?
I have to roll this about in my brain for a minute or two, letting the words sink in.

William. Is. Dead.

*Huh.*

"Didn't see that coming," I can't help saying it out loud, because I'm quite fucking stunned at this information. I'm even pacing my office, trying to let my mind accept what I'm reading.

William has kicked it. And that's a damn shame for me.

The report shows approximate time of death, and he had been well and truly pissed, sozzled, drunk, inebriated at the time of his death. The cleaners, when they got no reply to their insistent knocking, tried the front door. *Look at that*, it was unlocked, and they entered the house to be met with the smell of death and William's lifeless body. He had enough alcohol in his system to allow himself to be pushed down those stairs by that little bitch he kept.

Oh, I know it *all*.

I'm his lawyer, and he paid me well to keep my mouth shut. I'm well connected to the people he's connected to. There was no way either of us could double cross each other without severe repercussions. I would not want that wrath to come down on my head, and as wicked as William was, nor would he.

William, the clever monkey, had made allowances for his untimely death if that little bitch ever got the upper hand. His ego doubted it, but nonetheless, he still made arrangements. Even if he *was* stupid enough to fall down those stairs in his drunken stupor himself, he made sure she would not escape into the night like a ghost, which is what she has indeed appeared to have done.

*Score one point to Whisper.*

I know William had cameras around his home, and they must have all been taken care of, absolute proof of his cause of death never to be discovered. Nothing came out in the police report about anybody living in that home other than William.

Clever little bitch covered up her tracks.

Clever little bitch got her freedom.

*Or so she thinks.*

I knew her years were numbered. The one thing that sick son of a bitch didn't allow for was the tapes. His ego was far too saturated with her submissive, 'yes, Master' behavior.

He was only fifty-one years old, fit as an ox, no health issues what-so-fucking-ever, and kept under the radar of any danger to his person. He was expected to have a long life ahead of him. Her heart would have stopped beating once William was finished with her.

He'd hedged his bets on outliving her. I'd warned him. I'd told him to keep the footage off-site, but he was a glutton for Whisper, and the inconvenience of viewing her off-site was simply too much in his mind's eye.

*She was as good as gold,* he'd said. *Did everything she was told.*

William had bragged to me all the time of the goings on in that home. He had nobody to tell. He needed to boast and preen his peacock feathers as he strutted around my office, while I sat there mostly aroused, listening until I asked for proof. It would cost me some of the payment he gave me to shut me up about his affairs, but it was sure worth it. Each month, I got to see some footage. He'd only started showing me from the time she'd turned eighteen. I'd only found out about the girl when he couldn't contain himself any longer and he'd needed to reveal his sick little sordid stories to somebody.

*Where's the fun in keeping it all to yourself, when you can't brag about it?*

Now, the police have come and gone, I find it interesting there's no mention of anything linking William to his dark past. No mention of the little bitch, no mention of any tapes. She *has* to have had help. His home must have been wiped clean.

*How fucking convenient.*

*She got the upper hand.*

*Who else knows she was there?*

I do not mourn him. The only thing I will regret is my monthly footage to watch of that little beauty. I was paid in cash, so there's no link to me other than I'm his law-abiding lawyer. But then, I'm a lot of people's lawyer. There was nothing strange about my working relationship with William Dupré…to the outside world.

Sitting down in my office chair, I put my feet up on my table, hold William's file up, and can't help smiling to myself. He really was a sick fuck, but a very organized one.

It's time for me to play William's last cards. I have some detective work to do first, and once that's done, I will get out of Dodge for a while and lay low.

The orchestra is going to play William's last song, and he is the conductor.

In other words, the shit is going to hit the fan.

William sure knew how to keep me entertained.

# *Whisper*

## Green Thumb

### 3 Months Later

I've spent three solid months at Miss C's. Life has been quiet, peaceful, and there has been no danger lurking in the shadows waiting for me. I remain a secret, living under the town of Connard's nose.

My superhero never came for me, but that's okay. I feel better knowing it was all up to me in the end. I made the right choices and found people who I call family.

My past life is now locked away deep inside me. I only want to think about the present and how I have miraculously been granted freedom and a happiness I never knew was there for me.

To keep myself busy, I made a large vegetable garden for Miss C. It was something I knew how to do and it made me happy. I fenced it off and made a gate. Linc wanted to help me, but I needed to work the soil with my own hands and make it my own. Hard work never hurt anybody, and it was a soothing balm for my chapped and blistered mind.

Miss C would bring out freshly made lemonade for me while I worked away from morning to nightfall. Boxer and Linc got me the seeds I needed, and I became quite obsessed with filling that soil with them and caring for them. I made a flower garden for her as well.

I landscaped her backyard until I had no more room to dig and plant. It was therapeutic to my soul. It kept the boxes in my mind locked down tight. Soon, I will be able to start picking the fruits of my labor for her to enjoy.

I may not have had much more meat on *dem bones,* as Miss C calls them, but they are strong bones now. I have muscle, I'm tanned, and I work off everything Miss C tries to fill me up on.

I wanted to give something back to the old lady who has done nothing but care for me. She's very special to me.

Boxer has taken on this father-like role. He is a good man, a loyal man. If I understood love, I think what I feel for Miss C and Boxer is on its way to being that. I want to be able to voice that one day to them. It upsets me if I can't lay eyes on the both of them every day, even if it is just for a half-hour with Boxer. I can't lose these two people who have made my life worth living.

They saved me, treated me right from the minute they laid eyes on me, and my respect for them has never been challenged.

Lincoln has become my friend. He makes me laugh. I could see how much he wanted to help me landscape Miss C's property, but he also knew it was my thing that helped to keep my demons at bay. He watched me struggle with the fence posts, and I watched him having to hold himself back as I got blisters from stabbing the earth with my shovel and hammering every single post in by myself. I saw how proud he was of me when he dropped in to see how I was progressing.

Miss C would often sit on her back porch swing and watch me while she shelled her peas, rocking back and forth, an understanding look on her face. She knew I had to keep busy, and she knew I had to exhaust myself each and every day so the nightmares would be too tired to seek me out at night.

Miss Catherine got me to meet with Dr. Evelyn Castille for a check-up not long after I had arrived at her home. Dr. Castille came to the house because I couldn't get in Boxer's car to go to her. I tried, but the panic was all-consuming.

I had never had medical attention before, so I didn't know what to expect. She wanted to take me for x-rays, but the most I would allow was blood to be taken. She got to prod me while she hummed to herself and made notes. I just lay there like a scared rabbit on my bed. She wasn't too invasive; it was just a basic check-up. I wouldn't have agreed to anything more at the time, and Boxer had told me she would only examine what I agreed to. I didn't want to know if I had been raped. It was easier to lock it all down tight until I was ready. She hummed louder when she saw my lower back and the scarring left from William's beatings.

I haven't been able to set foot outside the perimeter of Miss C's property, and I haven't wanted to, but today is the day I will be taking that big step. I have gotten used to the comfort and safety her property has awarded me. I knew this day would come eventually, but I needed this time to myself, and now I'm ready.

Today, I'm going out with Boxer and Miss C to be shown around the town. I don't have to get out of the car if I don't want to. I'm not up for meeting people today, but I'm happy to find out about the place I live in and just drive. Miss C has packed us a lunch, and we are going on a 'road trip,' as she called it, for me to see a bit of Louisiana.

I'm putting on a face for these people who care for me. On the inside, I have to work every day to keep my past life tucked away. I know they all watch me for signs of any mental disturbance, but I'm not about to get locked away in an asylum.

I take every day as it comes, and look at the positives and ways for me to deal with my own anguish myself. I can't change it. I'm trying to be well-adjusted.

What's done is done.

I have a future to look forward to.

# EDGE

## Apparently, Blood Isn't Thicker Than Water

### 5 Months Later

**M**y bastard of a father is dead.
Thank fuck for that.

My hands shake a little as I read the letter from his lawyer, my rage for the man pouring out of my fingertips.

I was brought into this world by that bastard, who taught me how to grow a set at a young age. I've not seen the man in nearly twenty years. I had often thought about finding him and showing him exactly who I've become, but that's no longer relevant.

I was lucky because I got out from under him when I was eleven years old. The bastard was blackmailed into releasing...

But that's another story.

Over time, I've learned the apple didn't fall far from the tree in the end. That seed was apparently already sown, or I wouldn't have turned out the way I did.

His death had happened eight months ago, and it'd taken them a while to track me down. I'm surprised they found me because I sure as fuck didn't want to be found. Now, some bitch named Whisper has my fucking shameful inheritance.

No. Fucking. Way. Is *any* bitch taking that from me.

Who is she but some money-hungry old whore who got in good with him? She got her name on those papers, because he sure as fuck didn't want to give his only son anything but one hundred dollars.

Yeah, I hold in my hand a check for one hundred dollars and a letter with my deceased father's address on it.

It's like he's gloating from the grave.

Cocksucker!

My mother apparently left him when I was a baby, and he refused to talk about her or give me her name. She abandoned me to that man and no doubt got herself safe and sound away from his evil ways. I have no clue if she's alive or dead. I was never granted any answers, and I sure as hell knew only to ask once. I haven't even thought about her in twenty years.

I slam my fist down on my kitchen table, making my beer jump. What a pain in my fucking ass. I was gonna settle down tonight and get some sleep for once, but now I have this to deal with. I finish off the beer and toss it with enough force that it shatters against the inside of the bin.

"Motherfucker!" I roar at my ceiling.

*I hope he can fucking hear me, too.*

I'm pleased the bastard is dead, but there ain't no way some old, bitching whore is taking what's mine.

I snatch my cell phone off the table and punch in one number. I'm the fucking Soulless Bastards' enforcer. I know how to make bitches disappear. My president picks up on the first ring. "Hazard...yeah, good...I need some personal time for a couple weeks because I just found out my father's dead... Don't be sorry. I sure as fuck ain't," I grunt back and I mean every word.

"Hazard, I need to clear up some financial matters. Are we good if I take off immediately?" I know he won't have a problem with my request. I've given my loyalty to the club, and now I need to sort this mess out. He wants to know if I need backup. "Nah... this little misunderstanding will be easy to reconcile. Some random whore got dibs on my money." I listen as he curses at my injustice. "Just holler if you need me for a job. I'm heading to Louisiana…no problems, will do. I'll let you know when I get there."

I scrub my hand over my face. He wants to send a brother with me. I don't need anybody knowing about my past. "I'm good. I can't see how this will be any trouble for me. I'll be in touch." I disconnect and grab a few things. I'm always packed, ready for a job.

I stop off in the bathroom and look at myself in the mirror. I need to be careful because this isn't club retribution; this is personal. I worked hard at keeping my birth identity a secret for fear my adopted parents would be harmed.

By the time I'm finished, my long, light brown, shoulder-length hair is laying on my bathroom floor. I've used the clippers and shaved it close to my head around the back and sides, and left it long on top, so I can comb it back or tie it up. I've taken my thick beard and reduced it to a closely shaved scruff on my face.

I grip either side of the hand basin as I look at myself in the mirror, admiring my handiwork. I look different, and that's a good thing. Now, my own MC brothers would walk past me without a second glance. Without my cut on, I'll be just another civilian. I have to go in this way. I don't need the club brought into this.

My father would've been around fifty when he died. I've been gone nearly two decades, and I'm not Dallas, the eleven-year-old, scared, broken little boy.

I'm now Edge, a stone-cold motherfucking killer. Make no mistakes about that.

It doesn't take me long to head on out to my Harley and start the trip. I can get a few hours ride in tonight, and then I need some sleep. If I stayed at home and went in the morning, it would only set me back a night. I need to sort this shit out ASAP.

Albuquerque to Louisiana, here I come. My father owes me, and if this is the only way he can pay up, then so be it. I don't care if I burn the house to the ground, but some whore isn't getting it just because she was weak and slept with the sick fuck.

The bitch now has a price on her head, to be paid in full.

She's already dead.

She just doesn't know it yet.

# Whisper

## Life Is Good

**B**oxer and Miss C are my champions. Boxer, my forty-five-year-old British friend, has helped me get back into society with legal papers, although they're fake.

In the past eight months since I have lived with Miss C, many things have happened. I'm now a member of society. I exist on paper in a world, where before, I didn't. I'm now a human being with rights and identification.

I didn't ask how he made it happen, but I'm grateful I had stumbled across Miss C on that cold, rainy evening eight months ago, and that she trusted Boxer to know my secrets. I thank my lucky stars every day.

I will never know who my parents are or if I have anybody related to me, but I'm okay with that. There are still a lot of unanswered questions buzzing about in my head about my real parents. I try not to let it get to me too much. I know Boxer has tried. I worry about them and how they must feel having lost me.

There were no stories in papers that could be linked back to me. My birth date was given to me, a day that man cooked up. My colorings suggest I'm European. But who could give me those answers? The truth is buried six feet under.

My long dark hair and light olive skin make me look Italian, but the world is such a melting pot living among each other that I'm truly lost to my ancestry.

I don't want anybody claiming me and knowing what their child went through, the horrors that had been done to me. It's bad enough Miss C and Boxer live with this knowledge.

There's such a deep void of emptiness when I think about my parents, so I don't. I lock them away in a box. I am surrounded by people who care about me, and that will be enough.

I just want to start fresh and be plain ol' Whisper. I never offer my surname, if I can help it, as it is a fake. I'm simply Whisper, and my name is my voice. I never raise my voice. I speak quietly; it was how I was trained. I find it easier to be quiet and not a loud presence. I don't want to stand out.

I'm not looking for a man to notice me. I could be quite happy if I end up going to my grave single and in control of my own life.

I'm free. It feels amazing.

I'm Miss C's friend's daughter, and that is that. I simply appeared to have arrived in the small town of Connard one day looking for a job, and Miss C hooked me up with Boxer. I'm now his bookkeeper. I earn an honest, paid living. Miss C made sure the townsfolk welcomed me, and nobody questioned who I was. I was who I appeared.

All the hard drives of my life were in Boxer's safe room at the back of the bar. I eventually gave the hard drive I took from William's home to Boxer, and he promised he would not look at what was on it until I was ready to look at it. I put my trust in him that it would stay locked away in his safe. It was too soon to take all that on board, but it was mine to voice what happened to it.

For some perverse reason, I couldn't destroy them. I had to keep them, for I knew one day I would indeed watch those years.

Little did I know it would be sooner than later.

# BOXER

## Unplanned Family

A call in the early hours had me packing my bags and heading out for a few days. Now I'm sitting in a hotel room waiting for the intel we need to get this job completed so I can get back to Connard. Otherwise everything's been relatively quiet these past months.

Whisper has been coming out of her shell bit-by-bit these past months. She was like a frightened deer for a long time, but we all just kept coaxing her out of the dark place she was in. She was trained to be lifeless and God knows what has gone on with her body. I have been tempted to take that hard drive out of the safe and find out what she was subjected to, but I couldn't ruin her trust in me. Trust was a very big thing for Whisper, and I couldn't break that.

We were all very careful not to tell Whisper what to do, but to teach her. She had to learn her opinion mattered.

Whisper thrived under Miss Catherine's roof, and a strong, loyal friendship has built. I know that girl loves Miss Catherine, and I'm sure the old lady knows it too.

She has really blossomed around those she trusts. I think Miss Catherine would have had her heart broken if Whisper up and left her to explore the world that was waiting for her to discover, like any girl of her age.

I treated her like a daughter. I knew I shouldn't get close to her that way. She had every right to up and leave one day, but I too would have missed her.

We were an unplanned family.

I could see Lincoln hanging around a fair bit too. Once I knew the danger to her was non-existent, Lincoln wasn't needed anymore, but he still found ways to drop on by Miss Catherine's place and offer his services for repair jobs around her home. He is drawn to her like we all are.

Lincoln's only twenty-seven, and I trust him with my life. He is a respected member of my team. I can see he's very protective of Whisper and values their friendship, and would do the right thing by her, because she isn't ready for anything other than the friend zone.

I have gotten Whisper involved in training. I

personally think it helps to take her mind off things, and she's good at it, because she's disciplined. She comes over to the bar and works out the back with me on weights and the heavy bag. I'm teaching her self-defense because knowing she can look after herself will help to empower her mind into confirming she's in control of her life. A strong mind and a strong body is what she needs. I've taken her to the gun range, and she can now handle a gun. She's getting pretty good at it too.

The townsfolk have been great welcoming a new person among them. It helps that she's so likable. We have spun a good enough story for those who have enquired, keeping the nosier ones' minds at bay. Life has gone on without a hitch. Nobody would know the trauma Whisper has been through. She understands the importance of not letting her guard down and telling anybody. There's a lot at stake with my involvement in her cover up.

William Dupré's death is no longer gossip. His son didn't even come to the funeral, he was pretty much a phantom because nobody had ever met him, and as far as I can tell, the house hasn't been visited.

Whisper has taken to staying with me sometimes, and I've got to admit I like having her company. I may have missed out on having children, but having Whisper around makes up for it.

I know she feels she owes me some of her time as payback. I'm more than happy she's safe under my roof or Miss Catherine's. She needs the freedom to roam between our homes. It validates the fact that she can do what she wants. The first time she told Miss Catherine she was going to stay with me overnight, she got herself all stressed out about letting her know. Miss Catherine has this weird sixth sense, so she knew what was coming, and she set Whisper straight. Now she comes and goes as she pleases.

To aid in her independence, Lincoln and I helped her get her driver's and motorbike licenses. It was important that she acted like a normal twenty-one-year-old on the surface. Until we can get her a car, she borrows one of my bikes. She hasn't ventured very far, only to Miss Catherine's or the bar, or she goes riding with Lincoln on the back roads. I know she enjoys the freedom.

We have given her everything she needs if she wants to up and leave Connard, but she hasn't. For that, we are all grateful.

I worry she hasn't talked to a therapist about her time with that bastard. I watch her for signs of distress, and she holds it altogether well.

*Too well.*

I don't want to pressure her to talk to a stranger

in a room with a pad and pen, who will analyse her. She's smart. I know she will do what she needs to do when the time is right. It helps talking to me and Miss Catherine, but we aren't professionals at dealing with this type of mental trauma. We can only be here when she needs us.

Little the fuck did I know that was gonna be sooner than later.

# Whisper

## Creepy Café Break

Catching up with Linc at the Little Cafe in town is always a treat. We enjoy spending time together. I'm sitting here on my lunch break, waiting for him to arrive, while Lenny, the old black jazz musician, is playing his saxophone across the road. He plays beautifully. He just sits there on an upturned wooden crate on the corner of the street, having a smoke around lunch time each day, talking to the residents or playing his saxophone or trumpet for the town.

Miss Catherine told me Lenny turned up in Connard around twenty years ago. He's a little sweet on her, and she doesn't mind the gentlemanly attention he gives her when she's in town. I'm beginning to think they would make for a great elderly couple. She told me he was once part of a famous all-black jazz band. She's always polite when he woos her with a special piece of music every time she walks past his corner. It's like he's trying to talk to her through his music, but she never extends any invitation to him.

Sometimes, I see Lenny watching me curiously when I'm running errands for Boxer or taking a walk on my break. I'm not afraid of him. I'm more inquisitive of the looks he gives me and what he's thinking. He couldn't possibly know about my past, but he looks at me like he knows something. When I start to feel conscious of his watchful eyes, I look over at him, and he will be giving me a big, toothy smile, and that settles my thoughts. He will bob his head as he lifts his chocolate brown, felt, pork pie hat, and say, "Miss Whisper, nice day for a walk." Then I feel relaxed again.

Suddenly, an overweight, dark-haired man pulls the chair opposite me out, inviting himself to my table, startling me out of my thoughts. He is direct, holding his hand out for me to shake, which I do. "Whisper, I presume. My name is Jonathan Boothe. I am William Dupré's lawyer." He licks his lips. "It's a pleasure to meet you in person, my dear."

I snatch my hand back out of his and he gives me a sleazy smile. I don't like him at all.

"It has taken me a while to track you down, but now that the papers have been served to the other party, I must reveal to you a document that William had in place in case he departed this world before his time."

He raises an eyebrow at me knowingly.

*What does he know?*

"I don't understand." Nobody is supposed to know about my past.

"I'm just William's lawyer who is passing on this document to you." He gives me a smirk. "It took me too long to locate you...Miss Whisper...*De Ville*." He says my last name on a horrid sneer. "Where have you been hiding, my dear? I thought you had skipped town, long gone, but on a third attempt, to my surprise, I found you right here."

I need this man away from me because he talks like he knows things about me. He waits for my response to his remark. I give him nothing but silence. Boxer and Miss Catherine drilled it into me to never talk about my past, no matter what.

My hands are starting to tremble, and I can feel myself sweating. I want this man to leave me alone. There's something toxic about him; I feel it in my gut. I start to get up and move away because he's sending my mind into a tailspin.

He grabs my arm and wrenches me down hard onto my chair, my elbow slamming into the table top. He's a lot stronger than he looks. His calm façade is slipping as he grits his teeth together. "Now, now, let's not be hasty. I only want to talk to you...unless you want me to tell your secrets to the good townsfolk?" He lets go of my arm when he sees I'm not going to get up again.

*Did he just threaten me?*

I watch him lick his bottom lip slowly as he studies me, his mask firmly back in place. I do not like the way this man makes me feel. He's about William's age, and I want to get away from him now, but he knows things. The sooner I hear him out, the sooner he will leave me alone. I can hear Lenny has stopped playing his saxophone and I start to look over to him, when the lawyer continues talking.

"Listen up, missy." He looks over at Lenny calmly. "I can see I've already attracted a little attention around here, so I am forced to be brief." He takes an envelope out of the inside of his suit jacket and slides it across the table to me. "Take it and enjoy your *rewards*." He then looks back across at Lenny, who I can see has put his saxophone down and is making his way across the main street towards me, going as fast as his eighty-year-old frame will allow him, while he stops a car with his hand held up in front of himself. I turn back to the lawyer and he's gone.

"Miss Whisper..." Lenny's calling out to me as he

nears me, watching that horrible man as he hurries off down the road to his car. I stop watching him and focus on Lenny. I feel better now that the lawyer is gone and quickly fold the envelope and put it inside my bag. I will look at it later. I can't afford to draw unwanted attention that will bring questions. I need to stay under the radar in this town.

Lenny has reached my table, and he looks at where the lawyer has gotten into his car and driven off, and then back at me. "Miss Whisper, are you all right? I couldn't help noticing that man had sat himself down uninvited. I know you are waiting on that nice boy, Lincoln."

I put on a calm voice as I wipe my hands on my jeans under the table. I give Lenny a confident smile and tell him I'm fine. I give no more information, and for that, I feel bad. What could I tell him that wouldn't get me more questions?

I thank Lenny for his concern and tell him how wonderful his music playing is just as Linc turns up. He gives Lincoln a nod of his head and then leaves me to go back to his corner. I know he wasn't pleased with my vague reply and he was genuinely worried about me, but he was gentlemanly enough not to enquire any further.

"Hey, Whisper, sorry I'm late. I had a few last minute things that needed my urgent attention."

Lincoln has taken to giving me a peck on the cheek when he greets me, and today is no different. "What was that all about with you and Lenny?"

Great, now I have Lincoln noticing a little something was going down between the two of us. Fanny, our waitress, comes over when she sees Lincoln seated and notes our orders, and I take the opportunity to change the subject.

"Linc, why aren't there any people in this town my age? My only true female friend is Miss Catherine."

He thinks about my question. "This doesn't seem the type of town for young people to want to stay around in. There really isn't much to do here. I could see them gravitating to New Orleans, which would have the entertainment that young people enjoy and the job opportunities." He really is a beautiful man, very kind and patient with me. He's looking very handsome in black jeans, boots, and a long-sleeved button up.

"Why are you here in Connard?" I have wondered where he goes when he isn't here, but I never wanted to pry. From the look on his face, I can tell I have surprised him with asking a personal question.

"Look at you getting all nosy on me." He's stalling for time. "I sometimes work for Boxer, so I'm here when he needs me, and sometimes I'm here because

I want to be here, and other times I work somewhere else for a little while." He shrugs off his casual response to my curious question. I've never wanted to pry because Lincoln has never asked about my time with William, and I know Boxer has secrets too, so I can't help being inquisitive about the both of them.

Fanny brings over the coffees and sandwiches, and Lincoln, being such a big guy, starts inhaling his lunch. This looks like a snack for him, not a lunch.

I raise one eyebrow at him. "You cutting down on your food intake today or something?" He just laughs at me and shakes his head, while I nibble on my sandwich. I'm still not used to eating a lot of food in one sitting. Once he has finished his, I offer the other half of mine. Lincoln takes it, knowing my eating pattern. He never pushes me to do anything I don't want to do. He's very easy for me to be around.

I'm definitely curious to know more about Linc. I take a sip of my coffee, ready to ask my next question. "Do you have a girlfriend?"

He smiles a very knowing smile at me and replies, "No. I have a boyfriend."

"Oh. Wow!" I know my eyes must have gone huge because Lincoln's shaking his head and laughing at me again. I don't know what else to say, so I take another drink of my coffee. That will teach me to be nosy.

Lincoln pulls out his wallet and shows me a picture of a really nice looking guy wearing glasses. "That's Joel. We have been seeing each other for a few months. He lives in New Orleans and is a computer genius. You met him when he helped me with the armoire." He lowers his voice and brings his head close to mine across the table. "Boxer knows him, and we got together after he came to help Boxer clean William Dupré's home of your existence, and that's the only thing I'm gonna let you get out of me." He sits back and says louder, "We kind of hit it off. We enjoy each other's company, and we are exclusive."

I can see how relaxed he is talking to me about Joel. "I'm happy you're happy. You shouldn't be spending all this time with me, when you can be catching up with Joel."

"I enjoy your company too. You're a great girl. You should come with me one day and we can make a night of it in New Orleans with Joel and his friends."

I know Lincoln means what he says. "I would like that." I think I'm ready to be around a city of people and nightlife. This town and its small population have been good for me as I adjusted to belonging somewhere, but there are no people my age.

Lincoln gives me a serious face. "I do want to see

you happy."

I take his hand and squeeze it. "I really do like having you as my friend, my *only* friend, here in our twenties."

"Well, we better find you some more before you turn into a spinster with a house full of cats."

I laugh off Linc's comment, but is that what I have in store for me staying in this town? I want to travel a little, but I want this place to be my base. At the moment, I'm comfortable where I am and with the people I have put my trust in.

I know I'm free to do as I please, and this has been enough for me, but I'm young and I know there's a big world out there for me to one day conquer.

I think another change of topic is due. "Does Boxer know about you and Joel?"

Lincoln shrugs. "No reason to really tell Boxer. It's private. I don't feel it makes a difference to my work ethic."

He looks at his watch and pulls some cash from his wallet then sets it down on the table. "My turn today," he states. I go to protest, but I know there's no point. "I actually have to cut this lunch a little short and get going, but how about we go for a ride on the bikes later this week? I know Boxer's away at the moment and won't be back for a few days, and this will be the first time it's only you and Miss

# WRENCHED

Catherine—"

I cut him off. "We'll be fine. *I* will be fine." Having Linc here, I almost forgot about the document I was just given. I worry my bottom lip thinking about what I should do.

Linc watches me for a few beats, hoping I'll talk first. "Babe, what is it? I have to leave, but I gotta know what it is that's worrying you."

I exhale loudly because I can do this. I'm about to let a wall down and show Linc the letter. "Lincoln, Joel is so very lucky to have you. I just wanted to say that, and I'm so grateful to have you in my life. You really are my best friend."

I'm just about to reach for my handbag, when his phone starts ringing. He looks at the caller ID and holds one finger up at me as he steps away from the table to answer the call. He looks upset as he listens to the caller. Before he disconnects, I hear him say, "I'll be there as soon as I can."

I get up from the table and walk over to Linc's side. He's running his hand through his hair and pacing back and forth, clearly upset.

"Are you all right, Lincoln?" I know he isn't. I touch his back lightly before he spins to pace again.

He gives me a grimace, which I haven't seen on Lincoln before. "Whisper, what was it you wanted to tell me before?" He's changing the subject and trying to behave in a manner that won't alert me to his distress.

"Nothing, I'm fine. Do you want to talk about that phone call?" I forget my own worries because the caller has severely upset him.

"Whisper, something has just gone down and I don't have the time to talk about it now. I need to find out more information first." He sees my worried look and tries to reassure me he is fine by enveloping me in a warm hug. "I have to get going." He steps back and ducks his head to look me directly in the eyes. "Are you sure you'll be all right?"

I know he needs to hear I'm okay because this is Lincoln, my friend and all round good guy. I also know he needs to be somewhere urgently and I'm holding him up.

I brush off my worries. "Nothing that can't wait a few days. Please, you go and do what you need to do, and I'll be waiting for you when you get back." I give him another hug and a kiss on the cheek, something I never do to him. I just feel like he needs some comfort from me. He pulls away and I give him my most convincing poker face.

He checks his watch again and starts walking backwards, away from me. A black SUV pulls up to the curb a half-block up the main street, and Lincoln waves to me. "Later, babe," he says, then turns around, jogs to it, and jumps in. The driver executes a speedy U-turn and drives away from me.

All of a sudden, I get a chill up my spine. I put my dark sunglasses on and casually look around the street. I can't see anything out of the ordinary, but the feeling won't subside. I decide to head back to the bar at a brisk walk and get back to work.

# EDGE

## Can Of Worms

I've had too much fucking time to think about my past on the ride to Louisiana. I had blocked out that part of my life, even though it helped to shape the person I am now.

I'm ruthless.

I don't give second chances.

I get the job done.

Conscience plays no part in my world.

You fuck me or the club over, you are done for.

I'm indeed a soulless bastard through and through.

I'm grateful I was taken from my father, or God only knows what would have become of me.

Would I even be alive?

He should've been at the top of my retribution list. But, I had known if the bastard wound up dead, all bloodied and broken by my hands, then I would've been doing the people I call my parents a real injustice for all the kindness they showered me with. They were my kryptonite. I would do *anything* for them.

I may have had a bad start in life, but they tried real hard to make up for it. It's the one line I couldn't cross, for their sakes.

The couple that took me in were in their late fifties at the time. They were kind people, good people. They showed me I was loved.

But then that was taken away from me.

I have them set up in the best nursing home I can afford, and they're none the wiser to my Soulless Bastards life, mainly because they both suffer from advanced dementia. I'm a ghost of a son to them; they don't know me anymore. Bad things happen to really good people, and for that, I'm truly sorry. They saved me, and I can't save them from this fucking disease.

I'm an educated man, I have properties, and I'm ex-military. I've fought for my country, and I know I made them proud. It was important to me they got to see that before their minds were attacked and their memories stolen. I gave up trusting in a world that can give and then take away so cruelly when the two people who meant the most to me on this planet had their minds ravaged.

I'm without parents again.

I shake my head to get rid of these thoughts. This shit just can't be reversed. I've had too many hours on the ride over with nothing but my early childhood to think about on replay, and I'm on a cliff, teetering. No fucker better look at me sideways or they'll be wishing they hadn't.

I'm fucking furious this can of worms in my head has been reopened. That shit needed to stay buried. Now I have to sort this bitch out, so I can bury it all again.

There's no love lost. A man like my father should have been caged and the key thrown away.

I have vengeance on my mind, and I'm not taking on any jail time because of that slut. I'll do time for the club because that's where my loyalty lies, but I won't take it on because of my own stupidity.

I need to be clear-headed. I accelerate and hope the sounds of my Harley can soothe the inferno that's raging inside me.

# Whisper

## Possession Is Nine Tenths Of The Law

Once I got back to my office, I put the envelope on the table and let it stare back at me the whole time, while I finished off the day's work.

My phone rings and it's Miss C. I put her on speaker phone so I can tidy up my desk while I talk to her. "Hello, honeychile, I'm just checkin' in to make sure you are doing well. Dem old bones of mine are tellin' me otherwise."

I love listening to her talk. It soothes me. I don't want her bones to worry her, so I put on my strong voice. "Hey, Miss Catherine, don't you be worrying about me. I'm just a little off with Boxer away, and Linc got a call today that has me a little worried for him. I'm just gonna finish up here soon and do a workout then head on off to bed and do some reading. If you don't hear from me, it just means I'm having a test run at being independent. This is all new to me." I hope that sounded convincing enough.

"I understand. I'm your safety net if you need me. Don't hesitate to be callin' me any time of day."

"I know, Miss Catherine. You have a good night and take care. I'll check in to see how you are doing tomorrow." I know she doesn't want me fussing over her either. She's a strong woman to have stayed single and become so self-reliant. She's so proud of what she has achieved. I've watched Boxer keep an ear to the ground with Miss C. He knows she's old, and he knows she would be offended if he kept an open watch on her. She's alone in that house surrounded by open fields, the closest neighbor a several-minutes-drive away. She doesn't fear the isolation; she welcomes it.

"You too, child." Then she disconnects.

Tapping my fingers on my desk, I eye that damn envelope again that's quietly hollering at me to open it up. I have to read it to put Miss Catherine's bones at ease. I pick it up and slide my finger along the seal. It pops and the envelope rips under my sharp nail. I slide the document out and my eyes scan over it.

It's a letter from Boothe and Brown Lawyers. It's about William Dupré's will.

I'm confused as I read the document. I'm named, including my new surname, as the beneficiary to all monies, the house and assets, and that one surviving son, a Mr. Dallas Dupré, is to receive one hundred dollars, this being William Dupré's last will and testimony...*blah, blah, blah.*

I have to reread the words again.

William has a son?

I didn't know anything about a son. I couldn't imagine that evil man bringing a child into this world. I can't hide my shock that a son even existed. Does Boxer know? But where is he?

Why would William leave me everything and his son only one hundred dollars? He didn't even like me.

I go to put the envelope in the bin and something else drops out. A key.

This is the key to William's home. I have seen it before.

This is wrong. I shouldn't have any of this. I don't *want* any of this. His son should have it all. Tonight, I will go over to the house and leave the key with a note. I would assume if the son has received his letter, he won't be too happy about my name being on the will. I don't even like my name on it. It draws too many questions.

He might assume all sorts of things. I doubt he would know about my life with William. I was a secret to the world, as far as I knew. He might think

William and I were in a live-in relationship and that's why I've been left his assets. This guy must be wondering who I am, and I don't blame him. The death of his father will be enough of a shock, and then finding out he isn't entitled to his inheritance, only one hundred dollars…

I have a feeling he wouldn't have had a good relationship with his father. The man was evil, a murderer, a bully, an abuser. I'm glad his son didn't get to live under his roof. I don't know what his story is, but it has to have been a better one than mine.

I decide to let Boxer handle it all for me when he comes home. He'll know what's best, but for now, I don't want to even be in possession of the key. They say that possession is nine tenths of the law, and I don't want those nine tenths.

I shut the computer down. I have kept myself busy and had a productive day. I need to go work out. It's the only thing that releases the tension my body feels when the little boxes of memories in my mind are threatening to pop open. I need to center myself and let Boxer sort it out with the lawyer, so we can turn everything over to William's son legally.

It's his birthright.

*There's nothing to worry about at this stage*, I try to tell myself. I'll just refuse what has been given to me, and then my world will be back on its axis again.

# Jonathan Boothe

## Last Song

**My meeting with Whisper surprised the hell** out of her and she was as beautiful in person as her movie stardom dictated. I'm now headed back to Jackson. All the pawns have been dealt with and my source tells me the biker is on his way. Everything has been timed perfectly.

Even William could not have foretold the shitstorm that is coming for his little pet.

I really should get out of Dodge, but this is gonna be too good to miss.

The maestro has conducted his last song.

What could possibly go wrong?

# EDGE

## Knock Knock

**M**y Harley rumbles down the old oak canopy that leads me towards the weathered plantation home that once would have stood majestic and proud.

*So this is my father's home.*

During the day, the old oak avenue would be inviting, but under a pitch-black night, it's creepy, just like my father. Trust him to own this place.

I pull up to the front steps, letting the bike engine vibrate underneath my body. There's no light shining through the windows, no smell of cooking in the air. The house appears quiet, like nobody is home.

My rage is starving for justice. I've got my gun tucked into the back of my jeans and I'm itching to use it.

Tonight, I'm the bitch's judge and jury.

Her sentence?

Death by my hand.

*One bullet to maim and cause pain. The second, to be her reckoning.*

I park the bike and climb the stairs, regardless of the fact it appears nobody's home. It's too quiet as my boots pound each of the wooden planks, heavy with the injustice of my past life, heavy with the fate of the slut who dared to cross my path.

He must have loved this woman to give up everything to her.

I want to see the face of the whore who accepted my father for who he was. As far as I'm concerned, if you were with my father, then you too were a piece of shit, not worthy of being on the bottom of my boot, two fucking evil peas in the same fucking pod.

I knock on the front door. I'm a lost traveller looking for directions, and once I get my feet over the threshold into the privacy of my bastard of a father's home...

I can only assume the bitch lives here. After all, she now apparently owns it.

*What a fucking joke.*

I knock again and wait.

*Nothing.*

I walk around the perimeter of the house and

check in some windows. It's dark and uninviting. I go around to the back stoop and knock on the door.

*Nothing.*

I sit down on the step and notice the full moon has shed a soft silver glow over the backyard. There's a dead looking garden patch down the backyard. Nobody has lived here for months, or she simply couldn't be bothered tending the garden.

I could break in and see for myself. I rub a tired hand over my face. I'm not thinking straight coming here under the cloak of darkness. I've let my hatred for everything associated with my father lead me here without a clear plan. I haven't had enough time to think outside my anger. This needs to be clean and with no ties to me. My brothers will cover for me if I need an alibi.

I need a couple beers and to calm down, then I will come back here later tonight and see if she even lives here. I check my watch; it's only about a quarter to eight, plenty of time for justice to be served.

# Whisper

## No Point Stirring The Wasp Nest

The bar shuts down on a Friday at eight o'clock, Boxer's rules. I've told old Paco, the bartender, to go home and I'll clean up. I need to keep myself busy anyway, get my mind off that letter for a little while.

Paco's pretty much done everything already. I just need to sweep the floors and take the trash out. It will be my first time closing up. Paco thanks me and heads on out the door.

The town is so small that it really doesn't warrant being open late any day of the week. Boxer's times of trade haven't been met with any resistance. The townsfolk are too old. This is the town young people escape from as soon as they are legal, which doesn't bode well for it, turning it into a ghost town eventually. It seems like the kind of place where if you lived here, you had a good reason to want to stay. It feels like a place to hide in.

William had his secrets. I have mine, and now I'm beginning to wonder about Boxer and why he lives here. Maybe this is why the town's people keep their noses out of each other's business.

No point stirring the wasp nest.

The bar is empty, so I quickly sweep up then go on out back.

# EDGE

## Challenge Accepted

I've just walked into the bar and I'm in need of a piss, so I follow the restroom sign and notice along the way how empty the bar is, while the jukebox has some romantic country song wailing out of it. I could have relieved myself on my father's land, but even my piss was too good to be spilled on something he had owned.

I've taken care of business, ready for a beer, when I hear barely audible feminine grunts followed by smacking noises coming from up the stairs.

Call me curious.

I quietly climb the stairs, noting the *Private: Staff Only* sign nailed to the beam above my head, ignoring it as I walk toward the sounds, when I see her in a back room, punching a heavy bag in painted on, ass-hugging, little black workout shorts. I'm amused at first. My thoughts of revenge falling to second place as I cross my arms over my chest, propping myself up against the doorjamb while I watch her smack the bag with her toned arms as she makes those soft little grunts.

She has no idea I'm standing here observing her. I should walk away, but the more I stand here watching her, the more I can't take my eyes off her. She sure is a looker.

This female is so determined to break her thumbs that I have to step in and save them. She is lean, but she still has nice curves, like a slow-winding country road travelling up her body. Her tight, rounded globes have my dick's attention as she swings around the bag, concentrating so hard that she doesn't notice me, sweat dripping off her pretty face, determination written all over it.

I decide then and there I want to get to know her tonight. I have seen that look. That's the look of somebody who's working off stress…or working off *somebody*.

She is quick on her feet, but she is holding her hands wrong. She doesn't even have them strapped. She looks like she walked in and just needed to start hitting something. Her tits are a good handful, and her tight black workout top holds them secure. Her long brown hair is pulled back into a ponytail, perfect for grabbing onto, and she has these big, chocolate brown eyes a man could drown in while he fucks her senseless.

She is light on her feet as she rotates around again, jabbing at the bag with her back to me. In my current status of good-guy-civilian, I have to help her out.

I walk up to her and lay my hands on either side of her shoulders to calm her movements. She stops with a gasp, her body stiffening. I watch her reaction time. It's slow as her mind works on what to do next. She needs to get a little quicker with that.

Then it comes.

I'm ready.

She swings around, ready to shove her palm straight up into my nose, hoping to buy herself some time as she flees for help.

*Somebody has been taking self-defense lessons.* I actually find myself liking the fact that she has some knowledge about how to protect herself.

I dodge her predictable defensive response to my invasion of her space. Her palm goes flying through the air, hitting nothing. I twist her back around, keeping her arms locked down tight, and her back to my chest. "We can do this all night if you like, but I'm not here to hurt you. I came in for a beer and to take a piss. I've been on the road the last few days. If you'll calm down, I'll release you."

She thinks about my words and my actions and does as she's told. She's naïve, but I won't tell her that. Before I fully release her, I move my hands over hers and reposition her thumbs for her. "Like this." I soften my deep, rough, gravelly voice because I can be very intimidating when I want to be. "Little lady, I was just gonna tell you you're gonna break those thumbs the way you are hitting that bag." From her body language, I can see intimidation will get me nowhere. I need to behave like a civil gentleman, and not who I really am.

"You're not thinking about the care of your hands before you beat the heavy bag senseless because your mind is elsewhere." She's all kinds of frazzled about something, and this is an impulsive thing to do. She might have started out with good intentions, putting her workout gear on, but then it escalated to, 'Fuck my hands. I need to hit something, pronto'.

I fully release her and she immediately takes a step away from me, twisting around to take in who was touching her, who has invaded her private workout. Her eyes widen in surprise as she looks me up and down quickly. They don't linger too long. She just needed to assess me for any danger.

*Smart girl.*

All she sees standing before her is a clean-cut American guy. She would have given me a different look had she seen me in my cut, but for some reason, I don't think it would have necessarily impressed her. There are the chicks who would fear us, and then there are the chicks who can't wait to get in our pants. I'm not a hundred percent sure which category she was in at the moment.

I look her in the eyes. "I can tell this isn't your first time at the bag. You've let yourself get distracted, little lady."

"Thank you," she whispers to me. "You are right. I am distracted. I wasn't thinking clearly." Her eyes are now downcast and darting back and forth. "I'm good now, thank you. You can leave me to it."

I sense a challenge. I saw her look of appreciation before she looked away. I never have to work hard. I get fucked with ease.

"You shouldn't be up here. This is the private part of the bar and it's now closed. How did you get in here?" Her voice is soft-spoken.

"The door was unlocked and the jukebox was wailing. Also, it's only just eight o'clock. I needed a beer. What bar shuts at eight o'clock?"

"This bar," she mumbles. She slowly looks up when I don't respond to her two words, and then her eyes roam all over my body...again.

I'm neatly dressed and my hair is freshly cut. I'm wearing designer jeans, a checkered button up, and a leather jacket. I stopped off in New Orleans to get myself some civvies to wear on the way over. My cut is rolled up in my saddlebag on my bike.

I usually look dangerous and intimidating, but tonight, I need to be somebody else less threatening. I also need to be anonymous in this town, just a guy wanting a beer, passing on through.

Tonight, I'm nothing more than your average Joe Blow.

"Are you in charge of the bar?" I can't sense anybody else around.

"Not normally, but for now, yes."

She's deciding if she will allow me a drink. I know I look tired, and now I'm all kinds of sexually frustrated, since I've laid eyes on this female.

"If you want a beer, I can get you one." She's too trusting, but I won't knock her back. I really could do with a beer.

This new haircut is hanging in my face, and it works to my advantage, making me look younger. I scoop it up and over my head and give her a little smile. "You look like you need a break. Can I buy you a drink?" I'm all for smooth talking her to get what I want.

I can see her weighing up whether to let me buy her a drink. *Interesting,* she's making me work for it. I'm all for a challenge. She just made herself that little bit more of a game to me, so I offer up more information. "I'm just in town to visit family and decided to stop on by for a couple drinks before I head on over." A little white lie, but I can see I have to pull some half-truths here to get this one to take the bait.

"And they can't give you a beer?"

*Shit*. "They no longer drink." Well, that part is true. "Wouldn't be polite of me to show up with alcohol, when they're on the wagon."

I give her my warmest look, which I normally reserve for the people I'm hunting, because I need to pull on my resources for this female standing before me.

My brothers know if I get this look on my face I'm far more dangerous than when I look like I want to kill you. If I look like I want to kill you, then where's the element of surprise? But if I look at you like you are my friend and you can trust me, then you won't see me coming, *motherfucker*.

I need to take the edge off and get laid, and she just became my prey for the night. I'll be fucking her before the night is through.

I hold my hand out to her to shake. "I'm Edge, and you are?"

She puts her small hand in mine and gives my hand a little squeeze. "I'm Sara." I can see immediately she's lying to me. She has no clue how to lie. My name's Edge because I always have the upper hand.

She looks at me like she wants to say something more, her mouth opens a little, and then she says in a very small voice, "Ok. I'll be over in a few minutes. Let me just clean up a bit."

"I'll just go wait out at the bar for you." I have to strain my ears to hear her. "Take your time, little lady. I'll be waiting."

I can sniff a good girl out, and she's definitely a good girl, but can I get her to be a bad girl tonight?

I head down to the bar and take it upon myself to flip the closed sign on and click the locks. She's not used to closing up the bar because somebody else normally does this, and tonight, for whatever reason, she's been left alone to do it, and look what happens.

*I happen.*

I take a slow look around the bar. It's fitted out in wood and leather. A real old school kind of small town bar, with an old school kind of jukebox in the corner. The music has stopped, so I walk over to it, feeling around my pockets for a handful of coins, and I punch in several songs. The jukebox comes to life, clicking and whirring, and "One Of These Nights" by The Eagles starts playing.

I could have ducked behind the bar and gotten a couple of beers, but I don't want to appear more than who I want her to see. I want in her pants, and being Edge, the Soulless Bastard, isn't gonna cut it with this gal.

I take out my phone and text Hazard. I let him know I've arrived and I'll be tidying everything up soon. Whisper will be meeting an untimely end. We discuss some club stuff back and forth, and then end our conversation. I delete the messages, so my phone is clean.

I've positioned myself so I can see when she comes back into the bar. The jukebox clicks away as it chooses the next song, "Are You Gonna Be My Girl" by Jet starts playing.

She walks in, looking around the empty bar until she locates where I'm seated. She makes a stop behind the bar and holds up two beers. I nod my head, and she brings them over. I don't care about the brand; I just need a drink. I can see she's showered and has put on a clean white tank top, a knitted black zip-up, little denim shorts, and flip-flops. I'm amused at the flip-flops.

"Slide on in, little lady." I figure she'll sit next to me, but instead, she sits across from me. "Do you talk?"

"Of course." Her voice is so damn quiet against the

jukebox playing in the background.

"Darlin', you're gonna have to speak up because I can't hear you." She slides the beer over to me and I hold it up to her. "Thank you," I tell her, then take a deep swig.

She takes a long drink from her bottle and makes a little face while she looks about nervously. I need to go in for another swoop of getting her to trust me. This chick needs to chill. "Look, Sara, if you don't want to talk and have a beer, that's fine by me. I just thought you looked interesting and we might get along tonight."

"No. You are great. It's me. I've got a lot of things on my mind." Her eyes turn to me, but can't stay on me for too long. "I received some unwanted news today."

"Is that what the pounding on the heavy bag was all about?"

She nods her head. "My trainer would be disappointed all his hard work went down the peach pit the minute he left me alone."

*Peach pit?* I like this woman. "Is he your boyfriend?" Of course she would have somebody. I take a long swig out of my bottle, draining the contents. I'm about to cock-block my own dick and get out of here.

"Oh, no!" She laughs and I like the sound of it.

"He's more a father figure to me. He's away for a few days, and I was just feeling a little tense. He will help me sort it all out when he gets back."

I give my dick a mental double-thumbs-up, deciding maybe she's worth the challenge tonight after all. It's very rare a female doesn't push herself on me, or rub her tits in my face when I invite her for a drink. Actually, it's rare more than one woman isn't vying for my attention at the same time. This is something new to me. She's put a small chink in my ego.

When I'm hunting, I need to know when to back off and when to go in for the kill. This girl needs more effort, or else I will blow it before I can get to the finish line.

# Sara

## Moving Forward

I'm going to be twenty-two in a few months, and I want to behave like other girls my age. I don't know where I'll be in ten years' time, but for now, I'm happy being here, but I also want to grow up.

I have this man, who looks like he's around thirty, sitting across from me. We're doing a normal thing; we're talking and having a beer. I'm alone with another male, and I'm okay with that. His body language is relaxed and pleasant.

We talk. I lie a lot because I need to keep my identity a secret. I can't let that personal information out. I lie about my name, because I gave my real name to a stranger today, and now I'm saddled with a damning letter.

Tonight, I will be Sara, and she will help me move forward. I'm handing her the reins.

We talk about shallow things that are more a means to an end. I can see the interest in his eyes, and I can feel it in my body, how it responds to Edge sitting across from me.

I've watched enough movies to know how a guy makes small talk with a girl. I don't mind that he's doing it with me. He thinks I'm a mouse, but I have come a long way in eight months.

He's very attractive and I'm charmed by him. I saw the way his eyes looked at me when I walked back into the bar. He wants a beer, but he likes what he sees too. He doesn't frighten me.

*Maybe he should?*

He's now taken his leather jacket and button up shirt off. He's watching for a reaction. He looks more comfortable sitting here in his tight black T-shirt, which molds to his muscled torso. Tattoos cover his arms and he's well built, strong.

I felt like he was testing me when he took off his button up, like he was trying to show me his true self, shedding a facade. He's dressed one way, but then he sheds two layers and looks tougher and grittier, his tattoos exposed, his strength on display.

Boxer and Lincoln are both strong men with tattoos, and all they've done is protect me. I'm not intimidated by Edge. He keeps right on talking to me, and I'm okay to let my guard down and live a little.

I remind myself, *Tonight, I am Sara.*

We talk mainly about movies. That is our common ground. He's courteous, finding an interest I'm happy to talk about. We both stay away from being too personal. We laugh easily together about some of the movies we have watched.

I've sat and listened to him while simultaneously having an inner debate with myself. Maybe tonight's the night I take a leap, a giant first step, and let loose, go a little crazy, and behave like an adult. I know I don't act my age because I've had all that taken away from me. I act older, but at the same time, I try to hide how naïve I am. I want to find out what Edge wants, see where it leads. I can see in his steel grey eyes this man is attracted to me. He probably thinks I'm about twenty-five years old. Edge may be just what I need.

No strings. No promises. No boundaries.

I've paced myself and only have two beers, something I'm not used to doing in the first place. I tried to hide my disgust over the taste when it first hit my lips. I'm not a drinker, but I welcome the little buzz I'm getting. I don't like to not be in control; I have spent too many years at somebody else's mercy. So I drink cautiously. I know Edge notices, but he doesn't say anything. He doesn't seem the type to get a girl drunk so he can take advantage of her. He's respectful when I decline another beer, and he matches my pace. We are both in control of our bodies and emotions.

Tonight, I'm simply a young woman who was caught working out with her mind on other things, and a no-strings-attached handsome stranger set her right.

For tonight, the invisible tape is out securing the lids back down on the boxes of my memories and nightmares. I don't want anything spoiling this short time I have with this man, who is being nice to me.

This *feels* normal. *I* feel normal.

The thought crosses my mind that I'm entertaining a man in Boxer's bar after hours. Would he be okay with that? But I'm throwing caution to the wind. Edge has paid for every beer we've taken. I'll come clean when he gets back. It's not something I'm going to make a habit of because this small town has no young people for me to form friendships with. This is an opportunity that has presented itself, and I'm taking advantage while I can.

I tell Edge about my job, and omit details I find too personal from his questions. I tell him nothing of Miss Catherine. I know tonight's conversation is just a way of getting me alone. I've worked that much out. It means nothing to him, but after sitting here for a while, I think he's the perfect candidate to be reckless with and abandon my fears, if only for a few hours. I want to feel a little uncaring about what I want to do with Edge tonight.

We've been chatting for over an hour, when I decide to make the first move. It's what he wants anyway; that's why he's investing his time and money in me. I'd been lead to believe my virginity had been taken from me by William. That bastard never outright told me, it was a game to him, but I also knew I wasn't a whore. Boxer explained that to me. Whatever happened to me was out of my control. I was drugged and incapacitated. I had no choices in life. I had only rules and obedience. I knew no different. I won't ever be treated like that again. I want to be in control of tonight. I want this to happen, and I will say when.

I wet my bottom lip out of nerves and start to slide out of the booth.

"Where are you going?" He watches me lick my lips and those steel grey eyes darken with interest.

"I want to take you into the back room." I'm back to whispering again. It's a nervous thing. Boxer and Miss C set me straight when I regress. I set *myself* straight this time and say a little louder, "We both know what you are doing here with me, so I'm just going to speed it up a little." I sound confident. The jukebox has long stopped playing any songs. It's just two people in a quiet bar.

He slides out of the booth, grabbing his jacket and shirt, and follows me. He's a strong presence at my back. We climb the stairs, and I go to take him into the room I use when I stay here. It's a nice room. Boxer let me decorate it how I wanted to. It's simple, with a queen-sized bed and a dresser. It's decked out in nice calming colors of greens, creams, and pale blues. I hesitate, though, and walk straight by it. That's too personal.

I take him to the room where the heavy bag is and close the door. This is just going to be a 'hook-up,' as they call it, nothing more. No hearts and flowers, just a quick bang. I walk into the room a little more and turn around to face him. I'm nervous, but determined. This is what I need to get past William.

Sara is ready to do this.

# EDGE

## Sweet N' Wild

**W**ell, isn't she just a surprise package? I thought I was gonna have to change tactics, but she's ready and willing to fuck me. I walk towards her, noticing how the couple beers have loosened her up as she backs up against the wall, tilting her head invitingly at me.

I hook one finger in the front of her shorts and yank her towards me while I slant my head and go in for a taste. Her lips move with mine, while I pull her arms up around my neck and hold them there until she clasps her fingers around my nape. I push between her legs with my thigh so I can grind against her, letting her feel my hard cock. I can sense she wants to do this, but at the same time, something isn't right. I go in for foreplay to loosen her up more. She's still managing to dent my ego a little, and I'm not good with that.

She stops kissing me and turns her back to me, looking over her shoulder. I can see she's nervous, and there's this halo of mixed signals surrounding her.

"Is it all right if I face away from you?" Her confidence ebbs and flows.

"Fuck, little lady, we can do it anyway you want," I growl out.

I start grinding against her ass as she lets out a little noise of excitement. I take it as a green light when her fingers start pressing down and moving around at the front of her little denim shorts.

Fuck, yeah. We're on the same page. "Let me do that." I rumble against her ear. She doesn't need to get herself off. I pop her button and slide her zipper down so I can move my hand over her panties. They're already wet. I slide my hand out and she lets out a little whimper, which has my dick wanting to fight its way out of my pants. "Patience, little one." I move them up to her nose and tell her to smell herself. She inhales and her lips part in surprise, and I turn her head so I can see her eyes. Her lids have gotten heavier; she likes what she smells. She starts wiggling that little ass of hers again, rubbing herself against me as she arches her back to get the friction she's after. Definitely a green light.

"I want your fingers again," she whispers to the

wall. Her palms are pushing against the hard surface so I can get back down between her legs and inside her panties.

I cup her bare pussy in my hand, liking the way it feels, while adding pressure in the right place as my palm massages her slit. I let two fingers slip inside her, making her jump back a little against my chest, stiffening only for a heartbeat before the sensations leave her limp and pliable in my hand.

I'm kissing her neck as my other hand gets busy all over her tits. There are too many clothes in the way. I unzip her jacket and push the front of her tank top down underneath her breasts so I can feel her nipples poking through her lacy bra. I pinch the left one hard as I start to pump my fingers inside her. It only takes seconds and she's like putty in my hands. Her eyes have fluttered shut as she rests her head back on my shoulder, giving way to the pleasure of what she's feeling, and her little hips involuntarily start mimicking my movements.

Fuck, she's completely lost inside her arousal while my dick is hollering at me to uncage it.

I want to get her off before we go any further, so I step it up with another finger inside her. I know how big my cock is, and she's so small I want to prepare her for what's to come.

She's in the zone now, pumping her narrow hips

until she's almost doing all the work. Her lips are parted as she quietly pants from what I'm doing to her. Fuck it! I need to taste her again, so I angle my head until I can bite her top lip. Her eyes widen and she tilts her head so I have easier access to her mouth. I'm devouring her soft lips while her eyes stay focused on mine. I like her watching me. She's interested to see what I'm feeling, and I'm feeling all kinds of horny. She can't keep this up because she's about to come. Her long, dark lashes fan down to cover her eyes as her lips part, ready to cry out.

I pull away, burying my face in her hair. She smells like fresh apples mixed with a little sweat from her workout. She doesn't disappoint me. Her tight little pussy walls clamp down hard, and then my fingers are drenched as she lets out a sound that drives me crazy. I've never heard such a completely fulfilled sexual noise as the one that leaves her. It's like a breath of fresh air to hear a woman make a noise like that. It wasn't fake or exaggerated. It was full of unabashed ecstasy.

She opens her eyes and raises her head when her soft little pants turn to normal breathing, and she looks around as if to notice for the first time where she is, who she's with, and what just went down.

I don't want her thinking about it too long. I need some relief because my cock is about to pass out from the strain of wanting out of my pants. She just came in her panties, and I want to get inside her, ride her roughly, and hear that noise again.

My dick wants to hear that sound again.

I grab her hand, tugging her around to face me, kissing her hard on the lips. "Come with me." My voice is thick with deep, predatory desire. I don't wait for her to answer. I just take her with me, my hand gripping hers until we have made our way through the back exit I noticed earlier. I walk her across the parking lot to where my bike is parked in a corner out back of the bar.

The lot is empty.

Perfect.

I wouldn't fucking care if I had an audience. I know how to share. I like to watch.

The streetlight above us is so filthy only a dull glow escapes it, but it's enough to see each other. Her eyes go all big when she sees my bike.

"Do you ride?" I ask.

"Yes."

I can see she loves to ride just in the way she said that one word. I stop her beside my bike. "I'm only gonna ask this once, so be very clear with your answer." My voice sounds strained, but I don't rape chicks. I know what I'm capable of doing to a woman, and I don't get turned down. "Are you ready to be ridden hard?"

"Yes," she replies without hesitation. This is the most confident I've heard her all night.

I drop to my knees and strip her shorts and sodden panties off in one movement. She rests her hands on me as I bury my face in her bare pussy, eliciting a shocked little noise from her that gets replaced by a moan of pleasure when I slowly swipe my tongue deep inside her slit.

*Fuck, she tastes amazing.*

"Oooh..." Her lips make a little circle and she grips me a little harder. I come back for another slow, deep lick. A long moan comes out on a sexy, feminine purr.

*Jesus, this chick is hot.* She seems so innocent, not like any other woman I've had underneath me, on me, or wrapped around me.

I unbuckle my belt and my dick springs forward out of the top of my pants while the scent of her arousal sends me closer to the edge. I pull her hips to my mouth. "Spread your legs a little more." *Christ almighty*, she's turning me on. She's confusing the hell out of me with her innocent act.

Most females would be mounting me and wriggling their snatch in front of my face fully clothed. She's different. I groan at the sight of her pussy, lashing my tongue through her slit a few more times until she spills over so easily, so readily on a soft moan. Her fingers are gripping my shoulders like a lifeline while I lap her orgasm up, and her legs quiver a little from the pleasure.

*You got that fucking right, little lady. I can make you shake and tremble.*

My ego isn't so dented anymore.

Her scent is blanketed all over my mouth and it's driving me a little crazy. I wonder if she's ever been kissed by a guy after he's gone down on her? *One way to find out.*

I get to my feet and kiss her hard. She doesn't falter; so sweet one minute, and wild the next. I cover her mouth with mine and she meets my intensity, kissing me back just as hard. Her hands find their way into my hair, her fingers plowing through it while she devours my tongue, making a little humming sound as she tastes herself thoroughly.

My cock is standing up at attention between us. I wait for her reaction to it pressing on her stomach, expecting her to grab it and be all over it like other chicks would be... but she doesn't.

One minute, she acts so innocent, and the next, she's on fire. She's a little sexual bomb waiting to detonate.

I pull away and move so I can swing her leg over

my bike, and then I toss my jeans and boots where my jacket and button up lay on the ground. Her eyes are telling me how much she's enjoying the partial strip show I'm giving her. I grab the condom from my wallet before throwing it on top of my jeans. I tear the packet open with my teeth and roll it on then mount my bike behind her, sliding her forward a little, getting myself situated where I need to be.

"Step up on the bike pegs and lean forward so I can get inside you." She does everything I ask of her. I admire the view; she's something else. My rock-hard erection just got even harder, if that's possible. I grab hold of her hips and slam into her.

She cries out in pain.

I've pumped into her twice before I can stop myself.

*What. The. Fuck?!*

I still my movements. She doesn't move. Did I just break her hymen? "You okay, little lady?" My voice is low and unsure of what just happened. She didn't act like a virgin. Fuck, look at her. Who wouldn't have tapped this? I start to push her up and off me. There's no way I'm doing this to her if I hurt her.

The friction of me moving her up and her pushing back down on me has her making a little noise. "No. I'm okay. Please. I need to do this." She's breathless, and those mixed signals have come back.

I need to stop this. Her words sound unsure, and I won't continue. I move her up again, and she pushes back down with force. We both groan out in unison.

"Little one, if you keep that up, I won't be able to stop." I lay my head on her back. I need a moment. "Just let your body take me in. I'm big, and you are such a waif."

She looks back at me and nods her head then looks forward. This small movement from her body is enough to betray whatever her mind was just thinking and she starts rotating her hips. She wants the friction, and I need to go slower. She's never been ridden rough before; I don't care what she agreed to.

I won't be going hard tonight, so I gently thrust inside her, letting her move her body to get what she needs.

She's so *tight*.

I push her up because I need to see her face. She tries to resist me because she thinks I'm rejecting her. "Easy, little lady, I just want to turn you around so you can straddle me and ride me at your own pace."

She lets me lift her up, and we both want the feeling back the second we are separated. I help her turn around, with my feet planted firmly on the ground, and she slides back down onto me on a sigh, our foreheads leaning together as we take each other in. I let my hands glide down over her firm ass, feeling each perfect mound.

I want nothing more than to take her hard until she soaks my bike seat. It would be worth it just watching her get all wild in front of me. She might be quiet, but as the saying goes, it's always the quiet ones you gotta watch out for.

"Fuck, you feel good." I grit my teeth because she's wrapped so tight around my dick. I'm feeling a little animalistic at what this woman does to me. Her body calls to me, but I need to let her take the reins. I'm not used to someone behaving the way she is towards me.

I remove both her tops, dropping them onto the ground, and stare at her in only her little, lacy, black bra. Her breasts are perfect handfuls. I unsnap the clasp at the back and it gets tossed to the ground too.

*Jesus,* she's completely naked on my bike. Her nipples are so hard I whistle at the sight of them. "Nice tits, little lady". She responds by pushing them up closer to my face. I duck my head, swiping my tongue over one as she starts to ride me. I suck it inside my mouth and bite down on it, hard enough to have her arch up a little in pain. Then she offers me the other one. She's a greedy little thing, no longer playing the sweet card.

I pull her hair out of her ponytail and she shakes her hair out, which is one of the sexiest things I've ever seen. I have her amazing body naked on my bike while she straddles my dick, and her hair is flowing wild behind her as the mild breeze catches it.

*I need more.*

I slide my hands under her thighs, tug her legs up, and pull her a little closer to me. She lays back against the gas tank, moving so my balls will spank her rim. Then I take over.

Fuck, she's flawless.

"Grab hold of the handle bars." I sound like a caveman. I stand up a little, my feet pushing into the ground, and then I'm thrusting into her while my balls slap freely against her hole as she makes excitable little noises. Her breasts are bouncing, and I couldn't get any deeper if I tried. She's the sexiest creature I've ever let on my bike. She's wild, but in an innocent way. I know she would feel amazing without this condom, but we need this between us. I speed up and blow my load while she arches that perfect back of hers, her firm ass pushing into my seat, leaving her arousal all over it.

Fuck. Me. Drunk.

Her innocence concerns me. Any other female

would be making unnecessary noises and playing it right up to me, giving me dinner and a floor show. She doesn't come with bells and whistles; she's natural and sexy as all fuck.

I can tell from her response to what just happened between us that she has no idea how good she is.

We both need a minute before moving again, and I enjoy the view of her lying back, satiated on my bike. Her eyes are telling me how good that was for her. They have drooped lazily as she tastes her lips one more time.

And then I'm reminded of how she cried out. Looking at her now, lying back all sexually satisfied, you wouldn't believe it had hurt when I entered her. It felt like I broke her hymen, but that wouldn't make sense. Not to somebody like her. She was ready for this. I entered her so hard and fast, expecting a rough time. I wasn't paying too much attention to a woman's inner workings. I've never nailed a virgin. The whores that hang around the club are always experienced, and the other bitches I take had their seal broken a long time ago.

She doesn't seem bothered by it, and she was a sexy fuck, but now I need to move on. Enough of Joe Blow. I have to get this sweet piece of ass off my bike because I have a job to do.

# Sara

## Awkies

**E**dge slides out of me and lifts me off his bike. The sensation of him leaving my body is enough to make me come to my senses. I'm feeling shy, awkward, and confused. I'm the one butt-naked standing in a parking lot in nothing but my flip-flops, shivering from a mixture of emotions, not just from the cooling night, but also from what I had just allowed a man to freely do to me, and the realization that I was definitely a virgin.

I mumble my thanks and grab my clothes, dressing as quickly as I can, making sure I keep my back away from his eyes so he doesn't see the scarring. This would only lead to questions I don't need to be answering. He hasn't given me a second glance as he busies himself getting his jeans and boots back on, while my mind is bombarding me with questions I can't answer.

I don't understand. How could I have been a virgin all this time? William did things to me when I was drugged. He led me to *believe* I was taken every time. What did he do to me when I was hanging there?

Starting to feel sick, I grab my stomach and close my eyes as I try to center myself and keep my shit together. I have to lock these thoughts away until I can process them. I need a shower and to work through these emotions, and the only way to do that is to watch *those* videos.

"Hey, little lady," Edge interrupts my thoughts, bringing me back to what has just happened between us. "Sara!" His voice is sharp and concerned. He gives my arm a little tug. "Are you with me?"

I shake my head. "Yes." I look into those gun metal eyes.

"Are you okay?" He's watching me, waiting for a reply. The answer to that is on the hard drive because I'm not going to be okay with what I see on it, but I need answers.

"Of course, why wouldn't I be?" I lie and shrug my behavior off. This is my cross to bear, and nobody else's. "We both got what we wanted tonight." I give him a smile I hope is convincing. He lets go of my arm.

He's busy pouring water from a water bottle he's

taken from his saddlebag over his seat, wiping it down with a balled up T-shirt, giving me a mischievous grin. "You're certainly someone I could do this with again, so wild and innocent."

I should feel embarrassed at that comment, but I don't. I'm far from wild, but maybe I'm more innocent than I thought.

"Ok. I'm gonna hit the road." He's making his escape, and that's fine by me. I don't know what you say after a hook-up.

He's starting his bike, and I feel stupid standing here waiting for him to leave. I really should walk back inside, but I don't.

"Take care, Sara." He gives me one last long look, like he wants to remember my face, and then rides off. When he's out of sight I get that horrible feeling again, like I'm being watched. I scan the back lot and see nothing. I hurry inside to get cleaned up, so I can return the key and get everything back to how it should be, again.

I need my world back on its axis even more now.

# EDGE

## Twinge Of Regret

I smile as I leave the parking lot. She was a fuck I won't forget in a hurry. I could have had more of that sweet and eager conquest, but I have a schedule to keep. It's only ten o'clock; the night's still young. I'll take a ride over to the next big town and get myself something to eat, then I'll come back and get what I came here for done. Then I'll be gone, never looking back.

I've decided this time if the old bitch whore is staying at the house, I would go in quietly. If I have to fucking wake her up, I'm coming face-to-face with her before she meets an untimely end.

Leaving Sara behind has left a small twinge of regret tugging on my mind. To shed that feeling, I accelerate and ride like the wind.

# Whisper

## Take A Load Off

I've ridden over on one of Boxer's Harleys and parked around the side of William's house. This is the first time I've been back to it since I fled. Lincoln and I have driven past, but never to it. It was liberating riding down the avenue of oak trees toward the plantation home without having to feel afraid of anybody. I'm not scared, because there's no longer a reason to be frightened. Boxer and Miss C have shown me that.

I'm legally the owner, for a short time anyway. It gives me no joy. I'm not the rightful owner. I'm totally dumbfounded as to why William would have my name written into his will, much less leaving me the majority. It simply doesn't make sense. I honestly didn't believe I would outlive him and ever be free of him, so this simply floors me.

I climb the front steps, taking my helmet off and

hooking it through with my arm. I take the key out of my pocket and turn the lock. The *snick* of it unlocking sounds deafening out here, where I'm so isolated, but I feel empowered by being able to enter through the front door.

The door sticks, so I give it a shove with my shoulder and stumble a little over the threshold. The first thing I notice is how musty the house smells.

I try the light switch, but the power has been shut off, so I'm glad I came prepared just in case. I take the flashlight I brought along out of my leather jacket pocket I have on over my hoodie and click it on.

I'm confronted with the staircase that holds a lot of the answers to the questions buzzing around in my mind. My memories start to assault my mind, starting with William lying dead at the bottom. I gasp out loud because I can see him like a hologram, face down before me. I have to shut these thoughts down, now, because I don't need to be standing here in a dark house by myself with my little boxes popping open on me one-by-one. I shut my eyes tight and will them to stay closed so I can get down to business.

Once I have a hold of myself, I open them again and William is gone. The light beam hits the walls, which hold so many of my secrets, that I'm sure if you listened hard enough you could hear them whispering about me.

When I get back to the bar tonight, I'll go to the safe and find out what happened to me against that staircase. I knew a reason would come up to make me have to watch them, eventually. Then I will know everything. I'm strong enough to deal with what I see on that hard drive.

I simply have to be.

All I can now see before me is a lonely, old, dusty house. William would not be pleased to know his home was not clean and sparkling.

I know Boxer kept an eye out on this place and an ear to the ground. As far as Boxer knew, nobody had come back to the house to claim it. The son had probably only just discovered his father had died.

I'm happier trusting Boxer had everything taken care of, but there's no way he could've possibly known my name would come up on the will. I wonder if he even knows about a will. If he does, why didn't he let me know? All I understood was that he'd checked all the records and I was safe from being discovered. I can't help the questions that are banging away in my head, because none of this makes sense.

But here I stand under threat of being discovered

by the son who could quite possibly challenge the will. This is why it is important I set the key and my letter down. It is my way of cleansing my hands of it all. I know it is still on paper, but I need to show that I'm happy to walk away with this small gesture.

Why hadn't he visited in all these years, or he had, but I'd been drugged up and put into hiding? I'm going to go crazy if I don't stop doing this to myself.

I wanted to call Boxer, but it can wait until I get back to the bar tonight. He's done so much for me already. I'm giving the key back, which is a load off my mind already. It's been eight months since William died, and I haven't been discovered. That lawyer creeped me out, but there is no way he could have known everything about me.

Could he?

Am I being too gullible?

The will had my surname on it, the new one Boxer set up for me, and that is lurking in my thoughts like a dangerous plot twist. It's worrying my mind endlessly. Somebody knows about my new identity. The pieces don't add up, but there's nothing I can do about it at the moment.

The more I think about it, the more it all disturbs me. I'm hoping it's just a lawyer doing his job, making the appropriate changes to the document once he found me. Not that I know anything about wills. I've let Boxer do everything, when I should have asked more questions. How did the lawyer even find me?

Ignorance was bliss for me, because it was easier for me to try to forget, knowing somebody else was dealing with my troubles.

*Ughh. I need Boxer.*

I'll definitely call him when I get back to the bar. I won't be able to sleep until I know he's been told.

The other thing preying on my mind is what went down with Edge tonight. The opportunity crossed my path, and I just wanted to forget my worries, have a good time, and I did. My body's still humming from what that man had done to me. I don't regret what happened. He made me feel so good; it's hard to put into words what was going through my head when I was on his bike and he was inside me.

Edge made me feel alive in a sexual way I've never wanted to feel before. He unlocked something inside me that can't be taken back. With him, it felt right. It was amazingly hot, and I will probably never get that ever again, so I'm not sorry I did it.

I felt so fucking sexy on that bike. I did something tonight that made *me* feel good and *I* was in control. He didn't pressure me. I had choices. But he's now long gone. It was exactly what it was and nothing more.

Sara. Got. Laid.

I. Got. Laid.

I can't help the knowing smile from settling on my face until I remember why I'm here. Now is not the time to relive what was done to me tonight. I don't venture any farther into the house than I need to because this is *not* my home.

My phone beeps, startling me. I've got one missed call from Boxer, and he's just left a text message asking where I am. I'll reply once I've finished up here. We have a level of trust, and I won't lie to him. I can't tell him I'm here because he would worry. I'll be back at the bar in half an hour, and then I can be truthful.

I place the letter on the dining table and put the house key next to it. I hope my letter apologizes enough for my name being placed on the will, and I explain that I will be turning everything in my name over to the son.

I'm anticipating Boxer can sort this all out for me and help me contact that horrible lawyer so it can all be fixed when he gets back in a few days, and then that sleaze of a man can let the son know where to find the key.

The document I've received has the potential to threaten the story we have spun for the townsfolk.

It threatens the secrets I want kept boxed up. I want this misunderstanding cleared up, so all will be good in my world.

There's only one thing I want to do before I leave. I want to go and look at the garden patch because it used to be a little sanctuary for me.

The temperature has dropped, so I pull my hoodie up over my head as I head on down to my bike, placing my keys and phone inside my helmet, hooking it over my handle bar before I wander down to my little garden.

The way is lit by the full moon gracing the black sky. I don't need my flashlight on, so I click it off. I can see the silhouette of my much loved garden patch is dried up and withered from being unattended. I love watching something grow from a seed. I enjoyed tending to all the vegetables. It makes me sad to see it like this. We relied on each other for survival. I can tell nobody has been here, probably since his death, or the garden would be healthy.

I reach out and touch a crumbled leaf, which turns to powder under my fingers. I feel like I have let it down, left it to wither and die alone, while I thrived under the care of Boxer and Miss C. It's strange the things you hold close to your heart when there's nothing else to hold onto.

My eyes wander over to the old wooden slave cabin, which has been standing for a tremendously long time. Those wooden walls hold more than just my secrets. Other lives have come and gone, and had lived in that cabin.

There are a lot of memories trying to break through again, so I need to get away from here and never come back. It's not healthy being here. I came only to drop the letter and key off. I don't want to go near that horrible lawyer ever again without Lincoln or Boxer to assist me.

*"Whisper."*

My head swings to the side. Did I just hear my name called out?

I get that horrible feeling I'm being watched again. It's such a distinct feeling. A gut feeling that makes me want to run to the bike and ride away. I know I'm being silly, but this sense is ridiculously strong.

I hear my name called out again, floating on the breeze. *"Whisper."*

My natural instinct is to turn around. I can't ignore it, and that's when I hear the muted sound in the air that spears my left shoulder sharply backwards, while the rest of me goes with it, falling hard onto the dirt. Pain burns my shoulder in a blistering heat while I'm left staring up at the stars

flooding the night sky.
   *Please, God. Not again.*

# EDGE

## What The Fuck?!

*One bullet to maim and cause pa—*

"*Ooph!*" is all I can grunt out as I'm slammed sideways into the ground from the place I had been stalking my prey.

One second, I was aiming at the old whore so I could give her a taste of pain before we got down to business, and the next, I'm bulldozed sideways as I pull the trigger, my head bouncing off the ground like a crash dummy.

*What the fuck?!*

A heavy body lands on me, and then a jaw-crunching blow hits my face, which feels like a sledgehammer has tried to take my head off. I'm left dazed and disorientated in the dirt.

I was pissed before, but now I'm fucking furious. Rage has me twisting about on the ground, trying to see what the fuck just happened.

From the flat-on-my-back position I'm in, I'm trying to focus on the female I shot and the other threat that blindsided me. I can just make out she's struggling with a big guy. I slowly get to my feet, swaying all over the place like a goddamn drunk fool, when I'm hit hard from the back, my skull taking the full brunt.

*For fuck's sake, you gotta be kidding me.*

I go down like a sack of potatoes and the lights turn out.

# Whisper

## Inner Tiger

**There are two or three of them.**
My mind's playing tricks on me; it has to be. I thought I heard Edge's voice, and now I'm fighting with somebody.

Boxer's training slams back into me. I connect my palm with my attacker's nose, shoving it up as hard as I can. I hear a satisfactory crack and grunt come from my assailant, but before I can do another thing to save myself, a hard blow lands to my stomach, winding me, and another lands on my cheekbone in a classic one-two punch, and everything goes into slow motion. My head whips to the left and I go down hard on my side as the air is seriously knocked out of me. I'm gasping for oxygen like a fish out of water.

I lie wriggling about on the ground, trying to breathe, trying to calm the panic within me that wants to surface, but I know I need to get back up on my feet.

I command my body to listen and do as I tell it to. My inner tiger has emerged, and I won't be going down without giving it my best shot. Even with the agonizing pain in my left shoulder, my determination to survive outweighs everything else. I got attacked and I need to escape.

I push to my feet, not really in my right mind, because my body is on fire. My inner tiger is trying not to give up, but I'm feeling a little wonky and a lot woozy.

"Fuck's sake, lady, just stay down." The powerful entity has a voice. Boohoo to him. It sounds like I'm annoying this guy. I swing my fist in a ridiculous attempt at hurting him. He sidesteps my fist, grabs me around the neck, and strongholds me until I'm left gasping for the small amount of air I'd been allowing my body.

If I could have cried out, I would have, but nothing left my lips. I simply go limp from lack of oxygen until I feel myself passing out.

*So much for my inner tiger.*

# EDGE

## Ebony & Ivory AKA Bugsy & Deano AKA Benny Boy & Dean

**I come to on the ground, slowly opening my** eyes and trying to get the stars to stop swirling about like I'm looking through a kaleidoscope. Once I can see clearly, I assess my current situation and what has happened since I blacked out.

I never black out.

*What. The. Fuck?!*

A car has been reversed up, approximately ten yards from where I lie, and there's one guy carrying my revenge kill, dropping her into the trunk of his car.

*I don't think so. That's my body he thinks he's walking away with. Why is he so interested in my slut?*

I quietly get to my feet while he's busy with the body, and I get ready for another fistfight, because the cocksucker has stripped me of my weapons.

Then I see the second guy standing by a tree, puffing on a cigar, dressed up like a 1950's gangster, full pinstriped suit and fedora with a hankie, who's holding a flashlight.

*What a fucking clown.*

I'm not quite with it because of that blow to my head, but it now makes sense why I was taken unaware the second time. Why has my old whore garnered this much attention? What's the busy bitch been up to? Ripping somebody else off, no doubt. Call me curious, because I know these fools could have killed me. I would have killed me, but they left me alive for a reason.

I should just walk away.

But fuck, now I want to lay my eyes on her and see what all the body snatching is about.

I come up behind the guy who's about to pull the trunk down. He's more a run of the mill thug. Jeans, boots, jacket, nothing that stands out in a crowd… not like Bugsy. Naturally, he hears my approach, because I'm not doing a great job of being quiet, probably something to do with nearly having my brains smashed out of my head.

I'm a little off kilter. It happens.

Bugsy Malone isn't at all perturbed by my advancing on them, so he just keeps right on smoking his cigar.

Trunk guy turns around cool as a cucumber, a handgun with a silencer attached pointed at my head. "Ah-ah-aahhh. Whatever you were thinking, buddy, I wouldn't." It comes out all nasally, because he's copped a broken nose from the whore. He's even uglier now. Looks like the only job he could sign up for was *thug,* because he ain't got anything else going for him. You would have to be blind to want to fuck him. "We know you are a Soulless Bastard. We aren't going to mess with one of theirs, so make our life easy and play nice."

*What the fuck? They've been following me?*

"We've been following her. Not you." Then he shrugs at me. "Well, we've been tracking you. We knew where you were going when you left Albuquerque; we just used one as a precaution in case we lost you. We slapped one on your bike before you left. We had to make sure you got the letter and then headed on out. We don't want any trouble, so we'll take it from here. Think yourself fortunate; she's now out of your hands."

*Who is this dickhead, and what the fuck is he yabbering on about?*

I rub the back of my head, which is hurting like a family of flash grenades have gone off in it, and my fingers come away a sticky, dirt-clogged mess, and that just makes my patience non-existent. "What the fucking hell are you talking about?" I growl out to these motherfuckers, who are trying to walk off with my kill.

He just keeps on talking. "You were the one who was aiming to snuff the chick out." He shrugs casually again. "My boss wants her alive. William Dupré owes him...big. You would do well to keep your nose out of this and just walk away, my friend. We got no beef with you. We're just the delivery boys, and we want no trouble. We've got a job to do, same as you do."

I move slowly to the trunk, holding up my palms to show I'm not going to try anything. I want to know who he's fucking talking about, because my brain is off on its own merry-go-round at the moment and nothing's making any goddamn sense. "I just want to see why my father decided she was worth his time."

The gun's still pointed at my head, but I know he won't shoot me. His orders aren't to kill me.

"You fucked her, so you should know why. Did you just say father?" Then he starts laughing. "Hey, Benny boy, this is William's son. This keeps getting better and better. We got ourselves some father and son action." Bugsy Malone decides to come around and join our little shindig.

"What the fuck are you talking about?" How did

they not know I'm the son of William Dupré, if they made sure the letter was in my possession? They are just the delivery boys, as they stated, so their boss must not deem them high enough to know all the details. That means there may be another party involved issuing orders.

I tamp down my rage. I have to stay calm. If this guy sees me as too dangerous, then he won't hesitate to kill me if he knows it's either him or me—fuck his orders.

Bugsy's pretty confident his accomplice can handle me. He's standing watching us with his arms crossed, smiling at me with a very confident grin. He's dark-skinned, and he has extremely white teeth that are going all neon in the moon-light.

"Relax, delivery boys. I just want to see what she looks like."

Ivory's looking at me like I got hit way too hard, and that's gonna have to work for me. "You were the one fucking her in the parking lot earlier, which, by the way, I have told Boss Man she's everything he could ask for."

*I'm not hearing him correctly.*

"What are you talking about?"

"The beauty you were fucking on your bike. William Dupré owes my boss, and he's now collectin'. You've already damaged the package, and he'll be none too pleased, but if you walk away, there will be no hard feelings."

I pretend to sway a little.

Bugsy pipes up, "Deano, I think you hit him too hard. He's lost some of his memory. I sure wouldn't forget sticking my dick inside this little bitch. That was quite some show you both put on. I could have done with some popcorn." He actually grabs his crotch and starts gyrating his hips. "I nearly came in my pants watching her performance. Boss Man is sure gonna be pleased with the merchandise." Then he gives a low dirty laugh as he grabs hold of his dick again.

*Yeah, Bugsy, you've got balls...for the meantime anyway. I hope he isn't too attached to them.*

Now I'm getting beyond pissed off with all this blathering.

*Oh, for fuck's sake.* Ebony and Ivory underestimate my attitude towards them. The upper hand, remember? I play a role to get what I need.

I have to see for my own eyes. "Let me just have one last look." I give Ivory a little sneer. "She was a great fuck." This couldn't be Sara. "Don't do anything stupid because the Soulless Bastards don't forgive. My president knows where I am, and he won't give a shit who your fucking boss is." I give him a warning so I don't wind up in the trunk when

I bend over to take a closer look.

"Keep your panties on. Just take it nice and slow, and we'll all leave here tonight in one piece," Ivory says, watching me carefully. He's the smarter one out of the two, because Benny Boy is *really* misjudging me. I think that gangster outfit makes him believe he's bulletproof, but last I knew, Superman was no gangster.

My odds aren't too good at the moment of taking this guy and Bugsy out. I have no bones with these guys, or with my father's dealings. I came to exact retribution, and now everything has gone to shit.

Nothing is black and white anymore, except for these two morons.

Ivory shines a flashlight on her face. I rest my left hand on the trunk while the other pulls the hoodie back off her head, revealing her pale face to me.

*Motherfucker.*

It's Sara. She's got a bruise forming on her face and her eye is starting to swell shut. Her shirt has lifted up and there's a nasty bruise appearing on her right side. She's out cold. Her chest is moving, so she's still alive. Her hands are zip-tied together, and there's fresh blood staining her chest, which means she hasn't stopped bleeding from my gunshot, and they've obviously fucked her up more.

This really gets under my skin, and I don't know

why I'm feeling this strong emotion. If I had a gun, I wouldn't hesitate to use it on either of them.

Shit, I knew she was lying about her name, but it never crossed my mind my father would hook up with a girl so young.

What the hell is going on here? I need time to process, and my head's pounding like a bitch in heat. I just want to have a good look at her and see if there's anymore damage, but I won't get that time. I'm lucky he's even letting me do this.

My father was an evil bastard, but something isn't right here with Sara being Whisper. She's too young for my father, and she has an innocence about her that was hard to deny. Not unless she's a fucking award winning actress? You couldn't fake her sexual purity on my bike. She's no whore; I would bet my money on that.

*So who the ever loving fuck is she, and what did she truly mean to him?*

I slowly turn my head and look over my shoulder, putting on my hunter's face, the deadly one. "Why didn't you let me kill her? Why does your boss want her alive? To me, she's worth more dead." He's no longer shining the light in the trunk. I hope my questions will distract him while I casually pull my cell phone out from the left front pocket of my riding leathers. I pretend to lean heavily on the car, the movement allowing me the freedom I need to get the phone hidden inside the trunk.

I just hope like fuck she finds it and I can get to my Prez to let him know that nobody is to call that number. I need it to track this car with the GPS in it, not taken off her because it's ringing away in their trunk. They would have already searched her prior to dumping her in the back. That's just Kidnapping 101. I should be able to find where she's being taken.

"Consider her erased from your life. Whatever your beef with her, you got your cock wet, you got to mouth fuck her, and now she's got a one-way ticket. Boss Man will take it from here."

This cocksucker is so sure of himself and that I'm just gonna walk away, which puts me in another realm of pissed-me-the-fuck-offs.

Soulless Bastards have a reputation far and wide, but I still can't wrap my mind around Sara being Whisper and meaning something to my father. She's living at the bar. She told me that much when we were talking. She hesitated just a split second outside a room, which at a quick glance was feminine, but then she changed her mind before I finger-fucked her in the back room.

Previously, the name Whisper meant a money grubbing old whore, but now...I got no fucking clue what it means.

*What am I condemning her to?*

Earlier, this was my show, but now I've been bought out by another station. *Something is seriously fucked up here,* my gut is screaming at me. I need to be done with it all, just walk away, and burn the place down, but...something isn't ringing true.

Why is one of the best fucks I've ever had, lying unconscious in the trunk of their getaway car, bleeding from a gunshot wound I'd inflicted? This woman my father had shacked up with should not be a young female, and her real name shouldn't be Whisper, and she shouldn't have her name embedded on my father's last will and testament. She's supposed to be some old whore, not Sara from the bar, but repeating these facts to myself doesn't change anything.

I need more answers and information. For now, she's safe until she reaches their destination while my phone takes a road trip with her. They want her alive, and they are travelling by car, so they won't be going that far, and they *need* to keep her alive. My bullet would have gone straight through her shoulder. I was aiming to kill her with my second bullet once I'd talked to her. I'm not sure why I feel relief that I didn't get that far. If she's my father's whore, then she deserves what she gets from me.

But is she?

*Jesus Christ, what have I stepped into? Even in death, he's causing trouble.*

My phone is the only lead to finding out who is behind all this and why Whisper is involved.

"Move away and mind your own fuckin' business." Ivory's losing his patience with me. He's on a schedule, and I'm fucking that up. I can't win against a gun at close range pointed at my head. I move away and he slams the trunk down. "Don't even try to follow us." Then he shoots me in the foot. "Sorry about that. No hard feelings, just doing my job."

"Mo…ther… fuuuck…iiiing… ass…hole," I let out a deep groan as I go down on one knee. I had been toeing the line, playing the part, because it was as easy as him pulling the trigger to blow my brains out, and that silencer on the end of his gun would ensure nobody heard my death, but the fucker still shot me.

I know the cocksucker isn't going to let me watch them drive off. Just to add insult to injury, I have to let him knock me out. Such a predictable son of a bitch as he pistol-whips me across the head.

Just as I'm blacking out, I remind myself to find these two guys. They have just been added to my retribution list.

*Yeah, no hard feelings, Ebony and Ivory.*

••••

When I come to, lying flat on my back, my foot's throbbing and my head's pounding, and I find I'm having an inner battle with myself, knowing I should just walk away.

None of this shit is anything I need to include myself in. So she was a good fuck? I can still burn the house down now and be done with it all. So what if my phone is in the trunk with her? I can buy another one.

No, conscience isn't part of the Soulless Bastards fucking code. Whisper won't last long under the guy who wants her. She will pay whatever debt my father owed him, and then she will be done for. My world will continue the way it was revolving.

I roll to my side and pound my fist into the dirt.

*Fuck!*

There's too much blamelessness surrounding this woman that I can't ignore. I don't hurt innocent people.

My foot hurts like a thousand razor blades have been embedded in it as I stand up and hobble over to the house, when I'm distracted by a phone going off. I head towards the sound and find her phone lit up, lying a few yards into the trees. I scoop it up and check the caller ID. 'Miss Catherine' is showing up on the screen. I ignore it and let it ring out. I use the phone to first text my president with a code word to let him know I'm going to be calling on an unknown number, and then I call him and organize for nothing to be sent through to my phone. Hazard wants to know how it's all going because he knows if I don't have my own phone, something has gone down. I tell him everything just turned complicated, but it will get sorted. He wants to send a brother to help me out, but I decline.

I use the flashlight app to search for her bike keys, but I can't find them with a quick inspection of the area, and I don't have the time to search for them properly. They may even have kept them.

I head back to the house. There's gotta be something I can find out about her inside it.

Blood's dripping everywhere as I make my way into the house. The front door was left unlocked because apparently she has issues with locking doors behind her.

I had watched and waited patiently for her to come back outside from that house so I could end her life, and my mission would have been completed, but something felt off to me, watching her staring at the garden patch like it meant a great deal to her.

I still didn't hesitate to pull the trigger.

*If she was associated with my father, then she couldn't have been good,* was my last thought before I laid her out on the ground and the night turned into a free-for-all dust-up.

The house is dark, only barely lit in front of me by the flashlight app. It's enough to draw my attention to an envelope propped up on the dining table. I hobble closer to see a key sitting next to it.

The envelope is addressed to Dallas Dupré.

A red flag went up when I received my letter from the lawyer, because it was addressed to my new family surname, the one I was given to hide my identity from my father. The check was also made out to Dallas Masson.

*Christ, what game is my father playing?*

Something was off about the will and I didn't take the time to follow it through. I flew out of Albuquerque all hot-headed, instead of taking the time to think. That's a rookie's error.

I open the envelope and start reading. I can't read fast enough.

*Motherfucking cocksucker asshole!*

I shove the letter into my jacket pocket and also pocket the key. I have to get out of this house and get to a computer, but first I have to clean up the blood spilling from my foot, where I had trailed it into the house. I find some dish towels in a cupboard and I take the fucking time to clean up any evidence I have been here.

It takes too long.

Now, I can't get out the house quick enough as I try to work out where I can find a computer this late at night, so I can track where Whisper is being taken. I didn't want to let Hazard know about this clusterfuck. I can handle this shit myself. There's nothing I can't handle.

My bike's hidden in the thick trees to the right of the property. I had walked a distance to get here, and that was gonna come back to piss me right off.

I push Whisper's bike into the trees and then head off on foot to get to my bike.

Time is wasting away. My foot's exploding with pain as I jog as best as I can all the way back through the forest to my bike where it's hidden, and get back on the road and ride towards town. I've lost blood, and I'm having trouble seeing through the blinding pain from when the second prick knocked me out. Feels like the fucker used a rock on my head.

I'm speeding along the dirt road when my bike's light picks up a shadow on the side of the road, and then the shadow decides to step out into the path of my bike.

It's an old lady.

*What the fucking hell?*

I swerve to miss her at the last minute, which sends me careening off the road into a painful slide.

*Jesus Christ, this night just keeps getting better.*

I know how to let my body fall so the damage will be less, but it's still gonna do some damage. My helmet saves my head, and the leather jacket and pants I'm wearing save me from the impact of the ground sliding harshly underneath me. When I've finally come to a stop, I groan from the pain in my foot. It's wedged underneath the bike, which is lying sideways and partially on top of me.

An old face appears in my vision. "I'm Miss Catherine, and I'll be needin' your help, young man. I need to find a girl; it's an emergency."

"Christ, lady, I've just missed killing you and you want to have a chat?" *Un-fucking-believable.*

Then her name registers to me, it's the lady who was trying to call Whisper. I struggle to get up and see if the bike is still roadworthy. My response is muffled. "Lady, you should not be out here at this time of night. What the hell are you thinking?"

I take my helmet off, which is wet with blood, and assess the damage, ignoring the little old woman standing beside me, hovering. I stand the bike up and notice the tiny blinking red light of the tracker that has come loose and is lying in front of me. I'd forgotten about it. I pick it up, smothering a curse under my breath. As long as they think I'm not following them, this will work in my favor.

Miss Catherine puts her wrinkly hand on my arm, getting my attention as I look up at her. "It's Whisper. I know she's in danger. I was coming to find her. She didn't answer my call." I can see she's agitated. She holds up her phone then dials a number and Whisper's phone implicates me by ringing in my jacket pocket. It obviously survived the fall. Then she starts hitting me with her little fist. "Where is Whisper?" She takes a really good look at me now, taking in my face and the blood matting my hair, making all sorts of assumptions in her head. She's also noticed I was hobbling when I got out from underneath the bike and knows I'm hurt. She probably doesn't know I've been shot, but she doesn't hesitate to step on my foot as hard as her slight body will let her.

"*AH!* Shit, lady, I'm trying to find out. And don't do that again." Fucking hell, she might be old, but she sure is feisty.

She stares me down through the glow of the headlight. "Why do you have her phone?"

"She has my phone," is the only explanation I'm gonna give this crazy bat. Time is ticking away. "Do you have a computer at home?"

She eyes me up again then answers, "Whisper does. I got no use for one of dem things."

I can see she wants to ask a whole pile of questions, but we have no time for a get-to-know-each-other chat. I pay closer attention to the little old lady and notice she's only wearing a nightgown, slippers, and a robe. "Fuck's sake, lady, you shouldn't be out here dressed like this." Whisper must mean a lot to her to have left her home, searching for her without a second thought.

She stomps back down on my foot. "Mind your language, boy."

*Jesus!* "Enough!" I roar back at her. This gives her pause to reconsider her behavior with me. She's now dialling a number on her phone. I snatch the phone away from her and disconnect it before putting it in my pocket. I don't need this turning into a three-ringed circus.

I can see she's distraught about Whisper. "Look, lady...you are gonna have to trust me if you want to see Whisper again. Shit went down tonight and she's been taken by some bad guys, so we're gonna have to do this my way." I let what I've said sink in. "If I'm going to be able to find her, I need a computer, pronto." My patience is wearing thin with this woman. Whisper was my enemy, but now I'm not so sure.

"My phone's in the trunk she's laying in at the moment, being driven away by bad guys. If I can get a read on where they are now, then we have a chance of getting her back." If I know a thug's modus operandi, then they won't stop until they get her to their destination. They can't afford for her to die on them, so time's running out for me to find her. If they find my phone, they will ditch it, and then I will lose all means of tracking her whereabouts.

She grabs hold of my jacket. "Is she hurt?"

*Christ!*

"Yes. She's been shot, so I can't stand around shooting the breeze with you. I can either leave you here to make your way back where you came from, or we're going to your place. It's your call." I should just fucking walk away...but something is grounding me. I think I have grown a fucking conscience. My brain is needling me about this whole Whisper and my father's will situation. It now feels very orchestrated.

I get on my bike and hiss out a couple more expletives from the pain shooting from my foot when I start it up.

"Lady, do you think you can get on behind me and hang on so we can get to your place without any further shit going up against me?" I need her computer, and I need some answers from this woman. She knows Whisper, and she will make my mind up whether I let her rot and pay my father's debt, or if she's an innocent caught in the crossfire and I need my foot looked at as well.

"She could die?" Her voice has turned to steel.

"Fuck, lady, what bit of 'there's no time to explain now' are you not getting? If you're coming, then get on." She hikes up her clothing and deftly swings her leg over the bike. Christ, what more can happen tonight? I hand her my helmet, blood-soaked and all.

"Put that on."

# *Whisper*

## Monsters Come In All Shapes And Sizes

I regain consciousness inside a confined space. My shoulder is in pain, but manageable if I don't move too much, and my hands and feet are tied together.

I turn my head to get an idea of where I am. I listen to my surroundings. I gather I'm in the trunk of a car, which is driving along a road. My face hurts; it feels swollen, and my ribs are hurting. I try to look through the darkness for anything I can use to aid my dire situation, and I'm alerted to a blinking light.

*Is that a phone by my head?*

Who abducts somebody and leaves a phone in the trunk? I don't care, because it's just by dumb luck it's here. I move my body and groan with the pain until I can grab it between my hands. I roll onto my stomach, which makes my shoulder scream in agony, and something wet lands on my hands. I know what blood smells like, and I'm bleeding from my shoulder wound.

I can feel a hysterical giggle start to bubble up inside me, which I work hard at stamping down, because I may fear for my life, but the last thing I need to do is go into shock.

*What did I do to deserve this life?* I inwardly groan. I had happiness, and now my life has turned to shit again, and I have no clue why.

I really must have had an exceptionally fabulous life in a past one for me to be getting shit on so badly in this one.

I concentrate on the phone and try to stop my hands from shaking. I can press the buttons better in the position I'm now in. I check the time, seeing it's after midnight. I've been out for a while.

I can't think of Boxer's number. I am so used to pressing a speed dial button.

*Concentrate, Whisper.*

*Come on, think.*

I slowly start pressing the buttons for Boxer's number I hope I have right just as the car takes a sharp turn, and I go sliding, the phone slipping out of my hands.

I bite down on my lower lip to stop myself from crying out in pain.

*Fuck, that hurt.*

Once we straighten up again, I maneuver my body to get back to the phone. I start to dial again, but I have to disconnect, because the car has come to a stop. I need to hide the phone quickly. I work my leg around, preparing to slide it into my boot, when we take off again.

I decide to call Miss C instead, because I know that number and she will answer. I dial her number, and a male voice answers, "Sara is that you?" I don't answer. "Whisper, is that you?"

I don't know what to say. It's a male voice, and it's not Boxer's or Lincoln's. It sounds like Edge's voice.

*How? Why?*

"Edge, is that you? Is Miss Catherine all right?" I talk low into the phone. "I don't know what's going on, but you have to keep her safe. She can't be brought into whatever the hell's going on." I can't keep the fear from invading my voice. Miss Catherine means too much to me. I don't know why I've been kidnapped and am lying in a trunk, with what I'm guessing is a gunshot wound, but if it keeps her safe, then I will take this punishment.

There's a shuffling noise. "I'm here, honeychile. I am safe with Dallas. He be helpin' me to find you. Do as they say and give him time to get to you. I've tried Boxer, and I can't get through to him or Lincoln."

*Dallas?*

His voice is back. "Yes, it's me. Whisper, we need to talk, but now's not the time. We are tracking the phone I slipped into the trunk with you. You have to keep it hidden, and I need you to put it on silent. I want you to save the battery, because I need to be able to stay in contact with you."

*Edge?*

Something occurs to me in all this hellish mess I've found myself in. "Can Miss Catherine hear me?"

"No, I have her phone."

The pain in my shoulder is different to any pain I've experienced in the past. "Did I get shot?"

"Shit, Whisper, not now." His voice sounds rough and guilty.

Then it strikes me I thought I'd heard him back at the house, which has been confirmed, because I have his phone next to me. "Did you shoot me?"

There's cursing coming down the line. "There appears to have been a misunderstanding."

"I'll take that as a yes." There's silence at the other end of the line. "Did you want to kill me?"

Suddenly, the car comes to another halt. It feels more permanent. "I have to go; they've stopped." Just before I hang up, I hear Edge curse out loud and something smashes. I disconnect, put the phone on silent, and work my body so I can slide the phone into the side of my calf-length right boot. My legs are tied at my ankles, so I can get it in far enough to hide it for now.

I can't even process what all this means at the moment. He shot me? He must have known who I was when he arrived at the bar.

He was playing me.

Stalking me.

He was going to kill me.

*Why?*

I had sex with him.

I feel sick.

I quickly put all that into a box and pack it away in my mind. My immediate thoughts have to be on surviving whatever mess I've been dropped into. Miss Catherine will get through to Boxer, and he will save me. I don't want Edge anywhere near me.

Just before the trunk pops open I calm myself and pretend to be out cold. It's my only defense against what's coming for me.

I can't even afford to tremble in fear.

I feel a monster greater than William Dupré is waiting for me, and I'm fucking scared.

# WARPED

## HER DEBT OWED, #2

# EMMA JAMES

# CEZAR

## The King's Assassin

**I end the call, placing my phone down on the antique** hand-carved desk fit for a king, taking a deep celebratory puff of my Black Dragon cigar as I fall back into my oversized wingback. A smug smile creeps across my masked face while I enjoy this moment. All is going to plan.

The room is silent as the occupants await my next move.

Finally my eyes rest on Rose, my redheaded beauty. I drink her in as she waits patiently by the wall, hands clasped in front of her, head slightly bowed.

Rose serves as my courtesan, always available to fulfill my sexual needs, and when called upon, my assassin, ready to follow orders and eliminate the females in The Pen who are no longer required.

This latest news has spiked my need for a suck-and-fuck. "Disrobe, my angel of death, and come kneel before me." Her head snaps to attention as I push away from my desk so she has room to comply with my request, and I pat my leg. Taking another puff of the Black Dragon, my eyes flutter shut as I enjoy the exquisite taste.

The soft swishing sound of her silk robe fills the space as it floats down to the carpet, and I picture her lithe, naked body while she makes her way to me.

Rose never defies me.

Rose is my masterpiece.

She was so alive and headstrong when she was first brought to me.

She challenged me.

I *broke* her.

I dug into her mind until I found what I was looking for.

A cold-hearted murderess.

Rose learned what she needed to do to survive me. She is the *only* female I've chosen to keep for any great length of time.

A hand rests gently on my thigh as she kneels, and then my black Versace suit pants are unbuckled, the zipper slowly eased down.

I reposition myself in my office throne to get more comfortable as she releases my dick, stroking it, getting me harder and harder. My free hand winds around the back of her neck like a slippery serpent as her lips glide over the head of my cock, making me groan aloud at the sensations from her touch.

I let her adjust to the feel of my thick erection for precisely two seconds as it rests in her mouth. Rose knows what's coming. And then the slippery serpent strikes, forcing her head down until I hear her gagging.

*I love to hear her gag.*

She is suffocating on my cock. The thrill shoots through my body, spiking my arousal.

My head tips to the side, resting against the corner of my office throne, my dick touching the back of her throat. I don't need to look to know tears will be making a pathway down her cheeks while she gasps for air as I keep forcing her head down onto my cock.

When I know she's almost passing out from the way her head is shaking, her tears mixing with her spittle... I release her. Soft gasps escape as she searches for oxygen, quietly gulping down mouthfuls.

And then my hand strikes again, but this time, I pump her head up and down.

Up.

And.

Down.

And keep on pumping.

*Fuck, her gag reflex is amazing.*

I grab a handful of her hair, winding it around my hand, and jerk it, releasing her from my hard erection as I avoid my release, gritting my teeth as I get myself under control.

I withdraw the silk handkerchief from my breast suit pocket, holding it out for her to efficiently wipe the dribble from her mouth and chin, while I take another puff on the Black Dragon. I reach for her face, cupping it, drawing her closer to me so I can erase the salty droplets from her cheeks with my thumb. Then I push it into her mouth so she can suck it clean. The only emotion she ever lets slip is the salty droplets, which leak soundlessly from her eyes, a by-product from the gagging.

My long erection throbs, reminding me it wants to be swallowed up inside her velvet pussy. I am the only one who gets to fuck her. She stays clean for me.

*Because I own her.*

If I opened my eyes now, I would see her watching me, her face devoid of emotion. She would see a man in his late forties and fit. Today's hairstyle is cropped short and peroxide blond. I am a handsome man with an olive skin tone, and I'm immaculately kept.

I look expensive.

I wear a mask at all times when I am here. Today,

I'm wearing blood red silk that covers half my face. I change my hairstyle and color whenever I come back to one of my many hidden special places because I am king in this world, and I need to stand out. This is where I want to be noticed, but my true identity must stay concealed. My paranoia for losing what I have built has kept me behind a mask.

There are mundane people living outside *this* world I have created for myself, who are doing everyday things in their droll lives. They don't see the successful businessman, rich beyond their wildest dreams because I keep that life private, my value hidden in corporations. I don't draw attention to myself, but here I am, the center of my world.

I want to stand out.

Rose goes where I go; she is my secret pet, my slave. I am her master out there and in here.

She knows what is lurking beneath the surface. What my secrets are. What I am capable of.

I am a legitimate, respected businessman under my real-world name, but when I enter *this* world, I become somebody else.

My soul is wicked.

It has desires that need to be satiated. It has no love for *anything.*

I take another puff of the Black Dragon, enjoying the flavors as they fill my mouth while the thick, chewy smoke floats around us. Opening my eyes, I see her watching me... waiting for me to allow her to fuck me.

*So obedient.*

*Such a good pet.*

My eyes seek out Filip, the dark warrior who is dutifully standing by the wall to my left. Wisely, he doesn't make eye contact with me or watch what Rose has been doing. He is one of my loyal sentinels, an ex-MMA fighter rescued from the poorly financed underground fights. I note the bulge tightening the front of his suit pants and while he can't do a thing about it, I can give him a show he can beat off to in his private time.

I revert my attention back to Rose. "Straddle me." She complies and stands before me. I raise my hand, holding her off for a moment while I take in her dark red pussy hair, so carefully trimmed, plucked, and manicured to look like a rose. Her large breasts are firm and inviting.

I reach out, tugging both nipples hard until they pebble before me. She will want me to suckle from them, but I won't. Instead, I lean forward and inhale her pussy deeply.

*Ahhh.*

My erection jumps in appreciation. She smells like English roses in bloom. I am pleased she made sure she is scented for me.

I signal to Rose and she helps me lower my pants.

Her hands rest on my shoulders as she gets into position, her knees padding either side of my thighs as she prepares to mount me. She knows to be wet for me. If she's not, then her loyalty to me is in question.

Her tight pussy hovers over the head of my dick, letting me test her as her hips sway back and forth in a pendulum motion, slipping over my cock, coating it with her wetness. I nod my approval, and then she slides down my dick so elegantly, her hard nipples grazing my face.

She knows I won't ever treat her like a lover because she is only a possession.

She is here to serve me.

The others... they are disposable pussies.

"Fuck me hard, Rose."

She rises and slams down on me over and over as her strong thighs soldier on, helping her to thrust up and down like well-conditioned pistons. Not even my belt buckle, which will surely be uncomfortable, will halt her powerful thrusts. She will pound me noiselessly until I am satiated.

My hands white-knuckle the arms of my throne as the pressure builds until I can no longer hold myself in check. Jerking, I shout out my orgasm as I shoot inside her, coating Rose's pretty pussy as she milks every last drop. Her face is a stony façade until I have had my fill and halt her movements.

Rose does not reach orgasm.

I never allow it.

There is nothing loving in the way Rose services me. She is here to make me come when the urge hits me. Her other duties are to train the females in The Pen in what is expected of them and cull them on my orders. However, her robotic actions have me questioning her use-by date.

"Dismount and clean me up," I order her.

She slips off me, attending to both our needs at the same time. She knows how much I dislike mess.

Pleased with the news I had been waiting on, I rewarded myself with a fuck. William Dupré's pet had not fled and concealed herself from my prying eyes, as was originally thought. She was right under our noses the whole time.

Such a silly little pet for not fleeing and hiding herself away, but of course she had no idea of me, my station and power, nor William's debt.

William owed me on the contract he had been paid handsomely for in advance. I expected to receive his full services in that time, but the stupid bastard had gone and, according to police records, fallen down his stairs, breaking his neck.

I thought the money was lost to me, but then Jonathan Boothe, an easily bought lawyer William and I had in common, had to go and brag to Nicu during a recent business call about his own self-importance and dealings with William. Nicu has become my mediator when I need things attended to.

Whatever mind-fuck William was trying to have acted out after his death was immediately overridden by his debt to me. William's sordid little games were of no consequence to me. His need to have the last say had worked in my favor, and now I had just stamped a null and void across his antics.

The girl's last curtain call was postponed.

I brush Rose's hair with my fingers as she fusses about me, assisting me with my clothing. I had tried to acquire Whisper from William several times when she came of age, but he was adamant she was not for sale. I had to respect that at the time.

But now it was open season, much to my delight.

I have had plenty of beautiful girls passing through my gentleman's club over the years. Whisper was no more beautiful than the others, but it just stood to reason I would want her in the flesh with the debt hanging over her head. William had whet my appetite for her, brought her to my attention, and ignited my interest.

The girl will be a part of *this* world soon enough, forever lost to her newly found freedom, and apparently, she knows how to fuck like a wet dream.

She had been William's pet. He would have taught her well. Whisper knows the rules of ownership already. Rose wouldn't have to tame her like I had to tame Rose. Freedom, unfortunately, would have rejuvenated her spirit. No matter. She has been broken once already. It shouldn't take much to do it to her again. I believe Rose will have her ready for my next event.

*She will have to be, for Rose's sake.*

I take another puff on the Black Dragon and kick my legs up onto the antique desk, letting my mind wander. Maybe I will make her my new assassin. I haven't set myself a challenge in a long time. I would enjoy breaking her mind down into little pieces until she is nothing but a killer.

It would be a shame to lose such a beautiful subservient woman as Rose. I will see how Whisper turns out first before I set my decision in concrete.

For now, I will keep my options open. I am merely collecting on a debt owed to me, the principle of the contract being honored until completion. What can I say? I have a strong work ethic. Principles matter.

I have left orders for Jonathan to handle any loose ends he feels will be a threat to my plans as he sees fit.

I feel great excitement for this freshly acquired pen of women. It takes time and careful planning to net a worthy selection. It will be a busy time around here as preparations begin for my next get-together and readying all these females for their roles.

The men attending my masked event expect variety in the females and an exceptional experience from me, their host. If they know about my events, then they have contacts in deep, deep places. If they have the large sum it costs to attend and their background passes Nicu's high screening process, then they will be under consideration. There are only fifteen places per event, with a maximum two events per year. Forty-eight hours' notice is given upon acceptance, with time and meeting place disclosed. Enough time for all global participants to make their way.

Filip knows my true face because he's been with me since I birthed these events. He follows me into both worlds, traveling with me to all my different locations. Huge sums of money line his pockets for keeping his allegiance to me. Once my true face and secrets are known, the person is bound to me until their last breath is taken.

Nicu will see his first event. He gets to venture inside this time, having proven his loyalty enough to rise up on the podium.

"Filip!" His masked face snaps around to me. "You may escort Rose back to her room and send in Nicu as your replacement to stand sentinel."

Filip's eyes latch onto Rose, who has been standing by my side, a lascivious smile painted on his face as he leaves with her naked and compliant.

Underneath, she is as deadly a killer as he is. She will only strike on my command and he knows it.

I am law.

The people who surround me allow me to be all that I am.

My sentinels carry weapons and could shoot me dead at any time.

But... they don't.

One bullet to my temple, that's all it would take. But nobody does.

I have this type of Hitler mind strength.

They feed my power by lowering themselves beneath me.

I am a pompous man.

I am confidence and brutality.

I am powerful.

I am king of my castle.

I am Cezar Pavel.

# BOXER

## Fubar

My eyes flutter open, but I'm still met with darkness. I know I've been drugged because my mind is sluggish as it tries to breathe life back into my senses. Moving slightly, I hear the clink of metal against metal and groan at the uncomfortable position I find myself in. I test my movements again and realize I'm lying at an odd angle with my left hand handcuffed to a pole.

*Fucking amateurs should have handcuffed both my wrists.*

My throat is dry as I let my tongue pad its way around the inside of my mouth, searching for some moisture. The rest of my body is facedown on a cold stone floor. Shivering, I start to pull myself up when a sharp hiss of pain has me rethinking this moving thing. Agony spears from my right foot.

I halt my movements and carefully feel for my foot—well, where it should be anyway. What the fuck is wrong with my foot? It's facing the wrong way.

*Some fucker's clubbed my foot.*

Taking a deep breath, I lock my jaw together, threatening to break all my teeth as I manoeuvre myself into a sitting position. I curse and grunt through my clenched jaw, "Motherfucking, cocksucker, shithead assholes." It comes out unintelligible, but it sure helps me work through it until I can grasp the metal pole I'm chained to like it is a life preserver, vomit threatening to head north. The lack of movement and the vertical position help to settle my nausea, because it sure as hell was just about to blow.

I feel around my body and pockets. I've been searched and stripped of weapons, communication devices, and any personal items.

With my right hand, I pull at my left shoe, tearing it off my foot. I hold the heel part against my thigh, sliding a small, discreet switch, and then turn the heel counterclockwise until it opens *Get Smart* style. I feel around for the special-issue-handcuff-master-key that is held in place. I never leave home without a master key when I'm on a job, never knowing the situation I will find myself in.

*Blimey, it's pitch black in here.*

I insert the key into the little hole and twist, freeing myself from the pole, being careful not to jar my leg. Placing the master key back inside my heel, I return the shoe to my foot, and tuck the handcuffs inside my jacket pocket.

*Just call me fucking Houdini.*

Nothing but silence surrounds me. I don't need a light to work out I'm in an enclosed room. I move my sorry ass until I can locate a wall and prop myself up against it, panting from the agony of dragging my useless leg.

The last thing I remember is walking out of the Old Capitol Inn on State Street, Jackson, to stretch my legs around four o'clock. I'd cut down a quiet street.

Those wankers must have been light on their feet because the bloody knobs had a bag over my head pulled tightly, and I felt a sharp prick near my collarbone. Seconds later, I was no good to anybody. There had to at least been two of them to get me loaded into waiting transportation and here.

I'm no lightweight.

They must have been staking the Old Capitol, waiting for me to emerge. I just had no idea how they knew I would be there.

I may have let my guard slip a little because I was thinking about Whisper and this father-like need I had to call her up and check on her all the time, but I had been giving her space. As an adult, she doesn't need me worrying that she wasn't coping without me around. Whisper has Miss Catherine, and she would have notified me if there were anything up with Whisper since I had left for this job.

Running my hands through my hair, I tug on the strands in frustration at the predicament I find myself in. If I'd been paying attention, I would not be in this bloody situation. I would have heard the fucking blighters who snuck up on me.

*I am better than this.*

At least Miss Catherine is there for Whisper until I can get out of here. I've no fucking clue why I wound up here. There are no enemies I know of, and I can't say I've pissed anybody off recently. Everything has been legit with all the jobs I've been on.

*What if this has to do with Whisper?*

*How could it?*

I search the darkness, looking for answers that can't be found. *"Fuucck!"* I let out a low growl of irritation at my stupidity in winding up here.

Have I left myself too complacent after adjusting Whisper to the world she was deprived of? Has an enemy been lurking in the shadows?

Did I miss something?

I need to think this out.

I'd left Grady, a fortyish ex-detective who's freelanced on occasion for me over the past year, up in our room waiting for the intel for us to proceed on the job we had been booked for. We'd been holed up playing this waiting game, and I needed a break from the monotony. He suggested I stretch my legs, which wasn't unusual.

I took him up on the offer.

Now, I'm here.

*Where is Grady? Am I the only one in this dark space?*

I spend the next half hour or so in monstrous pain as I curse my way around the room. It's about a regulation cell size, six-by-eight feet, and all brick walls. The door is metal, so I can't break it down, and there is no handle on the inside, therefore, no lock to work on.

It feels too much like a dead man's cell.

They aren't as stupid as I would like.

*Motherfuckers!*

On a whim, I shout out to the darkness, "Anybody else here?" Good guy or bad guy, I hope for a response.

I give it another shot. "Hey! Any sons of bitches here?" I shout even louder.

"Boxer?"

Where did that voice come from? I already worked out there was only me, myself, and I in this room, but it sounded a hell of a lot like… "Lincoln?"

"Boxer?" There it is again. The voice is clear enough, close by, yet not. There's an echo about it, but it definitely sounds like Lincoln.

"Lincoln? That you, mate?" I wait and get no reply. Maybe I'm hearing things, the residue of the drugs playing with my mind. "Lincoln?" I shout out a little louder.

"Boxer, is that really you?" I hear Lincoln's confusion.

"Yeah, mate, it's me." Can't say I'm pleased there are two of us in here. What the hell is going on?

"Christ." He sounds deflated. "They got you too." His voice grows softer the more he talks. "Thought I was here by myself. I must have dozed off again for a bit." Lincoln sounds off. Then he moans like he's in real pain.

"You hurt, buddy?"

"They fucked my leg up." I curse under my breath. "Figured I was a loner in here, but you must have been brought in when I was all lights-out. I've been in and out of consciousness for a few hours I gather. Did they bust you up too?"

"Yeah, got a complimentary enjoy-your-stay clubbed foot, *Misery*-style. You know that movie?"

"Yeah, Boxer. I know the one. Must hurt a ton, huh?"

"I'll live." I work my right shoe off carefully, figuring it will alleviate some of the pain. Feels like I have a Shrek-sized foot. "I woke up cuffed to a pole, too."

"Houdini?" Lincoln is asking me if I pulled my

trick with the master key.

"Always," I reply, a smile in my voice. "Are you cuffed?"

"Was." This made me smile again because he was packing in his shoe like I taught him. "I think the brains behind this operation figured a bone sticking out of my leg wasn't enough incentive not to move around, had to cuff me too."

"*Motherfucking assholes!* You didn't say your leg was snapped. Did you get a good look at who did this to you?"

"Negative. Two guys jumped me and I had a syringe to my neck, and then I woke up here with a black cloth bag over my head and incredible pain in my shin. Something like a sledgehammer must have been used on it for the bone to push through my jeans. I hate to say it, but it's a fucking mess." Pain laces his words.

Time for a change of topic. "I can't see for shit in here because it's pitch-black. You got any light, man?"

I hear a soft, tired laugh. "Got it lit up like sunshine in here. If your cell's like mine, it has no windows and a heavy-duty solid metal door with no handle, so we can't attempt to open it from the inside, and we won't be able to kick it down. Not that we could anyway." Our captor is already playing mind games with us. One in darkness, one left in bright light. Oh goodie, let the games play out.

I keep on talking to keep his mind busy, because from where I'm sitting, it isn't looking very good for us getting out of here. "How is it we can hear each other?"

"There's an air vent along the back wall about ten inches long, four inches high, low to the ground. If you can get to it, I'll be a lot clearer."

I shuffle my way over to that wall until I can find the vent and lie down beside it. It's not far from where I was cuffed. I missed it on my first investigation of the cell. "Is this better now?"

"Read you loud and clear, Boxer."

"Have the bellends blessed you with water or a bucket to piss in?" I can hear Lincoln quietly chuckling to himself at the use of my British swear word. Humor is good for him at the moment.

"Nah, I haven't had time to renovate the place yet, got no minibar either. Sure could do with a cold one about now." I hear him hiss in a breath. I know he's giving me the watered-down version of the condition he's in. Lincoln is a tough guy, and I need him to stay strong.

"Maybe room service will oblige, mate." I hear another soft chuckle from Lincoln. "Do you know if anybody else is here?" I'm thinking of Grady.

"Haven't heard a peep since I was dumped in here... except from you."

Questions bombard my brain with two of us in here. "Linc, where were you abducted?" This is far too coincidental and organized.

"I was getting picked up by a guy who I wasn't familiar with. I was freelancing on another job. I got a call in from Grady the day before, asking me if I could take the job because he was with you. We'd stopped off around the halfway mark to Jackson for gas when I came out of the restroom and got jumped, and here I am. I put up a good fight, but can't argue with a syringe full of knock-out juice.

"I'd been to lunch with Whisper earlier and got a call about Joel. He's been hospitalized, beaten-up pretty bad. I haven't seen him yet." There is a lot of worry in his words. "Joel and I...."

"It's okay, Lincoln. I suspected you and Joel were more than buddies. I'm sorry he's been hurt, mate."

"Yeah... I figured you would catch on."

I can't shake the feeling this may have something to do with Whisper. "How was Whisper when you saw her?"

"She was good. We had a nice chat, but she did have something on her mind. I could tell it was worrying her. She clammed up once I got my call, and sensed I was upset about something."

*Jesus.* Sounds like I should've been there for her, which has my mind working over the facts surrounding the both of us being detained here.

Coincidence?

Could this really have anything to do with Whisper?

Could Grady have been compromised? The guy seemed solid enough when I did his background check a year ago. A friend of mine put a good word in for him, said he was looking to freelance. I have Whisper to look after now, and I only take on the big jobs that pay well because I have the bar's income too, so I can afford to be choosy.

"Lincoln. What are your theories on us being detained here?"

"One person comes to mind. I wish she didn't. I got no enemies."

*Christ, he's thinking it too.*

"Linc, let's not jump to conclusions, but if we were to use her as our first common denominator, let's think about this logically. You and I are the only two men Whisper is friends with and that she hangs around. She lives with me on and off. Joel has met Whisper and knows things. You watched over Whisper and Miss Catherine while I was cleaning William's house with Joel and Ghost. I called Grady in to watch Miss Catherine's house for any threats from the outside those first few days, as you know."

I take a moment to mull over some thoughts about all the people associated with the first days of Whisper's freedom.

Ghost knows things about Whisper. He only surfaces when I ask him to, and that's pretty much when I need somebody I can trust and rely on for special assignments. I know how to get in touch with him, but he's technically off the radar, and we go way back in the military. He's truly one of my most trusted confidants. Grady doesn't know what he looks like, and Ghost hasn't officially met Whisper but knows Miss Catherine.

I think about what information Lincoln just gave me. "You said Whisper was upset about something when you arrived at lunch. I was taken in the late afternoon, and you were taken before me. You got the call about Joel, who has allegedly been beaten badly and hospitalized, at lunch. Who called you about Joel, Linc?"

"Grady."

*Fuck!*

"Mate, you were on your way to a job in Jackson, separate to my job in Jackson. We were both on jobs that took us away from Whisper. Somebody wanted us both out of Louisiana.

"Joel's role in all of this is more by association at this stage as he doesn't hang out with Whisper, but somebody knew enough about you to know if you were told Joel had been beaten-up, it would be a mind-fuck for you. This knowledge would put you off your game."

I trust Joel; he's my computer hacker extraordinaire, and he's solid ex-special intelligence. He is in high demand and paid well. He knew about William's will, but none of this would make sense for him to be compromised. Why jump ship now? I refuse to believe he is part of this. He wouldn't allow his boyfriend to be hurt.

"The persons of interest to both of us in this equation are Whisper and Grady." I say his name with mixed feelings because shit is starting to stink. I know Lincoln would hear it in my voice. "Grady had previously put in a special request to be put on the next high paying job with me. He was renovating his place and wanted the money. I willingly obliged. He contacted you to offer you that job at short notice, coinciding with me being out of Louisiana." I don't like where my thoughts are heading.

"Have you spoken with Joel to confirm the beat down?"

"No. Grady was the one who contacted me and told me Joel was in surgery and to give it some time, which I never got as I wound up here." Lincoln swears as the dots start to connect and realization sets in that the job was probably bogus, just a means to getting him here.

*Has Joel actually been attacked?*

As Miss Catherine would say, *I can feel it in dem bones of mine,* because something is royally bent here, and the more I talk aloud, the more Whisper's life may be in grave danger. "They could have killed the two of us, but they didn't. The opportunity was there. That wasn't their orders."

Suddenly, there is a loud, slow clap coming through the air vent.

*What. The. Fuck?*

Are we being applauded?

Some motherfucker was listening.

"Who the fuck are you?" I growl out.

My question is met with piercing silence.

"Fucking smart arse."

And then he speaks. "Should I call you Sherlock? Come now. Are you going to ask the questions that are *really* playing on your mind?" The voice is southern, and at a rough guess, he sounds like he's in his forties or older, and definitely educated.

I'll play along. I need to know who I can no longer trust. "Where's Grady?"

He takes his time answering.

I'm a patient man.

"Let's just say he decided to get greedy. He became no longer useful. He sold you out for a price." He sighs dramatically. "Everybody *always* has a price. Amazing how you can turn a man when you find out he has a huge gambling debt he owes to some very unsavory types. You wave the right number in his face that has the power to wipe the debt clean and all his financial problems could be put to bed. Word on the street was a hit was going to be put out on him if he didn't come up with the money fast and he knew that. Desperate times call for desperate measures.

"The offer was too inviting. He just had to make sure he was placed on the next assignment with you, which I orchestrated, and make a few calls, and then my guys would step in and do the rest. Of course, nobody was supposed to get hurt, according to Grady. Sometimes things don't go according to plan. Unfortunately, he thought he would try to blackmail more funds out of me."

Jesus Christ! He only had to come to me with his troubles and I would have helped the guy out. Fucking us over only got him dead.

I think about my next question carefully.

"Somebody must have wanted Whisper pretty badly to have gone to all this trouble. We both know William Dupré has something to do with this. He's dead, and my guess is Whisper's in a lot of trouble as we speak. You needed us out of the way for that trouble to catch up to her. Is she alive?"

My heart pounds as I wait for him to answer. Will he answer me? Lincoln is silent. He needs to hear as desperately as I do that it's not about Whisper. But we both know it will be.

Naturally, this fucker is all about the drama and

suspense.

*I've time on my hands.*

There is a son out there alive, and there's that will we saw in William's files. Narrowing the field down to the non-friendlies who would have known about that will, I have to add the son in as he was mentioned, and William's lawyer.

And then there is Joel and Ghost. I trust them both to keep their mouths shut on everything they saw in that house; that's why I brought them in. They are solid.

Lincoln didn't know about the will. He was only told what he needed to know about Whisper because her past was her business. He knew enough to know she had led a life as a victim.

Grady didn't know about the will.

I don't trust the son, and the lawyer is worth a thought. The son's name was cleverly left off the will I saw on William's computer. He had nothing to lose; he was the sole heir. What would his interest in Whisper be?

"Is it to do with the will?" I throw that one in there to flush out a rat.

This leaves the lawyer, Jonathan Boothe from memory. It would make sense somebody like William would need a lawyer he could have in his confidence, who was willing to take on some nefarious deeds. It's not that far a leap to make a presumption knowing the players on the chessboard, or to at least narrow it down to suspects. That will wasn't meant for our eyes, and nobody interested in it would know we had seen the original. I have a copy of it.

I decide to push the envelope some more. "What does William's son have to do with Whisper and the other person of interest... Jonathan Boothe, of Boothe & Brown Lawyers?" My mind starts trying to fit any piece it can together to make a bigger picture.

*I hope the rotter bites this time.*

And then he finally speaks, choosing to ignore my questions. No doubt afraid he will give me some answers without knowing it, now he knows I know about the son and will.

"You know, I tried calling the girl earlier on your phone just to see if she was available to answer it. Alas,"—he sighs dramatically—"she didn't answer her phone, and I did let it ring out. I see she's not a fan of voicemail. Makes sense, considering her dirty little secrets."

*The fucker has my phone!*
*What dirty little secrets?*
*What does this arsehole know?*

I want to claw at these walls and bring them down so I can get to this cocksucker. Lincoln and I both curse the mother-fucker to hell. He's playing with us, wants us to choke on our fear for Whisper's safety.

"Sounds like Whisper might be having trouble getting to her phone, Mr. Boxer. Let me try and text the young lady and see if she responds. What would you like me to say on your behalf? Oh, I know. Let me type, *'Where are you?'* Keep it nice and simple, shall we? Now if she doesn't reply, the chances are… she may have been…."

*May have been what?* He deliberately trails off.

Lincoln and I roar out another round of curses, shouting at this cowardly bastard. I've pawed my way over to the door pounding on it, hoping to God I can break the fucking thing down, shred it from its hinges.

"Enjoy your stay, boys."

And then no more. All that is left is our empty threats in the air.

I make a promise as I slump against the wall. This mother-fucking arsehole has a death wish, and I aim to grant it.

# EDGE

## Q & A Time

**T**he first thing I did was make a detour to the closest hospital fifteen minutes away. I threw the tracker into the bushes right by their emergency entrance.

Ebony and Ivory would be clocking my moves. Considering the condition they left me in, it would be feasible I would seek medical attention. I wanted them to feel secure I wasn't following them, and I needed to keep the old lady off their radar. Once Ebony and Ivory were paid, they wouldn't give two shits about my whereabouts. I would be somebody else's problem then.

The old lady didn't utter a word the whole way. The only time she communicated with me was to point which direction I was to turn to get to the hospital and then back to her place. She must have been cold, but she didn't complain.

She was a tough one.

I knew she was sitting back there, her mind trying to grasp why Whisper had been taken and what my involvement in it was.

We made it to her small home, which afforded me the privacy I needed. I was shot and bleeding, my foot was screaming at me, and I had the mother of all headaches. I was realistic. I knew I wouldn't make it very far unless I got my wounds tended to. Blood loss is a bitch not worth tangoing with.

Now, after pulling up at the bottom of her front porch steps, we dismount and I follow her up. "Switch your outside light on for me," I grumble, sounding like a bear that's been poked one too many times.

She does what I ask without a peep as I drop heavily onto her wooden, two-seater swing. I take the sharp blade I'd already removed from my saddlebag and hack the shit out of my leather pants, making a slit up the side. Next, I hack the shit out of my black leather riding boot. I growl and swear like the biker I am while getting the fucking thing off. There ain't no laces or zipper on it, making this a fucking nightmare. Finally free, I peel my blood-soaked sock off.

When we'd first arrived, the old lady's eyes had grown when she came back outside, but she didn't utter a word at the mess my swollen foot was in. She just led the way inside, and I followed on behind as best I could and deposited myself on her cheerful floral high-backed couch.

She'd walked off and returned with two towels, which I was about to royally deface with my blood. With one towel rolled up and placed behind my fucked-up head to keep the damage minimal to her couch, the other was folded and my foot placed on top of it. The red already stained the yellow of the flowers.

And it was all done without a peep from her.

I knew she wasn't doing it to be nice. I was an unknown until she knew otherwise. She needed to give me a little of her trust and accommodate me because I was her link to Whisper, and she wanted to find out what the hell happened between the two of us.

I'm glad to be seated. Between my fucked-up head and being shot and knocked out, I'm not in a good way. Despite feeling the aftermath of the night, I can't afford to pass out though. I have to get back on the road. I just haven't decided which direction I'm heading: Away from my father's shit, or toward it?

The old lady walks off upstairs, and my eyes wander to the framed photos on the sideboard, standing proud, containing pictures of her Whisper smiling at the camera, the girl I had shot, the person who had introduced herself as Sara several hours ago. There are no other photos of people. This female means a lot to this old woman to have her on display.

*Something is so royally screwed up here.*

When we'd arrived, she hadn't even locked her front door, having left in that much of a hurry to find the female she treasured so much. She'd obviously taken off into the night without hesitation.

There's no man about the house. She didn't need to tell me she lives alone because her husband or family member would have gone with her, helped her, maybe even searched for her since she is no spring chicken. She had no one to turn to, no transportation, so she took it all upon herself to walk the dark, lonely road in the delusional hope it would lead her to her young friend.

What tipped her off? What made her leave her comfortable chair by the fire, where her craft shit had been discarded on the side table? Whisper sure as hell hadn't stopped to make a call for help during the time she was fighting for her life. She had stopped to drop a key off and have a nostalgic look at the dead garden, and then she was going to return to the bar once she had relieved herself of the burden of the inheritance.

The old lady proved to me she had no idea what had happened to Whisper, yet she went charging off into the night, ready to face anything head on in only a nightgown and robe, desperate to find her and make sure she was safe. That says a lot to me about their relationship. They are each other's family. This old lady respects this female, and she is of great worth to her.

Just as my previous thoughts of Whisper begin to rewrite themselves in my head, the woman comes back carrying a laptop and a tumbler of water, handing both to me. I am more grateful for the tumbler of water than she will ever know. I place it on the arm of the couch after nearly draining the contents in one gulp.

"Dallas."

"Excuse me?"

"My name is Dallas. Just thought you might be more at ease if you knew my name."

The old lady is wary but seems to think I'm not a threat to her. She turns her back on me, fussing about with the dying fire, breathing new life into it.

I start the laptop up and the screen reveals a headshot of three smiling faces: the two females I have met, the third, a man I haven't. It was a good day for them, from the looks on their faces.

I focus and get down to business wiping the data clean on my phone, that way, if fuckers one and two get a hold of it, they won't have my contacts. Then I set the GPS up for my cell.

It takes no time at all, and I'm linked up and have

a beat on Whisper's location. The fucktards look like they're headed for the Mississippi border. Not too far away for me to catch up.

Feeling overheated, I unzip my leather jacket, taking out Whisper's and the old lady's phones, and tuck them between my thigh and the armrest. I throw the jacket down on the couch next to me and strip off my button-up, leaving me in my T-shirt. I swipe my button-up over my face, wiping away beads of sweat and grime, before tossing it next to me.

I'm ready to chase down Ebony and Ivory, but I need answers. Due to my fucked-up state, I'm not being practical about the condition I'm in. I know I'm not thinking as clearly as I should be. I'm working off adrenaline until the crash comes, and it surely would soon. My body temperature is telling me that much.

I look over at the old lady, who has seated herself in her cozy chair as she observes me. She's wringing the fabric of her robe and is trying to hide how anxious she really is for her friend's safety. "Miss Catherine..." I needed answers now because this old lady's reactions to Whisper being abducted tells me I just made a big motherfucker of a mistake, and it won't stop scratching away at my soul. And then I lay it down hard. "William Dupré is my father." This is the only way to get an honest reaction out of her to see if she knew anything about him.

She physically blanches at this information I freely handed to her on a silver platter, letting out a little gasp of shock mingled with a look of pure hatred appearing on her old, lined face until she regains her composure.

*What the fuck has my father done since I last saw him?*

"You have nothing to fear from me. I haven't been associated with my father in twenty years. I was fortunate enough to be released from his care. I need to hear it all from you now, Miss Catherine. How Whisper and my father knew each other. And I will tell you what I know." *Well, not everything.* "Whisper's life is on the line, and I needed answers yesterday."

I hear enough of the sordid tale of Whisper and my father to make me feel sick to my stomach. So many fucking memories of my very own are being dredged to the surface. A rage is boiling inside of me, needing an outlet, and I've got nothing I can take it out on.

"How old is she?" I need to know how many years she's been subjected to his abuse.

"Nearly twenty-two. Came to me on her twenty-first birthday, but she be actin' much older. Her soul's been to hell and back."

*Around twenty years of his mind-fuckery. And she's*

*just taken another fucking road trip to hell.*

He must have changed states and stolen Whisper by enlisting the help of that dead bitch, not long after I was reluctantly released from his care. He needed somebody to fill my place.

Effectively, my freedom was the ultimate demise of hers.

My tainted blood has held her a prisoner, no doubt torturing her into submission. Christ! She'd only been free for a little over eight months. Now this has happened to her.

*I happened to her.*

She has already spent too long in those fuckers' hands. "I'm going after her."

The old lady is watching me, wondering if she can trust me.

"Is there anybody else coming to her immediate rescue? The longer we sit here, the farther away she gets."

She comes over and sits beside me. "If you be givin' me my phone back, I can be callin' Boxer and Lincoln. I trust dem with her life."

I hand it over. She makes a call and then another, and nobody answers either call. "Text them both the same message. Tell them it's an emergency and to call ASAP." She does as I request, and then I take the phone back out of her hands before she can utter a protest. I need to be in control. If either man calls back, I will answer. "Where are they now?"

She hesitates. I remind her time is wasting. "Most likely on a job."

"Legal kind?" Who the hell has Whisper gotten herself tangled up with?

She nods.

This is like playing 20 Questions. "Are they the type of friends who are capable of handling themselves?"

She nods.

"Ex-military?"

She waits and then nods hesitantly. "Somethin' like that." She probably only knows the bare skeletons of those closets.

"Your friends are the type to respond straight away to a call from you or Whisper, especially when they are away and it's past midnight?"

"Yes."

"They are never lost to you, correct?"

She nods.

"This is unusual for either of them to not answer your call or reply by text?"

"Yes."

Makes me wonder if something has happened to them. Ebony and Ivory had been busy tracking me, knowing my whereabouts—not that far-fetched to be thinking about after what happened already. "Would they be the ones who helped Whisper after my father died?"

She reluctantly nods again.

She knows she has to give me enough because I'm her fucked-up, knight in less-than-shining armor. I'm all she's got at the moment and she knows it.

"I need my foot cleaned and bandaged, and then I'm out of here. The bad guys have a head start, but I can catch up on my bike."

She's up then back with a generous first-aid kit and a basin and gets to work, while multitasking with her own questions. I grit my teeth while she cleans my wound.

"How did you meet the chile?" *Jesus.* I have to edit this for Whisper's sake. The old lady still thinks of her as a child.

*That was no child fucking me. She was a liberated woman.*

It's making sense now, her pain on my bike when she cried out and tried to cover it up. Whisper thought she'd had her virginity taken by my father, but for whatever reason, he hadn't yet taken that. He took everything else from her.

*I took her virginity.*

"She told me her name was Sara when I met her at the bar in town last night. After she closed up, we had a few drinks and talked." I'm not about to say we fucked, and it was one of the sexiest fucks I've had in a long time, if ever.

"I was in town because I was seeking out a woman named Whisper, who I assumed was some old whore my father had taken into his home."

Miss Catherine winces. "Why be assumin' this?"

"There was a will." I wait for her to acknowledge she knew about a will, but she doesn't. I explain there appeared to be two wills, and there was an inconsistency with my name, Dallas Masson, and Dallas Dupré on them. I hit her with the nutshell version of how I came to no longer be in my father's care, hence the surname change. I explain Whisper had been presented with her own document leaving my father's inheritance to her. Still, nothing registers on her face. She has no clue about any of this. Whisper didn't want to involve the old lady, or she didn't have time to tell her.

"In death, my father managed to get me tracked down because he wanted to play with me. About three days ago, I sped out of Albuquerque. I hadn't even cared how he wound up dead. Him no longer breathing was good enough for me." The old lady had earlier revealed how he'd died. It sounded too good a death for him. He needed to have met *No Mercy*.

The old lady's hands tremble as she attends to my foot, bandaging it up. "You said Whisper has been shot."

And we finally get to the money question.

"Who shot her?"

*How the fuck do I handle this and convince her I am trustworthy?*

And then her phone starts ringing.

She's immediately standing, hovering like an annoying bee you want to swat away, while I try to listen to the terrified girl who is trussed up inside a car trunk. All Whisper wants is for Miss Catherine to be safe.

This was the sweet and wild girl I got to know.

I allow the old lady a few words with the female she obviously cares so much for. She calls me by my birth name, which confuses Whisper. We both gave different names when we met at the bar. Would she put two and two together and work out I was the same Dallas she left the letter for, before her night turned to pain and abduction? There's too much to explain, and no time for explanations now.

I slide the laptop onto the floor, being sure to pick up Whisper's phone, and I'm up off the couch taking back control of the old lady's phone, moving away from her for some privacy. I start to sway about, reaching for the sideboard and grabbing a hold of it to steady myself.

*Fucking blood loss is catching up to me.*

I let her know she's being tracked as the old lady comes toward me with the glass tumbler. I take it, draining the last bit of water while I move away from her again as I respond to Whisper's comment, sounding guilty as charged. Then, I'm cursing at her next question, and all I can grunt out is, "There appears to be a misunderstanding." And if that wasn't the fucking lamest response to being asked if I had shot her. She assumes correctly that I did, and nothing comes out of my mouth because I can't deny it.

She asks me if I wanted to kill her. Anger consumes me for hurting her, and I'm cursing and hurling the glass tumbler onto the wooden floor, shattering it, because I *did* want to kill her after I extracted the information I needed out of her.

*I just didn't know it was my sweet and wild girl.*

I can't reply because the car has stopped, she sounds terrified, and then she's gone.

The old lady keeps one eye on me as she cleans up my mess, and all I can do is stand here feeling pissed at myself. I could possibly have prevented her abduction if I had taken the time to hunt rather than gone off half-cocked.

I replay Whisper's words in my head while I try to calm down. My foot burns like fire and brimstone is hailing down on it. A reminder of how fucked up the night has turned out, penance for hurting the girl.

There was so much confusion and emotion when she asked me if I'd shot her.

*Fuuuck!*

Sara was who I'd gotten to know for a few hours; she was a gentle, sexy female. We talked about movies. She wasn't like any of the bitches I'd fucked in the past. At the time, I had no clue Whisper was the one naked on my bike. I had no clue she was the girl I hunted. But they *are* one and the same.

Her softly spoken words may as well have been shouted at me with how deep they cut into my conscience.

And. I. Don't. Fucking. Have. A. Conscience.

Her words had sliced through the soul I thought was too rock-hard to let anything penetrate it, but they slid like a hot knife sinking into butter.

I'm not a guy who feels *any* remorse. I get the job done and I walk away.

*Fucking hell.*

I *did* shoot her, and shit wasn't black and white anymore. It never was. I was just too cocksure to slow down and take my time with the hunt. There was this whole big messed up area that had her blood and my blood tainting it, and that just pissed me right off.

*I shot a totally innocent woman.*

Now those two fuckers have stopped and are about to open the trunk, and I can't stop it from happening.

"Dallas!" The old lady snaps me out of my

thoughts. "Who. Shot. Whisper?" Her words are icy cold.

*"Motherfucker!"* I roar, making her jump, and she takes several wary steps back.

"I shot her. Are you happy now I've confirmed it? I was aiming to maim the woman who was my father's whore, and then I was going to kill her once she told me what I needed to hear."

"And what would be happenin' if she be refusin' to tell you who she be because she be protectin' her identity, her humiliation, her secrets?" Miss Catherine shouts at me.

"Lady... she would have told me her deepest, darkest secrets by the time I was finished with her. Make no mistakes about that." My words are dark and threatening.

She doesn't cower. A fortress has been erected around her emotions. She's now going into survival mode until Whisper is found.

She won't bow to me, and I need her to stay inside her fortress, stay rock-solid for me. I can't deal with her if she caves.

"Well, then you better be hearin' me straight, as sure as I am about dem bones of mine and when they be warnin' me. You'll be askin' for her forgiveness. I know your young life been a bad one. I make no bones about that, but as an adult, you be a grown-ass man. Whisper is nothin' but kindness.

She be livin' nearly twenty years under that bastard, and she never be nothin' but kind toward me and others. You been makin' decisions for what you deem right, but you been made into a coldhearted killer who hides his feelin's." I allow her to vent at me; it's what she needs to do. "Whisper *will never* be made into a killer. She be good through and through. She be an angel sent to me. She be my granddaughter without bein' my blood. There be a difference to how you and Whisper be conductin' yourselves... no matter havin' William Dupré in common.

"You be findin' her and rescuin' her, and she be comin' back to me. I need you to be promisin' me this right here and right now. That chile is comin' back alive and into my lovin' arms."

How can I promise she will be alive? But she needs to hear it from me. She would expect lies from a person like me after what I did to Whisper.

"I promise, Miss Catherine, whatever it takes." I fucked up and can't change what I did.

*The bad seed didn't fall far from the rotten apple.*
*Did he know me for the killer I am?*

Did my father know I was an enforcer for the Soulless Bastards MC? If he did, he would have known the kind of man I had become.

I played right into the dead fucker's hands. He could not foretell I was gonna aim to kill her, but I think the sick bastard hoped I would.

Did he want me to go down for murder of an innocent? I may never know my father's reasons for this game, but I aim to find out as much as I can. There is a puppet master now pulling *all* our strings, and that cocksucker is gonna get found out.

I lean all my weight onto my good foot, the pain my just desserts, and proceed to explain what went down. I owe her that much, omitting the sex, up until I nearly did a hit-and-run on the old lady, when she was out wandering the road in the dark.

I tell her the truth. I'm honest enough.

"William was left owin' this unknown bastard, and now he be wantin' payment in the form of Whisper?" She repeats it over to herself quietly, disbelief in her voice.

*Anger simmering.*

"What be givin' him the damn right to use another person as payment?" Her small, bony hands are fisted at her sides. "Hasn't she already paid enough in life a thousand times over? Slavery was abolished, yet man still be thinkin' it's his damn right to rewrite dem rules for demselves. Nobody should be touchin' that girl's life ever again. She shoulda gotten out of Connard. I be too selfish, wantin' her to be near me. She be such a special girl. Shoulda set her up someplace nice on the other side of the world, where bad men couldn't find her.

Coulda visited her. She be safe now, if my selfish wants had been ignored.

"Why you not be tellin' her your name was Dallas when you met at the bar? Could've stopped a whole lot of this mess goin' down. She was never goin' to tell you her name was Whisper because you were a stranger to her."

"Because Dallas Dupré no longer exists. I am not proud of that surname. I never wanted to see the man ever again. Dallas Masson hasn't been around for a long time either. The boy who grew into a man became Edge, and that was all anybody needed to know."

"I don't want to be relyin' on you, Dallas, but I have to at this stage." Her voice is determined as she glares at me. She has so much strength left in her soul. "Once my friend gets in contact with me, he be takin' over."

I let her believe that. "Maybe your friends are simply sound asleep?"

"No." She is very sure of that answer. "They both be answerin' their phones for Whisper or myself, any time of day or night. They be wakin' up if their phone be ringin'. Whisper be Boxer's priority, and he always be answerin' our calls or messages immediately. If he be busy, he be textin'. Simple. Nothin' be keepin' him from lookin' after Whisper. That be a fact."

Has something happened to the people she thinks are capable of handling a situation like this? The timing is too coincidental. Stealing Whisper was a bigger operation than I first thought. Maybe her friends were a threat to Operation: Abduct Whisper, which means they are a threat to me too, by association of me being my father's son.

"Have you exhausted all your contacts that could help?"

"I be only ever needin' Boxer or Lincoln. Don't know anybody else's information. Never had to have further backup in past eight months, never had to be worryin', all been quiet and harmonious."

I hand her phone to her. "Try calling again, and if they don't answer, let it go to voicemail. Then you have to be careful the information you hand out. Keep it simple and don't let on about me. If your boys have gotten themselves detained because of Whisper, better to play it safe until you know more, in case somebody who isn't a friendly to your boys has access to their phone. If they could contact you, they would have by now. Something is stopping them, and until they clock in with you, assume it's not a good thing they haven't returned your calls or messages."

She makes the calls and does what I ask of her. I hold my hand out for the phone. She hands it back begrudgingly with a look of pure annoyance, which

I don't care for. I type texts to both the men, putting in a couple military codes they should understand, and I keep the cell.

I take Whisper's phone and send a code to Hazard then text him. I let him know I'll be a few more days, and I'll be in touch.

"We be needin' a plan."

"We got no more time for Q & A, lady, and no time to discuss plans. I need to get on the road *now*." Whisper needs me. "That *is* the plan in a fucking nutshell." I make my way back over to the couch, snatch up my button-up, put it on, and then the leather jacket is next. I throw Whisper's phone down on the couch, keeping the old lady's with me because I need to intercept any calls or messages from this Boxer and Lincoln. I take another look at the computer screen and note where Ebony and Ivory are.

She grips my arm tight. "Trust and honesty are gonna be very important to me from here on out. Do you be understandin' me?"

*Really, she is going to make me answer her?*

I snag my fingers through my blood-caked hair out of pure frustration. "Yes," I grit out.

"I be knowin' if you be lyin' to me. I knew Whisper be in danger, and I will do *anythin'* to help her. Somethin' be goin' wrong all round, and I would rather be trustin' in those I know have Whisper's and my backs, but you are gonna have to be doin' for now."

"I fucking hear ya, lady, loud and clear, but for now, I am your golden boy, or you would be calling the police in and getting them intercepted right now. So let me handle things my way and I will get her back for you." I give her my don't-fuck-with-me face and stab a finger at the computer. "Stay on that laptop and be ready to text me if they stop or if there are any deviations. Stay alert, because you and I are her rescue team. This ends tonight."

I head for the front door, swing it open, nearly losing my footing, and make it down to my bike, weaving about like a goddamn drunk as I stumble the last couple steps and balance myself out. I take another step, and that's all it takes for me to start going down on my good knee, dizzy as fuck.

"Christ almighty! Not now!" I try to growl out my frustration, but it comes out as a virtually inaudible mumble.

And it's motherfucking lights out again.

# Whisper

## The Mystery Tour

**The muffled sound of the country music that's** been playing switches off as the car comes to a halt. I hear two doors open and shut and the shuffle of shoes making their way toward the back of the car. The trunk is about to be opened, and my fate is unknown. The phone is hidden, and I need to appear unconscious and a dead weight.

I *can't* afford to tremble in fear or pain.

My tie in my hair must have broken in the scuffle back at the house, so I make use of this and turn my head away, making sure my hair is covering some of my face, affording me valuable seconds to hide my vulnerability until they make the next move.

The trunk pops and fresh air rushes me. I want to gulp it down, but I can't.

I can feel myself being assessed.

"Is she dead?" one of them wonders aloud.

I feel a rough hand at my neck and my pulse is felt.

"She's still kicking," the other announces.

Unwelcome arms slide under my knees and armpits as I'm roughly lifted out of the trunk, the man huffing his breath in my face from the sheer exertion of scooping me out of my metal coffin as I try not to whimper in pain while I'm juggled about.

My hair hides the pain etched into my face as I almost pass out from the agony I'm in from the wound in my shoulder. I can feel it bleeding again, the metallic stench of fresh blood dueling with my captor's strong stink of cigar.

"We'll put her in the backseat, Benny." The other voice is close. "She's out cold, so she won't be any trouble. She looks like she would barely be able to swat a fly in the condition she's in."

Oh no, I want to be trouble. I need to be where I can make contact with Miss Catherine without being caught. I'm desperate to hear her calming voice again.

I make the snap decision to open my right eye because the left is so swollen I can't see out of it.

I use my bound hands to thrust upward into Cigar Man's face, screeching from the pain that shoots through my left shoulder as I grit my teeth from the spark that's ignited into an inferno.

Even though I took both men by surprise, this isn't Cigar Man's first rodeo. He is ready for anything as he throws his head back out of my reach, cursing me out.

I slow my breathing, working my way through the deep pain, keeping myself calm and alert, my eyes trained on Cigar Man, waiting for the repercussions of my actions. I am a prisoner in his arms, and at their mercy.

I gasp as I receive a hard smack to my head from the other assailant, who puts his ugly face in real close to mine. Instinct has me wanting to pull back, but I can't.

"Look at that, Benny. We've got a livewire. There's still a spark left in her after all." Through the sting, I notice to my great satisfaction I had previously done a number on this one's nose, busting it up real good back at the house.

"A little payback, sweetheart," he sneers, and then his hand clamps down roughly over my mouth, stifling the undesirable reply he knows I was about to give him. "Shut the fuck up, woman. I'm not in the mood for your shit. We have our orders, but if you keep on with this behavior, then I won't hesitate to put a bullet in your head, just like I put a bullet in lover boy back at the house." He gives me a wink.

*Edge has been shot?*

*Why call him lover boy?*

*How much do they know about me?*

He decides to make his point by giving me a 3D demonstration by unclicking the safety and placing his handgun against the center of my forehead, pressing down hard enough to no doubt make an imprint. "You aren't worth anything to us, only to the man at the top. There's been a change of plans. We're now getting paid to hand-deliver you to the next stop, and we're gonna uphold that end of the contract, so don't fuck with us again as we *always* keep our end of an agreement."

*Change of plans?*

He shrugs. "Although, in your case, I'm willing to make an exception, and I am sure Benny Boy can be convinced if you decide to be too much trouble. We can always make up some story about you getting yourself killed."

*What contract?*

I've been treated badly my whole life; these two were nothing new to me. Instead of feeling fear, my emotions have gone the opposite way and turned to pure outrage that this could be happening to me again.

*I was safe.*

*I was free.*

*I have friends.*

*I have a home.*

Boxer promised to keep me safe, and now I'm being held captive by low-lives who get paid to abduct people, and I have a gun to my head.

These are just paid thugs.

Henchmen.

Bullies.

I know this is nothing compared to what's coming, but my anger is boiling.

"And you can stop giving me that one-eyed death stare." He taps me on the head with the gun, which makes me wince and blink my one good eye. "Be smart, and you will live another day." Then he pushes the gun back into my forehead as a reminder of his capabilities.

I'm not dead, and that means something to me, and I need to wise up and survive this ordeal and escape.

Their orders have to be to keep me alive, and I'll bet he really won't kill me. He's all talk, to get me to fear him. He obviously knows nothing about my past.

My real nightmare is waiting for me at the end of the line. I keep my anger on low boil and my eye cast down.

He removes the gun and lowers it once he sees I'm now acting the dutiful prisoner then slowly removes his hand from my mouth. I want to spit the filth of his hand from my lips and wash my mouth out. I doubt a cold bottle of water will be offered if requested.

I move my head slightly, enough to see we are in the vacant lot of a warehouse, and I'm being carried towards another car, the light overhead showing my abductors the way.

My vision in my one good eye is fuzzy at a distance, and I can't focus on the license plate numbers clearly. I think I catch the first two letters, NQ, as I blink, trying to focus my sight.

I was used to being locked away by William for anything I did wrong. I want these thugs to lock me back inside the trunk, affording me the privacy I yearn for to speak to Miss Catherine. Will I have done enough to get my wish?

"Lady, you just scored yourself another bed in the trunk." The dark-skinned, cigar-smelling one sounds very pleased with himself, to the point of smug.

*Bingo!*

But then my stomach takes that moment to roll on me like a small boat in an ocean storm. I think I'm going to be sick, and preservation of my clothes has me trying to lurch to the side.

"Fuck, bitch, stop your wriggling." I'm shaken hard, which only makes me want to vomit more. It comes up before I can stop it, and I hurl all over myself and Cigar Man's suit. "Fucks sake, bitch!" he roars at me.

Through my misery, I can hear the other guy cackling like a hyena at Cigar Man as I'm dumped roughly inside the trunk, eliciting a deep groan of pain from me as I battle to stay conscious, and then that nausea wakes me right back up and keeps on tormenting me.

I roll, pushing my head over the edge of the sedan, and hurl all over the ground, splashing the laughing hyena's shoes, and he abruptly stops his cackling.

"Not so funny now, hey, Deano?"

I watch them both, unsure of what they will do to me.

Cigar Man is amused at his accomplice's bad fortune. He starts brushing the contents of my stomach off his suit with the handkerchief he swiped from his top pocket, and it rapidly changes to a disgusted look on his face.

All my mind can think at this moment is, *The guy is wearing a three-piece suit?* as I hang my head over, hoping I can keep what little is left in my stomach at bay.

I'm in bad shape, the worst I've been in a long time. I'd been granted a reprieve from the bad life I had led. Now I am back to square one.

I'm feeling clammy and exhausted, but my stomach is feeling better, and I lay back as gently as I can inside the trunk, trying not to draw any more attention to myself, panting from the efforts of puking and that horrible acid that comes up.

"She needs a muzzle." Deano is not happy with me. "But we can't afford to gag her in case she chokes on her own fucking spew."

Deano is pacing back and forth, throwing his hands in the air. "Fuck! I knew this contract was going to be a pain in the ass. The nomads normally take care of this shit." He points to me. "It's a fucking disgrace the way this kidnapping has gone down. We're behaving like amateurs on opening night."

"Stop your yapping, Deano. When we explain to the next team she's a feisty one, they will keep her under surveillance, and we can go have a few drinks and get laid." Cigar Man is watching me, waiting for me to react to this information as a smirk appears on his face. "Although, after what I have seen of this one, I wouldn't mind fucking her now." He licks his lips in front of me, but I don't give him the satisfaction.

Truth be told, I'm feeling really bad. I need to get them to close the trunk and start driving so I can contact Miss Catherine. I can't even care that I smell putrid. Miss C is my comfort in this storm I have raging around me.

"Don't even think about it. Shut the fucking trunk and let's get moving, Benny."

"It will be my pleasure." Cigar Man smiles and slams the trunk down. I am again cocooned in darkness. He thumps the trunk hard a few times, making me jerk, which does my wound no favors. "Enjoy the ride, bitch. It might very well be a bumpy one."

I lay in the darkness, waiting for the car to start up. When it starts moving again, the country music is turned up. I grope inside my boot for the phone. I had made my mind up that I was not talking to Edge anymore. I could not trust him. Miss C called him Dallas. I hadn't had time to process this information. The only Dallas I knew of was William's son, because his name was Dallas Dupré. It was written on the document from that creepy lawyer.

They couldn't be the same person?

*Could they?*

It might explain why I think he shot me.

*Like father, like son.*

The man I had incredible sex with was quite possibly a murderer like his father, out to make my life hell. I can't afford to think about all this at the moment. I need to think about myself.

This all needs to be boxed up for now.

Miss Catherine is my rock, and until Boxer or Lincoln, the only other people I trusted in my small world, can help me, then Edge wasn't gonna be my contact. This way, I also knew Miss C was well and unharmed if she was spokesperson.

In my head, I have this all worked out. Boxer is going to move Heaven and Earth to find me soon, and I'm going to be taken to safety because I'm being tracked. I'm not lost to them. Miss C is going to get through to Boxer or Lincoln and give them the information. It's the only good thing Edge has done for me. I can't even think about the sex we had together.

I close my eyes and go to one of my places in my head I haven't visited in a long time, and try to block out Edge and the mixture of blood and the vomit stench that is filling the trunk, and find my courage because I know I am going to need it.

Boxer will save me.

He has to.

# Miss Catherine

## Honeychile

He be out my door before I can be catchin' up to him, and then he be goin' down like a drunk bear.

The man be out cold, and I can't be movin' him back inside by myself. He be needin' a doctor. I take back my phone from his jacket and call the only person I know I can be trustin', Dr. Evelyn Castille. She be wantin' to know Boxer out of communication anyways. I know she be sweet on him, but not be allowin' herself that courtesy.

I look at the man makin' a bed in my dirt just when he thinkin' he be set to take off on that bike of his. Tough man's body be givin' out on him, and now I gots nobody to save the chile.

This night keep gettin' longer and harder.

I dial Evelyn's number, and she be pickin' up on the third ring. "Evelyn, I be needin' your immediate help, and you best be bringin' a strong man with you, one that can be trusted to be keepin' his mouth hush. I have a bleedin' man lyin' in my dirt with blood spillin' from him. Boxer would be wantin' you to assist, because he has up and gone out of communication for me, and dem bones of mine are tellin' me he be in danger."

Evelyn disconnects. I know she be on her way, and I just have to wait out a good hour until she be arrivin'.

I take another look at the man lyin' on his side all messy like, and retreat back up my stairs to get him a warm blanket. He was willin' to go after Whisper in the current state he be in, all beat up and shot, so I be willin' to get him the aid he be needin' because dem bones of mine are tellin' me Boxer and Lincoln ain't comin' home anytime soon. Truth be told, I be fearin' for them.

I fetch two blankets and the laptop and do my best to be coverin' him up with one of them. I sit down on the porch steps, folded inside my own warm blanket, and be preparin' to wait it out with the laptop by my side, the blue circle on the screen tellin' me Whisper is still movin'.

It's cold out, and I be watchin' the stars sprinklin' the night until my head slides to the side and I rest it on the handrailin'.

••••

I'm roused to consciousness by my phone ringin'. I'd claimed it back. *Shoot!* I must have dozed off. I don't be knowin' the number on the screen. "Whisper? Is that you, honeychile?" I run an eye over the prone man waitin' to hear her voice.

"Miss Catherine, are you all right? I needed to hear your voice. Edge hasn't hurt you?" The relief in her voice at hearin' mine is palpable.

"Don't you be worryin' about me, chile. We be good." She be breakin' my heart fearin' for me when she be the one in trouble. "I know he shot you," I say softly.

"He admitted it?" She sounds shocked.

"He be wishin' he hadn't done that to you, but that can't be changed. We need to be gettin' you home safe. He be payin' for his wrongs later. How bad you be hurtin', chile?"

"I could be better, but I'm okay for now. I've been shot in the shoulder," she quietly admits to me. I hiss in a breath as my hand covers my mouth. No good me lettin' on my anguish. My eyes roam over the unconscious man.

"Please listen carefully." Her voice clear and low. "They transferred me from one car to another in a vacant warehouse lot, and I think I made out part of the license plate number. It started with NQ. Please tell Boxer." Her voice breaks. "I can't remember his phone number."

"Don't you be worryin' about anythin'. You just be stayin' strong, honeychile." I move the mouse, and the blue circle is back up on the screen. "You've just crossed over into Mississippi." Edge can't be helpin' me now. "I be needin' to call the police. They can find you quicker than—"

"No! No police. Boxer promised me... *you* promised me my life would stay a secret. We did everything to keep it that way. Boxer has too much to lose now. He did illegal things, gave me an identity and hid things. You must *promise* me the police will stay out of this. Boxer can find me. I know he can, and *he will*."

Her voice is so desperate. I don't want to be leavin' her like this alone and in the hands of two dangerous men. "Promise. Me. Miss C." Those last words are said with such steel in them.

Ahhh, this be the hardest thing I be doin' in a long time. Boxer be mad at me if I leave her alone to be fendin' for herself.

"Promise me!" Her voice rises.

I bite down on my nails. Dallas/Edge told me she be needed to pay a debt, and she be more valuable alive than dead. I had to hope he be right.

"Pleeease." That one cried word nearly knocked me off the step.

"I promise," I concede. I pull the blanket tighter around me. I hope I be doin' the right thing by this chile and keepin' this promise. Trust and loyalty are so precious to her. "I be seein' your whereabouts on the computer screen right now. I be trackin' you along the bottom of Mississippi. We *will* be rescuin' you. You gots to be believin' this." It's all the comfort I can be givin' her, and I know it not be enough, but it is all I have. She be a survivor. I know she will stay strong.

"My abductors told me the man with you has been shot?" She sounds concerned for him. She don't be knowin' men enough to be knowin' the good stock from the bad. This man before me is not altogether bad, but he ain't altogether good neither.

"Don't you be thinkin' on him. He will recover." I be so afraid for her. Boxer won't be comin' for her straight away. I can't be tellin' her this. She be needin' as much hope as she can hold inside her. This man has to wake up, and *then* he be comin' for her.

"Whisper, anythin' you can tell me that be of value, now is the time."

"The battery is low, I..."

The line disconnects.

My hand flies up to my mouth as I try to stifle dem fears of mine, and then I hear a car comin' down my driveway.

A hopeful noise be escapin' me until I see the doctor's car approachin' and not Boxer or Lincoln, but at least Evelyn is here.

She be the only other person I can be reachin' out to and puttin' my trust in, and I *know* how she be feelin' about bein' roped into cagey affairs, so I be limitin' what I disclose to her.

I send one last prayer out to Boxer.

*Where are you?*

# Jonathan Boothe

## Hello. Is It Me You're Looking For?

I've entered the room where I can talk to the prisoners and take a seat by the little metal doors to the chutes. I got myself some shuteye, and couldn't help one last visit this morning with the prisoners in this cloak-and-dagger affair.

Boxer's phone has been ringing, and messages have incessantly been pinging over and over from Miss Catherine and Evelyn while I was trying to slumber. I ended up turning off the sound.

It was *so* annoying, helpless women practically begging for Boxer and Lincoln's help.

William's last song didn't go quite according to plan.

I had made contact with the bitch yesterday. Scared her, I did, when I invited myself to her table. I couldn't resist the face-to-face meet-and-greet. It was risky, but her sitting all alone was too tempting. She looked well and healthy, even happy until I creeped her out.

Little did she know at the time, but a web had been set, ready to catch those pesky flies that buzzed around her all the time. They were about to get swatted.

If I had been putting my full attention into William's wishes, I might have discovered her hiding place earlier, but it was a side operation, as I had other clients to look after, and let's face it, what William didn't know wouldn't hurt him. I felt I had time up my sleeve.

I'd watched who she hung out with once I had located the girl's whereabouts. The persons of interest were that Boxer and then the kid Lincoln, who had the boyfriend. They were the only concerns for me for completing William's wishes. I just had to separate them from her. It really was too easy to set it all in motion.

And then I just had to sit back and wait for the pawns to get knocked off the chessboard.

My conscience is clean.

I succeeded from my end.

Bravo.

R.I.P. William.

Nicu had contacted me with the change of plans. What a coincidence, William and I had a common acquaintance, who was now taking over the reins. I was open to dealing with clients who came in search of a lawyer to handle certain transactions of the less than legal kind.

The new orders came in and I had to roll over, just as Dallas was fulfilling William's prophecy. Dean and Benjamin had to step in and halt it. None too early either. One shot had already been fired.

Far too close for comfort.

If they had checked that fucking burner I had organized for them instead of having it on silent mode so they could get their dicks hard without being caught, watching the fuck-fest they had informed me about, they would have gotten the memo in good time and been able to abduct her straight from the bar.

I had to sweat it out from afar until those idiots put me at ease. It was going to be my neck on the chopping block, and I rather liked my neck right where it was, thank you very much.

Boxer and Lincoln are now tucked away nicely, unable to come to the fair maiden's rescue. Boxer has fed some of my curiosity surrounding the little bitch's ability to keep her dark past with William a secret. She got very lucky because the man had skills. He also sealed their own fate with his questions. He was already starting to work things out, and I couldn't have that. Originally, I had them both maimed, because I was going to set them free and it would have taken them an age to get help, dragging their poor broken bodies.

Boxer was too nosy for his own good and had a memory like an elephant. He had worked out that maybe Jonathan Boothe of Boothe & Brown Lawyers was a possible lead. Curiosity would get this cat killed. It's all making sense now, how that clever little bitch covered up her tracks. I have netted the man who made that all happen. He'd been into William's records when he wiped all evidence of Whisper from William's home.

No matter. These two will expire soon enough, and my financially profitable task will be complete.

The old lady was never going to be any concern to me, so she was left untouched, unnoticed to dubious eyes. But, should I be worried about her? I mean, how much trouble could an eighty-five-year-old be?

I have never gotten my hands so dirty before. I've pushed a dirty pen, but there is always a first time for everything.

Dirty deeds are a profitable business.

I did my best for William, but he's now six feet under, so he won't be able to call me on it.

I wasn't supposed to be here now, but I deserved a little fun for my hard investigative work. "Wakey, wakey. Rise and shine, boys." I wait for a reply. No fun if they are sleeping on the job.

"What the fuck do you want, arsehole, and when are we going to be released?" My, my... the British one is a tad grumpy this morning. How about I give them a little hope?

I place a water bottle in each of the chutes and listen to them rumble their way on home to their air vents.

"A little something to work on to keep y'all busy."

I catch the younger one's gasp of surprise when he sees what has landed. So close, but still unattainable until they can get the vent open. Boxer would have heard the noise of the bottles, but not be able to see what it is.

"What is it, Lincoln?"

"Water." The kid sounds a little dry in the throat. "The fucker has given me one bottle of water. I assume you have the same."

I interrupt their chatter. "You've got your own personal vending machines. If you can work on those vents, you might last a little longer in here." They don't need to know those water bottles are their last meal. It will be a slow death. The cleanup crew will be coming back for the bodies in a couple weeks.

Nobody knows they are here, and nobody will be coming to save them.

Bases covered.

I decide to taunt them one last time.

"Mr. Boxer, you're a popular man. Evelyn and Catherine have been begging for your help all night. I had to turn the phone off. They sure are persistent. Shame you can't help them. That goes ditto for you too, Lincoln. I might keep their spirits up." I pull out Boxer's phone and start typing.

"I thought I would stop them from worrying and harping on so much. I'm dropping Miss Catherine a text from you, Boxer. I'm going on, putting her mind at rest from your non-communication, and letting her know you will be back soon to her. Now isn't that nice of me? I doubt you will be able to work out how to get out of here soon, but that is something to aim for."

"Fucker, I'm coming for you." Boxer's roar is so loud it makes me jump in my seat.

*Doubt it very much.*

He *is* a little testy this morning.

The kid is silent. He seems to be conserving his energy, wisely.

"Now, the next noise you are about to hear is me destroying both your phones. There is a sledgehammer sitting in the corner of this room, which should do the trick." I'm not a very physical man, but I pick that hammer up and find it quite cathartic as I place both phones on the ground and bring the hammer down on them several times, bits and pieces flying off all over the place. I wipe my brow, satisfied with my work.

"I'll leave you both to mull on that little project. This is the last time I'll pop by for a chat, so I bid you both adieu."

I walk out to the sounds of their rage and think about the vacation I will be going on soon enough.

# Whisper

## Alive and Kicking

My body is weakening, and I don't blame it. I'm sweating and feeling the cold a lot more now. The temperature has really dropped outside, and the trunk isn't heated. I keep slipping in and out of consciousness, which helps with the pain management, but does me no good if Miss Catherine or Boxer is trying to contact me. I've set the phone to vibrate while the car is moving, so I can hopefully feel if anybody tries to contact me.

I *need* my family.

I am bruised from being inside the hard trunk. Most of it is a fairly straight drive, but I'm getting jerked around every now and then as the car swerves about sharply.

I can hear the men talking; it sounds like they are deliberately driving rough to shake me about in the trunk, as Boxer would say, *'For shits and giggles.'*

I heard Cigar Man laughing loudly and hooting

when he heard me sliding around inside the trunk. I think he's paying me back for puking on him.

I haven't phoned Miss C back. The phone has slipped out of my shaking hands more than once, and I feared their spontaneous, reckless driving would cause the phone to be smashed against the inside of the trunk. It took time to locate the phone in the dark and get it back into my boot, where I hoped it would be safe. I needed to conserve the battery life, so I held off on calling her back.

I've only used it to check the time. It is a small comfort I carry around in my boot, knowing I'm being tracked. I don't know why a man who wanted to kill me would now want to track me.

Is this a sick mind game of his, like his father enjoyed?

I had sex with the man who wanted to kill me.

He knew who I was and played a game of cat and mouse.

He must have had a hard time not laughing in my face when I told him my name was Sara.

I trusted him with my body.

*I feel so dirty.*

I dare to check the time on the phone again while the car is being driven law-abidingly, and I can see I've made it through the night. The sun would be rising.

I'm so thirsty, but at the same time, my bladder is

swollen and painful. I doubt a request for a restroom break would be accepted.

On a positive note, I'm still alive and able to fight for my life. I won't go down easily. I just wish these shakes would stop and the blistering ache that has taken up residence in my head would go away.

I'm half-dozing when the car eventually comes to an abrupt halt, sending me knocking into the wall of the trunk, making me feel all kinds of sick again. Maybe I can throw up on Cigar Man one more time.

I position my legs to hopefully avoid them noticing the flat bump in my boot, just before the sunlight pours in on me, Cigar Man smiling at me through it. My hands instinctively go to shade my eyes as they adjust to the early morning light.

"Morning, sweetheart. I see you are still kicking. It's time to rise and shine and get ready to go on a plane—far, far away, never to be seen again." He's sing-songing to me like I am a child.

My heart starts racing as he leans toward me, a sharp knife in his hand. I panic and my survival instinct takes over, and I'm wriggling as far back from that knife as I can get, which is pointless, because he lunges forward and grabs hold of my bound hands. "Now don't do something you'll regret, because this knife may just accidentally slip and cut you."

I hold still, and he enjoys my fear before slicing

away at the zip ties until they snap apart, and then he gives me a similar speech, grabbing a hold of my legs roughly. My heart's beating erratically, terrified the phone will be discovered as he slices through those binds.

He yanks me forward painfully without warning, my body stiff and hurting as he gets a hold of me, hauling me out of the trunk. He dumps me on my feet, where I almost topple over because my limbs don't want to cooperate, and I am feeling so dreadful. If he didn't have a tight hold of my good arm, I would have face-planted.

He gives me a sharp shake. "Fuck's sake. Stand up, bitch," he hisses in my ear. He's obviously never been shot, kidnapped, bound, and shoved in a trunk before.

I try. I honestly do. I don't want him touching me any more than he needs to, but these legs of mine aren't cooperating. They have decided to turn to jelly. I've got nothing in my tank giving me strength to stand up. Can't he understand that? Couple that with the shakes and sweats, and I am a sorry-ass mess about to topple over if unaided.

Just as I'm released and fear the ground is going to hurt a lot when I hit it, a woman comes into view. I can't see her clearly until she is right next to me. She has sad eyes, as she mutters to herself, "What have they done to you?" She ducks her shoulder under my good arm, propping me up against her. "Honey, let me help you." She doesn't even hesitate to come into contact with my filthy, smelly body. I must look like a grotesque mess, and her clean clothes will be rubbing up against me.

I grasp onto her kindness like a safety line, however frail it is. "Thank... you." My teeth chatter as I let her take most of my weight. "I'm... sorry... I smell."

"Honey, that is the least of your worries." Her voice is gentle, her kindness giving me false hope.

The woman and I are roughly the same height, and I think she is around the same age as me. She is beautiful and dressed in a white blouse and tight skirt. I can't help but inhale her long, dark brown hair as my head flops against her neck. It smells so fresh and clean.

She starts walking me away from the car. I raise my head a little, trying to absorb my surroundings. Anything I can tell Miss Catherine will be helpful. We are now in a big hangar, where a sleek white private jet waits and a tall, well-built man is walking toward us wearing a gray mask that covers half his face.

*Why the hell is he wearing that?* A giggle starts to bubble up because this just keeps getting more and more warped, but I stomp all over it, as laughing at him will only bring me more pain.

He stops the woman with a raised hand while assessing me. I do my best to look him in the eyes. I won't show him I'm afraid.

"Is this her?" He sounds almost disgusted by my condition.

She nods beside me.

He's looking me up and down while I return the favor, studying *his* appearance. He wears a suit jacket with a white business shirt underneath and jeans. His hair is brown and short, and he wears a longish beard. He has an accent, but his English is very good.

I kick my chin up at him. I might look like a pathetic mess, but these people have no right to take me.

"She stinks." His voice is much deeper than I would have thought.

*Give the man a prize.*

"She's not getting on the plane, smelling like that for the flight." He wants me to feel intimidated, but I won't give him the satisfaction. None of this is my fault.

I try to stand a little taller and sway hard to the left, forcing the girl to pull me closer, making me wince from the pain.

I direct my anger at this man. "You have no fucking right to take me anywhere. My friends *will* come for me." My threat is a pathetic croak.

He ignores me.

He radios for clothes to be brought off the plane and speaks to the girl. "Once you have the clothes, take her to the office, change her, and clean her up as much as you can."

She nods again. He walks past us, heading toward the two who brought me here, probably to give them their cash. She obediently walks me to the bottom of the stairs of the private jet, where an armed man descends, his gun casually slung over his broad shoulder. He is also wearing a mask, but this one is black. He meets us, carrying a small pile of clothes. Even though half his face is covered, I can still see part of a ragged scar extending from the bottom of the mask over his cheek. Our eyes meet, and his radiate evil as they pierce me to my core.

He jars my limp arm forward, shoving the pile of clothes into it. I grit my teeth, hissing through them from the sudden movement, my shoulder unable to move without blinding pain throbbing from my bullet wound.

He puts his finger to the side of my head like it is a gun. "Do as the girl says..." His finger moves. "Or *pow!* There goes your fucked up head." My aid's body stiffens and starts to quiver. She tries to hide her response by pulling me slightly away from this bastard in the pretense of getting a better hold of me. Then he marches back up the stairs.

Scar Face is a bad man, one to stay clear of. He is American. I feel it in my gut he likes to hurt women for the fun of it and without provocation.

She helps me across to a small room inside the hangar, speaking to me in hushed tones. "Honey, just don't ever give that one a reason... because he *will* hurt you."

We enter the office. I know I'm going to need a friend or ally where I'm being taken. I extend an olive branch.

"My name is Whisper." She looks at me with such pity in her eyes and ignores my words. I noticed she didn't speak to either of the men when approached. I feel this should be my first lesson.

"Lean up against the desk for support." I do as she asks, and she starts stripping me of my leather jacket, working efficiently. Her eyes flutter up to me as she works. "Look, names are too personal. I have lost too many friends. Please don't ask that of me."

I want to say something, but I don't know what. She scares me with her words. She starts unzipping my hoodie. I try not to let on how much pain I'm in when she starts to remove the sticky, no-longer-plain-white T-shirt I wore underneath. She ends up tearing the thin fabric to remove it from my body, while I try not to double over from the pain. Every time I move, my shoulder screams in agonized rage at me.

She doesn't utter a word when she sees the bloody, ragged bullet hole. Whatever she has been put through has desensitized her to my condition. I know she isn't here by choice. Her body language shows me she's a prisoner like I am.

She is simply surviving.

I want to ask her so many questions, but I fear what will happen to me. Can I trust her enough to risk the repercussions?

Her mind is elsewhere at the moment. She keeps looking out the window, watching the masked man as he talks to the two who brought me here.

She stops what she's doing, brushes my messy hair away from my face gently with her fingertips, and looks me square in the eye before she kicks her heels off. "I'm so sorry, honey. Please forgive me." She hurries to the door, shutting it quietly behind her, and then runs. There is another plane down the other end of the hangar, and she is racing toward it.

What is she doing?

Where is she going?

*Is she trying to escape these people?*

My eyes dart to the masked man in the suit jacket. He has moved away from my abductors, standing several feet from them, and is busy talking on his phone, while the two abductors wait patiently talking to each other, with their backs to him.

He hasn't noticed the girl has run off, and now I

know why. I gasp out loud when I see the guy pull a concealed weapon with something on the end of it out and calmly turn around, walking up to both of my abductors. And at point blank range, he shoots them in the back of the head, blood spraying as their bodies hit the floor at his feet.

I hear no gunshots. He used a silencer, just like what I assume Edge used on me.

They didn't even see him coming, just like I didn't see my shooter coming.

The killer is now talking to somebody on his radio. His head swings around to the office window; he knows I saw what just happened. He knows the girl isn't here anymore. He points to me and mouths, "Stay," and then he makes a run for it. He's been alerted to the girl's attempt at escape and starts legging it toward the second plane.

I've become frozen with fear as I watch this train wreck play out.

I'm William's submissive lost girl again. I can only watch on in horror.

He's fast.

*Too fast.*

I want to pray for her to survive, but I know these people won't let her escape.

*This is a spontaneous, desperate bolt for freedom.*

There will be a price to pay for what she has done, and it will be a heavy one, the crime not worth the punishment.

The girl has passed the second jet. The raised hangar door is her target, as far away from the masked man as she can get. Her hope of freedom is pushing her to get outside the hangar. Her mind thinks that once she gets past there, she is safe.

*Her mind is playing tricks on her.*

Masked Man is too fast. He will be on her before she gets much farther.

My heart is a tribal drumbeat pounding in my ears. I want the man to trip and fall. I want this to be a movie where she gets to run through an invisible portal, where she gets teleported to freedom.

I've just about convinced myself she knows of a way out when she hits the ground, lying face down on the hangar floor.

The tribal drumbeat falls silent.

The hushed bullet hits its target true because bullets are faster than any human can ever be.

The masked man has just caught up to her, his firearm in his hand. He lays the weapon down and turns her over, lifting her until her feet are dangling off the ground, her head hanging in defeat.

He looks like he's shouting at her, but she's not responding.

*She is now free.*

There is red staining her crisp white blouse. A bullet has pierced her back on the left side, cutting a path through to her heart.

Everything happened so quickly. Three people dead.

*Four deaths I have witnessed in my life.*

The girl was desperate to flee her captivity. Whatever evil awaits me, she made a decision to try to escape it. It was worth it to her.

Red washes my vision. A box has broken open, and I see William slicing my mistress' throat open as clear as if they were standing right before me. So much blood everywhere, a life taken without conscience. Mistress didn't see William coming. She was unable to defend herself. It was a great fear of mine, living under William's dominance, that at any moment, my life could be snuffed out and nobody would ever know I existed.

I just watched a man shoot three people dead. I bear witness to three people's lives taken in quick succession. My memories are now coated with their blood.

My breathing has escalated, my heart pounding, pushing blood through my veins. I'm awake and living this nightmare, and I can't get myself out of it. My freedom has, yet again, truly been stolen from me by people who have no right to it.

I close my good eye, trying to wipe my mind clean while steadying my breathing. I can't afford to freak out now.

I want to survive for my family; they are worth fighting for.

I repeat to myself a mantra. *I want to survive for my family—for Miss Catherine, Boxer, and Lincoln. They are worth fighting for.*

I'm standing here in my bra, pants, and boots, scared out of my mind. I need to focus on me now.

On *saving* me.

I look toward the office door, but running is not an option for me. I can barely stand. I would be gunned down by this killer too. I look back at the masked man. He's busy carrying her body somewhere.

Looking away, I concentrate on getting myself dressed. I unzip my boots, tugging them off, and place the phone on the floor beside my socked feet, and then an idea hits me. I unzip my vomit-covered pants and tug them down, making it look like I'm only taking them off, if anybody is watching me from the plane. I bend over, causing myself to feel dizzy as I hit up Miss C's phone number and watch it connect, a low battery message appearing on the screen reminding me of its own imminent death, and then I touch the speaker button. The office door is shut, so they can't possibly hear me talk if I'm quiet about it.

"Whisper!" Miss C picks up on the first ring. Her voice is loud, and she sounds so frightened.

"It's me. Please don't talk. I'm in a hangar." I croak each word out as I let my hair fall across my face, busying myself with undressing. "I am going on a plane somewhere." I talk as loudly as I dare. I glance up, looking through the curtain of my hair, afraid I will be caught. My eyes scan the private jet while I pick up the new pants and make a show of putting them on, ducking my head again. "There is a private jet here. It has no markings on it that I can make out. I..." I don't want to tell her about the executions; it will only scare her. "Is Boxer coming for me?" I want to ask her how Edge is, but he doesn't deserve my concern.

I check the window again. The masked man is now prowling toward me. He looks so angry. My skin begins to crawl like ten thousand ants are climbing on me. I feel like I am about to become his prey. I duck my head quickly.

"I've got to go. He's coming for me. I'm so sorry. I love you, Miss Catherine. Please let Boxer and Lincoln know I love them." My words are rushed and full of emotion, and then I disconnect.

I zip my pants up and hurriedly put each boot back on. I'm about to grab the phone and slip it inside my right boot, but the door to the office flies open with such force it's hinges creak in anger. I have a split second to react, kicking the phone backward through the small gap under the desk I'm leaning against.

I pray it is hidden.

I straighten slowly as he stalks over, glaring at me. His large hands are fisted at his hips. He looks like he wants to punch something hard. He positions himself in front of me.

I keep eye contact so I don't give away my guilt. "I'm nearly finished," I rasp out. My words are pointless, but I needed to say something.

I'm standing here in a stained bra, as blood from my wound is trickling down my chest and my back. The shakes have really taken a hold of me, and I'm finding it hard to pick up the clean shirt to put on. I start to sway with it in my hand, trying to hold my own ground. I don't know how long I can stay upright. My body needs to shut down, but I won't let it just yet. Pure adrenalin and fear has kept me going since the girl fled.

"I need water, please. It's been so long." I need to distract him.

He's still watching me, assessing me.

I grip the office desk, trying my damnedest to stay strong in front of this killer. My head is pounding to its own beat as I fight to stay upright.

I don't want to be here. I want my reality to become a dream.

This is *not* my life; this is somebody else's. It *has* to be, and I'm having a very bad, conscious dream.

It's the only explanation for the twist my life has taken.

He stalks over to the cooler I hadn't noticed was in the room, and fills a plastic cup with water and hands it to me.

I don't hesitate to gulp it down.

*It wasn't enough.*

"Please." I hold the cup out to him again. "My head is pounding, and I'm so dehydrated."

He puts his hand inside his jacket pocket and I shudder in fear. Is he going to shoot me too?

He pulls a bottle of Ibuprofen out and hands me a couple pills. I take them without a thank you, and he refills the cup and returns it to me. I gulp the pills and the water down.

I wanted more water. It still wasn't enough. "I need the bathroom. It's been a long time. Please," I whisper.

He searches the room. There's a mop and bucket resting in the corner of the office. He grabs the bucket and dumps the mop on the ground.

"Here," he growls at me, like I'm wasting his time, and shoves the bucket into my hand and ignores me, walking the few steps to the office window, one hand balled on his hip, his back to me while he radios the pilot, requesting the time of departure.

I use the plastic bucket. I think I sigh in relief then pull up my pants as quickly as my waning strength will allow. "Where are you taking me?" He ignores my question. "Please. Where am I being taken? Why me?"

He turns around, eyeing me up. "Finish dressing and take the boots off."

I hesitate, and that is all it takes. He comes at me, slamming me face first onto the hard desk. I can no longer keep up appearances, and cry out like a crazy person who has had fucking enough.

"Shut the fuck up, because your life is about to get worse unless you listen to me!" His voice is low and menacing in my ear.

I heed his warning.

He stands up and doesn't move. His body has gone rigid. I try to turn my head to see what has made him respond this way. And that's when I remember the old, raised, ugly jagged scars. The word 'PET' has been carved into my lower back among all the other scars. He can also see the mess the bullet has made of my back, and I know I'm covered in bruises.

Miss Catherine has never asked me about my back. I had placed what William had done to me when I turned sixteen in a box and sealed it down tight. I never looked at myself in a mirror if I could help it.

*A reflection never lies.*

Words slip from his lips in a language I can't

comprehend as he vents his anger at me, verbally abusing me. Then he's unzipping each boot, yanking them off one at a time, pulling my socks off so my feet are now bare to the cold cement floor while my chest is being forced into the top of the desk, held down by one strong hand.

He kicks it all to the side as my head is wrenched up by a handful of my hair. My head is turned toward the door and Scar Face, the armed man with the evil eyes, is standing there. He's watching me with a deeply satisfied smile on his face, casually propped up against the doorjamb and cradling his gun.

*How long has he been standing there witnessing my humiliation?*

"I can see you don't need my help." He looks at Masked Man. "Do what you need to do and then get her on the plane." He turns his back on us, leaving me alone with this killer.

*What is he going to do to me?*

And that's when I really panic, and my mind chooses to crack and I lose what little sanity I had left. My legs turn to dust as I pass out in an undignified position.

# Miss Catherine

## The Devil Be Sendin' Another Bastard After My Angel

**My hand grips my chest and I fall back into** my chair, tryin' to make sense of what I be hearin'. Whisper be needin' my strength to help her through. I need to be calmin' my beatin' heart for her.

I take a few slow, deep, shaky breaths. They not gonna kill her; she be needed on that plane. I have to be believin' we still have time.

I sit, watchin' the blue circle. It be all I have left to hold onto. My fear be a black hole in my chest and nothin' can fill it.

Evelyn has done her part and operated on Dallas. I be sittin' here waitin' on the dangerous man who looks to be my only advocate until he awakens. Infections and a concussion have kept him under, his body needin' to recuperate.

*And then it happens.*

My phone beeps and there's a text from Boxer waiting for me to read. My heart skips a beat in excitement. Boxer wasn't lost to Whisper. I read the text, understandin' now he was out of cell range, and they both be comin' back soon to help.

Boxer knows what to do.

He will save Whisper.

He has contacts.

I reread his message several times, and then I respond to it, waitin'... hopin' on another message in reply, but nothin' comes through. He's comin' and that's what matters.

*And then it happens.*

My worst fear be starin' me smack-bang in the face.

Whisper's blue heartbeat be missin' from the screen.

I frantically stare at the screen, willin' that blue circle to come back and be there for me.

I tap the screen with my finger, tryin' to startle it back into view.

*Please come back.*

I pray. I shake the computer, hopin' to knock the blue circle back up on the screen, but I know my prayers won't be answered because the devil be runnin' this show.

I look around, tryin' to find somethin' to grab

onto. I feel so helpless. My fear be a black stain upon my heart for Whisper and the hell she be put through.

There be a dangerous man with her, and she still be tellin' me she was sorry and that she loved me.

I can no longer stem the tears that be wishin' to fall.

How could an angel be sufferin' so much under God's watch?

How can one chile be receivin' so much attention from the Devil?

# Whisper

## My Life is a Bad Dream

**B**lood *is gushing from her neck like a release valve has been opened up. It flows down her crisp white blouse, soaking it. Her eyes are trained on me, begging me to help her. All I can do is watch in a horrified stupor.*

*Master William drops the body and heads for me. A storm was brewing.*

*I'm slapped hard across the face to get my attention, and then I'm being dragged through the house by my arm, the shoulder socket straining as he pulls me down the back porch steps. The skin on my knees and thighs rubbed raw as my dress rode up, catching the brunt of small stones and dirt as I'm dragged across the dusty, hard ground and into the slave cabin.*

*I'm chained up, and my dress is torn down the back in one rough yank, separating it, my bare back revealed. I hear my punishment being prepared as his belt buckle is undone and the sound of it swiftly coming away from his pants, and then he tells me to bow my back.*

*I do as I am told because he will make me regardless.*

*I can't protect myself.*

*And then it starts. Lashing after lashing from the thick metal buckle is rained down viciously upon my body.*

*"Please... Master," I cry out. "Please... I don't... understand."*

*"Whisper, you have made a disgusting mess. You will clean it all up when I come back for you."*

*He knew to keep the marks contained to my lower back. He didn't like to see what he had done to me. He liked them to stay hidden from his sight, as they were a blemish on my body.*

*"Please," I sob.*

"Wake up..."

My good eye slowly opens and a blurry figure comes into view. My instant reaction is to move away. I try to sit up, gasping in pain, my body shaking all over when a large hand firmly pushes me back onto the soft bed.

"Where am I?" I rasp out, barely recognizing my own voice, and only then noticing the body the hand is attached to belongs to the masked man who had slammed me face down onto the desk in the hangar.

I can see he's lost the jacket and has changed into a black tight T-shirt and fresh jeans, but he still hides behind that mask.

He woke me up. I think back and realize I must have allowed a box to come undone, releasing a memory that should have stayed buried. Boxes were boxes for a reason. You could shut them and tape them down so they couldn't be opened, but it only took something sharp to break the seal.

I don't like lying flat out in front of this man. "I want to sit up a little. Please." I feel too vulnerable lying down.

He wordlessly assists me into a more upright position, pushing another pillow behind me as his eyes take me in, and he quickly swears under his breath as he hands me a glass of water. I take it in my quivering hand. I am in a large bed, and the water slops onto the Versace emblazoned white, deep navy, and gold patterned bed coverings.

Annoyed with me spilling the water, he snatches the glass from my grip and holds it to my lips as a hand slides behind my head, holding me steady. I guzzle the water. It feels good on my parched throat, and then I'm coughing, the jolts spearing my body.

"Too fast," he grunts at me, as I get a hold of my coughing fit.

I look down, a reflex action from my submissive days with William. The coverings have slipped, revealing my naked breasts. This is what he saw before he handed me the water. He snatches the covers back up without a word.

I move my good arm underneath and feel about. I'm naked under the bedding. Just my underpants have been left on. I can't even feel the humiliation in being stripped without my consent.

The pain in my shoulder is a barely controlled fire, and I feel sweaty and uncomfortable. I don't know how long I've been out, and no idea where we are.

"You are on the plane," he answers my silent question.

I can now register the muted noise of the engines and notice the curved ceiling, and small window shutters have been pulled down. I've only ever seen planes in movies, never one with a bed in it.

"You were having a bad dream, so I woke you up. Your shoulder is bleeding again, because you were thrashing about, throwing your arms in the air."

I let my mind rewind a little. "The girl... her white blouse was stained red." My thoughts are spoken aloud. The guy looks away, running his hand through his thick hair.

"She was killed because she ran." I detect a note of regret. "You will be dead too if you try to run like she did. You have no clue what you are up against."

Fear starts to stifle my mind.

*No, I don't.*

"I can't be here," I plead to him. I *need* him to understand.

"But here you lay, beaten, shot, and weak."

"But why? My *whole* life, I was a prisoner to a bastard of a man. I escaped that hell to fall into another. What gives anybody the right to do this to me?" I am so angry.

He watches me, his mouth set in an unemotional line. He does not care for my loss of humanity, my loss of freedom, or my questions. He only cares for a paycheck.

I figure if he was going to kill me, he would have by now, so I tempt my fate. "You have assisted the devil in taking my life away from me again. Is your life that bad you need to help others to ruin innocent lives?" There is a flicker of something in his blue eyes, and then it is gone.

"I *earned* that freedom. I was free for a little over eight months, and now I am a prisoner again." I want to pound my fist in frustration, but I am so weak. I need to reserve my strength for when it counts.

I'm sweating profusely, and my breathing is coming in short pants as reality really sinks in. "I don't... understand why. I shouldn't... be here." I'm trying to convince an invisible jury.

This. Is. Happening.

He turns his back on me and leaves the bedroom.

When he comes back, he's holding a few things and dumps them on the bed. He places a cold cloth on my forehead. It feels like it has come out of an icebox, and it feels amazing as it soothes my scorching skin. He places another one over my swollen eye.

I look past him and notice the table with a bunch of white cloths piled on it. Has he been keeping my temperature down while I've been unconscious?

He doesn't warn me before he starts pulling the covers down. I instinctively grab for them, stopping too much of my chest from being exposed. "Relax, I'm not into cheap thrills." He peels the large bloodied bandage that is covering my bullet hole away, and I can't help but look down at the ragged, exposed wound. The skin surrounding it is red and angry-looking. An infection has set in.

He busies himself cleaning and placing a new bandage over my wound, getting me to move so he can tend the exit wound. He's not rough with me. I would go as far as to say he was being as gentle as he could, considering what I know he is capable of. He hands me two Ibuprofen pills and helps me drink from the glass of water.

He steps back from me, his arms crossed, one hand stroking his beard. "Why did you risk your life having that phone on you?"

*The phone! He found the phone.*

"You should have been searched. You would have been killed on the spot if it was found on you."

I owe him no explanation.

"I wouldn't trust me, either." He waits a few beats. "If you had somebody tracking your whereabouts, they will no longer be able to. The phone has been disposed of."

The tracking might not have worked in the air or from a greater distance anyway. I have no clue about these things, but it was a lifeline that has been severed, and it hurts.

"The scarred man, Kane... if he knew you had that phone, you wouldn't have lasted another second in his presence. He didn't hesitate to pull the trigger killing the girl, and he won't hesitate to hurt you. Remember that. I saw what you did when I entered the office, and I also saw when Kane got curious about what was taking me so long to bring you to the plane."

*This man standing before me didn't shoot her? He knew about the phone then and didn't turn over this information. Why? Because he needs to bring me in or his life is on the line too.*

"Kane would have disposed of you. Don't give *anybody* a reason to kill you." He holds my face still so I hear him and understand him.

"Don't give *me* a reason."

I tug my chin out of his hand and turn away from

him, dismissing him, and try to keep my body from trembling. I've lost the only connection to Miss Catherine, and I need to grieve the loss of my family.

The loss of my life, as I no longer have one.

*My fate feels set in stone.*

"Go back to sleep. You are going to need all your strength to survive what is coming your way."

I close my eyes and beg for sleep to take me under.

# MATHIAS

## We Are All Jigsaw Puzzle Pieces

I sit in the corner of *his* bedroom on his private jet, watching the girl float in and out of consciousness. I would have to remove all evidence she had bled and sweated all over his expensive sheets.

I am breaking a rule, but she needs to be alive or I'll be dead.

There was no other place to put her in the condition she was handed to me in. I also needed to keep her away from Kane, and this was the safest place where I could watch her, a door separating her from his insanity.

I've been looking at this mess of a girl and trying to figure out what is so special about her. In the condition she is in, it's very hard to tell what has drawn *him* to her. All I know is he wants her pretty bad, and he made sure it happened.

Those two clowns thought they were getting paid ten grand for how they delivered her to me. I don't think so. Better somebody else's head to roll than mine.

I contacted Nicu to announce I had her ready to board the jet. *The man* himself came on the line and spoke to me when the news was passed on. I've not been told his name yet. I haven't made it that far, yet he came on the line to speak with me. This girl is that important to him. He asked her condition. I told him the truth. He went quiet after hearing the girl had been shot, her face a damn mess.

I felt his silent rage through my phone.

His only words before he disconnected: "Kill them."

It was my pleasure to remove two more pieces of scum from this earth.

When we land, she will be going straight into the care of a surgeon, boss's orders. As long as she stays alive, I've got nothing to worry about.

I've worked too hard to have the rug swept out from underneath me.

And the other girl? The one who had taken off inside the hangar? She didn't even give me a chance to save her. Kane had radioed me and taken things into his own hands. He opened fire through the cockpit window, shooting her dead.

Nobody runs and lives.

# WARPED

You run, you die.

I lean my elbows on the small table I'm seated at, bowing my head and tearing at my hair.

*They always fucking die.*

# EDGE

## Tick Tock We're on the Clock

I wake up laid out in a hospital bed with a woman hovering over me, who gives me a warm smile. I run my eyes over her, taking in her slender fit body and blonde hair. She looks in her mid-forties and is very easy on the eyes. I know I've been in and out of consciousness, because I've seen her like this, watching me before.

"Hello, Dallas, I'm Dr. Evelyn Castille. You are now in New Orleans and under my care."

*What the hell?*

"Dallas, how are you feeling?"

"Call me Edge, Doc. I don't go by Dallas."

She nods at me.

I take a moment to think back and get my bearings.

Sara is Whisper. And then it all comes back to me.

*Motherfucker.*

The doctor is still talking to me, but I ignore her

and look around the room for the old lady from last night.

*Was it last night?*

The door swings open and she walks in. She sees I'm awake and a look of hope reaches her eyes.

*What has happened since I've been out?*

"How long have I been out?" I snap at her, still ignoring the doctor, who waits silently close by. The old lady looks terrible like she hasn't slept a wink in days.

*I can't have been here for days.*

My question goes unanswered, which just pokes my bear even more. I try a softer approach, which comes out in a more restrained, predatory growl. "Ladies, I *need* to know the God... damn... day... and... time."

The doc looks at her watch calmly. "It's after ten in the morning..."

*Fuck! I was out too long.*

"...on Wednesday," she adds quietly.

I let this sink in. It's been nearly five days since Whisper was abducted, and I've been here? I move into a sitting position, which is harder than first anticipated, tearing the IV out of my vein and pressing down on the needle hole with my bare thumb.

The doc shakes her head on a heavy sigh and nudges my thumb out the way, swiftly replacing it with a gauze pad from her medical supplies she has laid out on a tray close by, and tapes it down. She doesn't seem at all surprised by what I just did.

The pain will come soon, now that I'm off that cocktail that was being fed into me. I need to be able to think straight, and I can't do that with drugs in my system.

*Whisper needs me.*

The doctor is watching me closely for my next move because she knows I have one.

"Doc, can you get that damn thing out of my dick." It's not a question.

She gives into a heavy sigh and goes about her business until she has it removed and everything is tidied up.

"Let's talk about your injuries before we go any further. You got hit pretty hard by something sharp and jagged, and you were shot in the foot."

*Tell me something I don't know.*

My hand instinctively feels around the back of my head and touches a thick bandage. No biggie, I've had worse.

"My guess is a rock was used and you suffered a concussion. I've cleaned your head wound and stitched it up. Your foot has been operated on, and there are pins in it now. You were very lucky where the bullet entered your foot and exited. It could have done a lot more damage than it did."

*Has anybody gone after Whisper?*

My silence has the doc barking up the wrong tree. "If you are worried about being kept under the law's radar, you aren't my first patient, and nor will you be my last I've looked after. In case you are wondering, nobody knows you are here."

*Why does she assume I want to stay under the law's radar?*

I know I've been looked after, but I need questions answered pronto. I need a phone, and I need to know if Whisper is still being tracked.

I look over at the old lady. "Do you still have a beat on Whisper's whereabouts?"

Miss Catherine sadly shakes her head at me, and I think she just aged a whole lot more in front of me.

"Has the Calvary come through for you yet?"

"Boxer messaged me sayin' he be back soon; that been four days ago." She looks down and fiddles with the dress she has on. "He still not shown up, and his phone been disconnected." He isn't coming. I think that has finally sunk in.

I can feel my frustration starting to boil over for being shot by that fuckhead and not being in control of my life for days. I *hate* being laid up in a bed in front of these women and being dependent on their help. And as an added buy-two-get-the-third-free, we've lost the only thing that tied us to Whisper, that blue circle, the heartbeat that kept this old lady holding out hope.

I calm myself because this isn't going to get me anywhere with these two. No wonder Miss Catherine looks worn out. I can't imagine her sleeping with this knowledge. "Where's the computer?"

Miss Catherine starts chattering. "It be behind Dr. Castille on the over-bed table, under her tray. Before I lost the signal, there be a changin' of car along the way." I raise an eyebrow at her. "Whisper called me. She couldn't be talkin' long, and then the line disconnected. Then she be callin' me again a couple hours later, and she was gonna be forced to be gettin' on a plane, but the signal stayed for a while in the one place. I wrote it down. I hoped they be detainin' her there for a while when the signal wasn't movin'. Now I fear she be gone."

"Or the battery went flat." Trying to sound encouraging. I see hope and fear flickering in and out like a bad reception on her face.

I slam my fist down hard on the bed, cursing a string of obscenities for this FUBAR situation.

The doc interrupts our conversation. "Your bike is back at Miss Catherine's house, and I have the keys in a safe with your wallet. You need to calm down, because I deal with you guys all the time, and your behavior doesn't impress me or stress me."

"What guys?" I am intrigued.

"Ex-military. You think you can move mountains,

and usually do, but when you are hurt, you think you are invincible. I respect what you've done for our country, but whatever you are into now... I don't want to know. What I do know is that foot of yours isn't going to get you very far. These past few days have been nowhere near enough time to be back up on it."

"How do you know I'm ex-military?"

"Your tattoos for one, and yes, I checked you over. I needed to know if you were hurt anywhere else. And I know your type, been around them long enough." She glares at me. "Am I wrong?"

Fuck, this woman is too smart for her own good. I grunt as a reply. Then she surprises me.

"You need your president contacted?"

"Fuck, Doc, you gone through my things?"

"I did," the old lady pipes up. "You be under my roof and I had to be knowin' who I be harborin' as well. Your cut was in your saddlebag."

"I know where my cut was, and curiosity killed the cat."

This lady doesn't let up, still happy to keep on poking the wounded bear.

Miss Catherine ignores me, pondering her next words. I'll give her this much: she has grown a bull-sized set on her. She knows I'm a biker, and she doesn't give two shits about how dangerous I can be. I size her up for a moment.

*Really* look at her.

She might be old, but she is resilient. Life has taught her that. She has a story, maybe similar to mine, maybe not, but she has a past that has given her the strength to not be docile around somebody like me.

She looks over at the doc, who takes a deep breath, and then the doc is back on my tail. "I'm going to give you and Miss Catherine some privacy. The less I know, the better." She gives me a look. "And you're welcome for keeping you alive." And then she leaves, closing the door behind her.

*So I'm a prick for not thanking the doc.*

"If I'm going to have a hope of finding Whisper, I need to get out of here today. Too many days have been lost already, Miss Catherine. She went off the grid when?"

"The morning after she went missing."

*Fuck! Too long.*

"Already, Whisper's *alive days* have decreased. For us to get started, I need her last location from the GPS. That last breadcrumb is our only lead."

"The signal cut out at an abandoned airfield outside of Henrys Ferry, Alabama. The doctor has already Googled it. There be just a whole pile of fields and a whole lot of nothin' else, but this airfield been shut down since the nineteen sixties." Her voice is very shaky. "They could have killed her and buried her out there."

*I know she wouldn't have intentionally been killed. She may have died by my hand. She may have done something to provoke her death.*

"My take is she's alive until we know any differently. This is how we are going to treat her until otherwise proven. You've told me of her past. She's strong. She's had a shit life until recently, but she will draw on her inner strength.

"Deal is I'm getting up and leaving ASAP. I need transport to New Orleans airport, and I'll get on the next flight out to Montgomery, Alabama then take it from there. I need Whisper's cell phone back so I can use it, and I need my personal effects that have been taken from me. No wallet means no plane ticket.

"We will set your phone up with GPS, and you can track me on the computer and stay in contact. You can call me as many times as you want unless I tell you it's not safe to do so. The clock is ticking."

I watch the old lady try to keep it together. She doesn't want me involved, but she knows she has no choice and time is against us.

"Trust me, I know what to look for. You and your friends don't want any of this public, and I know how to be discreet."

She looks up at me with a determined expression on her face. "I be comin' with you and we be drivin'. By the time you get the next flight and then be gettin' out to Henrys Ferry, it be quicker to drive if we be leavin' now. You're in no condition to drive or fly, so I be your driver and that's final."

"I sure as hell can drive." I stand up to prove a point and sweat starts pouring off me as I tamp down the grunt of agony and wait for the room to stop spinning.

"No! I be drivin' you. Ain't done it in near on ten years, but it be like ridin' a bike. I'll get a car from Dr. Castille, and we be leavin' as soon as you be able. This be the only lead we have to findin' her."

"You still holding a license?"

"Not anymore."

"Well that's gonna have to be good enough for me, and you can call me Edge."

# Whisper

## Wing and a Prayer

I've been lying awake for a while in what looks like a real hospital bed. A hospital means people will help you.

Have I been saved?

Did Boxer find me?

There is a small light dimmed above my bed. The rest of the room is in the shadows. A medical machine monitors my vital signs, and the IV bag is full of goodies to make me feel better. If I stay calm, the monitor won't alert the medical people and they won't come charging in.

*Think, Whisper.*

What is the last thing you remember?

I concentrate, and my thoughts slowly come back to me. There was the man with the mask and beard, and we were on a plane.

Am I safe, or am I still in danger? Boxer or Miss Catherine would be here in this room if I were safe.

They wouldn't leave me.

I'm back in survival mode and thinking of how I'm going to escape. I look around the small room for any clothes because I'm only wearing a hospital-issued thin gown.

*Not good enough.*

My shoulder is sore but manageable. Whoever fixed me did a good job.

I'm about to pull the covers back and swing my legs over the side of the bed to test my strength when the door starts to open. I close my eyes and shut myself down, keeping my breathing even and relaxed.

*Please be Boxer or Miss Catherine*, I silently pray as I hear one set of soft footsteps approaching my bed, and then I am gently checked over.

"I know you are awake," an American female voice whispers in my ear. I must have given myself away with all the prodding. "We have only a couple minutes alone before Mathias joins me."

*Who is Mathias?*

My eyes shoot open and a pretty brunette in her thirties is watching me. I can see out of the eye that had been swollen shut. "I'm your doctor." She tries to give me a smile, but it doesn't quite make it to her eyes. "I will talk and you listen if you want to have any chance at all."

I can only lie here blinking at her. What is she

saying? Is she going to help me?

She pulls the bed covers back. "I'm going to remove the catheter from between your legs." She goes about her business quickly and efficiently, helping me into a pair of paper underwear before placing the thing she took out of me into a bin.

"If you want to live, you will find your inner strength and you will run. I'll do the best I can to give you time," she whispers, placing the covers back over me. "You are supposed to be moved in a few hours." She shakes her head, tears welling in her eyes. "I can't do this anymore." She swipes them away and composes herself, all the time keeping her voice a hushed whisper.

*I'm very confused about what she is saying to me. She mentioned running.*

"I'll make sure you are given time to escape."

*Escape?*

She releases my finger from the clip it is held in and turns off the monitor beside me. "I'll do my best to keep the skeleton staff here tonight occupied for as long as I can. There won't be a guard on your door. I'll handle that. Be as quiet as you can. Remove the IV needle first and apply pressure for as long as you can, but keep moving. Slippers are in the closet and you already have knee-high compression stockings on. Use the blanket on your bed for warmth wrapping it around your head to help keep your heat in.

"That's all you've got until you can find somebody to help you. You are very weak, you shouldn't be doing this, but you have no choice if you want a chance at surviving."

I want to ask her questions, but time is valuable. I need to stay silent and listen to her. My gut tells me I can believe this woman's words.

She stays still listening intently and then she quickly moves the chair over to the heavy curtain and peeks behind it. Satisfied, she stands on the chair, sliding her hand into her white coat pocket, pulling a small key out. Her hand moves behind the curtain and I hear a soft click.

The doctor hurries down, placing the chair back where she found it, and comes back over to me and picks up my chart. She starts writing in it as she talks in barely audible tones. "I will deny helping you if you get caught. I will be killed if they know, but I have to try. That window is the only way you will escape, and we are on the ground floor. I cannot help you any more than this. Find help quickly. You're not strong enough to make it far in the freezing cold weather. You need to head off—" She quiets down as the door handle turns.

I shut my eyes and focus on keeping myself still as she keeps writing things down. I have to place my trust in this person and take this lifeline she is offering me. I found help last time with Miss Catherine; I can do it again.

*I have to believe that.*

"Doc, how is she?" The man with the accent has arrived. I can feel his gaze drilling into me. I feel like I'm about to give myself away. I push my mind to the remote place that kept me countless times from being further exposed to William's torment when he entered my room to check if I was awake. He never touched me when he thought I was asleep.

"Hello, Mathias. She has a strong will to live. Let her fully regain consciousness and then I'll sign her out to you. Her wound looks good, and she's stabilized."

*She called him Mathias. Masked bearded man is Mathias.*

"She wouldn't have lasted much longer if you hadn't gotten her to me when you did. The girl should be awake within the next eight hours. She's been through a lot and her body shut down, needing time to heal."

"She's been here too many days already. I don't have the luxury of waiting that long."

"I'm the doctor, and my opinion should count for something. I get paid well to mend those he deems worthy. When she wakes up, she is all yours."

"I'll think about it."

"Please... I would never sign somebody out who

wasn't conscious. It goes against what I stand for as a doctor."

"You should have thought of that before you went on the payroll," he growls at her.

"Please... you can see she's weak." The doctor is doing her best to convince him.

"I said I'll think about it." Mathias isn't happy about her request. I have an itch to see if he's wearing the mask.

"You've virtually not slept the whole time she's been here. You need to rest too. She isn't going anywhere. Hell, lie down yourself for a couple of hours. She is out of danger, and you are dead on your feet. I'll wake you, Mathias, if there are any changes."

I hear an exhausted sigh like he's made his mind up. "I do need some sleep," he admits to the doctor.

I can hear their footsteps as she guides him away from my bed and toward the door.

"You can use my bed five doors down. It will be quiet, and I'll wake you in two hours. You won't miss anything in here. She's my only patient, so there won't be any other activity."

I hear the door open and close and their voices get farther away.

I open my good eye, peeking through my lashes, just to be sure I'm alone, and then I feel for the IV needle and carefully slide it out of my vein while applying pressure using part of my gown, bending my arm toward myself.

The doctor is hopefully keeping her word and covering for me, giving me the valuable time I needed. I had to believe I could get out that window without somebody storming the room.

I knew my escape was based purely on a wing and a prayer.

I slide my feet onto the floor, measuring how well balanced I am. I feel steady enough when I place all my weight on them and move slowly toward the closet, where I find a pair of white slippers and slide them onto my feet.

I grab the blanket off the bed and move over to the window area, carefully peeking behind the curtain. It is dark outside. I'm only going to get one shot at this. I wrap the blanket around my body, using some of it as a hood over my head as instructed.

The window quietly glides up without difficulty. The freezing cold air hits me and I gasp out in shock, small white puffs of breath floating in front of my face. I have no time to worry about the temperature. It's now or never. I climb out the window, careful of my injured shoulder, and land with a soft *thunk* as I sink into a few inches of cold ground.

*Snow?*

*I've been flown to a place that snows?*

I've never felt snow. It isn't soft; it crunches. It's also wet and really cold.

Instinct to hide has me heading straight for the shelter of the trees ahead, where I seek anonymity using them for protection as I try to get some bearings for the direction I should be fleeing. I have no idea which way I should go. I have never been out of Connard. I feel anxious and desperate and very alone.

There are two soft beams of light coming off the roof of the building from spotlights. I look around and notice a sign. A park backs up to the building I was in. I decide to head through it, wrapping the blanket tighter around me, and make my way through the freezing cold night, the high, full moon guiding me with its silver light.

I've been walking for several minutes and the shadows frighten me. There is nobody about. It feels too dangerous for me to be walking around in here. It's not lit up, just me and the trees. I make the decision to turn around and go back to find another way to somebody who can help me.

I come back around to the trees near the building and stand shivering behind one and listen. It is so quiet. I can't hear any cars or people noise. I move around to the side of the building, keeping to the shadows. I can make out parked cars ahead covered in a thin layer of snow, and once I take the time to look up toward the sky, I can see there is a city lit up with tall buildings farther down the road.

My teeth are starting to chatter, and I try to ignore how wet and burning with cold my feet and legs feel as they are subjected to the subzero temperature. I make a run for it, hiding myself between the sparsely parked cars. The snow is thinner here, so I can move a little faster. I take a quick look back at the building I was in. It is a printing business, so the sign says.

I keep moving, careful not to slip and do myself any more harm. This is my only chance for freedom, and the universe granted me this small mercy. Nobody is chasing after me. This is a good sign. I keep myself hidden as best I can, and then I walk out onto a quiet street and make my way around a corner, hoping to meet a kind soul who will help me.

I try lightly jogging, which is more of a fast-paced walk, as I hold my arm against my chest, trying not to jolt my shoulder any more than necessary.

Somewhere along the way, I have lost both slippers, and I hadn't even noticed because my mind was occupied and thinking about freedom.

I keep at a steady pace, excited for my freedom. I have managed to get away from Mathias. I'm breathing heavily from the exertion on my body, but I am facing liberty head on, and nothing will stop me from moving. I keep hurrying along at my steady pace down the sporadically lit street, when I hit a particularly slippery patch of ice on the pavement and go down hard, landing on my bad side. I swallow the scream creeping out of me and smother it by covering my mouth with the blanket.

I feel stitches tearing, but I get right back up, ignoring the pain, and make it past another block. I can't go back to being a prisoner. I'm shaking uncontrollably, but I push on. I am free, and I need to keep it that way.

There has to be a kind person like Miss Catherine, who will help me. I have to believe somebody will assist me. The streets are still quiet, so it must be late evening. I can see more lights ahead; it is busier. My heart jumps with joy. There are people crossing a road parallel to the road I am on. I tug the blanket down over my head tighter, trying to keep the freezing weather at bay, but it's simply too cold outside to keep my body heat contained inside it.

I'm making my way to another crossing when I nearly bump into two people who are walking around the corner and talking. I almost stop to ask for help, when I recognize the accent of one of the voices. I keep my head down and make it across the road when I hear, "What the fuck?"

I start flat out running, my blanket discarded. I just need to get to those people as fast as my body will take me.

The other person shouts out that he will get me, and I hear the click of a gun being reloaded.

Mathias shouts out to the other man, "No, Kane! Not necessary. Put your weapon down. I'll get her. This is child's play." Then I hear fast footsteps chasing me.

*I have to make it.*

I need help, but nobody is coming up this street. They are all walking parallel to my street, their heads down, huddled in their warm clothing against the freezing cold night.

Boxer has trained me well. I can normally run fast, and I'm giving it my all with my arms pumping hard as I ignore the pain. My legs are pounding the ground and I'm praying I don't slip again.

*I can't slip again.*

I've made it a block closer to the people, but it isn't going to be enough. I refuse to make it easy for Mathias to catch me.

*I have to try.*

I put everything I have into reaching these people before a pathetic squeal escapes me as I'm taken down. I expect to feel the ice cold ground smashed up against my face, but I'm rolled at the last second and he takes the full impact of our fall on an *ooph*. He then spits out several words in his language, which sound like he's cursing me to the devil.

And then his mouth is smashed into my ear, as he

snarls in English, "You fucking little idiot."

I can't move, because his arms have me caged in, so I let my head rest on his chest as I try to get my breath back, and my body shakes for so many reasons. From the cold, the pain, my fear, and beyond any of those things, my loss of freedom. I am so fucking mad at Mathias and these people.

I am indeed a *coo yon*, a stupid person.

And then something snaps inside me. I've had enough. "*You*... you are the fucking idiot for being a minion to whoever your Master is." I slam my head back against his chest, pounding it as hard as I can. "I am *not* the fucking little idiot for wanting to be free, for wanting to be happy, for wanting to be left alone, so don't fucking-little-idiot me." I don't know where that outburst came from, but now I'm spent. My heart is beating too fast and I need to calm down. I want to be fearless in front of these people.

*How is Boxer going to find me now?*

I feel like I have nothing to lose anymore, because how am I going to be saved when he has no clue where I am?

When he goes completely still underneath me, my gut instinct has the good grace to pay attention. I expect him to roll me over and strike me for my insolence and for escaping.

*I wait.*

But nothing happens, and then he moves a little

bit, and the next words he says shock and confuse me. "You stupid little rabbit, you should have run through the park." His growl is muffled in my hair.

I am replaying his words in my head when I hear the other man approach as Mathias releases his hold on me, and I'm brutally yanked up by Scar Face. This time, I do cry out in pain and wobble about as it finally becomes too much. Everything starts to get blurry and my balance is completely off-kilter.

I'm held brutally tight. I can feel his anger washing over me. I look down at the ground, trying not to let it show how much I hate him touching me.

"Fuck's sake, Kane, could you have picked her blanket up?" Mathias is pissed off. "Look after her while I get it for her before she undoes everything the doc did for her." Mathias is on his feet and running back up the street, leaving me with the man with the evil eyes.

I can't believe I'm hoping Mathias will hurry back. I am suddenly released and look up, thinking Mathias is back, just as a sharp, violent sting attacks my cheek, shocking me as my head swings to the side and I yelp pitifully.

"That's for trying to escape, bitch." He is boiling with rage. I can't look him in the eyes, afraid of what I will see in his soul. "You thought you could escape?"

I know this man wants to kill me in the most

brutal way, and he would enjoy taking his time.

This is the man I was warned to stay away from by the girl who was gunned down by this very man. My fear of him has taken a front seat as I whimper and stumble when he pulls me about by my bad arm. My good arm presses against the front of my thin white gown as it starts to get soaked with fresh blood while I try to keep the stitches from tearing anymore, and nobody is around to save me.

Not even Mathias.

"Start walking, bitch." I'm pushed forward roughly. I'm not prepared and I trip, skidding along the slippery pavement, my arms flailing when I feel a hard boot in my lower back propelling me forward. My hands come out instinctively to stop my fall and I land awkwardly. My left wrist snaps and I moan in pain when the rest of my body hits the hard ground. Blood sprays onto the light dusting of snow on the sidewalk.

A tear escapes, trickling down my face.

*I didn't think I owned any tears.*

I'm lying awkwardly on the freezing pavement, shivering and trying to turn myself over. The cold starts to freeze my tears on my cheeks and then my blanket is being draped over me as I'm turned over. Mathias roughly cradles me in his lap as he sits on the wet, frozen ground. His body is rigid underneath me and he doesn't utter a word.

He is stony, and I'm waiting to be yelled at, but instead, he grabs a fistful of my gown and slides it up my knees. "Don't!" I grit out between my teeth. I'm in too much pain and want this nightmare done with.

He ignores my protest and slides the sodden socks down my legs, peeling them off my feet. He surprises me when he starts massaging them. I can't look at him. I'm confused and waiting for the punishment for escaping.

"Kane!" he growls. He doesn't stop massaging my feet, trying to bring life back into them. I don't know why he is doing that for me. "Did you have to break her fucking wrist?" he roars at the other man, and I startle. "It's bad enough the damage already been done to her, but now we have another injury to explain away, a further delay in getting her to *him*."

"What? She slipped." It's then I realize both men don't have their masks on. I can see their faces. I can see the long angry scar going down Kane's cheek and those evil dark eyes that show so much darkness in his soul. I look at Mathias and notice the tattoo by his right eye, a symbol I don't understand, and how pretty his eyes are.

Do they even realize I can identify them now? I quickly look down, keeping my head bowed. I don't want to be able to identify them because they had masks on for a reason. They didn't want me to know what they looked like.

*What does this now mean for me?*

"Do you honestly think you are secure in your position, high up enough in the food chain to not have repercussions for treating her this way?"

The other man retaliates, "Fuck off, Mathias."

"Kane, you didn't fucking think of that, did you?" he spits out. "This is on your head, not mine. I've done everything to stop any more damage, and between you and this bitch, everything is unraveling. You've deliberately added to what the doc now has to mend."

I can't help myself. I dare a look at Scar Face, his eyes are almost demonic black, and if looks could kill, I would be dead. He bares his teeth at me like he's a hungry animal who wants to rip me to shreds, and mouths, *You're dead.*

"Stop playing with her, Kane, and take your fucking gloves off and give them to me."

Scar Face doesn't move.

"*Now!*" Mathias is barely holding onto his rage. I'm surprised he isn't dealing with this guy like he dealt with my abductors. He appears more senior. "I will not ask again." The words sound so cold coming from Mathias's lips. I want to be out of his arms.

Scar Face undoes his gloves and slaps them on Mathias's shoulder. He removes them placing one on each of my feet, securing the velcro. My feet had been hurting badly from being so cold, and now they were inside dry leather, fleece-padded gloves. The warmth is welcomed even if they are Kane's gloves.

"Take her from me so I can get up, and don't do anything else to bring fucking harm to her. I'm warning you. Do. Not. Test. Me. You saw what happened to those other two in the hangar at the airfield."

I'm jostled into Scar Face's arms, and I feel the pure hatred oozing from his veins. I don't want to be here, but I'm smart enough to keep my mouth shut and my head down.

He hisses in my ear, "Watch your back, bitch." I snap my head away from his mouth just as his teeth graze my ear hard. He would have had a mouthful if I hadn't moved my head.

Mathias gets up and his arms close around me as I'm scooped back into them. I lay cradling my wrist to my chest. He says nothing as he walks. His body is barely containing his anger.

I try to be as invisible as I can be and await my punishment. There is always a punishment for insubordination.

I bite down on my lip against all the pain my body is feeling. It's fully woken up from the painkillers I would have been on. I try to take myself to another place in my head and instead concentrate on watching the little white clouds my breath is making, wishing I was far away, hidden from the bastards of this world who find it a sport to track me down. A place that is safe from harm and nobody wants to hurt or capture me. Where there is no pain or suffering, only happiness and sunshine.

I want to take one last look at the city skyline and what freedom looks like, but I keep my head down. Freedom is simply not in the cards in this life for me.

The cold is now attacking me. Before, adrenalin pumped through my veins, keeping me from feeling too much. The blanket is not enough. "I'm... so... cooold," I chatter out. I didn't mean to say it out loud; it just came out of me.

"Give her your jacket," Mathias demands Kane.

I'm placed on my feet, but Mathias makes sure I'm standing on his boots, away from the wet ground. My body is flush against his. I will leave blood on him, but he doesn't seem to care.

Snowflakes have started falling fast. With my eyes, I follow some that are falling on Mathias's black beanie he's wearing and are dotting it, making it look spotted. I have this childish urge to reach out and touch one until I realize I broke my rule of looking at these two men in the face.

He tears his beanie off, pulling the blanket away from my head, and roughly pushes it down over my hair until it covers my ears. It is wool, and already I can feel its warmth. Then the blanket is stripped from my body and replaced by a far too big, thick warm jacket. I can't even think to complain that it belongs to Kane, because it staves off the cold.

*Instead of being punished, I'm being clothed?*

I keep my broken wrist held close to me while the large jacket is zipped up to my neck, cocooning my body against the cold. The hood is then placed over my head, trapping my body heat in, and then I'm swung up into Mathias's arms again like I weigh nothing. I've probably lost a lot of weight, not that I was much in the first place.

"Put the blanket over her legs." His words brook no disobedience; he is so angry. Kane reluctantly does what is asked of him and then snarls something about meeting Mathias back at the building.

This warmth I'm cocooned in is making me tired, so I close my eyes and let my head nestle into his neck. I'll worry about the repercussions of running later. I'm sleepy, and some rest sounds like a good idea.

"Hey, little rabbit." I'm being shaken. "Stay awake for me." I hiss in a breath of pain while his beard tickles my lips. The smell of coffee assaults my senses and falsely offers me comfort.

I know it would be better for me if I kept on sleeping and never woke up again.

But, I won't give in.

I open my eyes lazily when I'm shaken again.

"Stop that," I mumble.

"No!" And he shakes me again.

The movement is jolting my wrist and I need him to stop. I decide talking will help to keep me conscious. I no longer care if he's noticed I can see his face. "Where are you from? I don't know your accent."

He walks silently as he decides whether or not he will give me this little slice of information. I try my best to stay awake.

"Norway." His voice is a lot calmer now, more in control. I think Scar Face leaving to walk ahead has lowered his anger levels.

"Norway," I whisper. "I have a friend from England."

His arms do that tightening thing around me again. "I'm not your friend, little rabbit." His voice has dropped an octave. "I am a fox."

I make a little slurred noise like I can't help scoffing at his comment. I can already work out he's not my friend. "I have been with a Hell's bastard of a man my whole life. I know the difference between a low-life human being and a good person."

What more could these people do to me that hasn't already been done? What could a fox do?

"You may be sly and cunning, but I no longer fear you." I know my mistake when his arms tighten around me. I hiss in a breath when my shoulder gets squeezed into my body too much.

"Well, you should because I eat little rabbits." I inhale his coffee-scented breath when his head dips again.

I try not to fold inside myself at that comment. He wants to frighten the life out of me, but I am past the point of caring tonight. I know I should care, but maybe it would be better if I had been shot dead. I try to get a handle on my emotions. I am only alive, because Mathias's orders are to bring me in that way, and he has been trying hard to keep it that way, but I also know a phone call is all it would take to have me executed. I've witnessed what he is capable of.

I decide to challenge him to answer my questions. "Mathias, what did you shout at that girl in the hangar when she was already dead?"

He doesn't answer me straight away and keeps walking.

"Who told you my name was Mathias? Because I sure as hell didn't."

*Fuck. I have to think! I can't get the doctor in trouble.*

"The girl in the hangar... she also told me to stay away from Kane."

"She was correct. He was going to shoot you dead when you ran too. He thinks with his gun and not his head. You will also forget that you have seen our faces because it will only end your life. If *he* knows, then you have no more lives left. I won't be able to save you from him. He will take you out without a second thought. Do you understand me?"

I nod. I know how to bide my time until I can work out how I can escape. "What about Kane?"

"Leave him to me. He knows what is good for him, and your escape and seeing our faces will only get all three of us killed on the spot."

"Why are you doing this? My friends would pay you to walk away from this madness. Kane is gone. It's just you and me. Please. I didn't do anything to deserve this, and you don't need to do this. You have a choice right now. We could both disappear. Just a phone call to my family and you could leave me and disappear."

"Shut the fuck up," he roars in my face. "You have no fucking clue about me and what I choose. There *is no choice*. Do not utter another fucking word."

Mathias carries me in strained silence. We don't meet another soul on the way back. I can feel myself falling back to sleep with the rhythm of his pace, when he says quietly, "I called her a stupid little rabbit, because we are all foxes, and don't you forget that."

# MATHIAS

## Not On My Watch

I'm posted inside the girl's room, sucking on a hot coffee and trying to get comfortable in an uncomfortable, hard chair. Her window is locked, and she has her left ankle cuffed to the bed railing. She looks harmless enough and in no condition to make another great escape, but I'm not taking any chances.

The doc's eyes were filled with fear, a total giveaway when I walked in carrying a half frozen, unconscious, bleeding female in my arms.

To the outside world, she ran her own legitimate medical business by day in the city, and when called upon, she would be here in this fully equipped setup in one of *his* many properties. It was a front for a printing business and came with a small skeleton medical staff, who were all on the payroll.

The doc's behavior was more a nervous panic, with her eyes darting back and forth between

Whisper and me, which only tipped me off to her own guilt. There was a reason this girl was able to escape. She didn't achieve it all by herself, and she was so close to pulling it off. Only a couple of blocks were between her and freedom.

If I had been by myself, I may have played ignorance. After all, it wasn't my fault she escaped. The gods were on her side, and then she had to go and flee in the wrong direction.

*Stupid little rabbit.*

There is nothing more enjoyable to Dickwad-Kane than killing. Just give him a reason. She presented one on a platter for him.

I had been shown to the room by the good doctor for a much-needed rest, but I needed some fresh air and a walk and didn't want anybody knowing that.

Kane had a similar idea. He was out getting himself some fresh air and a coffee, unbeknownst to me, and I was out stretching my legs, getting a coffee and something to eat. What can I say? The doc supplied shit coffee.

I decided to take the longer walk back, giving myself some much-needed alone time, when Kane and I unfortunately crossed paths. I could have done with a break from the fucker. We kept on walking and all, but barreled into her. Our slow reaction time was enough to allow her to make a run for it because we sure as hell didn't think we were going to bump into our prisoner on the street.

The determination she has to escape can only bring her trouble, especially when *he* gets his claws in her. She is too headstrong and a fighter. She would have been tame once, and now she is wiser to life and no longer able to be brainwashed.

Being free for that small amount of time has taught her she will do anything not to be held captive again.

*Anything.*

And that means taking on freezing cold temperatures in fucking Alaska in the middle of November, wearing virtually nothing but a blanket for warmth.

The doctor had to push it by questioning *me* why I wasn't asleep, tucked up in that bed she had offered me. Nobody's fucking business why I hadn't quite gotten around to getting into it, and now I was going to forego any proper rest to keep this girl out of more harm.

I bided my time until the doctor re-stitched the female's shoulder and set her wrist before I slammed her up against the wall, my forearm pressing down on her throat. I didn't care that Whisper saw me attack the doctor; it would do her well to be reminded of what I was capable of. Things were getting out of hand, and that needed to stop real fucking fast.

I saw the terror in both their eyes. The doctor pleaded ignorance to it, and so did the girl. She was exhausted, but she still did her best to raise her voice to me, pleading it was all her idea, and the doctor just stood there letting her take the blame.

*I knew better.*

The doctor had cracked, and the guilt from the role she played among *his* minions had gotten to her. Hell, I was feeling bad about my role with this girl. She was so freakin' innocent; I could see that.

She had already told me a little about escaping from a life that was taken from her, and she had people who cared for her and they would be looking for her. She was a good person. If you were stolen as an infant, became a pet to a man for twenty years, and you had no identification, no worldly possessions, you were a nobody unless somebody helped you to become a somebody. Yes, she had people who would miss her and be looking for her now.

*He* was playing with fire with this one.

I'd released the doctor and took her aside, away from prying ears, and told her to run and stay hidden once we left the premises.

I told her if she valued her life she would need to burrow into the ground and stay there. She didn't even try to lie anymore. I knew she was thinking about her own safety and what the value of her life would mean to *him*. If you agree to be put on the payroll, don't expect to live a long life under his thumb. Whatever made her agree to taking his money is on her head now, because it was going to come back to bite her if she didn't heed my warning. It would probably bite her anyway.

*Once you wake up to what is going on in his world, the money is no longer so attractive.*

Now, we are back at almost square-fucking-one with Whisper, and time is up.

No more delay.

I've been piecing it all together, as much as I can, because nobody knows everything. He has contacts, who suggest women to him. They are normally loners, strippers, women who won't be missed, or who are runaways, but they are all beautiful.

He sends out his well-paid delivery boys to abduct them. I have recently climbed the ranks, and this female is my first-hand delivery. I'm about to make it to the man himself. I will finally get to meet him.

I've worked the shady world for two years. I knew who to put myself in front of to be noticed. He finds his sentinels in the MMA world.

I wanted in.

I was never a delivery boy. They are just thugs, lowlifes out to make some fast cash. They are dispensable.

I'm not dispensable.

I've been working toward this meet-and-greet for six months.

He has a maximum of two events a year, and he's got one coming up soon. Nobody knows when but his most trusted.

Nobody knows where but the man himself until he wants his clients to know.

He is paranoid.

He is seriously warped in the head, from what I've heard, and I will get to witness it for myself. The fucker is also very, very clever and unpredictable.

I move the chair closer to her bed and put my feet up on it, preparing to take a nap after I've finished my shit coffee. The doctor says Whisper will be out for hours with the juice she gave her, and I need some shuteye before we move her.

Things were going to heat up soon enough.

This female is a complication I wasn't expecting.

I am an undercover agent.

At whatever cost, I. Will. Bring. *Him*. Down.

# EDGE

## Just Call Me Miss Daisy

**W**ith all the snooping through my personal items, I had hoped a change of clothes had been brought for me from my saddlebag, but no, that wasn't the case.

We had to go back, waste time and get to my bike at the old lady's place. I had a few things I needed to get for the road trip to Alabama, anyway. Extra weapons and *No Mercy,* my small bag used to pry the truth from men's mouths, were both priorities. They were locked away in my specially made, hard saddlebag attached to my Harley, and I was the only one who could unlock it.

While I was getting organized, Miss Catherine went inside her home and freshened up after what looked like days of wearing the same outfit. She came back changed into slacks, a shirt, and a home-knitted button up sweater that old ladies seem to favor, with sensible granny shoes.

I stayed outside and threw on a clean, black Henley, my leather jacket, and a fresh pair of jeans. I was relieved to be out of that fucking hospital Johnny—nothing manly about that get-up. I felt like my dick and balls had been shoved up inside me wearing it back to the old lady's house.

I had to hack the jeans off at the knee with my hunting blade to allow for the moon boot I have strapped on. I gotta keep the awkward thing on for a couple months and use the crutches, Doc's orders.

The doc wasn't too pleased to release me, and then Miss Catherine announced she needed to borrow the doc's wheels. I'm not comfortable not being in control, and I prefer my bike to a cage any fucking day of the week, but we had to be prepared to accommodate more than two people.

And here I am now, being chauffeured, driven by the feisty Miss Catherine, while I navigate and play the role of a fucked up Miss Daisy, lying awkwardly across the back seat of the doc's BMW as we head toward Henrys Ferry.

We are the odd couple, driving in silence for the first few hours because this suited me fine. I wasn't in the mood for talking. Making small talk was just an aggravation.

Her friends still haven't made it back or contacted her. I'm beginning to wonder if Boxer had sent that message, or if it was a decoy message sent to play with her.

If I could, I would be working alone, because I don't need the added responsibility of an old lady to babysit when I don't know what we are walking into. I have my loaded handgun, complete with silencer, resting on the seat beside me, and I have a couple other weapons hidden on my body. I need to be prepared for a shit storm.

My mind shouldn't have been, but it kept wandering to Whisper/Sara and the night she came for me on my bike. She was a mixture of sweet, wild, and free.

I can see her perfect, naked body, her breasts aching to be touched as she rode me. The little noises that escaped her as she gave herself fully over to the intimate connection between our bodies, as she lay arched over the gas tank while I pounded into her.

She had let herself enjoy the sexual experience with a male who she *thought* wasn't out to treat her badly. She had allowed herself to use me, knowing I was there for the same reason. It was pure lust for both of us.

*I was her first.*

I've never had deep feelings for *any* woman. I've closed myself off from all that. I keep it simple. I like to fuck, and it comes with no picket fences or promises.

We were both consenting adults. She wanted to be fucked, and I wanted to fuck her. She wanted to feel normal, and I unknowingly gave her what she was seeking after a life of abuse, which now makes my stomach churn again.

At the time, I had no idea the trauma lying buried below the surface. My own blood had done things to the sweet and wild girl for a lifetime, things that were recorded, things she didn't even understand, things she could not let anybody else see until she was ready to know herself.

There can be no punishment for William's crimes, and this tears me up from the inside out.

I can't take it out on his cocksucking evil hide.

He got off *too* fucking easy.

She just carried that all with her silently and with a closed off dignity, watching me ride away, assuming we would never see each other again. She had no clue I was the son of her nightmares, but William had already set things in motion upon his death—our meet and greet.

It was inevitable.

After everything I've learned, Whisper had every right to take my father's inheritance and give herself a life. There was no compensation great enough to turn back time and return her to her biological parents and start the clock again, giving her the life she should have had with a loving, caring family.

There was no restitution for the known and unknown abuse, for the imprisonment, for the thousands of memories she keeps locked away in her mind. I know they're locked away because I have my own. But it would have been *something* toward her new life.

But she still didn't accept that fucking inheritance.

There was a son that was owed it.

She was honest.

The same son who shot her.

*Jesus Christ.*

I bow my head with remorse for my actions.

What have I done to the female that had shown me how innocent she was and freely showed me her wilder side? She couldn't have possibly understood herself at the time what it all meant; she was just following her own desires.

She had never been with a man properly to know. It had all been natural base instinct for her when she allowed herself that time with me. She had been with one of the devil's minions, and she still managed to show her sweet soul to me.

She is a good person, and I'm the fucked up asshole.

What could I have prevented if I had taken the time to observe my father's home and learn about the female in the letter? Learn about the town and take note? I could have hunted like I normally do, watching my prey, learning them, but instead, years of rage consumed me. It was like a bullet train of emotions that took the reins.

I let out a grunt of disgust at my actions.

I went hell-for-leather and assumed the worst straight off the cuff, knowing what William was capable of. I didn't stop to connect any dots and think maybe there was more to the person he left his inheritance to.

I instantly thought the worst.

It took over eight months to send me the news of his death because Whisper was always gonna be the target. He could not let Whisper have her freedom, even when he died. He needed her to be punished and dealt with, and I was the perfect assassin.

The son who'd been wronged.

He was a proud peacock even in death, strutting about and preening his feathers in front of me.

He knew I would be infuriated by his decision.

It was a trap.

I walked right into it, without question.

Rage had blinded me.

I'd had two parents at one stage. I had been told my mother had fled and left me. She *had* to have been desperate to leave me with *him*.

*She had to have been.*

Was it all lies?

Or was she dead by his hands?

Will I ever know?

I've only ever believed one thing because he told me. I was young and blisteringly angry and didn't want to learn more. He planted the seed and let it fester.

I fucking *hated* my mother.

Now, I wonder if I should be mourning the loss of her?

This epiphany hits me hard. So many questions I need answers to.

I want to learn more about Whisper. I want to fight for her life. Kidnapping a baby and forcing her to live her life with him under his demands was cruel. She had parents.

Did he kill them?

I look out the window, trying to slow down all these thoughts that are flickering in and out. My foot's painful, and I'm chewing on pills like breath mints so I can think straight. Ivory knew what he was doing shooting me in the foot, putting me out of commission long enough to get Whisper clean away, just in case I had any thoughts of taking off after them. Ivory had better start running when he sees me, because I'll be gunning for that cocksucker first, and then Ebony.

While I've sat back here for hours, something's been bothering me, and I couldn't put my finger on it until now. I place my hand inside my leather jacket and find the hidden pocket, pulling out Whisper's envelope.

My hot head hadn't absorbed the information at the time. I was shot, my head had been bashed, and then I discovered I had hurt an innocent woman who was two people in my mind. She had revealed in her letter to me that the lawyer had only just hand-delivered the letter stating the inheritance left to her that day, and apologized for the misunderstanding.

This is what has been bothering me, laying low in my mind. I can't remember the name of the lawyer firm on my letter. I need to know the lawyer's name who spoke to her because she doesn't state it in the letter she wrote to me, Dallas Dupré. Only that it would all be sorted out shortly. There were two different surnames of mine on both our letters. I needed to know what else didn't match. It feels like one is a possible decoy because one wouldn't want me coming after them if I found out I was being played.

*What the fuck is going on?*

I was so full of steam I didn't think to bring mine with me. I had put the address of my father's house in my phone, and that was it. I was hightailing it out of Albuquerque without looking back. I didn't need to know anything other than my destination and to find the female responsible for taking my inheritance. It seemed cut-and-dried at the time.

*"Motherfucker!"* I curse loudly, pounding the side of the car door with my fist.

"Edge?" The old lady looks at me with caution in the rearview mirror.

"Eyes on the road and keep driving." I'm sharp with her because there are too many unanswered questions floating about in my head. I try to gentle my next response. "We may have another lead. I need to make a call to my president." I want some information off my letter. It may be a lead I can pursue, especially if nothing turns up at this airfield.

I was never meant to see Whisper's letter. This was not accounted for in my father's far-fetched fantasy world of assumptions he'd played out in his mind prior to his untimely death. I was never meant to see the discrepancy.

The insane son-of-a-bitch was trying to role-play us. What kind of person does that?

Now, another puppet master wants his pound of flesh to be taken out on Whisper's soul.

I pull Whisper's phone out and put in the code to let Hazard know I'm about to call, and I wait for him to respond before I proceed.

"Hazard... Yeah, I'm good. Need a favor. Can you get one of the boys to get into my house and locate a letter on my kitchen table? Just need the full details off of it. It's from a lawyer firm. Get him to text it through on this number. It's safe." He asks me how everything is going. I reply with, "Fucked up."

He offers to send Lethal and Blueblood out, but I decline. Hazard knew things had gone beyond complicated, but he didn't push me.

I was a tough fucker, and he respected that.

Soulless Bastards were brothers who fought for each other.

We were family.

We died for each other.

I was too fucking stubborn to accept his offer at the moment, because then this toxic can-of-worms on my soul would be wriggling all over my body, burrowing into places I didn't need revisiting.

*Ever.*

It's all locked down.

I know how to be the person I had become. I wear it like a full body suit of armor. It fits well. I don't need any chinks in it, but I know I will be asking soon. I just need a bit more time to figure out what I'm dealing with and how deep it goes.

"What you be doin' for your motorcycle club, Edge?" The old lady breaks through my demons.

*Ahh, hell, here we go.* Somebody's been eavesdropping enough to start getting up in my business.

I let out a sigh. I thought we were going to make it to the abandoned airfield in peace until the old lady's need for chatter starts up, her silent thoughts stroking her curiosity to know more.

"I'm their enforcer."

She looks at me in the rearview mirror, an eyebrow raised. "Meaning?"

*I'm not a good guy.*

"I enforce bylaws, among other things."

"You have killed for your club?"

*More than you want to know.*

I rub my hand over my beat up face. "Club law is different to civilian law. I do what needs to be done when we are wronged."

"You choose to kill for a living?"

*Yeah, and I'm fucking good at it.*

"We've already ascertained I'm ex-military, which means I killed for a living. Our government's military told me who to kill, and I did because there is a war going on. It's acceptable in that environment."

She stays silent, letting me rant.

"If it helps your wellbeing, I don't go killing innocent people." Saying those words, I know what she must be thinking about Whisper. "Not deliberately," I add on for the old lady's sake.

"Why you be choosin' a biker gang over military?" The rest of what I know she wants to say goes unsaid.

*Because I watched good men die in front of me,*

*while I lived.*

*Because war fucks with your mind.*

*Because innocents got in the way.*

"Four tours were enough for me. War is acceptable when the enemy is recognized by the world." Not so much when it's a private war.

"Yet you still kill?"

Fuck these questions. I'm not used to being questioned.

*I* do the interrogating.

My eyes meet hers in the mirror. "Maybe... I'm the bad seed... who didn't fall far from the rotten apple," I say slowly to rein in the irritation that has crept into my voice.

I turn my attention to the window, watching the monotony of the landscape whizz past me, while some fucktard is doing god-knows-what to Whisper. I use these moments to calm myself the fuck down. I let out a heavy sigh because I know this old lady doesn't need this from me.

"I was protecting our country before, and now I'm protecting my brothers, *my* family. We look after our own. We right wrongs. I don't expect you to understand a motorcycle club and what these men mean to me. They're loyal. I trust them. I have a home. You gave Whisper a home when she needed one. I know you understand what protecting somebody means, and I think you know she would protect you too with her own life. Currently, where we stand, I think you would do what it takes to get Whisper back, and that means pulling the trigger on somebody standing in your way."

Her attention is only for the road while she absorbs what I've said.

*None of this is her fault,* I have to remind myself. She's only ever cared for Whisper when she needed rescuing. She put a roof over her head and gave her a future. She gave Whisper her life back and didn't judge her on a past filled with unthinkable horrors. She saw the broken soul lying dormant and has been waiting for the time she will be needed, when all those memories decide to eject from Whisper's mind and she falls into a heap.

I could use the enemy in war to take it out on. I saw my father in all those sons-of-bitches who were targeting the innocent. "We really are not that much different. It's human nature to step up and do whatever it takes."

Her tired old eyes flick back up to the rearview mirror. They are filled with determination. "Whisper be an innocent who's been wronged. She be needin' protection... the kind I can't be givin' her."

She watches the road again, waiting for me to acknowledge her message.

*Whisper has been wronged by my father, me, and now this new unidentifiable threat.*

"I will seek retribution for you. You have my word on that."

She nods her head, accepting my statement as truth. "You be a man who has led a hard life." Her statement is my reality. "You suffered under William Dupré as a child." She isn't asking me to confirm her comment; it isn't a question.

My hands clench into tight fists at my sides. "It's a life I got away from," I grunt out. I don't like talking about my childhood.

I *never* talk about it.

"You and I..." She hesitates before continuing, "We have more in common than you be thinkin', Edge." Her words hold a lot of muted meaning.

I hear her and don't doubt her words. She falls silent for the rest of the trip, acknowledging my directions until we pull up midafternoon in front of the high-chain wire fenced-off entrance to the abandoned airfield.

This appeared to be the area Miss Catherine had indicated as the last place the phone stayed before the signal was lost.

An old, rusty metal sign hangs on its last legs announcing we were at the Stephen Army Auxiliary Airfield #4 / Anderson Field / Anderson Airport.

There's nobody around for miles. "Stay in the car while I get the gate open." There is a padlock and chain on the ten-foot gate keeping trespassers out. I get out of the car, minus the crutches, and hobble around to the trunk. I pop the lid and rummage around in *No Mercy* for my lock pick.

That padlock didn't stand a chance. I open the gate and usher the old lady through. She waits on the other side, the Beamer's engine purring while I shut the gate, relocking it to keep up appearances.

I slide into the front passenger seat, knocking a little ragdoll out of the way onto the floor that was sitting on the seat, my temper peeking through as I try to ignore my throbbing foot.

The car isn't moving.

I look over at Miss Catherine, ready to tell her to get the fucking car rolling, but the look on her face stops me. Her eyes are locked on where the doll landed. And that's when I remember what she had told me about the only belongings Whisper had brought with her in her escape, and this was one of them.

I lean forward and scoop the doll up on a grunt, holding it until the car starts moving again.

*Christ! She's brought the doll along to give to Whisper, so I have to make sure I find her.*

I direct the old lady to drive me up the dirt road through a thick shield of trees. I grimly note the woods could serve as a great place to dispose of bodies.

*I should know. I've buried enough.*

Thick tall woods cleverly cloak the airfield, offering the motherfucker privacy. Fields for miles surround the area. No houses for nosy trespassers to get curious. It's the perfect setup.

The large airstrip comes into view, and I note how well kept it is.

*Too* well kept.

*Abandoned, my ass.*

The perfect place to traffic Whisper out on a plane. Grease enough palms with cake and you can do anything you set your mind to in this corruption-filled world of ours. Money talks. The bigger the slice of cake, the tastier the deal. I'll look into who owns this land because it's another possible lead.

We pull up beside the old hangar. It looks like it was built in World War II. There is a white sedan parked near the hangar. It's dusty and looks like it hasn't moved for a few days because there are no fresh tracks.

"Look!" Miss Catherine points to the parked car. "Whisper called and told me she be transferred to a car with NQ on the plates." She points to the back of the car. "This be the vehicle they be transportin' her in. Her eyesight be poor and she couldn't be makin' out the other part of dem plates."

It was enough. This is as good as we are gonna get for proof that she was definitely brought here, and this was the last place my phone was tracked to.

The locked gate makes me think nobody is around, but I can't be sure. Ebony and Ivory were here at one stage.

Whisper is either in those woods or was spirited out of here. Just the thought of the female being dead gives me a feeling I'm unused to.

*Deep regret is stealing its way into my soul.*

Before I can think on that emotion too long, the old lady's out of the car while I dump the doll on the backseat, and she hands me the crutches. I get out, my gun in my hand, and lean heavily on the car as I survey the area. It's very quiet.

I use the crutches for a few steps then throw them to the ground. They're a fucking nuisance, only slowing me down, keeping me from being at my most alert.

Miss Catherine looks like she wants to serve me up a speech, but she holds her tongue.

*She's learning.*

She's looking at the hangar; worry etched onto her face. She's afraid of what we'll find inside. Thoughts of Whisper being murdered will be swimming through her mind.

We make our way to the small hangar entrance door, which is part of the main hangar frontage, and I test the handle. It's locked. Which is a good sign we are the only two people here.

I stick my gun in the back of my jeans and pull out

the lock pick I had pocketed, inserting it and moving it around until I hear the satisfying click of the lock releasing.

I find the crutches hovering in my face, again. I grunt as I put them under my armpits and watch as the old lady opens the small door, ready to walk inside.

*I can smell death.*

I swing my crutch up against her ample bust, halting her.

"Wait. I'm going in first." The chances of somebody being inside a locked hangar alive and ready to kill is a long shot, but my caution has kept me alive in the past.

Always be the hunter, never the prey.

I toss the crutches to the ground, pulling the gun out the back of my jeans, taking the safety off, and positioning her behind me.

Opening the door has tripped an automatic light. The fluorescent tubes are flickering to life, blinking away as the inside of the hangar reveals itself. I don't look at her. "Stay here." My heart thumps with dread. Whisper is the only name on my mind.

I take a step inside; my gun raised and ready. I can't help coughing because the stench is indescribably bad. There appears to be no imminent danger, not unless the fuckers are invisible. It's empty except for a pushback tug, used to move planes in and out of the hangars, and it's sitting alone in the far corner.

The inside of the hangar appears smaller to what is depicted on the outside, and it's surprisingly modern. I observe the structure until it clicks what they have done.

The outside is simply a camouflage. The original hangar is blending into the countryside. From the air, it would look old and abandoned, but the inside is newer. The floor is polished cement.

*I'll be fucked.*

I'm in a hangar inside a hangar. And then I see what is making the fucked up smell. There are two pairs of legs sticking out behind some stacked up supplies to my right, fifteen or so feet away.

I move closer, my free hand covering my nose as two bodies come into view, lying beside each other on a tarp on the floor, and that's when I can see a third body lying covered beside them, up against the wall. A sheet has been laid over the much smaller, slimmer body, my guess a female.

*Fuck!*

I tense my jaw, grinding down on my teeth, and look away. It's then I can see the blood splatters and larger stains on the floor. At least two of the people were killed in that spot.

The old lady lets out a little gasp of horror when she sees what I'm looking at. I move to where she stands. Her small hand locks onto my arm as her eyes search mine for answers I can't give her at the moment. "I thought I told you to stay put. Don't move from here while I check the bodies out." She should have stayed outside.

"Do you think it's...?" She can't even say Whisper's name. She doesn't have to.

*Jesus Christ.*

"Just do as I say," I bark at her, and tear my arm out of her hold, making my way back to the corpses. Fear for Whisper's life has my temper flaring.

I didn't need to see the faces of the other two to know it was Ebony and Ivory lying face down; their clothes told me that much. Looks like I can cross them off my list. Lucky fuckers got it easy.

I hold off checking the other one, maybe because I need to delay knowing if it's Whisper underneath that sheet. She was last seen with these two. It isn't looking good.

I note the closed door to what appears to be an office farther down and bypass the bodies to quickly check it's empty. I don't need any more surprises or dead bodies.

I reach the door and turn a warning glare on Miss Catherine. She hasn't moved. She's just staring, entranced by the bodies. This has my mind wandering briefly back to the third person. I'm almost dreading checking who is under that sheet.

It can't be Whisper, not with a debt being owed. Not unless she died before they could get her on the plane.

I rest my head on the door and curse low under my breath. I need to keep my head in the game. I turn the doorknob and fling it wide open, stepping to the side, my gun raised. I can see well enough to know it's empty. I flick the light switch and give it a quick once over. It's clear. I'll come back to check it properly for any clues shortly.

I hobble back to the bodies. She hasn't come any closer. "These are the two who abducted Whisper from the house." I point to the uncovered dead. Ebony and Ivory were definitely executed. "These two were shot point blank range. You can tell from the hole in the back of their heads." They didn't even see their executioner coming. They were comfortable being close to their killer. They must have royally fucked up, or the top dog thought them dispensable. I would not have been so kind. Their deaths would have been torturous and slow.

"And the other?" The old lady's voice is quivering, but she hasn't moved.

I place a hand over my nose and mouth, trying to keep the stench of death away as I lean down awkwardly, peeling the sheet back. I let out a whoosh of breath I didn't even know I was holding in when I identify the corpse isn't Whisper.

I hadn't wanted to let on to Miss Catherine how great my fear was that it could have been Whisper's body lying here. And then I take a closer look, gently moving the stray hairs off the female's face.

"Motherfucker!" I shout, my voice ricocheting off the hangar walls. I hang my head. It's Santana. She was under the protection of the Lion's Den MC. She didn't deserve this.

*What are the chances Ruby, who is under the Soulless Bastards protection and disappeared around the same time as Santana, could still be alive and all three disappearances are connected somehow?*

"Edge?" Miss Catherine's voice cracks, riddled with fear.

"It's not Whisper," I call back to her. I hear the cry of relief from the old lady as she moves to come closer. "Stay where you are." My roar echoes before getting absorbed into the walls.

She doesn't need to see all the death. "This female is somebody the Lion's Den MC has been missing. She is under their protection, and she up and disappeared around nine months ago, and so did one of our girls around the same time. We knew nomads had abducted them. They were hoarding the two females' personal belongings in their possession like trophies. Tried to make them talk. Two of the most stubborn fuckers I've met.

"They had been lost to us. No more leads to

finding their bodies, so we were left with assuming the nomads had killed them for kicks. We located their parents, but both sets were drunks and drug users and didn't give a fuck about their daughters."

Were they taken because it was thought they wouldn't be missed?

Santana had been alive all this time.

Were they specifically handpicked and not a random act?

Was it thought that Whisper wouldn't have people who cared about her?

Is this what my father had assumed in that fucked up brain of his? That she was a nobody all her life, and upon his death, she would remain that way, a sitting duck for me to dispose of for him.

"I'm sorry, Edge." The old lady's words softly drift down to me. And I know she is. They are full of sorrow at the loss of this female's life. I'm sorry too.

I take out Whisper's phone and snap photos of the bodies and close-ups of their faces. There's nothing pretty about a stiff that has been dead for several days. It's totally fucked up, but I don't hesitate to check them over for anything that could give us more information, but they're clean.

Santana's wearing nice clothes. Her shoes have been removed and she was shot in the back. If she was trying to escape, then this is why she would have been executed. Dressed the way she is, she would have had heels on. It makes sense with the blouse and tight skirt. So where are the shoes?

Something had gone wrong for these three to be gunned down. All had been shot with the intent to kill with the first bullet.

Whoever did this wasn't fucking around.

Santana's body had been covered up, giving her a little dignity. The person who did this cared enough to do so.

I cover her body back up, saying a silent prayer for her soul.

Miss Catherine gives me a few moments then is by my side, handing me my crutches.

*The old lady does not listen.*

I put my gun away and take them off her. Only the dead are inside this hangar. My foot needs to rest because this doesn't end here today. I won't stop until I find Whisper, dead or alive, and take down the people responsible.

Santana's life was stolen from her, and Whisper is still a question mark if she is even alive. If she is, she is still in a lot of deadly danger.

"We'll take her body back with us. I can't leave it here. Torque, the Lion's Den MC's President, will have to be contacted, and they will get her body taken care of, give her the proper respectful burial she deserves."

These bodies should not still be here stinking up

the hangar. A cleanup crew should have come and gone by now, dispensing of the bodies if they couldn't take them on the flight and removing the car parked outside. So why have they not arrived?

"I need to check the office thoroughly because I might find something useful, another lead, because we've not got a lot at the moment. Wait over by the hangar door. I won't be long."

"No. I be comin' with you."

*Fuck's sake!*

"Lady, I'm not in the mood," I growl at her.

"Nor am I, Edge." I've gotta give her credit where credit is due. The old broad is determined, for Whisper. I have to respect that.

"She be like a granddaughter to me, and nobody be tellin' me what I can and can't be doin'. I haven't bowed to a man for over fifty years, so you better be gettin' that through your head right now. No man be orderin' me around unless I be allowin' it." And then she storms off toward the office, making me play catch-up.

*I guess that's settled.*

The first thing I notice on closer inspection is dried blood on the dark office desk, and then the pile of clothes that have been thrown in the corner by the water cooler.

I head straight for them and check them over, recognizing them as Whisper's. What she was wearing in the trunk. I note their condition, the bullet holes, blood, and dried vomit soiling them. She was in a bad way before she was put on that plane, mostly my fault. It doesn't escape my notice her T-shirt has been torn apart.

*What the fuck went on in here?*

The last item is a pair of expensive-looking black heels. Whisper sure as shit wasn't wearing heels, riding her bike. These would be Santana's missing shoes.

"They are Whisper's clothes," Miss Catherine confirms what I already knew, swiping away the tears with shaking hands, trying to hide her emotions, trying to stay strong. "Whisper would not have willingly taken her clothes off." She voices her fears to me.

The dried blood on the desktop doesn't go unnoticed by Miss Catherine. We both know she must have been hurt again in here, possibly for refusing to do as she was told. I need to believe she wasn't raped.

"My guess is they changed her for the trip in here." Better to think positively at this point. "Or maybe they were cleaning her up?" I have to say something out loud because the silence is too much. We are both letting our minds run wild with what went down in here.

I need to give the old lady hope. This was possibly

the last place Whisper spoke to Miss Catherine and she knows it.

I look across at the old lady, and guess what? She's examining each item of Whisper's clothing, noting the bullet hole that has gone through her leather jacket, hoodie, and T-shirt. She glares at me and I look away. The blood caked on the clothing fucking makes me feel sick because I did that to her. She was an innocent, and I became another man to add to her pain-filled existence.

I look over again, and she's placed all the clothing down in a heap except for the leather jacket. She's gonna take that with her; it means something to her.

Neither of us says another word while I hunt through the office and find nothing useful. It's fucking as clean as a nun. Whisper has just up and disappeared on a private jet, and I know I won't find out where in a hurry. A lot of money would have been used to keep it all quiet, but I will find somebody who will talk.

We have to get moving because my own nightmares threaten to invade my waking mind. The silence in here is like white noise to my ears, scratching away.

My father stole from me, and he stole too much from Whisper.

I *have* to find her alive.

*And then I will show this bastard from Hell the*

*devil I really can be, and I will rain my wrath down upon him.*

"We need to finish up in here and leave." I don't know when the cleanup crew will be coming, but they can't leave the bodies here indefinitely.

"What be her name?" Miss Catherine asks softly. I know she is asking about the dead female.

"Santana."

"It be a beautiful name. You be knowin' her?" The fearless old lady is now replaced with a gentle heart.

I shake my head. "I only saw her about. She was a stripper in one of the Lion's Den MC's clubs. She was only twenty-one. She was thinking of going back to college before she disappeared."

She places her small hand on my shoulder. "We will find who be responsible, Edge."

*She truly believes this.*

I take some photos of the evidence left behind; it may come in useful. "Come on, time is ticking. We need to get moving." My crutches are being handed to me. I take them and tuck them under my armpits and lean on them in relief. I know I'll be throwing them to the ground again when I put Santana's body in the trunk, but for now, giving my injured foot a rest is welcomed. I need to be as fit as I can for Whisper.

We make it over to the hangar entrance door, stopping along the way, taking a few photos of the inside and the blood splattered floor before we exit into the late afternoon sun. The temperature has started to drop. Nightfall is looming ahead.

We've only made it a few feet outside when I hear heavy metal music blaring, and then a car sounds like it's coming in fast.

"Miss Catherine, get back inside. *Now!*" I yell at her, just as she registers the sounds of the music, hesitating long enough for me to pull out one of my handguns I have concealed on me and hand it to her. "Safety is off and it's loaded. Point and shoot at the bad guys if they come for you. Shut the door, and if you can lock it from the inside, do it." I shove the crutches at her. "Car keys, now!"

She hands them over, and I turn and head for the doc's car. It's a long dirt road concealed by trees until they make it into this open area. I may still have time. I drive the car around the farthest side of the hangar and turn it off, getting out and quietly clicking the door shut. Is this the lazy cleanup crew? It takes at least two people to get rid of three bodies. The music volume means they are just about upon us.

I'm in position, watching around the corner as the beat-up, old, gray pickup comes to a standstill in a plume of dust, music still rocking on.

I move back out of sight and listen as two doors open and the music is silenced. Two male voices are joking about. They sound like full-on rednecks. They're now arguing over who has dibs on the female stiff. Who gets to *fuck the stiff.*

*Motherfuckers!* I bellow inside my head, my hand starting to strangle the butt of my handgun, itching to use it.

And then, to my further disgust, I hear them counting out rock, paper, and scissors. We have a winner, and he's pretty pleased with himself as he hollers in excitement.

I peer around the corner again with my gun raised and ready. They've gotten out of the pickup, which is parked about thirty feet away from where I'm hidden, and make their way to the hangar door, no guns in sight.

I step out, gun pointed as I prowl toward them. "Hands up, motherfuckers, and take it nice and slow."

And that's when shit goes down.

# BOXER

## Dehydration's a Bitch

"Lincoln, are you awake?" My question is met with silence. We've been here too many days already.

I managed to use the cuff master key to undo the screws on the vent and retrieve the bottle of water for myself, and Lincoln had done the same with the one in his heel.

Always be prepared; it could save your life in this line of work, but in this case, I think it only prolonged it.

We have rationed our water intake out, but still, one bottle isn't going to sustain us. I was hoping by now a miracle would have happened, and a rescue party would have arrived.

This is a deadly game I'm beginning to believe we will see to our demise. We aren't getting out of here alive. We have been left to die, with nobody the wiser to our whereabouts.

The coward couldn't even face us and shoot.

Fuck Grady, and fuck the arsehole who walked out, leaving us.

I'm fatigued and have a blistering headache—the joys of dehydration. I feel sad and pissed off the chances are diminishing every hour of seeing Whisper or Miss Catherine and Evelyn ever again.

MacGyver may have been able to make some mechanism to blow that fucking door off its hinges, but I have squat. The door is impenetrable from our end. It isn't looking good for us, and I can't help Whisper out of the trouble I know she is facing.

What must Miss Catherine be thinking?

What's happening to Whisper?

I have failed them both.

Lincoln is in a bad way, but he makes light of his injury and I'm doing okay. Not being able to get to him angers me. There was no reason to have separated us other than for it to be a game, a mind fuck.

*We're totally screwed.*

"*Lincoln!*" I shout out because I need to keep him awake, if only for my own sanity, my own selfish, lonely demise.

"Fuck off, Boxer." I hear him chuckle softly. My boy is still here with me and he isn't giving up.

"You out of water, buddy?" I pray he has been sipping like I have.

"Yeah."

"How you holding up?" I know he's in agonizing pain every time he moves. I hear the noises he makes.

"Same." I know he lies. It would be worse.

It would appear we're out of options. Not unless a fairy godmother comes and waves her wand and rescues us... we're royally fucked.

Nobody has a clue where we are, and that is the sad truth, or they would have been here by now.

"Hey, Lincoln, when we get out of here, how about I buy you a top-notch juicy steak?" We are being slowly starved to death, and that's not a pleasant thought.

"Sounds good to me." I hear another sad chuckle. The kid knows the chances are next to none.

I've been sending out a prayer or two for Whisper and Miss Catherine, hoping somebody is out there helping them, doing what I can't. I promised Whisper I would never let anybody hurt her again, and I have broken that promise.

"Hey, Boxer?"

"Yeah, mate."

"Wouldn't hurt to pray."

"Been doing it for a while now, Linc."

"Can you throw in a couple coldies with that steak?" The kid is keeping appearances up.

"Yeah, Linc, I think I can do that." I can't hide the

stupid smile that has leaked onto my face because a steak and a cold beer sound pretty good about now.

    We both fall silent, locked inside our minds.

    We've made our peace.

    We've said our prayers.

    It's just a matter of time.

# EDGE

## Checks and Balances

Concealed handguns come out in a blur, and the rednecks were all business.

*Two bullets to maim.*

Before they can even make a play for me, the muted sound of my gun goes off and I shoot the carrot top straight through his bare kneecap, blowing it out as blood spray paints the air, raining down. I'm instantly swinging my gun around toward the long-haired, dirty blond, ready to pump off another shot, but he's already falling sideways, holding his hipbone, moaning, and cursing. Blood seeps out between his fingers as I note out of my peripheral vision Carrot Top has dropped like the wounded fucker he is, clutching at his knee from the agonizing pain.

*What the fuck?*

I hadn't gotten my second shot off, and I was aiming for the blond fucker's kneecap.

I risk a quick glance over my shoulder at Annie Oakley, who has her gun trained on the dirty blond, more than willing to invest another bullet in him from the look of sheer uncensored anger mixed with triumph on her face.

*I gather she heard the gutter-assholes playing rock, paper, and scissors.*

I kick the weapons out of their hands before they can rise above the pain and come to their senses. My trigger-happy finger is ready for any sudden movements from either of these boys. "Hands up, the both of you, and act like statues. Grab for a concealed weapon, and I'll make the next bullet count."

The fuckers probably still have more weapons on them and may just want to grow a hero complex and reach for them.

Thug 101: Always carry more than one weapon on your person.

Hunter 101: Always be prepared for the fucker to reach for it.

They're your homegrown breed of redneck. They stink of cigarettes and moonshine, and they each have the makings of a genuine beer gut. They are clothed in open plaid shirts with cut-off sleeves and a wife beater underneath, and shorts that haven't seen a washing machine in days. They have faces only a mother could love without fault. Their hair is long and scruffy, and their teeth... even a dentist would run from those fucked up chompers.

Miss Catherine drops the gun into her knitted jacket pocket and is now taking it upon herself to use Blondie's head as a puck. She viciously hockey sticks one of my crutches into the side of his head, snapping it sideways, rendering him unconscious on an unladylike grunt.

*I'm impressed. Eighty-plus years old and she didn't hesitate to take him out.*

Here I was thinking the old lady didn't know the ass from the business end of a gun. I arch an eyebrow at her at what she's just done.

"What? You be sayin' to point and shoot, so I be doin' as you say. I be a fast learner, although I be aimin' for his penis." She sounds annoyed she missed. I suppose it's one less fucker to worry about.

I'm not used to being ignored, and I need to articulate I'm not impressed with her random, Annie-Oakley, gun-toting ways, even though I am. I won't admit I'm feeling a little proud of Padawan.

"I told you to fucking stay inside the hangar until I came for you." I grind my words out in a low voice. I need to be in control for her safety. "I had it under control. This isn't my first rodeo." If only she knew how talented I was, she would be running in the other direction.

I'm beginning to expect the unexpected with this old lady. She's much tougher than she looks. She's a fighter. Something ... someone in her past has made her this way. It's all hidden away until called upon. She's definitely seen darker days.

"I didn't listen." Miss Catherine has sass.

"Obviously," I say dryly out the corner of my mouth.

I watch on in slight amusement, as she gets ready to batter up again and take a swing at Carrot Top. I shake my head. *Did she not hear what I just said?*

I'm beginning to see she is a little unpredictable when push comes to shove. "Whoa there, Miss Catherine. I got this one. I need to be able to pry some information out of him, and if you knock them both out, then I have to go wasting time waking up one of these fucked up dickwads." I take the crutch away from her just in case she decides to take a whack at him and use it instead to steady myself.

"Bad Guy One, do you have a name?" I refer to Carrot Top. Fucker responds by howling a curse and spitting at my feet. I sidestep just in time. "I guess not. Names aren't important, but for my own amusement, I hereby name you Fucknuts, but don't get too comfy with it, because we won't be getting to know each other that well. I've just got some questions I need answering, and then we will be on our way. Not unless you want to attempt to draw this out?"

He ignores my words, baring his rotten teeth through his pain like a wild animal. I don't blame him; that's gotta hurt like the blazes of hell.

I've got things to say, so I pistol-whip Fucknuts across the face to make sure he is gonna pay attention to me, and remind him who's in charge, which of course has him cursing at me on a raging cacophony of anger.

I check the old lady's body language because I don't want to do too much to this asshole in front of her. She appears to be handling my behavior fine. All I get is a disapproving look for pistol-whipping the guy. I roll my eyes because she thinks I'm only playing with him.

*Think again, lady. This is a PG-rated show just for you. You don't wanna see what I can really do.*

I can be a scary fucker when I want to be. I need to get her away from here so I can get down to R-rated business. Every minute spent here is taking its toll on Whisper's wellbeing.

"Miss Catherine, could you go back inside the hangar and wheel out that comfortable looking office chair, so we can make Fucknuts here a bit more amenable. I was gonna tell him to get on his knees, but I can see that isn't gonna be conducive to him thinking straight, 'cause that knee's gotta be hurting like a son-of-a-bitch."

I have to hand it to her; she's a trooper. She goes and gets that office chair and wheels it back in front of us. I know I'm ordering her about, but I have to be the strong arm here because he would have that gun out of her hand in a shake.

I give her a tight smile because I know she must be worried about what my next move is... and so she should be. I'm only just getting started.

I would definitely label these guys wild cards. They have no self-preservation. I doubt there is a kindergarten IQ between them. They are cleanup boys, and sickos to boot.

I hand Miss Catherine the keys to the Beamer. "Bring the car back around behind me." She listens and does as I say without any deviation of her own. I think she has registered this guy is still a danger, and I need to keep him under control, and we need information.

"Now, Fucknuts, load yourself onto that chair without any fuss, and you may just make it out of here alive today. Let that be your incentive." I place the mouth of the silencer, trigger cocked on my gun, against the side of his head, so he fully understands the position he's in as he gets himself seated.

The car is parked behind me, and the old lady waits beside me for my next command. She knows I'm dealing with a sick fucker who needs to be kept on a tight leash.

"Fucknuts, before we get down to business, as there is a lady present and I don't want any surprises, do you have any concealed weapons on you?"

"No," he growls at me. Grumpy prick.

"Miss Catherine, pat him down for me, but stay behind him or the side of him at all times. Fucknuts, I need you to listen to her when she tells you which way to move, so she can make sure you're telling the truth. If you're not... the other knee gets blown out. Understand?"

"Yes," he snarls. The fucker isn't very happy with me. Miss Catherine does an excellent job of patting him down and he comes up clean. Then she pats down the sleeping beauty. Stupid bastards were too confident and turned up without reading the Thug 101 manual properly.

"Miss Catherine, there's a little black bag in the trunk. Could you get it for me? There are some things in there that will come in mighty handy." She walks to the trunk, opening it, and holds up *No Mercy.* I nod my head.

The guy is now death-staring me, which is kinda amusing, considering who has the gun trained on them. You would think he would wisen up to his predicament.

I repeat, *No self-preservation.*

The old lady brings *No Mercy* over to me and

places it on the hood. "Unzip it and take out the duct tape."

I enlighten Fucknuts, "Miss Catherine here is just gonna tape your hands and feet as a precautionary measure, and also your good buddy, just in case he wakes up from his snooze. It will also stop any wayward thoughts you may have of being heroes and getting your heads blown off."

I shift my body slightly so I can lean up against the doc's car, trying to unburden my fucked up foot, while I watch as Miss Catherine starts duct taping his hands together behind the chair good and proper, and then each foot gets taped to its legs.

"What... the... fuck... are you two... doing here?" Which comes out in a deep-south, toothless twang.

My guy is a real trooper, pushing through the pain, panting out his words, and somehow coming to the conclusion that an old lady and myself might not be that big a deal, and he thinks we owe him an explanation.

*He would be wrong.*

I ignore his question and watch Miss Catherine do a pretty neat job of taping him up, and then she moves on to unconscious mullet-man and binds his wrists and legs tight until he's trussed up like a Thanksgiving turkey.

"Fucknuts, you might wanna stop moving about so much, because the gun could accidentally go off."

I shrug. "No loss to me. I've still got another guinea pig to interrogate. I can wake him up from his nap easy enough." He grudgingly cooperates and keeps his head neatly on his shoulders.

These two rednecks have proven they have game. I'm not taking any chances with a conscious one around the old lady.

Miss Catherine has finished and joined me, resting against the Beamer, waiting patiently, if not looking slightly at ease with my behavior.

"Are you the cleanup crew? Are there more of you coming, and did I hear you two sick fucks straight? Were you two playing rock, paper, and scissors to see who was going to stick their dick inside the female corpse?" I nudge his head with the gun for good measure. "My hand is feeling mighty shaky at the moment."

"Okay... I'll answer... you crazy fuck." Pot calling kettle black.

*No self-preservation. He'll learn soon enough.*

"Be warned I'm very good at judging a liar. If you still have a head on your shoulders after you give me your answers, that means I believed you. Up to you if you wanna hedge your bets on whether your lie passes the test. The one thing you'll get used to in the time we'll get to know each other is... I only ask once, and then if I don't like what I hear or don't hear, I take action. I don't give second chances or respond well to pleading or begging, so man up and we will get along like a house on fire." I know the answer to the last question, but I gotta hear this cocksucker say it.

His mouth starts to open, but I've forgotten my manners. "Before you answer, allow me to introduce myself. I'm Edge, and I'm the enforcer for the Soulless Bastards Motorcycle Club. Ever heard of them?"

The fucker registers in that fucked up head of his the deep shit he's in. Is that a wet spot I can see on his pants? Did he just piss himself? He's definitely looking at me with a newly found respect.

"I thought you might have heard of us." I give him a pleasant smile, lean forward, and press my hand down on his shattered kneecap, his pathetic whimpering an embarrassment. "Now you can answer."

"Yes... Homer... was gonna get... to fuck the corpse." He lets out a hiss of pain as he talks through those ugly gritted teeth. "And we're... the only ones coming. We're the... cleanup crew." From the look of fear in his eyes, I know the quarter has hit the bottom of the gumball machine, finally, and he registers the deep shit he's in.

*We have a winner. The fucker is telling the truth.*

"You're the lazy cleanup crew, which should have been here how many days ago?"

He goes to nod his head and stops himself.

"Use your words. It will be a little safer for you." My trigger finger is barely containing the urge to shoot this sick fuck between the eyes so he can see it coming.

"Yes... we are. Shoulda been here a few days ago." I'm not sure if he's sweating buckets from his injury, or if I've got him scared shitless.

"See, that wasn't hard at all, was it, Fucknuts?" I remove the gun and slap him across the back of the head. "We're gonna get along just fine. Your laziness worked in our favor." I point to myself and Miss Catherine.

"There are always checks and balances for the things we decide to take on in life." I pause for effect. "For example, if you've undertaken the job of disposing of dead bodies for some bad guys, and you are a couple of lazy dickwads who get caught talking about fucking one of those bodies, then karma is gonna come and get you.

"Take me, for instance. I'm an enforcer, and I've killed many a bad fucker, never an innocent. I dispose of my own bodies, in a timely fashion. I dig my own holes, no sub-contracting. I really put my back into leaving no loose ends.

"Defiling those bodies doesn't even enter my head because I ain't a sicko. Know what I'm saying?" I'm using my hunter voice. Motherfucker has no clue what's coming.

"Speaking of which, one of those bodies inside the hangar is known and under the protection of the Lion's Den MC, and they have been missing this person. It also happens to be the female you were gonna corpse-fuck." I let that sink in and watch the asshole take a deep swallow. "My club is also missing a young lady, and as of recently, I happen to be missing another one. They're all under our club's protection, and we don't take these women going missing lightly. Hell, you and I are gonna get acquainted, and you will see how badly we feel about what's happened. The Lion's Den MC will be coming to claim the body you were contracted to dispose of, and their retribution list has just gotten a couple more sign ups."

*The fucker has the good sense to look terrified. He has every reason to be.*

"Now, I'm gonna send Miss Catherine for a walk around the back of the hangar, where she is gonna wait for me because she is a lady and doesn't need to hear the rest of our conversation."

I look over at her and give her a look that brooks no challenge. "Go take yourself out back and wait for me to come for you. This time, I need you to listen to me." I've got my calm-before-the-shit-storm hunter voice on. The deadly one, which gives the underlying message to her without any confusion of what is about to go down.

She nods she understands and wanders off around the corner. I hope she does as she is told this time. Anything is possible with her. There is no other place for her to go unless I put her back in that hangar with those dead bodies. If I could, I would be dragging this guy off into the woods. But I can't. I have to make do.

I turn back to Fucknuts. "Start spilling your guts. I want to know names, numbers, and addresses."

The idiot is suddenly hard of hearing, so I help his memory along and unzip *No Mercy* slowly. "Fucknuts, I would like to introduce you to *No Mercy*, my little bag I use for interrogation. See, it's not about size; it's often about the little things and where they get positioned on the body that can really hurt a guy into talking. Are you circumcised?"

"What... the... fuck!" The idiot suddenly regains his hearing and is a little confused by the turn of events.

*I thought I was clear enough.*

"I don't like repeating myself. You don't answer my question the first time, I take action." I snap on a pair of disposable blue gloves I carry around in *No Mercy* for such occasions and unzip his pants.

"Get the fuck away from me!" he hollers, spit flying as he struggles against his binds, while I dig around until I find his pathetic cock and flop it out.

I give him a warm smile. "Well, take a lookie at

that little slug. Not circumcised! Looks like you're in luck. I've circumcised a man or two in my day. I wouldn't say it was a medically approved job, but nonetheless, I managed to pull it off." I pause and admire my humor in the moment. "Well, look there. I think I just made a joke." I could almost laugh at that pun, but time is wasting.

I cut a piece of duct tape off and then lunge at him, clamping his neck in a headlock, and slap it over his big ol' mouth because this motherfucker is gonna scream to God and all the archangels for help. He might even sell his soul to the devil. "You might want to hold still for this. It's a tricky procedure." Then I hold up a small razor blade and watch his eyes bulge. I grab a hold of his foreskin and get right to it, slicing away, making a bit of a mess, because Fucknuts doesn't listen to instructions and keeps on trying to thrust his body away from me.

By the time I was finished, I felt we might not need to move on to phase two. He sounded like he was trying to tell me some information, so I ripped the tape right off his mouth.

"You were saying?"

I remove my gloves. The only name he had was Jonathan Boothe.

*Bingo!*

I believed him. He sung like his life depended on it, which he really believed it did. When another man has your dick in his hands and he's slicing that fucker up, you tend to fess up.

They were told to be on standby and await instruction and were contacted four days ago. Two keys were left under a rock by the gate to get in here and the hangar.

They had been told to take pictures to prove the job was completed to get paid in cash, and they were to front up in Jackson to receive payment tomorrow in a dive bar called The Pitbull at lunchtime.

"Did this Jonathan Boothe contact you for the job?"

"No. Some other guy. Got no name." Then he pants his way through the rest of his answer. "Done previous jobs... before for various people, our names... were known in many circles. We always... got the jobs done. Always a burner... phone used so client... kept anonymous. This time... we got given... a name to ask for at The Pitbull, to be paid."

Neither of the rednecks was wearing a wedding ring. "You two live together?"

"Yes."

"Alone?" Fucknuts knows where this is headed.

"Yes." He sounds resigned.

"You ever raped a living female before?"

He lowers his eyes to the ground. I lift his shorts up and slice at an angle across his femoral artery as he lets out a scream, cursing me to the devil.

*Actions always get me answers.*

He's now bleeding all over the ground. He has minutes until death and he will lose consciousness soon. He knows he's dead, so he might as well purge himself and answer me.

"Yes." That one word comes out resigned to the fact he won't be walking away from here today alive. His life source is being drained.

"Anybody else know you were coming here today?"

"No."

"Just so you know, I'll be leaving Blondie alive in the hangar as a present for the Lion's Den MC. They will make sure your body is disposed of."

Whisper's phone beeps and a text comes in from Lethal. He has the name and address of the lawyer firm on my letter. Eaton Dapusé.

I Google Jonathan Boothe, and with too many to choose from, I do the same with the one from my letter.

*Nothing.*

I try calling the number associated with the lawyer firm on my letter and get, "This call cannot be connected."

And then I look at that name again.

*Motherfucker!*

Eaton Dapusé... Eating the pussy. You've got to be shitting me.

I look over at Fucknuts, but he's an unconscious man. The reaper is knocking on his door.

I hobble to their pickup and find two wallets in the console. I check their driver's licenses and Fucknuts' name is Ellwood, go figure, and the other guy's name is, indeed, Homer. I check for a business card or any information with Jonathan Boothe's name on it, but there's nothing, only a few small bills in each wallet and a burner phone under the seat.

I ask Google about a Boothe lawyer firm and Boothe & Brown comes up in Jackson, Mississippi.

*What are the chances?*

I call the number using the redneck's burner phone and get ready to impress.

I ask for a Jonathan Boothe and get told he is currently out of the office for the rest of the week.

*Again, what are the chances?*

"Ma'am, if you wouldn't mind, this is Stephen Boothe, a relative of Jonathan's, and I have a sudden death in the family I need to speak to him about. I don't have Jonathan's cell phone on me, only his work number." I put on my upset-family-emergency voice. "I urgently need to speak to him. Could you possibly give me his cell number, please?"

The line is quiet as she contemplates getting into trouble for giving out his private number. She's also mulling over getting into trouble if she doesn't let this man talk to his relative. The good person inside of her will relent, thinking nobody would call and make this shit up. "It really is *very* important I speak to him as soon as I can, ma'am."

Like taking candy from a baby. She dutifully hands over Jonathan's cell number.

*Stupid woman.*

I make the call. The line connects, and my Ellwood-redneck prepares to kick into gear. "Hello."

"Who is this, and why the *hell* are you calling me?" Not even a hello. The man has no manners. Jonathan sounds a tad put out.

"Jonathan, it's the cleanup crew, Ellwood and Homer. We need to meet tonight. Homer and I would like our money. Things are heatin' up and we want to get out of Dodge for a while." Can I sound any more like Fucknuts? The guy probably has never spoken to him before, but I can't take that chance. This operation the Puppet Master has going on has a lot of players.

He lets out a string of curses. "We shouldn't even be talking. How did you get my personal cell?"

"Googled your name and tried a few until we got onto your lovely secretary, who was quite helpful." I'm just making this shit up as I go along. He just needs to believe it. I just need the meet and greet tonight. I don't give a flying fuck how I get it.

"I'm firing that bitch," he mumbles. "Is the job completed?"

"Sure is, three bodies disposed of. Wouldn't be callin' you if it wasn't." *Cocksucker.*

"Meet me at The Pitbull at ten tonight on the dot. Now, don't call me again." He disconnects.

*Fucking idiot.*

I shove Ellwood's chair out of the way and let it fall backward. I snap off some photos of the rednecks and the cars and then hobble over to the corner of the hangar. What a surprise, guess who's parked herself just around the corner eavesdropping? I shake my head in disapproval at her. "Miss Catherine, we need to get to Jackson. ASAP."

"What about Santana's body?"

"We have to leave it. I'll make a call and her body will be retrieved. Loose ends will be tied up here." I just have to hope nobody comes back here until then. I haul Blondie's body inside the hangar and lock the door. Fucknuts can stay where he is.

We make our way back to the Beamer, and Miss Catherine doesn't seem to show any signs of shock at what's happened to Fucknuts. She just picks up the crutches and gets in the driver's seat, and I scoop *No Mercy* up off the hood and get in the backseat because I need to put my foot up and rest for what's gonna go down tonight.

"Need to let Evelyn know where we be headin'," she says quietly.

"Miss Catherine, if we're gonna find Whisper

alive, we need to step on this lead, now. We can call the doc along the way if it makes you feel better. Head on out of here, and I'm gonna make some calls." This is starting to get bigger than just me and an old lady, and I need Santana's body taken care of.

*Fuck my privacy.*

Miss Catherine pulls out, and I send Hazard a code and wait for him to call me.

I have to get what I can out of this Jonathan Boothe. The trail is cold here. I fear Whisper may even be out of the country by now. This is also the first sign of hope for Ruby being alive. Too much coincidence in their disappearances being close together, one from my club, one from the one we have an alliance with, and now Whisper. Two out of these three missing ladies have wound up in the one place, this hangar. I can't help feeling my father has a part in this whole circle of women gone missing.

The phone rings. "Hazard, things have gotten more complicated. I need that backup now." He listens while I explain everything and let him know what I need done. The old lady can hear Hazard cursing down the line. I tell him about Santana, and he says he'll contact Torque, President of Lion's Den MC, and they will send club members on a flight out to get Santana and drive her back, and they'll clean up the mess of bodies. They won't need keys to gain access.

## WARPED

I set the GPS up on Miss Catherine's phone for The Pitbull in Jackson, and chew on a painkiller and close my eyes for a bit. We got a three-hour drive ahead of us.

If Homer's still kicking... he'll wish he wasn't.

# BOXER

## Boom Boom Boom Shake Shake the Room

*BOOM!*
*BOOM!*
BOOM!

I roll over on the hard cement. Christ sake! I know I've got the mother of all headaches working overtime pounding my gray matter to a pulp, but it's not this loud.

*BOOM!*
*BOOM!*
*BOOM!*

I'm starving, dehydrated, and weak.

I listen again.

There's nothing but silence and my throbbing headache.

I croak out weakly to Lincoln, "Linc... mate, you awake?"

There's no reply.

*Jesus Christ!*

And then it starts up again.

*BOOM!*

*BOOM!*

*BOOM!*

I drag myself over to the door and put my palm flat to it.

*BOOM!*

*BOOM!*

*BOOM!*

There's silence for a few minutes.

I think maybe I'm dreaming this shit up. I'm not feeling too good, so I let myself lie back. My eyes drift shut and then...

*KABOOM!*

*That sounded like an explosion.*

Wait, I thought I heard a voice. I concentrate on listening.

"Fuck! Lincoln!"

That was definitely a voice hollering through the air vent, not unless the hallucinations are playing with me.

"Wake up!" Nope, not hallucinations, I'm definitely hearing a voice. "Aww, thank Christ." The voice sounds relieved. "Lincoln, buddy, here's some water. Open your mouth a little and take it easy." It's a familiar voice, and then I hear Lincoln coughing. I run the voice through my memory bank.

*Ghost?*

"Ghost?" I croak into the vent as loud as I can muster. "You... really here?" My lips are so dry.

"Joel, quiet down. I can hear someone." There is a pause. "I'll disconnect unless you put a lid on it. He's safe now. I need to listen, so zip it."

Am I hearing things? Is my mind indeed playing tricks on me? He's talking to Joel?

*"Joel?"*

Odd. Can't hear Joel talking.

Everything's gone quiet. I try again, hope burrowing its way inside me. "Is Lincoln okay, Ghost?"

"Boxer?"

"Yeah. Air vent. Talk... into it," I rasp. I have no saliva left in my mouth. It's as dry as dust. "Linc?" That one word comes out on a beg. I need to know.

"He's alive, Boxer. Just passed out on me again. Hold on a sec, buddy, just talking to Joel on the phone at the same time. He's pretty anxious to hear you've both been found." I can wait a few more minutes. "I've got them both, Joel. Just gotta bust Boxer out of his cell now. He's gotta be in the next locked room," I hear Ghost's deep voice relaying to Joel. Call me back in a few minutes." Everything goes silent for several beats too long.

"Getting you out next. You hurt badly?" Ghost's deep voice is booming at me through the vent.

We. Had. Been. Found.

"I'll live." I try to chuckle, but I only end up dry-coughing.

"Boxer, mate, stay by the air vent. Gonna blow your door. You got me?"

"Yeah. How… did you find… us?"

"Short version, Joel's in the hospital. He got a hold of me when he was able to, and being the genius hacker he is, he found a breadcrumb on your phone's last location and Lincoln's. They matched and here I am. Took a bit of figurin' where you were exactly, because you are underground. Clever fucks have it camouflaged."

"Grady… double-crossed us. He got… wasted." I want to tell him a whole lot more, but I just don't have it in me.

I hear a mile of cursing. "Save it for later, Boxer. Time to get you free, so stay clear."

I can't even give a fuck about the stench Ghost's about to walk into. I've pissed and shitted in this cell. Nothing to be done for it.

Thank fuck we've been found. I can now get onto finding Whisper.

I'm so tired I don't even brace for the *KABOOM!*

# EDGE

## Mocha-chocolate

We're staked out a couple cars back from a street light across the road from The Pitbull. It's definitely a dive bar. Perfect place to meet up and not be noticed if you're a redneck; not so much if you are a suited up lawyer. Makes me wonder why he chose this place.

I know who we're looking for because the smug fucker has his picture up on his website. We've been out front for forty-five minutes and haven't seen him enter, and it's just now ten o'clock. Time to take a walk inside.

I'd filled the car up with gas and bought a couple chargers for the phones once we hit Jackson, and then we picked up food at a drive-thru burger joint. I hadn't realized how hungry I was for real food because all I've had for days is IV juice. I've swallowed more pills to ease the pain in my foot, but I'd get shot in the other foot if it meant bringing

Whisper back alive for this old lady.

I've just swapped Whisper's phone for hers, just in case Hazard tries to contact me while I'm in The Pitbull. She knows to send a two-digit code to her phone, and I will respond. I also want it in case her lost boys try to contact her, and I'm not around to manage the response.

"Miss Catherine, you are to stay put and lay low keeping the doors locked." I give her my don't-fuck-with-me-this-time stare from the front passenger seat and give her back the handgun. "It's loaded." She's proven herself capable and knows how to use it. "No heroic stuff. If a bad guy is coming for you or your life is threatened, drive off, or make the bullet count. You got me?"

Her hand shoots out and grabs my wrist. "Be careful." I look down at her crooked fingers for a beat and then get out of the car and make my way to the bar. Christ, I hope she listens for once. I can't be worrying about her safety and whereabouts while I'm inside.

This fucking moonboot actually works for me with my look for the evening. We'd stopped off and I got myself decked out in some genuine redneck attire. I wanted to be Ellwood and didn't know if this bastard had met me before and would recognize me, but from a distance, I might pass until I can get a better hold on the situation.

I haven't shaved in days or had a proper shower. I was cleaned up under Doc Evelyn's care, but that's been it. I look like a man who needs a strong drink.

I pull the cap down low over my eyes as I enter the dimly lit bar. A couple dozen patrons are scattered about. I carefully scan the joint, but I can't see the cocksucker anywhere.

Maybe he's doing what I'm doing, blending in?

I make my way to the end of the U-shaped bar and take a seat, positioning myself so I can see anybody entering or leaving. I order a beer and take another closer look at the drinkers at the tables. Nobody resembles that fucker's picture, and nobody is paying me any attention.

I spend twenty minutes waiting. By now, I figure he's not coming. I signal to the old scruffy-looking bartender to get his attention, thinking the prick might have sniffed a rat and either dropped a package off for Homer or Ellwood earlier or ran out on their contract. I'm contemplating our next move when Miss Catherine's phone rings.

*I told her to fucking code me first.*

And then I feel a gun low in my side as a big man slides onto the stool next to me, and the phone is snatched out of my hand.

"Where's Miss Catherine?" a deep, smooth voice says against my ear.

*Christ! Now the fucking Calvary's decided to show*

up. *Must have finally gotten around to tracking her phone.*

I'm nudged in the side with the gun. "Take a walk. Nice and slow, Edge. Move!"

*Knows my name. My guess, he has been speaking with Doc Evelyn.*

I'm not holding the deck of cards, so I have to play along. "Hold your horses there, buddy. Sounds like we are playing for the same team. You can remove that gun and we can have an intelligent conversation."

*Formal introductions have gone by the wayside.*

"Maybe so, but not going to happen. Doc Evelyn says Miss Catherine's traveling with a man, and you got her phone. We tracked it to here and looks like I just made it in time to catch up to you. Got no time for shenanigans, because the lives of Whisper's friends depend on me getting you outta here ASAP and locating Miss Catherine."

I go to get up. "Don't do anything stupid. Doc Evelyn's given us your rundown. Know who you are and be respectin' you are dangerous, and I also know you are ex-military and trained, and so am I...." He pauses for effect. "And just as dangerous." Cue rolling my eyes. "Miss Catherine and Whisper are our top priorities. Where is the lady?" He works himself up to a deep growl.

"She's safe outside in the car. I'll take you to h—"

"Nope. Saw Doc Evelyn's car, but nobody inside. Want to rethink that answer?" The gun gets pushed harder into me. "If you've laid one—" And cue the threats.

I slowly turn sideways to look at him. A mocha-skinned, big, pretty military type has now got the gun against my lower abdomen, and he's not fucking around from the grim look on his face. I wouldn't be fucking around either.

*Why does it not surprise me she didn't stay put?* And then a more sinister thought hits me. *Or did something happen to her?*

"Edge! Ghost!" Our names come out in a hushed, anxious tone.

*Thank fuck for that.* A sense of relief washes over me. At least a bad guy hadn't swiped her.

"She just doesn't seem to get the concept of doing as she's told," I mutter, and see a hint of relief touch the big guy's eyes, but they don't leave me. He's all business as she makes it over to us.

"You are well, Miss Catherine?" He doesn't take his eyes off me, nor his finger off the trigger when she stops next to him.

*Smart man.*

"Of course, Ghost. Good to see you." *Ghost?* Fucker's got a curious handle. She gives him a one-armed hug at his side. "Just been terrified for Whisper and worryin' about Boxer and Lincoln."

She lowers her voice, moves a step closer to where I'm seated, and puts a hand on my shoulder in a show of solidarity. "No harm been done to me. I been safe with this man.

*Fuck's sake, like I'm out to beat up on old ladies.*

He hands her phone to her and she pockets it. "Ghost, put your gun away and be leavin' him alone. We all be on the same page. I be vouchin' for this man. Dem bones of mine never lie."

*Dem bones?*

"He's got some explainin' to be doin', some regrets to put to bed and some forgivin' to be requestin', but now's not the time or the meetin' place. More importantly, have you found Whisper? Where's Boxer and Lincoln? Are they all right?"

"No. They're here. Not exactly," he replies in a nutshell.

Then she looks at me, assuming this big guy is going to take her word straight off the bat, put his weapon away, and have ourselves a tea party. "Did you get what you be comin' in here for? I been worried." From the look on her face, I believe she was actually worried about me.

"Nope. Just about to have a word with the bartender." I ignore the gun and turn, signaling for the bartender to come over.

"Package for Ellwood or Homer?" I bring my best redneck to the table.

The wiry old guy looks me over and shakes his head in the negative. "Been here since opening and no package been dropped." His gravelly voice sounds worn out from smoking and drinking. Jonathan just put himself on my wanted-man list. Fucker's got answers I want to be hearing because now the bastard ran scared from my earlier call.

I know Mocha-chocolate is listening. I settle my tab and get up. We all move toward the door. Mocha-chocolate positions himself next to me, keeping Miss Catherine on his right. That gun will be hidden, but still trained on me as he directs the conversation toward her.

"Heard you decided to go on a road trip with a total stranger. Doc Evelyn briefed us. Now, what's Boxer gonna be thinking about that?" He looks at the old lady with affection.

"Nobody else be available to be helpin' me. Couldn't be sittin' about waitin' when Whisper's life been on the line. Edge been lookin' after me."

*This guy doesn't seem the wiser about my original intentions and follow through toward Whisper.*

He stops outside the bar. "Before we go over to our car, I need to warn you of a few things. Joel's been beaten to a pulp. He has a lot of internal injuries, so he was out of commission for a few days and is still in the hospital. He managed to sweet talk a nurse into letting him borrow her computer, and he's been helping me from his hospital bed."

"He be okay?" She's worried for this Joel. He's a friend, but not close enough to warrant swapping phone numbers.

"He'll live. Tough guy." He rubs a hand over his closely cropped dark hair. "Cutting a long story short, Lincoln and Boxer been MIA, as you know. After not being able to get through to Boxer or Lincoln, Joel called Doc Evelyn to see if she heard from either of them. She let him know about what had been going on from your end." He arches a dark eyebrow. "The limited amount you cared to disclose to her.

"Joel's next plan was to hack my personal information and get a hold of my cell number. Never had a situation for anybody other than Boxer to need my personal details before." He shrugs. "I'm a private man. He'd already hacked their phones and found out the last breadcrumb, the last location those phones were at." He looks over at me, deciding whether I should be listening to any of this. "How they got into that mess, I'll explain later.

"Doc Evelyn has a thing for Boxer, even though they both won't admit it, and she arranged a set of wheels to come to Jackson as soon as she could. And Joel's been keeping her up-to-date on everything." He taps his ear. "He's listening in right now.

"This brings me to Boxer and Lincoln. They've

both had it pretty rough, with broken bones and being left to starve to death." Miss Catherine's hand flies up to her mouth. "They'll live. Done what I can for them. I picked up a bag of medical supplies Doc Evelyn had organized for me to collect after I gave her their medical update of injuries that I could physically see. Was on my way to meet up with Doc Evelyn, and she'll be able to look after them better than the makeshift job I've done for them."

We start walking again and make it over to the Beamer, where a black, fully tinted SUV has boxed us in.

*No prizes for guessing whose.*

I can see through the front window there are people inside the car. One is in the front passenger seat laid out horizontally with the seat jacked back and part of another body is lying across the backseat. Neither appears to be moving. The old lady tries to get to the back passenger door, but the guy holds her arm, stopping her from getting any closer.

"I'll warn you, they look bad. I found them in a large bunker underground in the woods outside of Jackson. I got to them in time. Doc Evelyn knew you two were headed to Jackson, so Joel got the GPS working on your phones and here I am. I didn't call you ahead..." He looks at me. "Didn't want the man with you to know I was coming in. We realize none of this was coincidence. It was a cleverly hatched plan to get Whisper alone, and we're hoping you can fill in some blanks." He lets go of her arm.

Miss Catherine hurries to the back door, swinging it open, while I follow on behind. These are her people, but I made a promise to her. She opens the door and then kneels down next to a guy who looks to be in his mid-forties and is out cold. I take a good look at the two unconscious men buckled up. Both have fucked up legs and are hooked up to IV bags hanging from the oh-shit roof handles.

Before anybody else can get another word out, a car pulls up beside us in a hurry to stop, and my concealed gun is out swinging in its direction.

And then a gun is shoved into the side of my head. Mocha-chocolate is the voice of reason. "Easy, Edge, lower your weapon. It's Doc Evelyn to see to Boxer and Lincoln. Joel's been feeding her our location, and those men need her immediate attention." I only have to hear Doc Evelyn's name and the gun is being holstered, and I no longer have one at my head.

She's out of the car, running over to the SUV with a bag, and starts checking them over, mumbling to herself. Sounds like she's cursing their day job.

Mocha-chocolate gives me a rundown. "Lincoln, the blond, younger guy, is Whisper's best friend. And the other guy, Boxer, is as good as Whisper's father." I don't like hearing her best friend is male. It actually sends a streak of emotion through me I don't want to identify, and I've only spent a few hours with her. I only know her favorite and least favorite movies, that she really isn't a beer drinker, and she can't lie for shit.

And... she's *my* sweet and wild girl.

*I don't know where that came from.*

"Edge, we're gonna take it from here. You can go back to Albuquerque. Whisper is no longer your concern. Appreciate what you have done for Miss Catherine, and she can fill in any missing blanks Doc Evelyn couldn't, which I assume is a fair bit. Not unless you got anything you want to add?" Mocha-chocolate thinks he has this all worked out.

"'Fraid I have to beg to differ... hot shot. I've made Whisper my business."

*Fuck you very much.*

Now, I appreciate these people are her people, but I am now involved, whether they like it or not. We glare at each other, which does nothing for anybody. Too much testosterone in the air for my liking and that shit makes men dangerous.

"Ain't leavin' Jackson, got a man to locate with a cell number and would appreciate a little heads up on his whereabouts."

We continue our stare-fest.

Mocha-chocolate waves the white flag first.

"Boxer's been mumbling the name Jonathan Boothe over and over before he completely passed out. Seems like the name was mighty important to him. Joel and I concur and now remember seeing it on the original will." He raises an eyebrow at me. "Any of that ring a bell to you?" He's baiting me. Sniffer dog is out.

*Ding! Ding! Ding!*

"Jonathan Boothe is a name we have in common." That's all I am willing to concede at this point. Miss Catherine hasn't jumped in to announce who I am. Mocha-chocolate hasn't shot me, so I gather I'm still under the radar for my sins against Whisper and my biological connection.

*Why?*

Sounds like she didn't divulge this information to the good doctor, or she would have told this guy already.

*Wouldn't she?*

I will take what's coming to me once she is safe.

I need to get moving. "If you can get your boy onto the cell number I hold for Boothe, I'll be on my way. Just need a location to get started. He can stop tracking Whisper and Miss Catherine's phones, because she's in possession of them, and stay on that one for me. It's the one solid lead we have at the moment." Miss Catherine hands over a piece of paper she jotted it down on to the guy, and he starts rattling off the numbers to Joel.

"I'll be sure to let you know what I find out tonight, Miss Catherine." She looks like she wants to say something to me and Mocha-chocolate isn't liking I'm getting all bossy, but I don't give a fuck. "We can work together to find Whisper." He's still eyeing me up.

"What's your stake in this... with Whisper?" he asks me, his tone deadly serious now. "Before, you were Miss Catherine's only help, found her on the side of the road. Had your own troubles prior to that meetup and got yourself bashed and shot in the foot."

*So that's the magical mystery explanation of what went down. Fuck's sake, ladies.*

"I ain't buying that explanation. Your enthusiasm for Whisper and her plight isn't sitting well with me."

I don't suppose he'll believe, *'Many hands make light work.'* I start to tell him William Dupré is my father, but Miss Catherine starts chattering.

"Because he be makin' a promise to me to find her and he been keepin' it." She's trying to give me an out, but I don't need protecting from an old lady.

*Far from it. I made my bed.*

I can pay my own bills.

I look the big man directly in his eyes. "Because William Dupré is my father and that fucker has hailed shit down on Whisper for a lifetime, as I have just discovered, and here's the kicker... I shot her in the shoulder."

A thunderous noise fills the street, and I watch a lion heading my way, still roaring as he aims to fuck with me good and proper.

On an *ooph*, my body's slammed into the hard road, and I have to let the guy have his due as he swings punch after punch down on me. I can't fight him because I would do the same if the roles were reversed.

*I would do worse.*

*Much, much worse.*

I feel a tooth dislodge itself, my lip split, and a black eye or two will reveal themselves soon enough.

*Nothing I haven't survived before.*

My mind drifts away and I'm the young boy again, weighed down by my father as he hammers me into submission. I used to fight back, kicking and screaming, trying to protect myself, until I learned to take my punishment because I surely deserved what he was windmilling down on my body. No father would do this to their child unless they had done something so bad they needed to be set right. The thing is, I could never work out what that was.

My cheek is smashed to the side, bringing me back into the present, as I lay with my hands at my sides while he gets a few more solid hits in... until he realizes I ain't fighting him back. This is just a down payment for my past actions toward the sweet and wild girl.

*The fucker sure can hit hard.*

He yanks me up to my feet, blood pouring out of a gash on the side of my head, blinding me in that eye. I can feel my stitches have opened up on the back of my head. I would assume I look a right fucking mess about now.

*Penance can be a painful pill to swallow.*

"*Enough!*" the old lady screeches, and fuck if that doesn't stop Mocha-chocolate in his tracks as he shoves me back a few steps and I plant my feet, steadying myself. "I know what he gone and done. I be knowin' from the first night he be in my home. I'm not happy about it, and Whisper knowin' he be the one who shot her, but she be the one in danger. Let us not be forgettin' that. He be doin' wrong, but dem bones of mine be tellin' me to take a giant leap of faith and trust this man to be doin' the right thing from here on out."

*What's with 'dem bones' again?*

"That's all he been doin' since he made his big mistake. He be knowin' he did wrong. He not even fightin' you, Ghost. It takes a man who be knowin' he's at fault to lay there and let another man pummel him when he be quite capable of layin' you out with a bullet to the brain. I've seen what he been able to do to a man. Whisper be makin' the judgment call on whether she be forgivin' him or not. That be what he has to look forward to and be livin' with.

"I be explainin' in more detail once we get Boxer and Lincoln seen to. They die because you be takin' the time to beat up on a man who is beatin' up on himself enough in his mind over what he gone and done... do you think Whisper be any happier? Do you think bein' William Dupré's son been easy on him? Do you think he didn't get his fair share of William's insanity rained down upon him?"

*Time for the rant to finish; this is getting too close to home base. She's assuming correctly far too much.*

"Miss Catherine, I don't need you to step up for me. Ghost did what he needed to do. Would have done the same thing if I was in his shoes." I spit out a bloody tooth. "The good doctor needs to get moving, and I need to find a man and have a talk with him."

Mocha-chocolate still isn't finished. "Miss Catherine, you agreeable with Edge going lonesome dove and approaching this man of interest?"

"I am. You be knowin' full well you got enough on your plate with dem boys."

Mocha-chocolate wants to ride my ass. He's snorting like a bull who wants to keep charging, but he knows he's gotta look after his men and has two ladies to keep safe. He's done the math, and he's also got another man in the hospital, and he knows I'm gonna be *nobody's* tag-along. I'm not turning tail either.

He paces about because it's not sitting well with him. He doesn't like it one bit that the old lady is feeling shit *in her bones* when it comes to me. She has this man's respect, and she knows it.

I give him my most direct no-bullshit look. "You have my word I'll keep you in the loop. Sometimes, in a situation like this, it's all a man has to offer is his word. You take care of Whisper's family because she will need them. I'll call for backup when I need it. At the moment, I'm just sniffing around. Whisper's disappeared, and I aim to get some answers soon. You need to be briefed on what Miss Catherine and I have been up to."

Fucker is looking for a reason to go another round. I won't be so accommodating this time around because this round won't be about me shooting Whisper. This round would be purely letting off steam, and I ain't nobody's punching bag.

"I promised Miss Catherine, and I won't break that. She will fill you in, but whether you like it or not, this has become two motorcycle clubs' business too. Whisper is missing, and she's your people, and we're missing two ladies. One just turned up shot through the back, dead, and the other is still a question mark. Seems like there could be a link.

"Your computer genius can start by finding out who is the owner of the abandoned airfield out at Henrys Ferry. Miss Catherine has the details. My guess, it will be buried deep, because the fucker who masterminded the kidnapping doesn't want to be found out. Any flight plans for Saturday morning out of that airfield that can be found will be a lead. We believe Whisper was flown out of there. Could be in the country still, or could be out of the country."

Mocha-chocolate gives me one last glare and walks off to calm down, with Miss Catherine following a few steps behind. Doc Evelyn hands me a small towel so I can wipe myself up, and then I hold it against the gash. She grumbles about not having time for this gorilla shit.

From her absence of shock, I can see she knew what I had gone and done to Whisper already, but she still let the old lady leave with me and gave me her wheels... because I was better than nothing, and *dem bones* have sway.

She sharply pushes my head down, checking the back of it. "I don't have to like it, but the more people looking for Whisper can only be a good thing," she mumbles away behind me, as she tears the old bandage off. "Stitches nearly gone and done their job anyway. I'll use some Steri-Strips to keep it held together. Stay still."

"Why didn't you rat me out?" I ask softly.

She doesn't answer straight away, just goes about patching up the back of my head. "Miss Catherine has her thing where she simply knows something in her bones. She believes in you. She knows you made a mistake, and those bones of hers are steering her when it comes to you. I've decided, after all I've seen over the past few years when it comes to you ex-military types, her bones are worth listening to. Don't prove me wrong for keeping my thoughts to myself."

She moves around and starts to work on my face, but I hold my hands up. "No thanks, I can handle the rest myself."

She lets out a little grunt of disapproval, the doctor in her at war with wanting to fix me, but there is no time. She's spent enough time fussing over me, but still hands me some Steri-Strips and alcohol swab packets. "Edge, you need me to take a look at your foot?" Her voice is low, concern laced through it.

"I'm good. No different from earlier today. I'm taking the pills and I'll get it looked at." She looks like she wants to argue, but decides against it. I get in her line of sight. "Thank you for everything. You go take care of your men." She gives me a sharp nod and walks away.

The old lady approaches me. She looks a little sad

she knows our Bonnie and Clyde run together is over. "How you be leavin' here?"

I wave the burner phone in the air I swiped off Homer and Ellwood. "I'm a big boy. I can sort myself out. I've got people." I give her a half smile.

She looks like she has more to get off her chest, so I let Ghost know I'm just going to have a quiet word with her. He doesn't take too kindly to that idea, by the way he starts to prowl back toward me.

Miss Catherine holds a hand up to him. "I've been perfectly safe with Edge. You get ready to be leavin' and I'll be followin' on behind in Evelyn's BMW." Now, I could have laughed out loud at the look on Mocha-chocolate's face when she told him she would follow on behind. She looks a little put out as a hand lands on her hip. "How you be thinkin' we got from New Orleans to every other damn place we been to, Ghost?" She sounds like she wants to give him more lip, but holds her tongue.

He just holds his hands up in capitulation, walks off, and waits in the SUV, so we can talk. I take her around to the back passenger side of the Beamer and get busy with removing my things, including *No Mercy*.

She hands me the ragdoll which was laying a top of Whisper's carefully folded leather jacket and she's places it inside a plastic bag. "For when you be findin' her. She be knowin' I gave it to you. Her name's Jenny. Bring Whisper back, Edge. I know it be you to be doin' it." She puts her hand over her heart. "I know it in here."

She gives me a tight hug, which surprises the hell out of me. Opportunity has presented itself for the picking. I dip my hand smoothly into her pocket and lift her phone.

"Be stayin' in contact. Boxer be needed by Doc Evelyn's side to get well. You need Ghost, you just be askin'. You need anythin', you contact me on that phone you just be stealin' away from me."

I shake my head at her comment. She doesn't ask for it back. I do something without thinking which surprises me. I give her a swift kiss on the head in reply and then try to cover up my action by turning away and grumbling out, "Time for me to leave."

Mocha-chocolate beckons me over. "He's at the Quality Inn North, room 213." Joel knows how to get information. "Hasn't moved since we've been yapping, might be asleep. Expectin' to hear from you tonight."

I give him a sharp nod. Before he drives off, he hollers through the window, "Joel's sent you a present," and then he drives away.

I wave Miss Catherine off, watching the convoy of cars depart, just as a cab pulls up in front of me, the window peeling down.

"Yo, you Edge?"

I swing my bag over my shoulder and grip *No Mercy's* handles tight.

*I most certainly fucking am.*

••••

Jonathan was indeed at the Quality Inn. Picked my way into the room and found the twin beds—one of them had been slept in—moved at angles like there'd been a scuffle. The phone was poking out from under one of the bedspreads on the floor. I checked the bathroom and found Jonathan laid out in the tub.

Needless to say, he wasn't breathing. Couldn't see any reason for his death until I looked extra closely and saw a small needle mark at the side of his neck.

Somebody wanted ol' JB out of the picture, possibly a loose end.

He was executed, and there goes another fucker who had escaped my wrath.

I called Whisper's phone and passed on my findings to the old lady, which was simply a dead body. JB had his phone clean. He wouldn't leave a trail on his personal one for the shit he was neck-deep in.

*Back to square fucking one.*

The room is completely clean of any of JB's things. I made sure the cabbie dropped me off a block away from the Quality Inn, and I was careful not to touch anything when I arrived. I quickly wipe the handle clean and shut the door, pulling my hat down tight over my face.

I need to find a place for the night to bed down, one that won't be looking to ask questions about my beat up face and work out my next move.

*I'm not one for praying, but I will pray to even Buddha if it gives Whisper strength to hold on.*

# Whisper

## Welcome Mat is Rolled Out, Evil Villain Style

"Let me do that," he murmurs in my ear. My button pops, and then the zipper's being slid down and his hand is moving over my underwear. I don't know if I should feel embarrassed about how wet they are, but I know I want more. I let out a little whimper when he removes his hand. "Patience, little one." I don't want to be patient. I want more. "Smell." Oh, my God, he's offering his fingers up, coated in my scent for me to smell. I inhale. My lips part at the sweet smell of my arousal. I feel so wanton.

He turns my head. My eyelids feel so heavy with this power he has over me. My body voluntarily moves closer to the part of him I know is supposed to give me so much pleasure, backing up against his hard bulge so I can feel him that much nearer to where I need him to be. I had been forced to watch enough porn to understand a great feeling can come from a man and what he can do to a woman.

"I want your fingers again." I'm speaking aloud, but this voice is not my own. It's too breathy, but he already knows what I need. He's already there. Two fingers have slid inside me, which makes me jerk back in shock at the way I feel, his wet lips kissing along my neck. It all feels so good.

Oh, God! He unzips my jacket and pushes the front of my tank top down, and then my lace-covered breast is pushed up and over it. My breasts feel like they are straining against my bra, wanting to be bared to him. My nipples harden, and just as I wonder what it would feel like to have him touch them, he pinches one hard as he starts pumping those fingers inside me, the pain mixed with so much pleasure, and everything goes white. I'm seeing stars my senses are so overwhelmed. There is so much hitting me at once my eyes flutter shut, my head feels heavy, and my hips start dancing for him.

I want more of this man.

I need to be closer.

Oh, God, this feels so good, and then he adds to all the sensations that are flooding my sensitive parts by sliding another finger inside me, and I can feel myself starting to pant, trying to stay in control while he adds to the pleasure by biting my top lip. My eyes widen from the sheer surprise of him doing this, and *it is in no way an act of violence. It's sensual.*

*He's now assaulting my lips with his mouth; he's devouring me. Our lips are lost to this fast dance, while my hips grind against his fingers, and I can't take my eyes off him. I'm in a trance as I feel my body starting to take off. I've watched women about to orgasm on the porn sites, but it doesn't do it justice to what is happening to me.*

*I felt nothing watching the porn.*

*I didn't believe I was capable of feeling aroused, but I can feel myself clamping down hard on his fingers as my lashes force themselves down. The power of this feeling is getting too much for me to stand. I'm going to explode from all these intense feelings my body is being subjected to at once. I have a volcano growing inside me, and it's about to erupt and overflow and I can't stop it.*

*I don't want to stop it.*

*I cry out when I can no longer stand the ecstasy my body is being subjected to, and let it have the reins as I shudder from the sheer euphoria of my release. I don't even understand the noises I am making. They take over and reveal themselves unashamedly to this man.*

And that's when I wake up to my panting breaths easing, and embarrassment consumes me before I realize I am alone.

I allow my eyes to take in where I am. There is a

small light overhead illuminating the room with a soft glow. I'm in a single bed, and not with the tattooed man in Connard who brought me so much pleasure in the safety of Boxer's bar. That had to have been a figment of my imagination, because how can Edge have changed from being that sexy man who gave me all that, to finding myself alone, coping with the pain he has inflicted on me, and strangers who have abducted me.

I know it's real because here I am. He doesn't deserve to enter my dreams. He stalked me and shot me after having sex with me. I'm confused by his actions. He now seems to want to help me.

I note how different this room looks to the last one. Where have I been taken?

Where is Mathias? He's surprisingly become a small comfort I have grown used to. He is dangerous and a killer, as I've bore witness. He has roughly manhandled me, but he has also looked after me. There is something about him. I don't know how to explain what I feel with him, but I have to go on my gut instinct.

*It's all I have.*

A shiver runs down my spine as I wonder what web I have now been caught in. This room is deliberately cold and uninviting. There's no window for me to look through, only four dull gray stone walls holding me captive.

It's a cell.

I. Am. A. Prisoner.

I move to sit up and groan as pain shoots through my shoulder, and my body protests from everything it has been put through. I decide staying still for a little longer has its merits.

I don't know how long I've been here, but I need to get out. I know I can't lie here like a sitting duck waiting for my fate to be revealed, waiting for somebody to control me again.

The urge to flee this horrible room is too strong versus playing a sitting duck. I swing my legs over the side of the bed and stand. I give myself a moment, letting my right shoulder fall back against the wall beside the bed, supporting me until I feel sure I can walk a straight line.

My broken wrist is in a cast and has been placed in a sling. I am clothed, but it is a poor attempt at covering me up. I've been dressed in a ridiculous, virtually transparent, flimsy piece of black, lacy, loose flowing, thigh-length lingerie. My wound is bandaged.

I look around for something to cover myself up in, but there is nothing. There are no cupboards or a closet. The room is bare, with nothing but a bed in it.

This is indeed a cell.

My bare feet feel the chill on the stone floor, but

it's dry and doesn't burn like the cold of snow, which is a positive. I start walking across the room when my skin gets that all too familiar crawl to it. I know that feeling. I snap my head up, searching the corners of the room, and notice the red blinking light.

*I am being observed.*

My face flames. Did they see my dream play out? Was I loud?

*Does that mean they know I'm awake?*

These thoughts do not stop me from defiantly walking over to the door and twisting the handle, and to my utter surprise, it turns, and then I go for broke and pull on the handle. The door swings open.

I stand there for several heartbeats, staring at a curved corridor ten feet wide in front of me, and another stone, windowless wall.

I am about to walk out into the unknown. A prisoner who was left unattended in an unlocked room raises a mighty red flag that is flapping in my face, begging me to pay attention to it.

But I don't.

*Fuck them!*

I face the camera, determined, and give *them* the bird. I owe nobody my manners or my emotions.

This is a game.

They want to see what I will do next.

I will show them I am not afraid.

What more can they do to me that hasn't already been done?

And then I stupidly walk out the room, because there was indeed so much more they could do to me.

And they would.

I had no concept of how far I had gotten when I'd left that room. The hallway was curved and it had an arched roof. It felt medieval, because the outer wall was also made of stone, and I hadn't come across one window.

*Was it night or day?*

The inner wall was broken up with doors like mine every so often. I felt like I was walking in a constant semi-circle, as I tried to find an exit that would lead me out of here.

It almost felt like a curved tunnel that had been burrowed beneath the ground, with a central hive of rooms at its core.

My heart stutters when I see a striking, long-limbed, redheaded woman dressed in a black catsuit, looking like she belongs in a Marvel comic book, walking toward me bare-footed. My instant reaction is to call out to her for help, because Miss Catherine was kind and helped me when I was in need, and then I notice the look on her face. My skin prickles, and I suddenly feel like I'm her prey, and it is me she is hunting.

I start to back up when she hastens her pace, and

then I awkwardly run back from where I came.

I have no clue where I'm running to, and I should have tried some of those doors, but I was afraid they were just more cells. I need a way out, not a way into another room.

I'm too slow. She catches up to me in seconds, her hand at my nape, slamming my face against the wall on my barely healing side.

"Ugh!" I cry out, as I pant from the exertion of running. My broken wrist is pushed hard up against the wall, trapping the cast against my chest, while my other is pulled up high behind my back. I can do nothing but wait for what is to come next as pressure is applied, making my shoulder throb in agony. She wants me to cry out again, but I won't. Instead, I bite down on my lip, her warm breath fanning the side of my face.

The silence is broken by the heavy, clipped footsteps on the stone floor getting louder and more condemning as they approach us.

And then they stop behind me.

Nobody moves.

*Let the mind games begin.*

I want to roll my eyes at this show of drama because my give-a-fucks at this stage would have flown out the window if there was one in sight. But, I keep a lid on bringing any further unwanted attention to myself and getting the shit piled higher against me.

*Disobedience always comes with punishment.*

I know this play is all about bully tactics and eventually trying to bring me back into a submissive mindset, which is what William had trained me to believe was my position in life, but Boxer and Miss C showed me it wasn't.

"Rose, my darling, you may turn her around," a smooth, deep, accented voice orders the woman. I make my mind up as I'm released and pulled away from the wall, and turn around. I'm going to put a halt to showing any more fear because these people thrive on it. It strokes their ego and swells their confidence.

A slim arm slides around my neck, holding a long, cold blade to it, as I'm forced to confront my new enemy. The brutally sharp blade bites into my soft throat, a reminder of how fragile my life is.

That trigger has been activated again, and my breathing hitches, my legs threatening to give out on me. I wish I didn't react like this, but I can't stop it.

*So much for not showing any fear, because I can't be held accountable for those fucked up boxes.*

My past has a way of taking the lead and overriding my initial intentions. I don't see my enemy because the box bursts open containing the memories of my mistress having her throat slit, and my vision becomes bathed in a blood red thick coat of paint.

A strong arm holds me up, the sting of the cold metal slicing into my stretched neck deeper until it is pulled back.

I'm lost in my memories. They have taken me hostage as I watch my mistress' death play out to me in slow, precise motions.

I can hear Master William talking to me, but can't understand what he is saying over the blood-filled gurgles of my mistress as she fades away. I inhale and can smell the metallic scent in the air, which makes me want to throw up, so I shut my eyes, try to block the memories, and repackage them.

I'm being shaken while a deep voice is talking to me, and I don't care to listen. It feels good zoning out. I seek out new images and force Miss Catherine and Boxer's smiling faces to slide their way in, locking the other memories back inside their box. I want to be home so badly. I've got no clue how long I have been lost to my family.

*A week or more?*

I just want to wake up to the smells of one of Miss C's breakfasts and go check on the gardens I have made around her house. Take a ride with Lincoln on the bikes.

Pain explodes across my cheek, snapping me out of my safe oasis I had taken myself to. I blink a few times at the woman now standing in front of me. The blade has been removed from my throat.

*What is with all the bitch slapping? I am so over it.*

My annoyance helps to balance out my fear as I regain my footing unassisted. The male voice is back, but he isn't revealing himself to me as he stands behind me again. "Rose, assist her back to her room in The Pen. I will give her this one small measure and converse with her privately."

Without hesitation, I am being marched to my cell, the dagger hovering over the layer of skin that could so easily be sheared wide open, ending my life if I disobey. I know blood is trickling from the cut, and no matter how much I want to wipe it away, I can't.

I have not yet laid eyes on the man issuing the orders. He's stayed behind us the whole time, while Catwoman keeps my feet moving one in front of the other.

Guards would have come for me before I had gotten as far as I did if I was being watched on the camera, surely. Had it been dumb luck I had made it this far? Or was there simply no way out for me and I was not at risk of escaping, hence the unlocked door?

*Was it a test?*

We come to a halt, and the door opens, revealing the room I walked out of. Rose lowers the blade and holsters it then shoves me toward the bed, and I collapse onto it, moving myself quickly into a seated position, conscious of my nearly naked body.

The ridiculous piece of clothing I've been dressed in is see-through, and I was aware of my naked breasts being visible. Thankfully, I've been allowed a scrap of material for underwear. I'm far from comfortable with how I look in front of these strangers, and that is very deliberate. They want to see my humiliation. It is all a part of the mind fuckery. I badly want to cover up, but I won't show them my discomfort.

I dare not acknowledge the cut to my throat. It will only show weakness. The thin trail of blood continues its path south to be lost in my cleavage as I sit defiantly in front of these people.

Catwoman stands, arms crossed, glaring down at me like she would readily kill me rather than bother with me. I match her stare, trying to look into her soul and see if there is anything humane left inside of her.

*I fear there is nothing.*

"Rose, you can stand down and wait by the door." The man enters the room, and for the first time, I dare to look at him. He is wearing a thick black leather mask. My skin itches as he takes the steps needed to sit on the bed beside me.

Instinct has me starting to move away from him.

"Stay where you are." His command reminds me of William. I know there will be a punishment for not doing as he orders while the woman named Rose is in the room and appears to be his weapon to command, so I halt my movements. I need to choose my fights.

He reaches out, trailing one manicured finger along the cut at my throat, swiping it across the injury, and bringing it slowly to his lips. He sucks his finger clean. He thinks he is unsettling me.

*He would be wrong. I want to murder him.*

"My name is Cezar, and I own you." His words are matter-of-fact. He waits for me to let that sink in. He wants me to cry out in rage.

*I won't.*

*Been there, done that, had one Master already.*

He continues assessing my behavior while looking for a crack in my armor. "Your room is in the area I like to call The Pen, and because you've been delivered to me," he looks me up and down, "not in the condition I would have liked, and through no fault of your own, you will be given a grace period to rest. You will not leave this room unless assisted by Rose or one of my sentinels. Rose will introduce these men to you later."

*Sentinels? This guy's ego is so shoved up his ass.*

"There will be no lock on your door because you *will* obey me. However, there is the camera in your room I noticed you have already observed. Leaving this room unassisted will lead to a punishment you will sorely regret."

He pats his pants softly. "Rose, darling, come sit on my lap." She does as he requests, positioning herself to look at Cezar. He holds her by the back of her head and turns it to face me. Her eyes are glazed over; she isn't really seeing me in this moment. I know that look. She's in survival mode. "Open your mouth, Rose, and stick out your tongue."

She opens her mouth dutifully, looking like a beautiful, soulless ventriloquist doll. I stare in horror at the hacked off piece of muscle that has been left behind. She has no tongue to stick out.

Cezar just scored a direct hit, and I start to shake in rage. I wrestle with the urge to look away. I want so badly to launch myself at him, fight this animal, cut out his tongue, and stuff it down his throat until he chokes on it. I look over at the man controlling her. He's gotten a reaction from me, and his eyes are hungry for my fear.

"You can close your mouth now, Rose." He pulls out his cell and makes a call. "Meet me now in Whisper's room." Then disconnects sliding it back into his pocket.

I visualize tearing the mask from his face so the coward beneath it can be revealed.

"Now, as you can see, it took Rose a little

convincing when she first came to me. She had spirit." He pats her hair. "She was a fighter, but she had to be broken in. I saw the potential in her like I see the potential in you. Your previous master had bragged about you. I wanted to buy you from him, but you were his to covet and were not for sale. Fortunately for me, you became available."

His smile is creepy. This man is the definition of a functioning insane person.

"You've had training, whereas Rose hadn't when she first came to me." He starts combing his fingers through her hair while this shell of a woman stares vacantly at me. "She is my pride, having been brought to me the same age you are now." He starts to turn Rose's head toward his and I see her come back to the surface from the depths she had taken herself, plastering a passable look of interest on her face for the man in front of her as he bends down, kissing her full on the mouth.

*He is an exhibitionist.*

Her back has stiffened ever so slightly, and I catch a glimpse of her hand and the little fist she is trying so hard not to form. Cezar's eyes are closed as he passionately claims her mouth. He is blind to what I can see. Only a person like me would be able to recognize the shell of a person in front of them.

He is used to her obedience and is comfortable around her, and also, he knows the camera in the corner will be capturing all our movements, but she knows how to hide her tells from the mechanical prying eye, her face tilting just enough not to be caught.

This woman has been so repeatedly traumatized she is on autopilot, obeying his commands as her mind silently fights him, unable to have her voice heard.

I understand the lies a victim tells themself to survive.

His hand has moved up to the zipper on the front of her catsuit and he starts peeling it down, the soft hum of the metal teeth opening up until he can get to her right breast. Her chest is naked, and I don't want to watch, but I fear what will happen if I look away.

He is surely testing me.

*I will not bend, but I will not concede either.*

He opens his eyes and watches me as he fondles her generous breast, tugging at the nipple until it hardens.

My eyes may be open, but I am no longer seeing this vile masked man who is too lily-livered, as Boxer would say, to show me his face. He has abused this woman so much she is inwardly dead to his touch.

Rose has mentally switched off but knows how to keep herself alive. She is too many shades of her former self, but she is still alive, keeping up appearances. It's what is keeping her breathing and she knows it.

He wants to get a reaction out of me, but I close my mind off to this sick showmanship.

He releases her breast when I don't give him what he is looking for. "I see you have conditioned yourself over the years, being around William Dupré." He studies me, cocking his head to the side like he's trying to work me out. He has thankfully stopped groping Rose in front of me. "I was recently informed you were a wet dream, yet your features aren't schooled enough to hide the distaste for what I am doing to Rose. Interesting."

*Who told him I was a wet dream?*

"William had bragged about all the things he has done to you, yet you sit there looking uncomfortable by my display of affection for my Rose." His hands start tucking Rose's breasts back inside her catsuit and then he pulls her zipper up, the whole time watching me.

"Has freedom left you high and mighty and erased everything you were taught?" He pushes Rose off his lap and she stands, automatically moving to the side.

A loud, impatient knock interrupts the mood of the room.

"Come in," the only person in authority who can

speak replies because I now know Rose can't talk. She is mute.

The door opens, revealing Mathias, complete with a mask covering half his face. He takes a step into the room dressed in a dark, expensive-looking suit and tie. He only has eyes for Cezar's masked face, completely ignoring me.

"Ahhh, here is one of my newly appointed sentinels." He gets up from the bed, moving to the side and placing his hands behind his back.

His attention is back on me. "Mathias informed me of Santana's demise. You will take the hit for my loss. Mathias, please assist in holding her down and her head firm."

In a flash, Mathias is on me, pushing my good arm to my side and putting his shoulder into my chest as I'm slammed onto the mattress, flat on my back. He straddles my lower body, keeping my legs from kicking out while one knee slides into position, resting painfully on my right forearm, wedging it by my side while one hand grips my damaged arm, ensuring no free movement. He's not using his full weight, but it's enough to keep me in place.

Fear starts to bubble up inside me.

"Keep her head steady."

Mathias complies and his spare hand presses down on my forehead, paralyzing my head. My breathing speeds up as I start to panic.

*What the fuck is wrong with these people?*

"Rose, you know what to do. You may have the honors." She moves toward me.

*What honors?*

I watch with frightened eyes darting about as the dagger reappears, and I can't hide my fear anymore.

*Oh, God!* What are they about to do to me?

Rose's other hand forces my mouth to open by squeezing my cheeks with carefully applied pressure using her thumb and fingers. I can't hold my mouth shut. I can only watch in horror.

My body begins to quake as it starts responding to these people and their actions. I have no rights. I am at their mercy.

*What the fuck is she trying to do to me?*

Rose reaches in, grabbing my dry tongue, and that's when I understand I'm about to lose it. An animalistic noise leaves my throat as the dagger is raised into the air. My natural reaction is to buck Mathias off me and tear my face out of Rose's grip.

But. I. Can't. Move.

*I can't fight these people.*

*Get the fuck off me*, I want to scream out. My eyes water when I feel the burning sting as the cold blade is brought down on my tongue, slicing into it.

A gurgle of pain and blood leave my mouth as my head and cheeks are released. Rose is no longer in my vision. I start to retch as blood coats my throat, threatening to choke me. I need to get it out, so I turn my head to the side, allowing me to breathe better as blood sprays onto my bedding as I cough it up.

When I realize Mathias has let up on the restraining pressure, I roll my body as much as his weight will allow, dribbling and spitting blood until the coughing ebbs. I can't stop myself from shuddering beneath him, as my body can't control the spasms of shock at what these people have done to me.

My eyes are watering from the pain, tears mixing with my blood as they too spill onto the bedding. I turn my head, swiping my trembling hand across my face, vanquishing the tears. I won't let these warped people have them.

*And then I see it.*

A phone is poking out from underneath part of my thigh. It must have slipped out of Mathias's pocket, and I covered part of it when I moved my body. I pretend to have another major coughing fit with blood spraying about and cover it completely with my thigh when Mathias slides off me, his blurred body standing tall, dutifully waiting for Cezar's next command.

I need to keep this phone hidden. I lean on my right elbow, turn my head toward the bedding, and allow these people to believe I am starting to break as I cough up more blood and spit.

These people are insane, and insanity is so

unpredictable. *They are all warped in the head.*

I had almost forgotten Cezar was in the room until his deep accented words hit me. "Mark this as your one and only warning, Whisper. On my command, Rose will cut it right off if I hear of *any* disobedience, and she's very good at it, as you have just witnessed. She made the mistake once of thinking she would get a second warning, and she was punished for it, as you have seen. You will do everything asked of you without complaint."

My only response is to cough more blood up, the burn painful, but I've felt worse.

My mind is strong. I won't be broken ever again. What this crazy man doesn't realize is how strong Rose's mind is too. She shows him what she needs to keep breathing, and the rest is survival mode.

Rose has been treated far worse than I had; I can see that from her reactions. There has been a lot of irreversible damage done to her soul. She is robotic, but her eyes show only me her rage that was hidden below the surface for Cezar. She might not care what happens to me, but she wants to live and will do whatever it takes, including ending me.

She has spent too long under his command. She looks mid-twenties, and I fear for the shell that will be left of this woman if she is able to walk away and get her freedom one day. Rose has been through too much, made to do too many bad things.

I have learned I may still have been a virgin, but there are many ways to abuse a woman's body and mind.

This Cezar commands Rose, but there is a part of her mind that never obeys. Her clone is his puppet. She has learned to separate her true lost soul and keep that small part for herself when she needs to keep going.

I can become Sara. She will get me through this.

The evil man lets out a dramatic sigh. "Mess is something I have a low tolerance for." He holds out a white square of fabric. "Here." I grab onto it and try to mop myself up. "This was just a warning shot; the next will be permanent. If anything happens to any of the other women, it will be on your head. Somebody will always suffer for any insubordination, for any fuck ups. Santana was a fuck up. Let's just say it is my way of keeping you all in line."

*There are other women here?*

He claps his hands together in one loud smack, making me jump.

"Well, Whisper, it would appear I must cut our little meet-and-greet short. Just remember, the debt William owes me comes at a heavy price. There will be no more marks on your exterior body. I assure you of this. I will not stand for it. Just don't test me. Underneath all that bruising and swelling and mess is a beautiful woman who will pay William's debt off. You are my new prize and need to be in pristine condition in a short time for my high paying guests."

He lets that comment sit in the air for a few heartbeats. I am counting them, trying to calm my shattered life and what it has now become.

*Am I to become a prostitute?*

"Rose will come back later and assist in cleaning you up and clothing you, as you've made a mess of yourself. For now, you will sit and think about what we have talked about. Rest."

I want this sorry excuse for a man to shut the hell up and leave. I know Mathias is watching me now. I can feel his eyes on me and I can't look at him. He helped do this to me.

He is my enemy. I must remember that.

Cezar starts for the door. "You know the cameras are always watching. Don't give me a reason." He beckons Rose to walk in front of him, the bloody blade being wiped on another white square of fabric he's handed her as they exit my cell. Mathias follows, shutting the door behind him.

I stay still, scared somebody will come back. I haven't touched the phone yet, so I haven't done anything wrong.

Conscious of the camera in my room, I curl up on the bed, my back to the blinking light, and pretend to shudder and cry and cough. I reach up for the pillow and pull it down to me, pretending to cuddle it for comfort, and tug as much of the bedding up over me as I can, working the phone up my body. Somebody may be watching me at all times, or they might just check the footage every now and then, but what I do know is I won't have much time until Mathias discovers his phone is missing.

*Then what do I do?*

# MATHIAS

## Place of Trust

*Fuck!*
*Fuck!*
*FUUUCK!*

I got there as soon as I could.

I couldn't stop that sick bastard.

*FUCK!*

Now I have to walk beside this motherfucker to his office with this calm look plastered all over my face after what he just did to Whisper.

I *had* to obey him.

I *wanted* to turn on the fucker and put a bullet in his sick brain.

I have to keep my eye on the job at hand. I can't jeopardize the years I've spent undercover working my way closer to this cocksucker. I've only just made it into his inner sanctum. I can't be blowing everything I've worked toward, infiltrating his paranoid network, to throw it all away on a beat up girl because I feel so goddamn sorry she is being put through this, and I want to save her.

I saw all three of them while I was checking to see if she'd woken up on the screens in the security room. There is no volume, so I had no clue what he was saying to her. And then he summoned me.

*Jesus Christ!*

How much more does she have to endure until I can get his operation shut down?

Answer: A fuck-of-a-lot. This nightmare has only just started; the rest was simply a preview.

The look of fear and disgust on her face at what was being done to her matched mine, but I couldn't show it. I couldn't do a thing to derail it.

Rose, from what I've heard, could take me on. She is trained well. She is a killer. This place is heavily under surveillance and guarded. I could kill Cezar now, but then I would be killed.

Nothing would be accomplished, because it wouldn't stop his event from going ahead. It wouldn't stop these ladies from being taken. These girls are never seen again once Cezar is through with them. That fucker Filip, who is Cezar's most trusted, would just slide up into the role of head motherfucker in this highly secretive organization.

I don't even know where *here* is. I was blindfolded at the last pit stop by the guy I know now as Filip, who came and met me and then a syringe was stuck in my neck. Kane didn't make it to where I am. Got no idea where he is. I'm still new blood here, and Cezar is gonna protect his hidden lair. I now have this head fucker's name.

Whisper can't get in the way of what I've worked for. I'm now in a place of seniority, of growing trust. I've made it to The Pen, his holding place, until the highly secretive, exclusive event. I want every last one of his secret lairs around the globe. I want *all* the players taking part. There will be records. I want them all, every last one of the fuckers' names. They are all part of a network of high profile businessmen and millionaires, some who are married men with an appetite for what Cezar has to offer.

She has to believe I'm capable of ending her life. She has to believe I'm one of the devil's foot soldiers.

I *will* bring justice for all the lost lives.

# Whisper

## Desperate Measures

This will be my only chance to make contact. I don't know how much time I have so I need to make every word count. There is no time for punctuation.

I place the phone on silent and text Miss Catherine, letting her know it's me, with trembling fingers. She replies instantly. I so badly want to hear her voice.

> **Miss Catherine:** Can u talk if I call?
>
> **Whisper:** No camera in room
>
> **Miss Catherine:** Where r u?
>
> **Whisper:** ? Cold place. Plane trip. Snow at printer place in city where had surgery on shoulder now in another place lots of stone

Miss Catherine: Names?

*Something isn't right here. Miss Catherine has a way of talking, the same as she texts.*

Whisper: Who is this

Miss Catherine: Edge

*What?*

Whisper: She ok

Edge: Yes with Ghost, Boxer, Lincoln.

Edge: I'm sorry.

I know what he is sorry about, and he can get fucked.

Whisper: Fuck u

Edge: I'll find u.

Whisper: Want Boxer

Edge: He's hurt bad. Lincoln's same. Won't stop until find u. They'll live, need time. I need more information, anything.

*Oh, God. Boxer and Lincoln are hurt.*

**Whisper:** Event coming up I'm trophy more girls somewhere here.

**Edge:** Names!

**Whisper:** Cezar in charge rose broken weapon mathias bad guy.

**Edge:** Delete this conversation

I do as he says.

**Edge:** Call me. Don't talk, just listen.

I call him, because I'm desperate and, it would appear, weak of mind.

"Whisper!" He sounds relieved I rang. "I'm going to talk. If you say nothing, I will take that as a yes. Cough if it is a no."

The sound of his voice makes me break down crying loud sobs.

"Whisper, baby, you need to hang on." Guilt laces his words. "I promise I'm coming for you, and I will slay down any fucker in my path. You *will* be coming back to Miss Catherine. I'm sorry I shot you. I'm sorry my father put you through hell. I didn't know." I disconnect. I'm too upset. How dare he call me baby? But I can't help hanging onto every single one of his words and then the screen lights up with a message.

**Edge:** U still there?

**Whisper:** What day and time

**Edge:** Thursday late afternoon. It's been a week since the bar.

*What he isn't saying is since we had sex.* I shake my head a little to stop those thoughts.

**Whisper:** They cut my tongue warning b obedient

**Edge:** Fuck I'm so sorry. How bad are u?

**Whisper:** Ok

**Edge:** How did u get phone?

**Whisper:** Man held me down on bed dropped from pocket he will come for it I'm scared.

**Edge:** Hold onto seeing Miss Catherine again. I have Jenny to give to u when I find u. Delete conversation again, place phone where u found it and ignore it. Do it now. Little lady, I'm coming.

I delete the conversation again and work the phone back down my body as the heavy sobs keep coming, the taste of metal in my mouth.

    I shut my eyes, quieting my sobs, as I wait to see if I have been found out and what punishment will fit this crime.

# EDGE

Fuuuck!

*S*MASH!

Roaring at the ceiling, I throw the first thing I can get a hold of, which happens to be a glass, and smash it against the wall in my room.

Whisper is in deep trouble, and we've still got nothing to go on.

Her sobs were killing me.

Fucker. Cut. Her. Tongue.

That motherfucker is gonna *pay*.

I've kept in touch with the old lady. She hasn't let on to the others that I have her phone, and for that, I am now truly grateful.

Whisper managed to get that phone and keep it hidden while she was going through hell, and now we have some names.

It's a start.

Joel and all his genius wasn't able to turn up a name of ownership that wasn't the government for that abandoned airfield. Fucker must be using it rarely, and no one seems the wiser. Doubted the government even knew, not unless somebody's hands were being greased.

Flight plan was a no-go too.

*Unauthorized?*

I'd slept longer than I should have, spent most of the night awake communicating with the old lady and her people. Crashed near dawn, my body needing to recuperate, Whisper's call waking me. I feel guilty for sleeping half the day away when she's going through shit she shouldn't be.

I palm Miss Catherine's phone and send a code to Slade, letting him know he's got an incoming call coming.

He knows if I'm digging his number up, shit has hit the fan.

"Slade. Need you buddy." And then I give him the location and disconnect.

I need to assemble a team. I need me a whole lot of muscle, but more importantly, I need what skills he can offer.

Always be prepared in advance, because I have no doubt...

*Shit is gonna blow.*

# CONTORTED

HER DEBT OWED, #3

EMMA JAMES

# Whisper

### Opportunity May Knock Only Once, But Temptation Leans on the Doorbell

My thoughts are bloated with everything Cezar did to Rose in front of me. How he commanded both her and Mathias to do his bidding.

I'm now nursing a warning in neon lights that I could wind up the same as Rose, silenced. I know I had it bad with William, but I never had to hurt another person on command. Who would I be now if I had? This man has the power of control, only using words among his people, and that is a very dangerous thing for me.

The burn of the cut is nothing compared to the knowledge I am in deep, deep shit with this crazy, extremely unpredictable man. I am used to a camera watching me day-in and day-out. I know how to live with one.

I move the pillow so I can spit out saliva and blood onto the bedding, the small bit I have covering my legs falling away. The blinking eye in the corner of my room will tell on me if it knows I can see the phone, so I must play the game and play it well.

I stay in the fetal position, pulling the pillow back to my chest, dismissing the phone's existence. I lie here under the guise of sleep, while waiting it out until Mathias comes back to claim it.

*And he will.*

I fill my thoughts with knowing he must be sweating bricks because he is a stupid man for making such a blunder. A small win for me, although I'm too afraid of the consequences if I were to gloat in his face.

I hug the pillow a little tighter. It was so good to let somebody know I was still alive, even if it was Edge. They know I still exist.

I rewind the phone call from Edge in my mind. I've done exactly what he asked of me so my messages can't be traced at first glance.

He said he has Jenny, my ragdoll. Miss Catherine *must* believe in him to hand over my precious doll, a possession she knows means a great deal to me. Jenny had seen me through a lot of hard times. She was the only friend I had as a little girl. I held her when things got too tough, when sleep was evading me, when nightmares enveloped me, when evil hurt me.

*Jenny kept me from falling.*

I need Jenny now.

Miss Catherine wouldn't have given her to Edge if she hadn't formed some kind of bond with him. I *know* Miss C. If she trusts Edge, then is it possible he meant what he said about coming for me and being sorry?

I dab at my eyes, removing the moisture still leaking out. I hate that I have been reduced to a teary mess. I *am* stronger than this.

Questions keep flipping through my mind as I huddle, waiting for my enemy to walk through the door. Is Edge *truly* sorry for what he did to me? How he played me? Boxer and Lincoln are too injured to come after me, and my heart bleeds knowing this, but Edge said they will survive. Why were they hurt? Was it because of me? Who hurt them? My kidnapping has to be linked to their troubles.

I badly want to hear Boxer's British voice. He's the closest thing I have to a father, and Lincoln is my best friend. I miss them so much. Had I gotten them almost killed? Is my very existence putting their lives in jeopardy?

*Am I cursed, never to know happiness and peace?*

Curling my body around the pillow, I try to calm my anxiety and fear for the people I love. The best thing I can do is try to get some rest before all hell breaks loose.

*And it will.*

I'm walking a narrow tightrope of hope. Even though I've wobbled about, I haven't yet fallen off. I have to believe I'll be rescued. It happens in the movies, against all odds, and this is like one epic never-ending movie filled with betrayal and violence playing out in my life, because this just doesn't happen to other people.

*Does it?*

I lay in the painfully quiet room, my shoulder a dull reminder of what I have already been through. Only my frightened breath can be heard through the piercing silence, a constant form of torture ready to burst once my enemy arrives.

The minutes keep ticking by, turning into at least an hour. I'm beginning to think Cezar is keeping me isolated for the rest of the day. He told Rose to give me time to think—in other words, stew in my own pot of despair. She can't be coming any time soon.

I want so badly to reach for the phone, convincing myself if only to read the time. Maybe Mathias hasn't noticed his phone is missing. Have his duties kept him occupied?

Knowing I can talk to Edge again, it's a strong temptation lying by my thigh, the only link to *my* world, a world I may never ever see again.

As time keeps ticking by, my hand is greedy to

pick up the phone and hear his voice again. I want to ignore his betrayal, if only to have one last chance before I am cut off, maybe never to be reunited again with Miss Catherine, Boxer, and Lincoln.

My fingers twitch.

I make the decision.

*I can't help myself.*

I tempt fate once more and carefully grope around until I clutch the phone. A small sound of comfort reveals itself inside the four confining stone walls as I tuck it by my face.

I know it's wrong, and I could be badly punished if not killed but call me super crazy because after everything that has happened to me, I *need* the contact. Even if it is with a man I shouldn't feel this pull to talk to. This temptation I'm feeling is a drug I need another hit of to feel calm, even if it may cause me to OD.

I hit the keys for Miss C's number and wait. I just want to hear his voice. It rings twice and connects.

"Whisper?" My name comes out on a soft growl. I say nothing. "Baby, I want you to make a little cough now if it is you." I try to cough, but it comes out filled with saliva and blood, and then I can't stop coughing as it turns into retching. "Christ, what have they done to you?" He's angry, but not at me. "Take deep, slow breaths, darlin'. Listen to mine if you can."

I close my eyes and concentrate on doing as he

says, matching my breathing with his. Any kindness, I am cloaking myself in to warm my beaten soul. *This* Edge is the man I met in the bar who talked to me like an equal.

"Fuck, darlin', you shouldn't be calling. Somebody will catch you." He's gruff and angry again. "Please," he sounds desperate, "you have to disconnect for your own safety."

I wipe the tears that are still leaking from my eyes, the traitors. "Edth—"

"You shouldn't be talking. Your mouth...." He curses. "Your bullet wound." Those three words are racked with guilt. He cares I'm hurt. I'm not imagining he's sorry.

I know I should disconnect and put the phone back, but I can't... not yet. I *need* this connection to keep me from losing it. My mind is fragile; everything keeps piling up, and the boxes are already full. There's no self-storage space left for any more boxes of nightmares in my head.

I try again. I should text, but that takes time, and I don't know how much more time I have. "Edth... I...." My voice is barely audible, and raspy from my coughing, his name a slobbering mess on my ruined tongue. I go to repeat myself. "Edth—"

"Fuck, baby," Edge cuts me off, "you're frightened and hurt, and I know you need this contact, even if it *is* with me, but I want you to stay as safe as you can, and this isn't fucking safe. This is fucking suicide if you get caught."

My fingers peeking out of my cast move nervously across the cut at my throat. It has stopped bleeding, a shallow gash left as a reminder of what will happen if I step out of line. I don't think it needs stitches, but I couldn't trust anybody to stitch me up here anyway.

"Edth... *pleathe*... I can'th do thith again." My words are slow in my endeavor for him to understand me. I thought I could be brave, but this is becoming too much the longer I lie here. Twenty years of captivity was enough, but this... this is too much. Everything is catching up to me, how much I've endured.

"You can and *you will*." He understands me, even though my sentence is all messed up. His words prop up my limp self-doubt. He's determined for me to stay strong. "I'm coming for you, Whisper. *Believe* me when I say this. I have friends, and we are working on locating you. Do as you're told. Don't fight them, no matter how hard it gets, and it will get *fucking hard*." He goes silent. I'm afraid I've lost the connection, because I can't hear his breathing.

I stare at the screen, the seconds counting away... and then he's back. "Stay alive for your family. You survived my father. Don't forget that." How much does he know? "Please just do as they say, because

Joel is working on finding you."

*He knows Joel?*

"I won't let up until I find you, and Boxer won't let you down... not like me." He sounds ashamed of himself.

I am reminded of the family who loves me and won't give up on me. They won't forget me. Boxer gave me a place in society, and he broke the rules to give me a voice in this world. Before, I was just a whisper floating through time, an abused secret.

"I fucked you over." His voice has dropped an octave. My face heats under the double meaning. "I could have kept you from all this, if I had known about my father. I didn't keep you fucking safe. I hurt you and let those fuckers drive off with you in the trunk."

*He'd been shot.* I mentally check myself and stop my conscience from making any more excuses for him. Nobody should just go around shooting people and then ask questions later.

Although this man has taken so much from me, it doesn't halt the insecure words flying out before I can stop them. "Doth leathe me here." I am so alone. I want to believe the same man who hurt me will help me.

*I want to believe he is sorry.*

"Fuck, Whisper, hear me when I say I may have tainted Dupré blood running through my veins, but

I *will* be coming to save you and I'll be bringing a small army with me." His words are a fierce growl. "Shit, babe, you weren't who I thought you were. You're innocent and brave. I am sorry for my father's sins against you, and I'm sorry for *my* fucked-up sins against you, too." His voice is full of pain and regret. I want to believe him, even after he broke my trust.

I need to tell him about the girl. "Girl wath killed in hangar. Trying ethcape." I cough and spit out blood.

"I know. I found her body," he says quietly. *He was at the hangar?* "Her body has been buried and shown the proper respect. Her name was Santana. She was under the protection of the Lion's Den Motorcycle Club. She went missing from their club over nine months ago." I've seen seven seasons of *Sons of Anarchy* with Lincoln which taught me a lot of what a club is about. They are violent and dangerous.

He answers the silent river of questions flowing through my mind on a fast current. "I was there with Miss Catherine. She's one tough old lady. She loves you and is fighting for you. We have tried any lead we can find. I'm now in Jackson, Mississippi, waiting for another lead. I'm only a few hours from Connard."

I know this is my last desperate hope to tell him

everything I forgot to tell him earlier. "The men wear mathk. Kane ith dangerouth. Enjoy hurting women. Mathiath ith Norwegian. Tattooed thymbol by hith temple. Thick beard. I tried... to... ethcape... cold... city. Kane broke... my writh." I don't know how much he can understand with my lispy talk, but from the sounds of rage and cursing coming down the line, I gather he understands enough.

"Masks? Fuck's sake, who are these people?" he rumbles, as though he is only speaking to himself.

I keep talking, too scared I'll forget something vital that could help him, even if I'm dead and he can save the other women. "Think I'm undergwounth."

"Underground?"

"Yeth. Loth of thone. No windowth."

"Lots of stone? No windows?"

"Yeth. Curved corridor. Rothe ith dam-ed." I try and repeat the word again, "Dam-eeed." My mouth hurts so much to talk, but I have to keep going.

"Damaged? Rose is damaged?"

"Yeth. Thurviveth in her head. Needth thaving thoo." It is so hard to talk with my tongue a piece of hacked meat, and blood and saliva adding to my messed-up words, making me feel nauseous.

There is silence for several heartbeats, as though he is choosing his words carefully and keeping his anger in check. "Understand this. All our concentration is going into saving you. You can't think about this Rose, because she is one broken bitch. I don't fucking care if she is surviving in her head. She's hooked up with this cocksucker, so she's just as bad as him."

"No!" I cry out a little too loudly. "Pleathe. Thave... Rothe. Promith. Other... girls... too." My words have slowed down, begging for him to understand clearly. I'm desperate for him to help them too.

"Has she hurt you?" His anger is barely contained. I know it isn't directed at me. "Yes or no?"

"Edth—" My sentence is cut short.

"Yes. Or. No. Whisper." His words are clipped.

"Yeth." I know how much weight that one word will hold for Edge.

"Who cut your tongue?"

I won't waste anymore time. "Rothe. Cezar ordered her." I can barely understand my own voice. "Prom... ith," I can only whisper with a broken voice.

I wait several precious heartbeats for him to answer me. "I... promise."

*Thank you.* My eyes close, relieved.

"Whisper?"

"Yeth?"

"Remember your favorite movie?"

"Yeth."

"I promise you will get to watch it when we get you out of there."

I want to smile a little at this thought, but I can't

trust it to be true. Tomorrow isn't even a guarantee. Everything is unpredictable and to be feared. There is no safety for me anymore.

He takes a deep breath. "Just so you know, I mean what I say. I'm the enforcer for the Soulless Bastards Motorcycle Club. Trust that I have people who can help me locate you and get you out. Everybody is fighting hard to find you. If you don't believe in me, then believe Boxer will find where you are."

He is in a biker club? *An enforcer?*

I don't know how I feel about knowing Edge is a biker.

"Hang up, baby, and save yourself. Do as I say." He sounds like I'm stressing him out by staying on the line.

*I can't.*

"Hang up, darlin'." His words are softer, almost gentle, but he isn't going to disconnect until I do. I want to listen to his breathing just a little longer, because it comforts me. His rich deep voice grounds me. I feel as though he's listening to my breaths as well.

Edge was right in telling me to stay strong. I must tolerate what is thrown at me to buy myself time, to buy Edge time. No matter how hard that is going to be.

He interrupts my rambling mind. "Now, for the love of God, please hang up before you get caught. I can't lose you."

*What?*

I don't understand why he said that, but I know I'm pushing the limit. I've gotten this far without being caught. I need not risk my life any further. I'm just about to disconnect, when a noise behind me makes me turn my head and look over my shoulder, a frightened noise escaping me.

*"Whisper!"* Edge's stricken voice can be heard roaring inside my small room as the phone is snatched from my grasp. *"Motherfucker!"*

And then there is silence as I steel myself.

Because.

I. Am. A. Survivor.

No matter the cost.

# EDGE

## Helpless is One Fucked-Up Pill

**H**er deep, throaty scream hits me before it is cut off. *"Whisper!"* I shout, dropping the phone onto the well-worn carpet, and raise my right arm, my rage needing an immediate outlet. I put the full force of my body weight into pounding my right fist over and over until my knuckles split, punching an impressive hole through the cheap hotel's wall.

My anger douses a little as I stand back, looking at my handiwork, allowing my gasping breaths to return to normal. My hand might be a bleeding mess, but I don't feel any physical pain, just the sharp, soul-deep terror for Whisper knifing through me. She was discovered with that fucker's phone in her hand. What is being done to her now?

I start pacing like a wild animal as I try to calm the beast inside me that needs to feed again. I am feral because I am helpless. She risked that second call, and now she will be punished because I didn't get her off the phone in time.

As if she hasn't been through enough already being shot and bruised when I left her in the trunk of that car. Then a broken wrist and her tongue nearly severed... and now....

I clench my fists, and roar like a warrior before battle until I run out of air.

I keep pacing, trying to get a handle on my emotions, because I have nothing to battle, no puppet master to take my vengeance out on. I can't get my hands on *any* of those cocksuckers who have hurt her. I've got nothing to feed my beast. I'm stuck in this hotel room with no leads and an amped-up temper.

I sit down on the bed, hanging my head, trying to control my rage. My father buried that seed inside me, I know that. It lay there dormant, waiting to be awakened.

I'd been sitting here for the past hour, thinking about everything we knew so far, which wasn't much, and trying to find a thread I could go on instead of doing nothing. But everything is a fucking dead end.

My imagination's going wild with what could be being done to her right now, throwing my own memories into a time machine and transporting me back twenty-plus years. I find myself watching my ten-year-old self suffering at the hands of my father, because I was too small to fight back.

*"Boy!" he hollers in my face. We're in my room. "You leave me no choice. You are wild and need to be tamed. You don't escape from your room. You think you're clever, picking that lock, but I chained you to teach you manners. To show you I'm your master and will do as I please to you."*

*I look up at the crazy man who is bent over me, his fist raised again, ready to hammer down on me. He is dressed in a black hooded shirt, the one he always wears when he wants to go all insane-father on me.*

*I cower like the small child I am, because angering my father, who I must call Master, will only get me more beatings.*

*I silently watch as his fist comes toward me again, and wait for the connection. My body moves through the air effortlessly and slams back down on the hard ground. I am a mess, with my arms and legs spread out as I take in as much air as I can, blood trickling from my injuries. My stomach is on fire as I gasp for air. That black place I hope to get to starts to pull me under, but not quite. I haven't been hurt enough yet. I'm strong of mind, and my body tells me I'm not ready to be released from this nightmare and put to sleep where nothing hurts. He's taught me well. Every beat down makes me stronger, more able to cope. I am being conditioned.*

*I close my eyes for a few seconds in a private prayer, begging somebody to save me, to take me away from this evil man. I want my mother, but she fled, leaving me alone with him. I don't even remember her, because I was only a baby, but he keeps reminding me my own mother didn't want me.*

*I open my eyes, hoping I have been transported to a loving, normal home, with a mother and brothers and sisters and grandparents and maybe a pet dog, but all I see is the screwed-up face of William Dupré from a few feet away as his anger bleeds around him.*

*I lay waiting for the next punch, and it will come, because I'm not unconscious. He will only stop when his beast calms or my mind beats him to it and takes me under.*

*I watch him as he approaches me, satisfied I won't run, and confident I won't make a sound. To cry would be like asking for a far worse punishment than his fists. I am past feeling any new pain, because my body is one ball of agony. I am the only thing that can calm the animal inside him, and the way that happens is by letting him beat the shit out of me until the monster is no longer ravenous.*

*I have tried to understand his rules and be everything he wants from a son. I am homeschooled and smart for my age. I soak up knowledge. I am a good student.*

*I just needed the toilet. I only wanted to pee and get back inside my chains before he noticed. If I peed my pants, I would be given the belt. Many times, I had successfully made it unnoticed to the toilet and back without being caught. I knew how to use the toilet brush holder to fill with water and tip into the toilet enough times to wash my urine away. If I flushed the toilet, he might hear me.*

*Today was not my lucky day.*

*I always try to keep the peace and make him happy, but I can't seem to do that all the time. Today, there will be no broken bones. No belt marks on my body. Today, I will just have bruises and places where my skin breaks open.*

*Today is a good day.*

I shake myself back to the present and look around, taking in the low budget hotel, probably not even measuring in at a one-star rating. When questioned about my rough appearance, I explained to the young bubble-gum-blowing female at the front counter with the big hair that I had lost my underground fight last night.

I previously let Ghost run his fists over me good and plenty, and I looked the part of the guy who had lost the fight. She didn't seem to mind the condition I was in the way she was licking her lips and eyeing me up. I think she would have offered herself up to me if I had shown interest.

I was so fucking not interested.

I could afford a nice room with all the bells and whistles, but if I rocked up to a fancy hotel looking the way I did last night, the police may have been notified. Staying in this dump afforded me a certain amount of anonymity.

Now, here I am with nothing but time on my hands and memories to keep locked down, and all I want to do is get a hold of these people Whisper spoke of, and do very, very bad things to them while taking my time doing them. I always have the upper edge, but this time, I am *not* in control by a long shot, and that is a hard pill to swallow.

I'm a fucking hunter, and this motherfucker is laughing at all of us, because he's pulling the strings, staying well hidden. He's a clever mofo who leaves no trail.

Adrenaline is pumping through my veins with the names of the scum being added to my retribution list. I made a promise to get this Rose bitch out. I didn't promise not to punish her for her sins against Whisper.

*She fucked over what's mine.*

Scooping the phone off the floor, I check the time. My palms thump against the wall by my bed as I let my weight push into it. I bow my forehead to the wall, touching it as I absorb the realization I can do nothing, absolutely nothing, to save her from what is being done to her now.

I feel so guilty, because I would be lying if I didn't fucking soak up that sweet voice of hers. I could hear her breathing, and that was the most beautiful sound. She was hurt, but she was alive.

And now? I don't know what is happening, and the onus is on me. I should have just fucking hung up on her.

I push off from the wall and head for the shower. I strip off my boxers, shove the well-used curtain aside, and turn the taps on that have seen better days, and then step under the spray. I tug the curtain closed, watching the bloody trail from my knuckles swirl around the discolored white tiles at the bottom of the shower.

Like a good little boy scout, I will have to phone in this information to Miss Catherine and her people. I know how much it means to her to know I have spoken with Whisper.

I'll call it in once I've calmed down. She doesn't need to hear my current state of mind. Won't do her any good knowing I'm losing it.

I have to remind myself Cezar needs her for his event. She is his trophy, and he won't damage his trophy beyond repair. He needs her sparkling. He is a businessman and needs the debt paid before he disposes of her.

Once clean I shut the water off and yank the curtain back, grabbing for a towel. A good hunter has to be patient. This has to work both ways. Whisper's people need me as much as I need them; we can't rescue her without the other party.

I dry myself and get dressed. I can't help wondering if my father organized for Ruby and Santana to be stolen.

*Coincidence?*

One female from our club and one from our allied club within seventy-two hours of each other. It's not a stretch to think he discovered where I lived and who I became, and his twisted mind wanted revenge.

Was it a punishment for me leaving him, including the Lion's Den MC as a smoke screen? I won the first round by getting my freedom and a life. Did he need to take back that win? To take from both our clubs would be a clever, underhanded move, one there would be no retribution for, because he was dead.

I should have killed Whisper for him. Loose end tidied up, me possibly in the slammer for her death.

He would have thought of himself as rather clever devising the back-up plan and having the last laugh because he got his son to kill an innocent, therefore ending the rest of my life as a free man.

Was William receiving payment for handpicking

women? Was that the debt Whisper was paying off? Will I ever know?

This hotel is home for me now, and I will stay in this shithole until I know my next move. Thank fuck Slade is coming. I'm going to go batshit crazy until he arrives. One thing I can do is organize both clubs and have them on standby.

For now, all I can do is call Miss Catherine and hope Joel-the-genius-hacker can find something on this Cezar and his minions, because she's one small needle to be found in a world full of hay.

# MATHIAS

## A Penny for Your Thoughts

"Mathias!"

*What now?*

I school myself into the cold and professional demeanor of his sentinels and nod my head, acknowledging the pompous, evil bastard who just snapped my name.

"You will no longer be liaising with Jonathan Boothe, because I had him executed."

This news does not surprise me. Lives mean nothing to Cezar. I want to ask why Jonathan has been executed, but questions would bring unwarranted attention my way. I simply have to do my job and not get caught to end this once and for all.

"I'm feeling unsettled about Santana's urge to escape. I need you to check on all the girls in The Pen and let them know Santana will no longer be taking them to their exercise classes. I want you to note how they each behave and get back to me. I don't need any more of them thinking they want to be brave hearts and stage a coup. Tell them she was given her freedom, because they will wonder about her non-attendance. This news will give them false hope, working quite well for me. And another thing, they will no longer be able to fraternize with each other. All bathroom and exercise rooms will be met with a schedule, leaving the girls without any further contact with each other." He takes a puff of his Black Dragon, looking quite the pompous idiot. "And you can advise Whisper that Santana's death is our little secret to keep."

*Yes, sir. Three bags full, sir.* I turn to leave.

"Oh, Mathias?"

*Fuck's sake, what now?* I turn back, schooling my features.

"Send in Nicu to stand sentinel."

I nod as he dismisses me with a wave of his hand and resumes doing whatever the fuck he does. I go to pull my phone out of my pocket and realize it's not there. I curse a hundred expletives in my head, because it's not on me. I cover my blunder up by confidently opening the door to leave the room and closing it quietly behind me.

*Fuck!* I pat my pockets. Nothing. It was definitely on me when I entered Whisper's room earlier. *Shit! Did I drop it in there?* No. We all would have heard it land on the floor.

I stand like I'm protecting Cezar's door while my mind replays the short film of what went down in that room. It must have slid out of my pocket and onto the bed.

*Fuck!* First thing's first, I need Nicu ASAP. I can't summon him with my invisible phone and I can't leave my post outside this evil fucker's office until I swap with Nicu.

Wondering what miracle will bring Nicu to me, the man himself rounds the curve of the corridor and is headed straight for me. Luck has washed over me like a cooling balm.

"Nicu." I raise my hand. "Cezar needs you in his office." I throw my thumb over my shoulder. He gives me a sharp nod as I wait for him to reach me and I stand aside, allowing him to open the ornate door.

I have come to realize the man shares very few words. Even though we all wear masks here, it's like he wears another invisible mask, cloaking himself even more. He's a very hard man to read. I shove those thoughts to the side with more important things to worry about.

I make my way to her room double-timing it, stopping only to scoop up a bottle of water for her. I look over my shoulder, checking the corridor is clear before I open her door, quietly entering and closing it behind me, my eyes never leaving her. I've been told to check all the girls, so this makes me think Cezar has everybody busy, affording me this gifted time.

She looks so small, her weight having dropped considerably since we first came face-to-face in that hangar. She appears asleep. I hope to search for the phone and get in and out without her knowing. I noiselessly take those few steps to reach her bed and....

*What the hell?*

She's holding my phone, totally unaware of my presence, listening to somebody talking. What a fucking fool I am; as if she could sleep through the pain she must be in. I'm about to snatch my phone out of her hand when her head turns, her eyes filled with fright.

And then her mouth opens, and my hand shoots out, anticipating what was gonna be her next move, muffling her cry before she can get much volume. Fuck, she's gonna get us both killed. I pray nobody is in that surveillance room watching. We're screwed if they are. And that's when I hear a man's voice roaring her name from the phone.

*Goddamn it!*

I disconnect the phone and pocket it. "Shut. Up!" My voice is low, gruff, and nasty, my back deliberately angled at the camera so nobody can see what I'm doing to her.

*I have to protect both of us. She can't take another hit for her stupidity.*

I let out air I didn't realize I had been holding. "I'm going to take my hand away, but so help me if you scream again...." I pause, watching her trying to get a read on whether she will do as I say. She nods, and I release her mouth, wiping my hand clean of bloody spittle on the bed coverings. She shuts her eyes and a tear rolls down her cheek.

*Christ's sake. I'm the good guy!* I want to yell at her.

"Who the hell did you just call?" I growl low. Her eyes fly open, a fierce look in them. She does not want to answer that question, and I know she won't, because she knows I fucked up and she's gonna test me to see how I handle this situation.

I lean a little closer to her. "Who. Did. You. Just. Call. Rabbit?" I'm not fucking around now. She's gotta believe I will hurt her as I sneer at her, bringing my clenched fist up to her face.

Her body is visibly trembling now. *Finally*, it is hitting home, the damning situation she is in. I am no longer the guy who will cool her fever or stop her from landing in the cold snow. This is a whole new playing field, and her opposing team hasn't lost a match yet.

*And I don't like to forfeit a game.*

"I hope you remember what I'm capable of, little

rabbit." She's not even blinking as her mind starts playing over my part in what happened to her. "That was a man's voice shouting your name." She knows we both heard her name from my phone. "Little rabbit, I won't ask again." My voice is threatening her with a consequence for her insubordination, and just when I think she really is contemplating not answering my question, she gives in.

"Doeth ith mather?" She sounds so defeated as saliva leaks out the corner of her mouth, dribbling onto the stained pillow she's clutching like a lifeline, her broken wrist cradled against it. Her face is marked with tear tracks that I helped put there, her eyes sadder than I have ever seen. Before, she had fight in her, and now, that has been physically sliced out of her.

"Yes, it fucking matters. Sit up. Jesus Christ!" The words come out in a hushed bark. She has no clue what I am trying to do here. What my mission is, what I can't fail at.

She does as she's told, moving so her back is against the wall, watching me, waiting for what's to come. I am her enemy. I have now cemented that in her mind. Before, I wasn't so much the bad guy, but a man following orders and bending them along the way. She was letting her guard down around me. That wall is now up and solidified.

*Good girl. Be afraid of me. It will make my job*

*easier.*

This is the second time she's used a phone that I know of. Somebody would've scoped out that hangar, looking for answers by now, because it's way too easy to track a regular cell phone these days if you have the knowledge, and she had somehow gotten a phone into that trunk she was in. They would have found the gate locked, but I doubt that would have stopped them.

I stand here watching this frightened girl, wondering why her abduction isn't plastered all over the news reports and media. I've been checking, but no reports have been listed of her being a missing person. No police investigation appears to have been brought from her disappearance, which makes me question why.

I let out an irritated sigh. What does it really matter who she called? What can I do about it?

My hand squeezes the forgotten bottle of water. I need to be gone from this room. I drop it carelessly onto the bed. There's the tiniest movement as she squeezes the pillow to her chest a little tighter. She wants the water, but won't reach for it while I'm here. For now, she needs to protect herself the only small way she can after what Rose and I did to her.

I've been in here too long. I rip the pillow away from her chest, and she gasps in shock, her eyes huge. I throw the pillow to the end of the bed and eye her scantily dressed body. Her breasts are not hidden beneath the sheer lace as she brings her knees to her chest. I want her to think I am just like those other men, although all I see are her bruises everywhere. I still haven't seen the trophy of a girl revealed. It is hidden under the physical trauma her body has been put through. Her gunshot wound is healing well, and her broken wrist is on the mend. She needs a good, hot shower to clean herself up and some real clothes to keep her covered, away from the other sentinels' eyes.

This was just all part of Cezar's mind games, trying to make her feel exposed. None of the other women are dressed this way in only a piece of lingerie. All the other beautiful dolls in here are perfect, no physical imperfections, but Whisper has those scars on her back. That previous fucker she talked about must have cut *PET* into her lower back. I saw it when I slammed her face into the table in the hangar. She had permanent marks from repeated beatings. Whisper was damaged, yet Cezar had her up on this strange pedestal in his mind. She was the only one who had been physically marred, yet when he saw the imperfections on her body when she was brought in, he didn't bat an eyelid.

The woman in stall five was more likely to be trophy fodder for Cezar than this underweight, scarred girl. A private joke among the sentinels was to refer the women's rooms as stalls inside The Pen.

She picks up the water bottle, trying to hide the slight tremor in her hand as she tries to undo the lid with only her right hand.

"Here." I snatch it back off her and unscrew it. She takes a small sip, hissing at the sting, which ends with her coughing up blood and spit all down her front.

*I can't show her I care.*

"Nobody knows where you are and my phone is untraceable. If anybody finds out about this, your life will be over." My words are darkly threatening. They cut into the last threads she is holding onto, making her lower her eyes.

*Good girl. Stay scared of me.*

She is a brave girl, but she's learning to pick her fights. It will keep her alive being more submissive. I'm about to turn away, when she bends over and coughs her guts up all over herself and the bedding, and then her body is shaking uncontrollably.

She needs medical help immediately. I watch her for a moment longer, and then abruptly turn on my heel and swing the door open hard, bolting through it. If I stayed I would have wanted to help her.

And. That. Isn't. Gonna. Happen.

"Just stay under the fucking radar, and if you've got
any self-preservation, you'll remember the cameras

are watching," I mutter to myself, when I smack straight into....

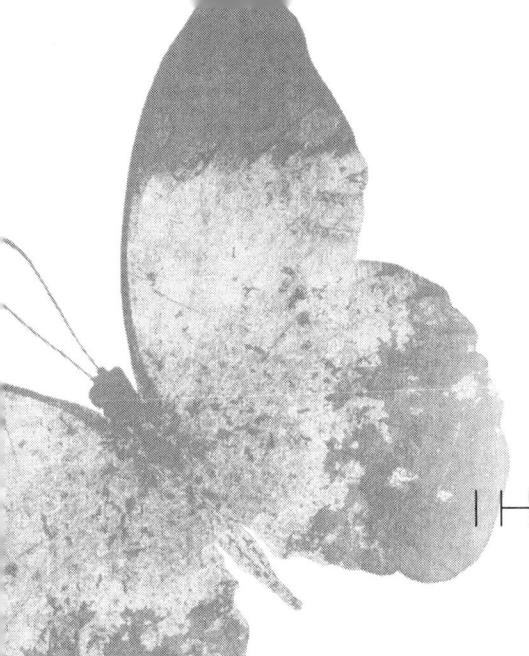

# ROSE

## I Have My Very Own Sasha Fierce

**I walk the silent corridor of the stone tomb, not seeing** another soul, which is around a gridiron-sized circular length. I'm carrying a bag of things to attend to Whisper.

Somebody had to pay for Santana's insubordination. Cezar bided his time, waiting for Whisper to wake up, giving her no breathing space before laying his law down. Santana broke the rules. She had been given the role of flight hostess for deliveries and had lasted nearly as long as me, but I knew her time was up after this upcoming event.

Whisper had to know straight up that escape was punishable by death, and somebody always had to pay for another's fuck up. It was the balance of scales in his eyes.

I am not naïve. I am Cezar's first courtesan, and I won't be his last. His insane kingly-role-playing needed to be fed, and so the position of courtesan and assassin was recently born.

At least I can stop the other women from being violated until I can no longer protect them, and that is when my soul turns another shade of black. I take no joy in fulfilling his commands, but I too have a role to play.

I haven't had to cut any of the other women, just this one. She may have come to us battered and shot, but she is strong-willed and that is dangerous. I saw her determination to survive written all over her face. He saw *me* in her when I had first arrived at one of his lairs. I was strong, determined not to become a victim, just like he read in her defiant eyes. He cut my tongue out to teach me a lesson, and I've folded to his every whim from then on.

I became a machine.

I've killed for him.

I am a shell to be fucked.

Every time I do his bidding, a bit more of my true self dissolves away, never to return, but I am unable to stop without being taken down.

*I am trapped in a vicious cycle.*

I am allowed to freely move around The Pen area when he chooses, this being one of those times, because there is no escape for me. All exits are locked with security-coded panels. Cezar takes no chances.

The other girls here have already been given their information booklets. I can't teach them with speech. They needed to study them and learn why they are here and their part in this contorted game of Cezar's.

Their heads have been filled with promises of freedom, and they are all willing to believe it, because they're all in survival mode. Hope will keep them in line, keep them obedient and submissive.

All I have to do is plan the event and let Cezar know what I need, and he gets it sorted for me. His outside persona has no ties to this hidden world.

I've planned one event before this one. Filip and Cezar used to plan them, but he decided a woman's touch was needed to take it to the next level. I had to perform or be executed, because he can't really bring in an event planner.

This upcoming event *has* to be more spectacular than my last, and worthy of the over-the-top money these rich, wicked fuckers fork out, or I'll be signing my death warrant sooner than later. Cezar will not be made a fool of.

All the girls have to do is look beautiful and tempting on the night of the event and let the best man reap his reward.

*Simple, right?*

Not so much. They haven't been told the truth. They think they are going to be pretty things to be admired and not touched.

*The not-knowing is far better than the knowing.*

I am unmasked here while the men hide like cowards, most of their face hidden from the women's eyes. They are to look imposing and dangerous, and I am to look like you can trust me until I am ordered to do otherwise. There will be no fictional ending where they walk away with a happily-ever-after, with me as their comic book superhero.

*Not this time.*

That fucked up information booklet I coerce them into signing their name on the dotted line for their services and their release is all a ruse, but they are all too scared *not* to sign.

They badly want to believe they will survive.

They *believe* in me.

I am their hope.

Instead, I am their damnation.

When Cezar decides it is time to merge back into his other self, revisit the outside world and regain his respectable place in the business world, it is then my time to perform.

They don't even know I'm coming for them. They think their contract is fulfilled and Cezar is going to grant them their freedom, because they've played by the rules of the booklet. They haven't been able to identify him or his sentinels due to the masks, so they convince themselves they can survive their ordeal.

*Never.*

I was granted one boon. It's his way of caging any thoughts I have of rebelling. I'm allowed to choose the method for their demise, and I choose death by a lethal injection. It's the best I can do for them. I wait until each girl is asleep, drugged into a carefree slumber by a sedative administered in their last drink, and then I *end* them, mercifully and without fear or torture.

I am a silent murderess in the night, handing their souls one-by-one to the Grim Reaper. I say a silent prayer for them and their families while I wait for their heart to stop, telling them each how sorry I am for my part. Knowing I am not forgiven.

These deaths are on my head. They all trusted me. I was their mistress who didn't lay a finger on them, but I was deceitful. I was almost a friend to them, as their minds became more attuned to Stockholm syndrome, the feelings of trust or affection felt in some cases by a victim towards a captor.

I play my role well.

Cezar would have handed them off to Kane, who had previously been the one to dispose of the girls, if I hadn't accepted my role as assassin. He would again be allowed to take great pleasure in draining the blood from their bodies while torturing them lifeless, and I too would be executed violently. I've made myself temporarily useful in Cezar's eyes. I'm an asset.

I make their short life in captivity as comfortable a lie as I can. Every girl in The Pen receives two coloring books and a packet of crayons and fine line markers. The crayons, she can keep at the end of each day, but the markers are taken from all the girls, counted, and returned each morning, because we can't have anybody making a weapon out of them. I also sharpen their crayons daily and must return the sharpener to Filip or one of the other sentinels at the end of each day. The razor part could be used to slit their wrists or my own, and Cezar can't have that. Everything is always accounted for. I too am left with only crayons every night.

A man like Cezar leaves no untrustworthy loose ends that can warn the world of an unidentifiable evil creature that exists, although I have been the recent exception.

Filip taught me how to fight. He trained me until I became as much an equal as I could become, weighing much less than him. I'm now strong, but he can still kill me, because he's built to survive a bullet train head-on.

When I'm not being beaten to a pulp until I've learned to defend myself and fight back, I'm with

Cezar, slowly losing myself as I'm sexually abused, my body debased.

I am under no illusions. I know I have a use-by date. I have a goal to take down the sons-of-bitches involved. I have been taking mental notes of everything. I've been searching for a way to escape this nightmare I've been thrown into, but it appears impossible.

I dream of escaping into the *real world* and revealing this man and his operation. I pray every night that it will come true and there will be enough of *me* left inside this hardened shell to try to bring justice for the lost lives. It's the only thing that keeps me going in here, or I would have turned one of those lethal injections on myself a few months ago, if it weren't for a sentinel watching me closely administer it.

I've been made to do very bad things, and deep down I know I couldn't live with myself on the outside, even if I were to be set free. My soul is marked for death, and I've made my peace with this. The vile things this man is getting away with and all the evil bastards paying to enjoy it... somebody has to bring it all crumbling down.

I have to *believe* it is possible.

I reach Whisper's room and am about to open the door, when it swings open and my face is smashed against Mathias's hard, muscular chest as he finishes muttering to himself. All I can think for a second or two is how nice he smells of soap and masculinity, and then he steps back from me and my bag falls to the floor.

I look up at him, although his face is partially covered, he is a handsome man. He's tense and wired, growling an apology as he gathers up the bag, shoves it into my hands, and then pushes past me. I look to my right, and he's storming away, his back rigid.

I know I don't have any allies among the sentinels, nobody I could trust to turn on Cezar, but this new man, Mathias, intrigues me. I am wary of him and pay him no visible attention, but I have watched him these past few days, and he isn't like Filip, or Kane. I don't have a clear read on him, but I sense he is different. Mathias isn't deliberately cruel. He follows orders, only. Yet Cezar trusts Mathias enough to bring him into his inner sanctum, which is saying a lot, because the man is paranoid about the secrecy of his wicked life.

Mathias must have done a lot of impressive bad things to raise his profile to get Cezar's attention and be welcomed into the fold of sentinels. I need an ally in here, but how can I trust somebody who has worked their way up the food chain to become a sentinel? I can't.

I shut the door, place the bag on the bed, and open

it up, getting out a medical kit, coloring books, black yoga pants—without the drawstrings, in case the girls get any bad ideas—a white tank top, and a plain fleece hoodie.

Whisper's body language is that of a petrified statue. Fear keeping her immobile. What just happened with her and Mathias?

I brush the thought aside, because it is not for me to know, and yank on her legs without warning, moving her body down until she is lying flat. The last time I was here with her, I hurt her badly and she doesn't trust me, but she doesn't fight me.

She is a quick study.

I grab her face and motion with my own mouth for her to open up. She complies. A torn, bloody, swollen lump of mutilated muscle stares back at me, and I get to work. She doesn't make a peep, but the silent tears escaping her sad eyes tell me enough. I was once, not that long ago, in her exact situation, scared out of my mind and spitting up blood.

I had been stolen.

I was once Ruby Rose.

But I had to leave Ruby behind and become Rose.

# Evelyn

## Sometimes Wrong is Right

I move the chair a little closer to my queen-sized bed, in one of the rooms I keep above my offices and stroke his hair, trying to calm his restless behavior. He's having a very active dream.

When Ghost called me with the news of Boxer and Lincoln, my heart nearly stopped. I was so afraid I would never see the man I have loved from afar alive and well again.

Boxer has shown himself as a man of integrity. I've watched him work toward settling down and becoming something more to Whisper, someone solid in her life she could rely on. He has made a family for himself, while I've looked in from the outside.

Every excuse I had before for not being romantically linked to him dissolved into thin air. It's not until you nearly lose somebody that you realize how lonely and sad your own life has become.

All these hidden feelings I have locked away resurfaced, and now I haven't been able to leave his side. He's been in and out of consciousness, nothing sensible to be made out of anything he's said over these past few days. Even now, he's making noises and calling my name, muttering things I can't quite make out.

He keeps repeating "Ev," the shortened version he hasn't used in a long time. The one he reserved for flirting with me, until I knocked him back so many times I became plain old "Doc."

I wanted to accept his flirting and agree to his advances, but I simply couldn't. It wasn't the right time, and when the right time could have been *the right time*, it appeared he was past there being anything between us. I wasn't brave enough to put my feelings out there or test the waters to see if there was still a thread of interest from Boxer.

As far as I could tell, Boxer hadn't gotten himself a girlfriend. He seemed too caught up in his work to have one of those, and I didn't want to be a booty call.

My brow furrows with concern. He's getting so restless now that I get up out of my chair and hover over him, trying to listen to what he is saying. I bend down a little closer to try and hear more of his jibberish, when I let out a surprised squeak.

*What the hell is he doing?*

Before I can stop him, I'm splayed across his body, his hands weaving their way into my hair, tugging on the strands, and it feels so sensual.

*Oh, lawd.* Now he's nuzzling my neck, his lips locking onto me, and *wow*, they feel so good sucking and kissing me there.

*Oh myyy.*

My eyes roll into the back of their sockets, my fingers finding purchase on his hard chest as I feel my body beginning to respond to his touch, and I can't even care he's unconscious.

I should care.

I should pull away.

I should be professional.

Boxer's my patient, and he's caught up in what I can only assume is an erotic dream, the way he's behaving, with me as his co-star.

I need to stop this, the evidence in my panties a warning sign I'm getting in way over my head. And then his lips rise from my neck and I hear him say ever so clearly, "I've got all the time in the world, Evelyn Castille." His husky words purr to me, and then he's marking me again, his lips insistent as they move against my skin, pulling and sucking, his tongue expertly working my neck while my head rolls about, wanting him to never stop.

I try to think coherently and be conscious of my body weight and his broken foot. I want to help out by spreading my legs on either side of his hips so I don't knock it, and bear some weight on my knees, but I'm having trouble concentrating on what I should be doing and what is happening. My natural reaction is to want to grind myself against him, my body wanting some relief from its arousal.

"Boxer." I can only pant his name in a pathetic attempt at waking him up, because he's stolen my breath. I need to pull my neck away from his mouth, but I can't seem to find it in me to do so. Just when my conscience is getting the better of me, I feel his hands glide down my spine and over my ass, cupping my butt, and I find I very much like his hands there.

"Ev," he breathes against my neck on a moan. I want to tell him I'm here, but I'm afraid he'll come out of the dream he's having and come to his senses and stop.

The little wanton devil sitting on my shoulder doesn't want him to stop, but it would be nice if we were on the same page and he was conscious and fully aware, instead of me taking advantage of this situation.

"Need you closer, Ev." And then I'm being pulled up higher until I'm gently rocked over his very hard erection, the bed coverings and my clothing not much of a barrier.

I think my eyes just rolled back into my head again, because I can't see anything. I can't mute the soft little noises escaping me as the pressure builds inside me the more he rubs me against himself, and my hips have a mind of their own, because they want in as they start to groove to his beat.

*What am I doing?*

I let the angel on my other shoulder speak to me, *Ev, pull yourself together.* I start to pull away, to do the right thing, my mind at war with what my body wants, what is ethical, but I can't seem to find the rulebook. I close my eyes, trying to block out how wrong my behavior is, when his hands tighten on me and he starts to grind harder, trying to find my core.

I groan loudly.

*Who am I?*

I will pay for my sins later. My mouth lunges for Boxer's, connecting, and I'm kissing him with the intent to have the rulebook thrown at me. I'm all sex-starved female, deprived of intimate contact for far too many years. I thought I was a dried-up raisin, but it appears my raisin is still fresh, because I am so close to liftoff.

*I am going to hell for this.*

And that's when my lips are no longer quite connected to Boxer's, and I hear a deep, satisfactory sigh breathed across our parted lips. It's the same moment my brain has caught up with the memo it has been trying to deliver and I realize exactly what I have been doing and how unprofessional it is. My eyes swing up, and my face feels like it needs a bucket of ice thrown on it.

*Shoot!*

I hadn't even noticed Boxer's eyes were open, and they are a mixture of hungry and amused as they watch me.

*He's awake?*

I bite Boxer's bottom lip in embarrassment, because it's the only thing I can think to do, hoping he will release me so I can regain some sense of pride instead of acting like a randy forty-plus-year-old.

He doesn't help the matter by broadening his amused look into a full-on grin, white teeth everywhere, blinding me.

I'm abusing my patient/doctor relationship, and I try to untangle myself from Boxer's arms. "Hey", he whispers to me, with a now toned down silly grin on his face. I'm not sure if he even knows what's been going on. I pray he's still dreaming. Some people dream with their eyes open. Don't they?

*Shoot! What have I done?*

"Evelyn, I thought I was having a hot dream until I woke up a few minutes ago."

Yup, he's still grinning. *A few minutes ago?*

"I think we just became an item." That damn sexy British accent. He gives me a sure-of-himself wink and then his eyes wander over my shoulder.

I face-plant on Boxer's chest as another voice I so do not want to hear starts talking. This just keeps getting better and better.

"Oh hey, Doc, sorry." Ghost's deep voice doesn't even sound the least bit sorry.

*Lawd, save me from this embarrassment, for I shall not live this down.*

"My bad… should've knocked. I see you're busy." He coughs a little like he's trying to smother a laugh. "I heard noises and was checkin' in to see if everything was all right. You look like you have things under control here."

I can now hear the laughter he isn't even trying to disguise. Thank God I am fully clothed.

"I'll just be going, seeing you're in safe hands." I turn my head and give him the stink eye, which only has him shaking his head and laughing out loud. "Good to see you are fightin' fit, Boxer."

"Hey, Ghost." Boxer looks around me and gives his good friend a small wave. I make a mortified noise and look back at Boxer, who seems to really be enjoying himself.

"Good to see you're awake and makin' up for lost time. That cocktail the doc's got you on seems to be workin' wonders. I'll catch up with you later on." And then Ghost is gone, and I'm left with a man with an erection digging into me, and I don't even know where to begin with what just happened.

*Awkward much.*

I prioritize my thoughts. The first thing I should do is get off Boxer. I try to roll away, but he's not having any of it, as my hips are gripped firmly and held in place. "Let me go, Boxer. You were dreaming and you pulled me down onto you, and that is all that happened," I lie, because I can't face the truth.

"From where I'm lying, it was a pretty good dream, Ev. Not one to be dismissed so readily." He raises a fingertip to my neck, gently rubbing the spot I know will be red. "Looks like it played out in 3D. You seem to have been marked, and I seem to remember, in this dream of mine, putting it there and you liking it." He pulls my face up to look at him, and I am hit with a shot of heat like I'm a crème brulee getting prepared to be eaten.

*I need to fan myself.*

"I know it," he begins, and I try to commando roll off him, but I'm tugged back into place. "And you know it."

I can't make eye contact, because he's right, and I don't know what this truly means for us from here on out.

"Ev, look at me." He waits until I raise my eyes,

and... what beautiful eyes he has. He's such a handsome man. He's lost weight from his ordeal, but he'll be back to his strong self in no time. "Are you with me, Ev?" If it's possible to blush anymore, I think I just did. "No more pussy-footing about. It's you and me, love."

I nod while he puts a very smug smile on his face, and then he kisses me again, and all I want is out of my clothes.

My body responds, seeking out the hardness of his crotch, and I rub myself against him as he moves the best he can to help me out, but then he stops kissing me. I want to whimper at the loss of his lips.

"Ev, I've always only had eyes for you, love. You must know that by now?" I want to sigh the way he says 'love' with that British accent of his. "A man doesn't keep coming back if he's not interested."

*He does keep coming back.*

My only response is to grab either side of his head and start kissing him again. Whatever this is right now, it is worth trying. I nearly lost the man I have loved from afar, too afraid to step up to the plate. Now, I'm taking the run at the bases.

Without releasing our lips, I start undoing my sensible blouse. I need out of it. Once it's discarded, flung somewhere, I try to roll off him again. He misunderstands. My hips are gripped again, holding me in place. I tug my lips away from his. "Do you want me out of these pants or not?"

I'm literally thrown to the side of him, and then I wriggle out of my sensible slacks and kick them away. I look up to see the molten desire in his eyes, and I'm not sure what my next move should be.

He takes that decision away from me by sliding his hand down my belly to the top of my panty line, my hips moving to get closer to his hand, but then he slides that hand right back up my stomach, unclasping my bra with a flick of his fingers.

My breast spills into one hand as he cups it, thumbing my nipple, coaxing it to get harder before his tongue licks the little bud, making me exhale on a sigh. My hips start getting restless as I squirm, needing more, a fire in my belly demanding to be put out.

"Boxer." I'm begging, I know. He adjusts himself so there are no longer any barriers between us, and tears the hospital gown over his head, leaving him gloriously naked, but still attached to the gown.

"Careful, you'll rip your IV out." I help him to thread the bag through the sleeve and untangle himself from the fabric.

"It would appear, Ms. Castille, you have more clothes on than me, now. Care to play fair?" I quickly relieve myself of my bra and go to shimmy out of my not-so-sensible matching panties, when he pulls me toward him so we are lying turned inward. "I can take it from here." He can't help looking satisfied with himself as his eyes roam my face. "Beautiful," he murmurs.

I try not to smile back, when I feel his hand cupping my panties from the front and one brow arches. "Ready for me, Ms. Castille?" His hand is inside the lace barrier, feeling my almost bare skin while my hips impatiently tip, trying to find his fingers. I need relief from this maddening arousal that has taken over me.

My foot slides up the bed, bending my knee to give him more access, letting my hip swivel out so I can spread myself for him.

"Ms. Castille...." I like the way he says that, it sounds dirty. "You sure about this?"

*Surer than I've ever been.*

"Yes. Let me show you how much. I don't want to go another day without trying you and me."

"We can take it slower, whatever you need, but this," he points between us, "it's going to happen, and I'm bleedin' over the moon it is."

And then he kisses me with his eyes wide open, our pulses accelerating as our hands move frantically, touching those intimate places, our lips colliding urgently as we taste each other, our climaxes fast and euphoric.

We finally pull apart, and I lay my head on his chest, listening to his heart beat, so strong and alive.

This feels right. My heart laid its roots down a long time ago.

We stay like this for a few moments lost in the connection and then his body jolts as though he's been shocked when he remembers where he is and why. "Ev, is Whisper safe?" I sit up and give him space as he processes everything he can remember.

I think I need to send in Miss Catherine and get Joel on speaker with Ghost. There's a lot to explain, and he isn't gonna like any of it. "Boxer, you need to rest, and then we can all talk with you."

"No! I need to bloody well know what's happened to her, Evelyn, because I can gather from your answer that she's not safe." His tone has changed to a pissed off man who needs his girl back. All sexual tension has been forgotten, and fear for Whisper is filling the bedroom.

"Okay, Boxer, I need to get dressed and then I'll go get Ghost and Miss Catherine and they can fill you in." I get up off the bed and quickly slide back into my clothes while I keep talking. He knows from my tone of voice he isn't going to like what he hears. "But you need to promise me you'll hear them out and stay calm, because I will stick you with a sedative quicker than you can blink if I think your health is in danger. You've only just regained consciousness. Waking up for sips of drinks and potty breaks don't count. This is the first time you've been fully alert, and you need your rest, and we shouldn't have just done what we did. Edge is doing his best to find another lead, and he isn't stopping until he gets one."

Boxer's body has gone ramrod straight at the mention of Edge's name. "Who the fuck is Edge, Evelyn, and why does he have anything to do with Whisper?"

"Ghoooost! I need you in here, stat," I holler. I'm buttoning my blouse up just as Ghost comes charging into the room. Boxer is getting agitated and ready to move, and I don't think he even realizes his leg is in a cast and he's still naked. "Ghost!"

"Who the fuck is this Edge?" He's looking to Ghost for answers.

*Shoot!* Boxer is on a warpath.

"You might want to sit back, buddy, and I'll tuck you in for this little bedtime story." Ghost tries to defuse the situation and get Boxer back into bed, but I know Boxer, and so does he, and the road is about to get very bumpy.

I don't stick around, leaving to get a sedative, because Boxer is going to need one when Ghost gets to the punch line.

# EDGE

## I've Decided There's No Virtue in Patience. It's Fucking Torture.

***C****hrist,* **the not knowing is hard. Here I am** drinking a beer in the Pitbull, waiting on Slade to arrive. It's been too many long, fucking frustrating, unproductive days since I set things in motion, calling in Slade and my club, who are on standby. I'm just about tearing my hair out with how useless I have been to Whisper.

I had Slade fly into New Orleans and stay overnight in a hotel, leaving him instructions to meet up with Miss Catherine at a café the next morning. I thumb through the images on Miss C's phone and find the one of Slade looking deadpan, wearing the bright, almost too tight, I LOVE NEW ORLEANS T-shirt, making him look ready for Mardi Gras. It was his ID for the meet-and-greet at Miss Catherine's request. I figured she wanted to see if Slade would do whatever it takes. It was her little test. I had returned the favor with a happy snap of my transformed look, bruises and all.

I needed my bike, and she wasn't going to let a stranger into her home overnight and let him raid her freezer without meeting him and letting *dem bones* of hers talk to her. I realized it was important to me she trust Slade, because he is going to be one of the team members swooping in to help rescue Whisper.

Boxer and Doc Evelyn were keeping Miss C safe at her office, so the old lady had to come up with an excuse to duck out to meet up with Slade in private. From her phone call to me, her bones approved of the mountain of a man.

While Slade was at her home, board and food were payable by watering Whisper's garden. She hadn't been back to her home in too long and was fretting about Whisper's garden dying on her. Keeping that garden alive meant much more to Miss C than vegetables and flowers. It represented Whisper. I also thought it was another test she was giving Slade to see his reaction.

I have been talking with Slade on the phone, catching up over the past days on what had changed in our lives since we last saw each other.

I haven't been without a physical visitor. Doc Evelyn's professionalism weighed in. She called a 'friend', who came to my hotel room, saw to my injuries, checked my foot over, and made sure I was taking my painkillers and using the crutches.

An older man, who looked a lot like Doc Evelyn, same blond hair, same eyes, greeted me at my hotel door with a no-nonsense look on his face. If I were a betting man, I would say it was her father.

He went about his doctor business in a professional, methodical way and behaved in that same manner as Doc Evelyn, not wanting to know the ins-and-outs of my medical situation, and then he left with the passing comment to let Dr. Castille know if I needed any further medical attention. His intelligent eyes were all too knowing.

The Lion's Den retrieved Santana's body and cleaned up the mess left behind. Drill worked on Homer, a.k.a. Blondie, but he knew nothing. Homer paid the Ferryman and wound up buried in the wooded cemetery surrounding the airfield, no doubt keeping company with a lot of other souls.

*Fucknuts included.*

We couldn't save Santana, and I have to hope Ruby isn't buried among those woods or anywhere, but I doubt she is still alive.

I've stayed put in Jackson, because where else was I gonna go? I was midway between where Whisper lived and where she flew out from.

Word is Boxer has woken up. I'm expecting a powwow with him soon enough. No way we're gonna be best buds after what went down with Whisper. I can't redeem myself in his eyes, and I'm okay with that. Shit is done. My priority is Whisper, and I know his will be too. Our unfinished business can wait.

Ghost and I have been staying in contact like a parolee and his parole officer, nothing forthcoming about a new lead.

The waiting is getting to me. It's a slow torture that is eating me from the inside out. I take another swig of my beer, looking the part of a fellow patron in the bar with the jukebox playing songs I'm not interested in listening to.

This asshole is going about having women abducted, and the world keeps right on revolving.

I can't stand not knowing what to do about it, where to even fucking start. It's like Alcatraz how securely locked away any leads are. This Cezar has everything sealed up tight, and I'm almost rocking in a corner with how fucking worried I am that I can't fulfil my promise to Whisper and Miss Catherine.

*I can't fucking fail.*

Not. Gonna. Happen.

Joel-the-computer-genius couldn't tap the keyboard into magically revealing this Cezar or any information surrounding him, because all I had was a fucking first name, and she had been held in a cold place prior to wherever she is now. She could be in fucking Antarctica for all I know. Believe me, Joel tried there for anything.

*Fuuuck!*

My hand clenches around the cold beer as I take another swig, checking Miss Catherine's phone with my other hand for any news updates.

Nothing.

*Always fucking nothing.*

The cops will be running in circles chasing their tails, trying to piece the motive together for Jonathan Boothe's murder. Doubt they are gonna find anything, because according to Joel, Jonathan's office was burned to the ground shortly after I called in his murder, his corrupt little secrets were incinerated.

*Equaling no lead.*

Could this be anymore FUBAR?

I look up from the table, letting my eyes settle on the front door of the bar. It's time for Slade to show.

And then he appears. He's around my age, thirty-one, with watered down Irish blood swimming through his veins. He's one hard, muscular unit, tall and built like Dwayne Johnson, without an ounce of Polynesian in him. The man looks after himself. He could be a poster boy for fitness magazines, with his brown hair and blue eyes and the pure mass of the man.

People have no clue what he can do. What you see is camouflage. He looks like he works out for six hours a day, no tattoos, save for the one inked over his heart, which simply states *HONOR*. He's a man of few words, unless he wants to spend them on you, and he's one reliable person who will always have your back if you earn his loyalty.

I watch him get a lock on my location and head for me, taking powerful strides. I stand up and clap him on the back in a one-armed hug. "Slade Malone, the years have been good to you. It's good to see you, brother." And I mean it. He was a fucking true soldier, a warrior for his country who landed on his feet and chose Ocean Beach, San Diego to tend bar and live an honest life. He'll show everybody that side of him, but he's got investments, he's got smarts, and when he's ready to let you in, you will know the *real* Slade. The man *behind* the bar.

He sizes me up, paying particular attention to my face as he takes off his leather jacket and puts it around the back of the chair he's slid out. "And you, brother." He lifts my scabbed over hand, the knuckles healing. "Looks like you've been bar brawling. I can see why you called me in, because it seems you're losing your touch." Slade injects some humor, because he knows damn straight I got problems that need solving.

"Something like that," I give him a wry smile as

we both sit down, our chairs loudly scraping the floor, but nobody pays us mind. Not even with a man who looks like Slade sitting among them, a man who should surely draw attention, but not in this dive bar. And that is why I chose the Pitbull to meet. I've come in every night, chatting to the regulars, becoming part of the fixtures, hoping to catch wind of any stories among the seedier clientele that may have been of interest to me. Everybody minds their own Ps and fucking Qs in here, but I couldn't just sit around in that hotel room doing nothing. I had to at least try.

I slide the cold beer I have waiting for him over, watch him drink half of it down, and point to my face. "I fucked up, paid the down payment, and I'm looking to settle the balance. I shot an innocent female, and I deserved everything I got and more." Slade's not gonna poke about with a response. He knows me well enough that if I'm admitting my mistake, then that is enough said. I saved telling him that part over the phone, wanting to do it in person.

Over the next beer, I get him up to speed, including my foot accessory, which I also omitted telling him about in the various phone calls we had prior. When I get to the part about Whisper's tongue getting cut and the last phone call, his fists clench on top of the table and he looks like he wants to crush some fucker's neck. But, the man responsible won't be getting off that easily.

There will be *no mercy.*

There will be debts to be paid by any fucker who touches Whisper and harms her.

He hasn't had much to say in response, other than grunting and growling. The more he understood what had been happening to my sweet and wild girl, he knew I'd fucked her in more ways than one.

Raising his cannon-sized arms, Slade stretches, his back muscles cracking as his black Henley pulls to the max across his hard chest. He's releasing the pent-up tension from everything I've revealed to him.

"Tomorrow's a new day, Edge. We'll get the answers we need to find your lady." Slade is full of confidence.

*My lady?* I doubt very much she will see it that way. We both stand up. "How's my bike traveling?"

"Got a few scrapes on her from the night you nearly cleaned up Miss Catherine on the side of the road, but other than that, she's a sweet ride."

I agree. "Hasn't let me down yet." I leave some bills on the table and we start walking toward the door. "Got a cab ride here. Figured you could give me and my moon boot a ride back."

Slade finds this amusing and shrugs. "Your bike, but you can keep your hands to yourself."

"I didn't plan on wrapping myself around you, big

guy." I grin for the first time in a long time and mean it. "You got a woman?"

Slade rubs his cropped hair with his hand. "Working on it." He widens his big blues. "You'd like her."

*And you'd like Whisper.*

# Whisper

## Color My World

**I sit cross-legged on my bed, picking up the** markers as I shade with bright colors onto the page of one of the two coloring books I've been given to blow away the lonely hours in seclusion. A subtle tactic to keep us mentally stimulated.

The only luxuries I have been given in here are packs of clean underwear, and a toiletries pack containing tampons, hair care items, a toothbrush, and toothpaste. Everything else is magically waiting for me when it comes to bathroom time, and food is always delivered to my room. I receive a pound on the door, and then the meal is waiting for me on a tray on the floor when I open it. The temptation to cross that threshold is great and very deliberate. It is a game to show it is possible to walk outside the room, but we wouldn't dare.

My tongue is better, my bruises nearly gone, and my shoulder doesn't bother me. I am healing well and have been obeying the rules. I am biding my time.

I'm currently busy transforming a black outline of a snow scene with the Ice Queen from the Chronicles of Narnia into a ridiculously over the top mashing of brilliant colors. Nothing is white. I have had enough of no color in every room I have been taken. I *need* color.

I look over at the page I have finished of Prince Caspian. He shouldn't have fuchsia hair, but he does.

I resume turning the snow scene into a blaze of color. I've completed some of the pages in the Venetian Carnival coloring book. I went wild with the pallet in that one. The pictures have been transformed from black and white into vivid art. The Narnia book is now looking almost comical, an outlet for staying calm and busy.

I've been trying to count the days since I've been here. My calculations tell me I missed my first Thanksgiving with my new family and now it's rolled over into Black Friday.

I was looking forward to reaping the food in Miss C's garden and helping her make the dishes for my first Thanksgiving dinner. I had so much to be thankful for with my freedom, my new family, and friend, Lincoln, but then all that disintegrated.

Miss Catherine and I had discussed a trip into New Orleans for Black Friday sales, and I was going to spend some of that money I was saving and splurge on a new wardrobe for myself. I was really looking forward to it, my first ever outing into New Orleans and away from Connard. The farthest I would have traveled... until now.

What I wouldn't give to be with Miss Catherine, trawling the sales and then going on to have drinks with Joel and Lincoln and meeting their friends. A celebration for giving myself permission to embrace my freedom and leave the safety of Connard.

*Or the place I* thought *was safe for me.*

I had good people who loved me in my life. I was ready to take my freedom to the next level. Lincoln would have been there with Joel to keep me safe. Boxer thought it was a brilliant idea. I knew he was happily going along with our plans because he trusted both men to watch out for me, and I was good with that. It was a blanket of security that a father figure needed to know existed.

Boxer must be going out of his mind with worry. At least I knew he and Linc were safe, and that was enough for me.

My time since I made contact with Edge has been spent with healing, reading that booklet of expectations and understanding my place, and coloring like a child. We are being pacified, and that is frightening me, but I can do nothing about my fears.

I have had no contact with Cezar or Mathias, and

Rose escorts me daily to a room set up with state-of-the-art gym machinery for an hour's workout. My muscles feel good to be doing something to stave off the continual isolation and silence that surrounds me.

The walls are so thick I can't even hear if there is somebody next to me. My day is Groundhog Day. Rinse and repeat. I eat three small meals, color, work out, color some more, and sift through my good memories in my waking hours. It is only a small folder in my mind, but they are so precious to me and put me in a better place.

My sleep time is a different story. My dreams keep circling back to Edge and the one night I thought I had met a good man, one who turned my world upside down with sexual pleasure, only to flip it on me.

I am at war with myself for continually thinking about him and that night. He enters my dreams before I can shut the gate and barricade him from entering them. I rouse, panting and hoping the camera isn't capturing me. I am always wet for him, and I hate how my body responds so willingly.

I have to keep reminding myself Edge told me he was coming for me. Boxer won't let me rot. He will find me.

I haven't let my guard down; if anything, it is higher. We are being lured into a sense of false hope.

I had to sign on the dotted line a contract releasing me from my captivity at the end as long as I do everything that is expected of me.

*It is all bullshit.*

But I play the game.

You don't get kidnapped, told you are a debt to be paid, and then every day since has been uneventful. This is where the real fear hits me, because I know things are going to turn ugly, and I don't know if I will be safe once it is all said and done. I am a debt owed, and I've had time to heal enough and work at getting healthy again. I am stronger. This is a smokescreen for what is really coming around the corner. It is the calm before the storm. There is a tsunami coming, and it will leave dead bodies in its wake.

Cezar keeps changing everything around to confuse me, scrambling in my mind the approximate time of day, as nothing is set. Everything is always the same every day, except the order I do it in. The only constant is my bathroom break in the morning, because it has to be morning... doesn't it?

My door opens suddenly, and I swing my legs over the bed, ready for anything. It's Rose, decked out in the same outfit as me her red hair up in a ponytail. I haven't seen any of the other women, but I know they are close by. I can feel their presence.

Rose yanks me in front of her and ushers me out the door, where a masked sentinel I've not seen

# CONTORTED

before tags along.
    I guess it's gym time.

# EDGE

## The Crossover is Evident
## *wink*

**W**hen Miss Catherine's phone rang, I had it palmed in seconds. I missed the ping of the text message showing on the screen, coded to let me know Lethal, the club's vice president, was calling. It was nearly 3:30 in the morning. I'm wired tight as I accept the call and hit the light switch beside my bed.

It has to be a good sign. I look over at Slade, who has rolled to his feet in one action from his bed in just his black Tommy Hilfiger trunks.

"Edge, *hermano*?" There's excitement in Lethal's voice. I hit the speaker button. He's part Hispanic, part all-American white boy.

"You got good news for me, Lethal?" I know he's not calling me for an early morning wake-up call. He has to have something for me to go on. I'm barely hanging on mentally at this point.

"Yeah... another woman named Joy Parker, a friend to the Lion's Den, was the center of a botched abduction attempt several hours ago in the back lot of Coyote Cooter's in Fort Worth, Texas."

*Christ.* And that's when Slade and I get serious and start pulling on warm clothes.

"Billy, a friendly to the Lion's Den, passed on information to Torque, their prez, which sounded like it had your woman's disappearance mentioned. Blueblood and I were close by on a run, so we responded."

"Did you get the fucktards?" I'm breathing fire as I nod at Slade, who's getting all this loud and clear.

"We got the *conos*." I hear the satisfaction. "Fucking team of nomads again, they spilled their guts, in a manner of speaking, but didn't know much other than the destination for their delivery. Here's the clincher: they were supposed to be dropping her off at that very same airfield you found Santana." I suck in a breath and stop what I'm doing. I catch Slade's eye, and then we start stuffing things into our bags as we listen to Lethal.

That's another team of nomads. Too fucking coincidental after Ruby and Santana went missing at the hands of a nomad team, and it's the same airfield where Ebony and Ivory had taken Whisper. Shit is adding up, and I need a face-to-face meet-and-greet with that flight crew.

"You gotta haul ass over to that airfield at Henrys Ferry ASAP. Drop-off for the female is for seven this morning. I'll explain everything else in detail later, no time now. You have time to get there. We're too far away, so it's just you two going in without backup."

I ain't arguing. We're out of here ASAP.

"You still got your man with you, Edge?" None of my brothers have met Slade.

"I'm here, Lethal. The name's Slade Malone. I've got your boy. How's the female?"

"Good." Lethal knows if I've called in a friend who's a nonmember of a club, I must trust this man with my life. "She's pretty banged up," he tells us, and we both let out a string of expletives. "But she's got good people watching over her at her home in Crowley. A guy named Levi Donovan is stuck to her like glue. Joy and this Levi are pretty tight. He's got the thumbs up from the Lion's Den men and Joy's grandfather."

"Levi Donovan?" Slade prompts. Sounds like he knows the man. "Good-looking guy who wears a prosthetic leg?" He's watching me with a confused look on his face.

"Yeah. Viking, vice president to the Lion's Den, filled me in. Apparently Levi was at Coyote Cooter's Country & Rocker Bar with a posse of friends. Their females were at a concert at the establishment, and

Joy was waitressing. She left to go home with Levi, but he got waylaid talking with somebody while she walked on down to the back part of the lot to her car. Then shit got real. Levi and co found her hiding underneath a car. She was beat up and scared shitless. Fuckers tried to snatch her."

I look up from balling up a shirt and stuffing it in my bag to see Slade's stopped packing as he listens to Lethal continue. "Joy has a prosthetic leg too. It's what saved her life. Dumb fuckers thought she was defective, not good enough for the fucker running the show, which worked in her favor."

A low, angry noise is vibrating deep in Slade's throat. He's pissed. "I know Levi Donovan, and there won't be anything defective about Joy, and there's nothing fucking defective about him either. He's a solid guy and one of my friends. I'll check in with my crew later to see how Joy and everybody are doing." Then he resumes packing and mumbles under his breath something about cupid has struck again.

"Slade, we need to hit the road."

"I'm good to go," he rumbles out.

"Where are you now, Lethal?" Adrenaline is flowing through my veins. We can't fuck this lead up by missing our chance for a rendezvous with the flight crew. I can smell their blood already.

"I'm about to leave for Coyote Cooter's. We've just finished up with disposing of those two nomads. We got their burner phone and ascertained from those dumbasses that they didn't have time to make the call yet, announcing their empty pockets, which works in your favor. We are ready to take the call when it comes in from their contact, who will be waiting for those two dicks to turn up, and I'll see what we can get out of him.

"Blueblood and I are heading on over to meet up with Torque and three of his men now. I'll speak to Hazard, let him know what's going down. We'll rest up, and then all head out to meet with you when you know where you'll be at." He goes quiet for a heartbeat. "This is the lead you been waiting for, *hermano*."

"Thank you for acting fast, brother. I appreciate everything everybody is doing for me, for Whisper." My club knows how private I have been about my past. Now, it's an open book.

"Brothers to the death," Lethal says quietly, and disconnects.

Slade and I are out the door and heading toward my Harley.

*Brothers to the death.*

••••

We arrive at 6:53 in the morning. I hardly notice the cold I'm that pumped. Sunrise was roughly twenty minutes ago, the day not been given a chance yet to let the temperature rise. Slade cuts the bike's engine and we leg it a short distance, because Harleys are loud and it's so peaceful out here at this time of morning. We're going in blind to how many fuckers we're coming up against and what firearms they have, so we don't need to announce our arrival.

I pick the lock on the fence, making sure to leave it undone if we need a quick getaway.

We hide the bike among the thick forest of trees, and I grab the handles of *No Mercy* and hurry the distance to the hangar, the crutches long forgotten in the hotel room we abandoned. We need to jog, and I'm not doing too good with that exercise with this fucking moon boot attached. I look like a bandy-legged drunk.

We clear the road and can see a sleek, white private jet resting inside the open hangar, which has my hunter heart hammering an intense beat. This time, I need to be smart. I need to be the predator I know how to be.

Slade has binoculars up to his eyes, one of the supplies we picked up during the week, and holds up one finger, telling me he has one man in his sights, and then he hands them to me.

One armed man is all we can both make out as he paces the hangar like he's impatient to get moving. We know there has to be more, a pilot to fly and at least one person to watch the prisoner.

We've already spoken about our plan of attack and have our guns, complete with silencers, raised and ready, our phones on vibrate. I give Slade the signal, and we split up, making our way closer to better gauge what we are dealing with from different angles.

The armed man in the open has a mask on top of his head pushed back, revealing a face that is scarred. He looks like a mean motherfucker. He's not expecting any trouble by the way he's not on full alert and his gun is slung over his shoulder carelessly.

*Motherfucker, trouble just arrived.*

I can see Slade from my vantage point and am about to signal him I'm going in, so he can cover me, when I see another man make his way down the plane's stairs. He has a baseball cap pulled down low over his face.

I hold up a hand signal to Slade, telling him to wait. I want to see what this one is up to; we might learn something. I hold the binoculars to my eyes, but can't see his face. It's like he's deliberately holding his head so I can't get a lock on his appearance. I scan his body, but from what I can see, he's not outwardly revealing a weapon. He might be the pilot. Both men are dressed in nice suits. Appearance means something to Fuckhead Cezar.

"Hey," he calls to the scarred one. He's American.

"I'm just gonna stretch my legs and take a walk around the hangar." Baseball cap guy makes a show of stretching his neck and back muscles. "Need to be alert for the flight back. That was a long trip from Alaska. You good if I take fifteen?" His voice echoes around the hangar.

*Alaska? What the fuck?* Whisper said she was in a cold place. Could she be in Alaska now?

The scarred one stops his pacing and nods his head in understanding. "Yeah, I'm good. Don't want you crashing the fucking bird." He continues pacing, thinking that was the end of the conversation.

"You heard from those two delivery boys?" Baseball cap guy is walking backward in the direction Slade is spying from, giving him time to ascertain the path the pilot will take and get into a better position.

"Not yet. Fuckers better be here on time and have her in one piece. Cezar was not happy with how that Whisper bitch was delivered."

My body is on full alert hearing her name from the scarred one's lip.

*Was he on the last flight with her?*

I aim my gun at the scarred one's head, my trigger-happy finger ready to squeeze, ending his life in one muted nanosecond. No maiming this time, no wasting a bullet. I've got the other guy to question. Don't need two guys to tell me the same thing. I only need one of the fuckers to torture answers out of, but I hold off, this moment too important to get anxious.

No matter how much I want to drop this fucker for even saying her name, I grip the gun, taking a deep breath, and hold myself in check. I relax my trigger finger and give the fucker some bonus minutes on his life's expectancy, hoping to hear more of their prattle. These dickheads are on borrowed time; they just don't know it yet. I can't afford to fuck up the *only* lead we've had all week.

The scarred one is still yabbering. "Cezar wanted retribution for losing Santana. Fucking heads will roll if we can't deliver the last female."

*Did one of these men kill Santana?* My finger gets twitchy again, a bead of sweat trickling down my face.

"Somebody's gonna pay for that, and you better hope it's not you." The pilot points a finger at the scarred one, and I catch the barely contained snarl on his face as he glares back at him.

*Stiirriike!*

Sounded like Baseball cap guy pitched a little warning his way. Not a lot of love there.

My phone vibrates. I look over at Slade, and he holds his phone up. I check the incoming message.

> **Slade:** Don't shoot any of these fuckers. Trust me. I need to check something out

first. Wait until you hear from me again.

He's right. I'm losing my mind over Whisper. We don't know what we're dealing with. I need to get a hold of those reins and pull myself up. I swipe at my brow, clearing away the stress that is evident on my mind. No point jumping the gun, they aren't going anywhere in a hurry.

I look up to catch Slade waiting for me to agree. I move my head in annoyance, because I really just want to rattle the snakes' cage and drop one of these fuckers to see how many come slithering out. We're close to getting answers, and I need to remember that and not become prey. Fuckers are totally oblivious to the dickwads not making their delivery date.

Baseball cap guy gives a short wave and heads off for his walkabout. Slade signals he's gonna follow the stroller, while I keep an eye on the scarred one. Makes sense, because I'm not the fastest or the quietest of the two of us with this fucking moon boot.

I turn my attention back to the scarred one. Whisper's relying on me, even though I really want to pop this fucker between the eyes solely because he called her a bitch. Instead, I make use of this time and take some snapshots. Anything that can lead me to Whisper is worth documenting, and then I send one on to Lethal.

The minutes tick by as the scarred one keeps marching back and forth along the side of the plane. The longer he has to wait, the faster he paces.

I text Lethal to let him know one of the flight crew is getting impatient for the delivery and that phone he's got in his possession will be getting a call anytime now.

And then I sit tight.

# SLADE

## Honor Can Be a Double-Edged Sword.

I follow the man as I silently creep forward. A warning bell is going off inside my head, alerting me to the fact I feel like I'm the one being lured away. Self-preservation instincts kick in and I aim my gun, my voice pitched low as I step out into the open once we've made it clear to the back of the hangar.

"Motherfucker, I want your hands raised and slowly turn around." My voice is deep and threatening. "My gun is pointed at your head and I won't miss." The guy turns around in a fluid motion, deliberately knocking his cap off, and gives me an apologetic shrug as he reveals his face to me.

*Son of a bitch!*

"Adam?" I breathe out, while my head cocks to the side as I take in the man standing before me. "What. The. Fuck?" The look on my face is a clear indication

I'm totally shocked at seeing my ex team leader standing before me. There have been some small cosmetic changes, but there is still enough of Adam Balan shining through if you look hard enough.

"I saw you from the cockpit, Slade." He keeps his voice low. "You're a little rusty on your stealth." He gives me a rueful smile.

Are those contact lenses? His nose is no longer crooked, and his hair has grown out and is salt-and-pepper like his close beard. His hands are tattooed, and he's definitely aged. He looks older than his mid-thirties. I watch him, taking in the man I once respected so much.

"I'm still here underneath." He sounds weary and sad. What's he got to be sad about? I can't help being deeply hurt by this man's betrayal of honor.

I don't lower my gun, no matter how much of a natural reaction it is for me to do so. He and I were as much brothers from another mother as Edge and I are. "You better start explaining what the fuck you are doing here." My hand tightens on the grip. I'm so fucking mad he's involved in trafficking women and God only knows what else. Edge will lose his shit. "How many of you are there?" I hiss at him.

"Just the two of us on this trip, and keep your fucking voice down. I lured you out here for a reason, because I sure as shit didn't need a fucking bend-and-stretch." He jerks his head to the side. "I gather you weren't stupid enough to come here alone and you've got a buddy at least out there watching Kane so we can talk?"

"Edge is here," I spit, not hiding my disgust for my former team leader. This man was once one of the best, loyal without fault, fearless, and a brother I would lay my life down for.

"Christ, Slade. Stop looking at me like that. It's not what you think. I'm unarmed. I deliberately left my weapons on the plane so you would trust me enough for a quick deep-and-meaningful. Now keep your cool. I'm going to lift my shirt and spin for you, and then I'm going to lift each pant leg and let you see. You can hold that gun of yours to my temple and feel me up if you choose, but I came out unarmed to talk before you did something stupid to jeopardize all my hard work."

He does a twirl for me, showing me he appears unarmed. I take no chances. "Place your hands on the back of your head," I order, and then I approach him and hold the gun—which Edge and I picked up as part of our supply run—against his dick and pat him down.

He doesn't move a hair.

When I'm satisfied, I push him forward, and he turns and faces me. "Don't fuck with me, Adam." We go way back to our time in the Special Forces. "You're playing for the wrong team now, and there is no fucking honor in that shit."

My faith in this man has taken a beating. He saved my life on more than one occasion. I'm so fucking disappointed to know he is part of whatever this hell is that women are being forced into.

The more I look at him now, the more I can see the strain on his face. Whatever he's been up to is taking its toll. Finally, he speaks. "Come on now, Slade." Moving one hand over his heart, my gun mimics his movement. "It hurts you think I would so readily bat for the other team."

*What does he expect me to motherfucking think?*

"It's been a long time, my friend," he says. The smile he tries to feed me doesn't quite reach his face, but it gives me a glimpse of the Adam I once knew, just in that small expression.

"Don't call me your friend. No friend of mine would be a part of this, whatever it is. You better start talking before Edge finds us, rips your balls off, and makes you choke on them."

His hands slide to his hips as he looks me in the eyes. "You remember I had a kid sister named, Eve?"

I nod because how could you forget they were named Adam and Eve by their parents who must have thought it was hilarious.

He looks right into my soul, like he's deciding whether he should trust me.

*Trust me?*

"I have reason to believe my sister was stolen a couple years ago by these fuckers."

*Motherfucker.* Not sweet Eve.

He doesn't give me a chance to reply. "Why are you here with Edge?"

I don't hesitate in replying. "We're here, because Edge's woman, or the lady he thinks is his woman, has been abducted to pay a debt to this motherfucker named Cezar. Whisper is her name. Seen her about?"

Adam looks away, cursing under his breath at this news, and then he looks back at me. "You've been doing some homework, I see. I know of her presence. Look, I'm deep undercover, so deep I didn't even remember my own name until you said it out loud. I know this is gonna be hard, but you need to walk away, now. Grab Edge and leave. Whisper is alive and well."

*Undercover?*

"She had her motherfucking tongue slashed. I wouldn't call that well."

Adam curses again. "How the fuck do you know that?"

*The tables have turned.*

"You've got your secrets, and we've got ours. The woman you were supposed to pick up today isn't coming, because she has a prosthetic leg and your delivery boys didn't know until they had assaulted her pretty badly."

Adam looks genuinely concerned for Joy. "She going to be all right?" This is the Adam I know.

"Yes, and just for the record, those two delivery boys are dead and buried." I hook my thumb over my shoulder. "Your buddy should be getting a little impatient right about now and giving a call to the ghosts." We're also running out of time before the other man wonders what's taking Adam so long to stroll around a hangar. "Keep walking. If by the time we get around the other side I'm not convinced of what you're telling me is true, then you and I are gonna have a really big problem."

Adam sighs and starts walking, while I listen, and I talk, and I listen some more.

*And then I walk away.*

# EDGE

## Ready to Crack Skulls

**I've gotten as close as I dare. The scarred one** has had enough of waiting. He's checking his phone and cursing the invisible delivery boys. I quickly text Lethal to tell him the show is about to start.

"Where the fuck are you two idiots?" Dipshit barks down the line in greeting. He's forgotten all about Baseball cap, who's still not surfaced, nor has Slade. I know he can handle himself.

"What do you mean you've been held up? What the fuck are you being paid to do? Be the fuck on time, is what!" This dickhead is fuming. Lethal must really be acting up. "She was a no-go? What does that even mean?" Dickhead is cursing like a pro into his phone. "All you fuckwits had to do was bring us a pretty girl, and now you're telling me she had a fake leg and you just let her go? You didn't pop a bullet in her pretty ice-blue head? You fucking incompetent *idiots*!" Now he's hollering at the top of his lungs. I hear the deadly impatient sigh. "How far away are you from the airfield?" He wants to know so he can end the nomads.

*Too late, fucker.*

He listens more to Lethal, who is putting on a pretty convincing show. "No, he doesn't have fucking time for you to find another. Fuck you, assholes." There go his bad manners again. "I would enjoy making you two scream, and I would draw it out slow until you wish you were dead." Another round of curses starts up. The dickhead needs anger management courses, and maybe some social skills. "You better hope we never cross paths, or you can consider yourselves done for."

*Keep pushing him, Lethal. The angrier he gets, the more he will slip up in rage and spill some secrets.*

"Can't wait another night, idiot. Gotta be back into Anchorage tonight. He needed just one more gal for The Pen, and you two can't fucking deliver, which means I can't fucking deliver, which means you've made a very big fucking problem for us."

*The Pen? Is this guy fucking serious?*

His arm is flying around like he's a maestro. "Shut up, asshole," he squawks, really losing his lot. "You've got no idea who you're playing with and what this fuck-up means to *him*."

*Asswipe... you got no idea who* you *are playing*

*with.*

"We're expected to return with a pretty, young, fuckable thing who is undamaged, unlike the last one, who was half-dead when she arrived in our hands," he bites out. "That bitch was a handful trying to escape in the freezing cold. I fucked her up so she would think twice about running," he boasts his achievement in hurting Whisper, who had already been shot.

*Is this man Kane, who Whisper said likes to hurt women?*

I hear the animalistic growls coming from me, threatening to expose me. I quiet down as Slade messages me to abort and meet him back at the bike.

*What. The. Fuck?*

I'm ready to crack skulls. Shove things in places that will hurt. Cut places that will drain the life essence out of a person. Make a fucker talk. *No Mercy* is ready to come out and play.

Dickhead growls down the line. "Fucker, you talk too much." The realization he's saying too much hits. Lethal has pushed him for too much information, and he's gonna run. "Forget I told you Alaska. Forget we've even had this conversation." And then he disconnects and starts pacing again.

I've heard enough. My grip tightens on the handles of my little black bag of tricks, the urge strong to break all my rules of Hunting 101 and just go motherfucking Nazi on these two men, because I have no patience left in the tank. It's empty.

I've known Slade a long time, and the last time I remember, which was fifteen minutes ago, he had all his marbles. Why the fuck would Slade ask me to abort?

Baseball cap reappears holding his hat in his hand, looking straight in my direction, a deliberate action. I snap off a couple pictures. I shove the binoculars to my eyes and I jolt back a few steps.

*Adam?*

I'm about to do something stupid, when a hand slides over my mouth and across my chest, crushing my trigger-happy arm to my side. Slade's a beast of a man and knows he's got more mental and physical strength than me at the moment.

"I. Said. Abort." Each word is ground out with an invisible full stop into my ear.

I'm straining against his bulky body. My brain hasn't caught up with the memo yet. I hear what Slade is saying, but we came here to make heads roll and get answers. This isn't getting answers in my book.

*That guy looked a little like Adam, but it can't be, right?*

"Time... to... walk away... brother," Slade grunts each word, because my body has a mind of its own and is fighting his hold. Nobody has had their hands on me like this in a long time, and it is setting my nerves on end.

I'm hearing him, but the math still isn't computing, because my memories are at war with my mind, threatening to spill out, and they need to stay locked down tight.

I'm glaring at the two men, who are now conversing with each other in the hangar and then Kane-the-fucker has his back to us and is heading for the pushback tug. They are preparing to leave. Those fuckers are right within our grasp, ripe for the picking, but what Slade is asking me to do sounds fucking nuts.

*Is that really Adam?* I'm floundering in my mind, because it does and doesn't look like him. And why would he be here of all places?

I put more effort into my struggling. This is our shot to find out a lot of information, to exact some motherfucking retribution for Whisper. To make a fucker bleed, as Whisper has, as Santana has.

*An eye for an eye.*

I'm being dragged backwards by Slade's sheer strength into the hidden safety of the trees. "Fuck, Edge, stop fighting me for a second and let me talk." I hear a heavy sigh of relief from Slade when I stop struggling against his hold, but he isn't fooled by my compliance. He's still convinced I'm going to buck him off me. "Do you trust me, Edge?" His voice has this deep, soothing timbre to it. I've never known Slade to steer me wrong. He's by my side now, because I know he is loyal to a fault. He won't fuck with me. "Are you with me, buddy?" He gives our mashed-together bodies a shake.

Of course I fucking trust him. He wouldn't be here if I didn't.

"I said, are you with me?"

I take a moment, and then begrudgingly nod, because I do trust Slade, but this doesn't make sense. How did he come back with a whole new plan? We had a motherfucking plan, and it didn't involve walking away without busting some chops and getting answers.

"Not a peep from you when I remove my hand from your mouth, but I'm still gonna be hugging you like a bear. Got me? I ask you a question, you answer in hushed tones. You can't fuck this up now, Edge. I'm warning you. This is for Whisper's safety and return to her people. I have intel that will make that possible."

I nod reluctantly. *Yeah, yeah... not a fucking peep.*

He removes his hand, and I don't wait for a question, but I do use his requested hushed tones. "Answer me this. Was that Adam Balan?"

"Yes, that was Adam. He knew I was out there watching, and he was trying to lure me around the back, which he succeeded in doing. He's still one crafty motherfucker." There's great admiration in Slade's voice.

*What. The. Fuck?*

"I'm gonna take my hands from around you now, and I need you to listen, stand down, and let me explain once we get back to the bike. Can you do that for me?"

"Yes," I growl.

"Christ, Edge, you better mean it, because regardless of what you are telling yourself, this is the best thing for Whisper. You want her rescued, then you will do as I say. I promise you, on my life, I'm not fucking around with you. This has to go my way this time."

*Well, fuck.*

I begrudgingly agree again, and his hold loosens as he steps away. And then we make our way back to the bike with me taking the lead, fuming and confused why Slade had been talking with Adam and why we still aren't storming that fucking plane.

I'm the bear that has been poked too many motherfucking times in the last few weeks.

"This better be a fucking Oscar-winning speech."

# GHOST

## They Don't Call Me Ghost for No Reason

**I**'m all decked out in my camouflage gear and have stayed hidden, my sniper rifle ready to take out any threat as I observe the plane from my vantage point. Nobody will find me unless I want them to.

I arrived before the private jet landed. And have been taking notes and photographs of the usual suspects once the plane landed. There appeared to be only two people on board. I held my special issue parabolic microphone up perfect for eavesdropping on conversations, but couldn't pick up any other voices but the two men who got off the plane in my headset.

Boxer had me bug the hotel room Edge and Slade were stayin' in. Once I got wind of that phone call, I had a ten-minute head start on the two of them. I'd previously attached a tracker to Edge's Harley, so I knew they stopped for gas, giving me extra precious time to get hidden and set up. I probably broke the speed limit a few times gettin' here, and I know a thing or two about breakin' and enterin' and not gettin' caught.

The rental car is parked up the road in the other direction, the hood left up to look like a break down. Not unless you were specifically lookin' for it would you go out of your way to locate it.

Things got real informative when this Slade guy came along and had a very interesting powwow with Mr. Walkabout while Edge was out there stewin' with the need to go Rambo on the one named Kane.

That major fucker was lucky I didn't take him out. The piece of shit was beggin' for a bullet neatly between the eyes, but we couldn't afford to fuck this lead up and blow Adam's undercover work or lose Whisper.

Adam gave up the motherfucker runnin' the show's full name, being one Cezar Pavel. Even if that isn't his real name, it can be thrown around in a very elite hacker's circle Joel is privy to. He knows the best of the best, the type the government wants to put collars on, if they could catch them. Boxer can call in some markers and ruffle some high-up suit's feathers, while Joel is workin' his genius and I'm out in the field layin' low, doin' what I do best, leavin' nothin' to chance.

Adam was our way into the event that was happenin' in a couple weeks. Slade had pushed for that much; loyalties still existed between them. He was a good negotiator.

He also got himself a contact for this Adam on the outside, who Boxer could work with on the grounds that his cover wasn't blown.

Adam knew he had to play along with Slade, now he had been enlightened on the two motorcycle clubs who were fully invested in the mercenary mission. And nothin' was gonna stop Edge.

Gotta give Edge credit where credit is due. He is a man of his word. He is fightin' for any lead he can find. I've watched him tearin' his hair out for the last week from afar. He's a man fightin' to right his wrongs. He's kept up his end of the bargain by sharin' information, up until this dash for the airfield.

A man like Edge is one like myself. We fuck up, we need to do what we can to un-fuck it.

He took my ass-whoopin' without a fight. He admitted what he did, and he's done nothin' but try for any leads to find Whisper. He hasn't withheld information. He's not tryin' to be the Lone Ranger. He knows he needs all the help he can get, but he wants to be her knight, and not because he wants to look good in her eyes. He really does need to try to fix what he broke.

I turn the parabolic microphone towards where I know Slade and Edge are and shake my head slowly, fightin' a grin at what I can hear playin' out.

I gotta say I like these two more and more as I learn them.

The plane won't be hangin' around much longer. It's time to pack up, blend back into the thick woods, and wait for Edge's next move.

# EDGE

## Why, Oh Why, Can't I Fucking Shove Something Into a Painful Cavity?

Slade, his hands on his hips, gives me *the look* I guarantee is telling me I'm not going to like what he has to tell me next.

"Edge, we're gonna sit it out until Adam flies that bird out of here." He backs his words up by smacking his ass down in the dirt and looking at me to follow.

"I'd rather stand. You fucking asked me to walk away from the one who broke Whisper's wrist. The one who likes to hurt women." I squeeze the handles of *No Mercy* a little tighter.

"I did. But you and I both know we've got nothing to gain by outing ourselves and using armed force to overtake Adam and that motherfucker. Because he is the fucking good guy who has been working from the inside to bring an end to the shit that has been going on for far too long, and he doesn't know enough. He's got no clue where she is being held, because even they get stuck with a needle and blindfolded until they wake up in this place Whisper is. Cezar protects his secrets well.

"We can't storm the plane and get them to fly us back to their hidey hole with them at gunpoint. Shit can go down at the other end, causing alarm bells. We don't know what eyes are watching in the private airport, and if word gets out, then Cezar runs, and we lose all the women."

*I hate he's making sense.*

"Let's say you tied up the scarred one and you get your little bag of tricks out and go to town on him. Adam already knows as much as that guy, and we don't have to torture him, because *he's the fucking good guy!* We do this Adam's way and nothing can get fucked up."

*Would Adam's suits want us involved?*

I don't give a shit if they don't. I volunteered my services to the bring-Cezar-down club, whether the suits like it or not.

"Adam promised to send a code to my phone, only if Whisper's life is in jeopardy. Otherwise, we're to assume she's well." Slade gives me a solemn smile. "A word loosely termed in this case."

"She's not fucking well." My anger is growing. I

don't need to tell Slade this; he already knows, but I have to get pissed at somebody, and he's it. "Adam can't risk me fucking with his undercover work, nor can the people he works for, and I do get that." I give Slade a determined glare. "But *nobody* is stopping me from getting dirty in that big fucking playground full of happy-to-fuck-with-Cezar players. The suits may want Adam to play his role for another year... ain't fucking happening. This shit gets dealt with, done and dusted, during this event. I ain't sitting back twiddling my fingers until they deem it the right time to take down these fuckers."

*Hell no!*

Cezar ran his dark world cloaked in a need-to-know basis. I see all these hurdles only as a challenge. We hear the engine noises and look to the sky to see the private plane getting air. Kane is now lost to me, but not forgotten.

*Until we meet again, fucker.*

The plane disappears, and I message Hazard with a meeting place and to pass it on to the rest. Then I contact Miss Catherine. Everything else can get discussed when everybody is in the same room.

We walk back to the bike and roll it outside the fence line of the airfield, padlock back in place.

"Where to, Edge?"

"Connard, Miss Catherine's house, where we regroup with a team."

## CONTORTED

He starts the bike up and I sit on the back. Slade heads back onto the road, letting the bike roar to life.

Boxer and I need to meet. He has resources, and we need to sit around Miss Catherine's table and be all kumbaya with each other.

My father started all this.

I'll end it.

*Church will be in session.*

# CEZAR

## You Haven't Seen My Bad Side Yet

"**R**ose, my office. *Now!*"

I smash the phone down onto my desk, my anger a ferocious beast, hungry for vengeance, impatient for blood. This is the first time a delivery hasn't made it. A new beauty, the last addition for The Pen, should have been on my private jet and on her way here. This team of nomads couldn't commit to their contract. They dared to fuck with my plans. I pound my fist into my desk, my rage finding no peace. My fury overtakes my rationality.

*I always get what I want.*

"Filip!" I roar. He tips his head lazily to the side in acknowledgement. His arrogance will one day catch up to my wrath, but not today. He will enjoy this too much if he stays and watches. "Leave the room and send in Mathias."

He swiftly turns, swinging the door open and

closing it. Filip will only get a stiff dick with what I am about to do to Rose. Nobody needs to be rewarded for my loss. I need to balance the scales, and I know just how.

I remove the plain satin black mask I have on and place it on my desk. Then, I prowl over to my tall, antique, ornately carved set of drawers, sliding the deep top one open to reveal a mask lying on a bed of rich black velvet.

My hand reaches for it, and I allow myself a moment to gently pet it in admiration of the intricate craftsmanship and artistic detail. There are three faces on it, but only two sets of eyes. The left side has a sad face, the right, the smiling face, and in the middle, there are two hollowed eye sockets from each of the happy and sad faces, where they both meet. It is very much a three dimensional mask, which allows my mouth to be freely seen, to look happy, sad, or enraged, letting my wicked desires purge from my body on a roar if I so choose.

The mask is white and hand-painted with real gold, which coats both sets of lips and the three delicate and intricate gold masks that cover the two sets of eyes, giving the illusion of three masks, three faces.

It is one of my most prized Venetian carnival masks. One I have not had a reason to use... until now.

I pick it up, holding it with reverence, and then I place it over my face, making sure it is fitted and secure, and glide the drawer shut again. I walk over to the lovingly handcrafted gold-framed mirror hanging on the wall, one Donald Trump himself would envy, and seek out my reflection. The mask covers the sides of my face, almost engulfing my entire head. I turn my head side-to-side, making faces. I smash my palms into the wall on either side of the mirror and silently roar at my reflection, showing my teeth, stretching my lips, and then I close my eyes and let its power soak into me, giving me the strength to perform. My flattened palms ball into fists as I let my anger fully engulf my mind.

I am furious, and somebody must pay, which is the only thing that will soothe the wicked beast's thirst inside me.

The door opens, and I turn my head slowly to watch my tall courtesan walk in, ready to take what I am about to give her, with Mathias following at the rear. I lick my lips, because I am so hungry for Rose's blood.

*I need to taste it.*

"Mathias, strip Rose of her clothing," I order, leaning against my ornate desk, my arms folded, my ankles crossed, and watch him peel her out of her catsuit. She doesn't fight him. She works with him, and there is no bulge in Mathias's pants. Maybe he isn't in to women? I hadn't thought of that.

My courtesan is bared to both of us in her naked glory, and even I'm not sporting a hard-on.

*That needs to change.*

Payment must begin for this utter fucking mess. I needed the right number of women, and now I don't have that. There is no time to get another. I am seething, wanting my dark, wicked side to come out to play. I need it to take the reins, and I want to ride it hard.

*Oh so fucking hard.*

I stand aside. "Rose, bend over my desk and spread your legs." Mathias has placed her weapons on the floor atop her catsuit. "Rose...." My lips are by her ear as I move her hair over one shoulder so her neck is bared.

"I've just discovered the last female for The Pen won't be delivered to me to complete my collection. This does not make me a very happy man." I pause for a little drama, letting my finger trail lightly over her nape. My hands move to her lower back, touching it, caressing her soft, naked skin. "Apparently, she was defective, something about only having one leg. The moron's who screwed up can't pay for their fuck-up, because they skipped out on my sentinels. It is, of course, not the sentinels' fault the girl was not delivered. They did their job. They were on time, waiting patiently for the delivery boys to arrive under the correct assumption the contract was to be given its full commitment." I pause again, letting her anxiety for what is to come tether her nerves while my hands massage her tense back muscles.

*There is a storm raging inside me, and she's about to become the eye of that storm.*

"Rose, I can only be a respected king if I show my loyal subjects what severe punishment insubordination brings. Somebody has to always pay. It is the balance of things in my world."

My blood is pounding through my veins at the sight of her perfection. "Bow your head and arch your spine." My dick is starting to harden, my mind practically dancing with excitement.

And then a random thought grabs me. "Before we proceed, the silly season starts in just a few days. Why not a little Dean Martin to pass the time?" This is not a question that warrants an answer, because I am Cezar Pavel.

With a giddy smile, I approach the set of drawers and roll out the one with all my favorite vinyls. I select the one I think will elevate my spirits the most during the next few moments I spend with Rose, and place it on the turntable I have on top of the drawers, lifting the needle gently and lowering it again. Hearing that crackling sound, I go pick up Rose's blade, unsheathing it as Dean Martin's jolly

## CONTORTED

"Let It Snow" begins to fill my office.
*Now, where was I?*

# ROSE

## Oh God!

**M**y heart is knocking around in my chest as I let Mathias undress me. He's methodical, and even under the mask he wears, I can tell he's not showing any interest in my body.

Cezar is behaving differently. He's wearing an over-the-top mask I've never seen him wear before. He hasn't moved from his position. He just keeps staring at me in that horrid three-faced mask, the rest of him dressed in his uniform of an expensively tailored suit.

Ever since he cut my tongue out, he's never been angry around me. He's never had to be. Everything always goes in his favor without question. But the vibe he is giving me now is far more dangerous than anything I have seen before with him.

I am repeatedly sentenced to fuck him, raping my soul when he summons me. I thought that was what I was in for now, but something or someone has upset him. I can see it in his manner, the barely contained rage that is hiding under the surface.

Nobody upsets Cezar.

*I am frightened.*

I do as he says and bend over the desk, spreading my legs wide, expecting to be abused sexually. I am one-hundred-percent Rose and never Ruby when I am summoned to play out my role as courtesan, because none of this is consensual. None of this can get to Ruby; only Rose can handle what happens to me. Ruby hides deep where he can't get to her, and Rose does as she is ordered.

Cezar is babbling on in his manic way, when he scares me even more by wanting to play Christmas music. He has never played music before. I hear my blade being unsheathed just as the perky music starts to play.

"Mathias, hold her forearms together against the desktop. *Firm.*"

He moves into position and does as requested, without showing me any interest. His attention is focused on Cezar.

My body tenses as Cezar takes up position between my spread legs. His bulge in his suit pants is rubbing against me, wanting a reaction from me.

I'm confused.

*Something very bad is coming my way.*

*Oh God, what is he going to do with my blade?*

# MATHIAS

## Rattling the Viper's Nest

I thought he was going to fuck her. Instead, he starts cutting her. I want to put a bullet in his head. I want to turn that blade on him and gut him, *slow...ly.*

What the hell is wrong with this fucker? I can only stand here and watch him carve a *P* into the skin of her back, the flesh unzipping and spilling a bloody trail over her bottom.

The madman is humming to himself, wearing that ridiculous mask, as he carves away, totally oblivious to the pain Rose is in. He isn't even in his head. He is somewhere very dark, with the irony of Dean Martin crooning away happily in the background.

I watch him start an E, and then it dawns on me this sick fuck is branding Rose the same as Whisper had been by her former master, with the word PET.

Her hands manage to wrap around my forearms as she holds on. I'm anchored to her while her eyes glaze over and her teeth gnash together, saliva pooling onto the desk as she tries her hardest not to show this deranged man the pain she's in.

Not that he would notice. He is fucking contorted.

I grip her tighter, watching her bite down on her lip to hold in her mindless pain, which silences the noises that would surely have escaped. Not willing to give this twisted bastard any of her sorrow. And all I can do is watch and keep my rage and disgust buried, willing him to hurry the fuck up and finish.

If I reach for my weapon and put a bullet in him, there's no way I can get any of these women out safely. Sentinels would come running. We would be slaughtered and no intel would get out. Hell, they are probably eating popcorn, watching this barbaric display on the monitors somewhere. I know there is a camera in here, but who is keeping tabs on this office?

*Nothing* would be achieved.

I have to just stand here, watching her being tortured. Even though Rose will still be breathing after his cruel hands are finished, another part of me will sink deeper into the darkness.

*Will I be able to live with myself once this is all finished? Will Rose?*

He finally finishes the T—thank fuck for that. His hands are smeared with her blood, his expression no longer filled with darkness, but a creepy awe as he lifts his fingers to his mouth and sucks them like lollipops. The mask adds to the crazy picture.

Her blood runs in random pathways down her naked body, dripping onto his carpet. I loosen my grip and change our hands before he notices she's been holding onto me.

The mad fucker is now standing back, eyeing his handiwork, blood staining his mouth. The word PET has now been branded onto her flesh six inches tall.

Her body has gone limp, her chest lying flat against his desk, her breathing heavy, her legs barely holding her up. She is in such a vulnerable position if he decides he now wants to fuck her.

"Mathias. Take her away and clean her up." He sounds disgusted as he moves toward the door to his private bathroom. "Send Filip back in here." The bathroom door clicks shut.

"Rose, can you stand?" She doesn't move. "Rose?" I wrap one arm around her back and gently pull her off the desk when she doesn't respond to me, careful not to touch her deep cuts. There's no way to carry her without hurting her more, so I swing her arm over my shoulder and take all her weight, which is nothing. She's so thin. Her head tucks in under my chin, her breaths slowing down and feathering my neck.

I pull my phone out, letting Filip know Cezar's orders, and then stow it in my pocket, freeing my hand to wrap around her narrow waist. I take the necessary steps to the door, opening it, and walk her out into the corridor, leaving her clothing and weapons behind.

I shield her naked body with mine as best I can when Filip rounds the bend. He sees her bare flesh and a dirty smirk appears on his face.

"Uh-oh. Somebody's been bad." He plays with his groin.

I want to knock that look off his face, but I simply nod at him and I keep walking Rose closer to her room, to her sanctuary. She will have peace for a while, because Cezar won't call on her for the rest of the day.

"Rose, you with me?" I whisper. I duck my head, trying to see her face, but her hair has fallen across it. "Rose?" She still doesn't respond. My hand curls tighter around her naked waist as I gently tip her head back to see if she's conscious. Her eyes are open and set to the ground. "Rose, you take the time you need. I'm here, and you're safe with me." I shouldn't fucking show her this side of me, but she needs to hear I won't hurt her or take advantage of her.

Rose is in her safe house inside her mind until she is ready to come out. I know she will leave a bloody trail as she bleeds down the length of her body, but the fucker can deal—*he cut her*—until I can get it attended to.

We're passing the medical supply closet, and I stop to collect a first-aid kit with the things I'll need. I prop her up against my side the best I can without adding to her pain, and gather what I'll need before we move on.

We arrive at stall eighteen without making contact with any other sentinels. I've always wondered how many of us are here at any one time, but he keeps us mostly separated, answering his orders. If we aren't assigned a girl to watch during the exercise program, then we are on bathroom and meal duty. We individually rotate them, making sure they are never allowed to make eye contact with the other females in The Pen.

I turn the door handle just as Rose comes back to me on a little whimper, and I whisper, "It's me, Mathias. I've got you, Rose. We just arrived at your room, and I'm going to clean you up. Nod if you understand me."

Her head flops forward and bounces a couple times. The tables have turned. Not that long ago, she was the one doing the cutting. I hated her that day, and now I pity her. I can see she has no way out. Rose is merely surviving the only way she can.

I make sure my back is to the camera as I walk her into the room. "I'm going to lay you face-down on your bed and cover you before I clean you up. You're going to need stitches."

She can't verbally reply, but she nods in understanding. I take out the medical supplies I'll need, putting down a sterile blue sheet beside her, and start cleaning the blood off. I want to put a fresh towel underneath her body so her bed would stay clean, but I can't show that kind of attention. I need to get her stitched up and leave. I lay another sterile blue sheet over her naked buttocks and try to cover her as best I can, affording her some dignity.

Next, I swab her down with antiseptic and then get to stitching her up. I can't leave these wounds gaping to get infected, but I'm no trained medic. "Hold on now, Rose."

I've threaded the needle and make the first of many punctures to her skin as her hands squeeze into tight fists, while she takes the assault of this new pain in silence. I keep puncturing her skin and sewing, knowing this is going to take a lot of stitches.

"I'm sorry." The hushed words escape me before I can stop them, when I see the tears gliding down over her cheek. And then my phone sings, cutting through my conscience.

*Fuck.* It's Cezar. Is he watching me now? "Hel—"

I'm cut off as he orders me to stop what I'm doing and bring Whisper to him, and Filip is going to come finish up with Rose. Her body tenses when she hears his voice and the order he is growling loudly down the line, and then a whimper of fear escapes her. Her body can't hide its trembles from me. The one thing I've picked up about Filip is the man has gone well into the darkness. He is a hard man through to his core, and I don't trust him alone with Rose.

I'm not thinking like a loyal sentinel should, before I blurt out, "Sir, I'm just about done with Rose, and then I'll be at your office with Whisper." I've got a long way to go, but I can't trust Filip, with her so vulnerable. He's got enough of us standing about doing fuck-all during the day. Cezar doesn't need me specifically at this moment. He just wants to order somebody around, keep on shuffling us around like pawns on a checkerboard in his hideaway.

My response is met with the silence of an enraged beast, because you do not question his orders. Rose's fists are no longer white-knuckling as her hands unclench, because she knows very well what I have just done for her.

"Stay! Come see me afterward. Knock and wait before entering." Then he disconnects. His voice was eerily calm. It's hard to gauge how I will be received when I arrive. I will explain, and hopefully he will understand.

I slide the phone into my pocket securely and get back to work. I watch Rose the whole time visibly let go, her palms flattening onto the bed covers as she turns her head toward me.

There is a silent thank you in her pretty green eyes. I avert mine away from her, back to the task at hand, but I know she doesn't look away from me. The only sign of discomfort she shows me is her hands spread wide, pressing into the covers as I repeatedly puncture her skin until she is sewn up, and then I place gauze and bandages over the stitches.

I start packing up the medical supplies, when her hand shoots out and grabs at my wrist. "Aank-oo." The side of her face toward me flushes bright red at the mangled sounds she makes. I bet she doesn't ever try to talk in here.

I apologize, "It's not the best job."

A tear slides down her cheek. "Heee wuu a bee wor."

Filip *would* have been worse, in more ways than one.

Everything is packed away. I shake out the blanket folded at the base of her bed and place it over her body, and then I leave, shutting the door behind me and dropping the medical supplies back in the closet.

I hope I haven't rattled the viper's nest too much. Whatever reason Cezar has for seeing Whisper and me I will deal with it. It will be worth having seen

Rose's gratitude.

Who knows how I will turn out if I stay here long enough? I too will be ordered to do unthinkable things. Cezar chose not to order me to cut Whisper's tongue or Rose's back, but if he *had* ordered me, I know I wouldn't have been able to decline.

Human monsters aren't always born a bad seed. They can also evolve into a monster through conditioning.

The cards are currently stacked in my favor, but I know unless I can find out the location of where this place is, then I'll be ordered to do deplorable things to these women.

He's the monster who will be brought down, even if I have to take my last breath doing it, but I can't promise no bad will be done before the good can be seen.

*For now, I've got a meeting with the devil.*

# Whisper

## The Monster Within

**I'm surrounded by silence, sitting cross-legged** on my bed, doing the only thing to amuse myself, and that is coloring, when the door suddenly swings open on a loud slam and a masked man comes for me.

I know his name is Filip. He's watched me in the training room a few times. He has dark skin like one of the men who abducted me from William's property, and black, tightly curled hair cut close to his scalp. His throat and neck are tattooed, and I imagine his body would be covered in ink. I try not to allow my eyes to linger on him for too long whenever he's watched me.

He's a very dangerous person. He frightens me, because he's such a strong-looking man, a true fighter. He could easily break me in two. He's dressed in an expensive-looking suit, like all the sentinels, and I know he is armed. His body would be a weapon all by itself.

Filip takes a few long, powerful strides to get to me, and I can't help but throw my broken wrist away from him, protecting it as he yanks me off my bed on a yelp. The pages of my coloring book are kicked across the bed as my legs flail, and I half fall, half get dragged to my feet.

"Stand up, girl!" He has the same accent as Boxer.

I do my best to regain my balance, and then I'm shoved forward, his hand pressing into my lower back, and I'm out my room and in the corridor that seems only to go round and round in an infinite loop. The illusion given is that we are all trapped. I know there is a way out, but it is not for us to be shown.

"Where am I going?" The lisp has completely gone now; time has healed my tongue. I hope for an answer. I shiver, not from the crisp temperature but out of fear.

"Cezar wants to see you now, and that's all you need to know."

I hurry ahead of him, not wanting him to touch me again. I haven't seen Mathias in many days. No matter what has gone down between us, I would rather he be taking me to Cezar than this man.

I try not to fret over what is about to happen to me. I have done nothing wrong. I have obeyed all orders and been a model prisoner.

# CONTORTED

*I can't be in trouble.*

I am pulled backward when I'm about to walk past an ornate wooden door. I have not been this far from my room before. "Wait!" The order is sharp. Filip knocks on the door, and another masked sentinel I've not seen before opens it.

I gasp out loud when I am pushed roughly over the threshold, with Filip following me in. He didn't need to shove me. I look over my shoulder, and the sentinel who greeted us is leaving, the door shutting with a sinister thud.

I look back to find Cezar watching me from behind a very impressive carved desk. His hands are steepled under his chin, his elbows pushing into the leather top.

"Lovely to see you again, Whisper." His smile is creepy, his accent I still can't pick. The mood in this room is deadly. I feel like something very bad is about to happen.

Filip is standing close by, a silent threat to behave. I can *feel* him waiting for my reaction when I find out why I am here. He is taking great pleasure in his position.

My eyes stray to the carpet in front of his desk. Is that fresh blood that's been spilt? I look up, catching Cezar observing me.

"I must apologize for the mess." He waves a hand dismissively in front of himself from where he is seated on what looks like a modern day throne. "I haven't had time to redecorate." He sounds amused with himself.

*Is that real gold on his chair?*

It is such a big, opulent high-backed seat, one you could lounge sideways in. "Whose blood is it?" My heart pounds a drum between my ears, because I didn't mean to say that out loud.

Cezar gets up, ignoring my outburst, collecting something in his hand, and secreting it behind his back as he walks toward me. He simultaneously taps this *something* on his back as he takes steps closer to me. He's wearing a full black mask, with a large mouth opening on it.

These men are never without their masks. I want to yank them off their faces. They are cowards not showing their identities.

He stops in front of me. Too close. Deliberately right up in my personal space. "You are looking well." His head tilts to the side as he inspects my face, his breath smelling of flavored smoke. "I see the bruises have all cleared up, and underneath all that swelling is the beautiful woman I knew you to be."

I hold my ground, trying not to look defiant and uncomfortable in his presence. I have learned to play along. I am buying time for my friends to find me, for Edge to find me.

I am thankful to be wearing the yoga pants and a tank top, my hoodie zipped up high. I have on my armor. I am covered from his prying eyes.

"Oh, look at you all up in your head." He childishly taps me on my temple with a finger and squats down a little to my eye level. "I can see you want to do bad things to me, young lady. You want to hurt me, don't you?"

I go to look away, because my eyes are selling me out.

He roughly grabs my chin, holding my head in place. "You need to hide your feelings better, Whisper." He releases me and taps my nose, and I want to flinch away, but I don't. He's more amused by my emotions. "This is your lucky day. I'm feeling most gracious toward you, because you're about to do something for me, and it will give me great pleasure to watch you carry out my order."

My skin starts to prickle in fear and I take an involuntary step backward... into Filip's rock-hard chest. I'm now sandwiched between these two men. They have come together like a vice.

*Another game of intimidation.*

I can feel Filip is hard, and *it* is pressed up against my lower back. He smells blood in the air, and he's the type of man who enjoys dark sensations and my discomfort. He gets off on it.

The game has gone up a notch since I walked in. I

think of Edge telling me to do as I'm told no matter how difficult. I need to save myself. I want to see Boxer and Miss Catherine again. I'm afraid of what Cezar is going to ask of me. Will I be able to do it?

*No matter what?*

I look past Cezar's shoulder and can see on his desk rests a hideous three-faced mask, as if he had recently discarded it. It has red spots on it. What went on in here?

Cezar turns his head, following my line of sight. "Don't worry your pretty little head about that mess." He turns back. "All will be set right soon enough."

There's something far too calm about this man. I don't like how my gut is starting to churn. He takes several steps away from me, allowing me to sidestep away from Filip.

"While we wait for Mathias to join us, come kneel at my feet, Whisper." He points to a place free from the blood marks he's now standing by. I can do nothing but obey him, so I walk over and kneel before him. "Hands on your thighs and bow your head." I do my best with a broken wrist. "Sit back on your heels."

I can see his feet moving as he steps back, and his ankles cross as he props himself up against the wall, his hands still behind his back. If I looked up I would expect to see him looking down his nose at me.

*So arrogant.*

We stay quiet like this for some time, except for this constant tapping noise coming from Cezar. I'm beginning to wonder how long I have to sit here in this submissive position, when there's a sharp rap on the door.

"*Ahhh*, here is Mathias now. You, my darling, are going to teach my newest sentinel a lesson on manners and respecting his king. Come now, you don't have to avert your eyes." I look up, and his hand is held out for me to grab onto. I reach up and allow him to help me up, pulling my fingers free once I'm standing. I turn my body slightly away from Cezar, trying to put as much space as I can between us, my head bowed at an angle. What does he mean I'm going to teach Mathias a lesson?

"Let him in, Filip."

Mathias walks in. I look out the corner of my eye, my head turned ever so slightly, and I see his eyes glide over me. He shows no signs of being surprised to see me in here.

*Did Cezar find out about his phone?*

I'm clutching at straws as to why I am in here. My belly starts getting all nervous again, and I can feel myself starting to overheat with the stress of what is about to happen in this office. I'm feeling dizzy. I shut my eyes and wait for it to pass.

"Yes, sir?" Mathias steps out of Filip's reach, a

deliberate move, and keeps enough space between me and Cezar.

"Mathias, thank you for coming along as requested." I hear the politeness in Cezar's words, but I'm not buying it. William had taught me many times that polite words don't equal a happy, sane man. It is often a man barely containing his anger. "Whisper has been invited to help out with something for me. Would you be a good sentinel and come stand and face the wall, palms flat to the surface."

"Sir?" He doesn't move.

I look at Cezar, who gives Filip a nod. He swiftly ambushes him from behind and throws him against the wall on a resounding *'ooph'* from Mathias. "Cezar said palms flat," he grunts. Mathias doesn't fight Filip; he does as he's told.

I try not to show my shock at what is quickly escalating badly for Mathias, while my mind is a jumbled mess as I try to think why Cezar is turning on Mathias. With his palms flattened against the wall, he can only wait quietly as Cezar walks up to his vulnerable back while Filip moves away.

"See, this is what you are still doing wrong." He talks over Mathias's shoulder. "You are questioning me, first with bringing Whisper to my office when asked, and now with doing as I request of you again."

My eyes shoot to what has been making that tapping noise. Cezar has a long cane behind him, and he's tapping it against his back. "This means you need double the reminder of doing what I ask the first time without question. You aren't paid to question my orders. You are here as one of my sentinels, because you have earned the right to be here. I understand you've had a little lapse in judgment. You aren't used to working for me, but now that you are here, you don't question *anything* I ask. Is that understood?" He's still being far too calm and polite.

Mathias cocks his head to face Cezar. "Yes, sir. I apologize."

"I do understand you felt the need to continue with the original order I had given you, but I am prone to changing my mind. So let me hear you again."

"Yes, sir!" Mathias responds in military style, like men you see in the movies with their heads looking dead ahead and shouting their agreement to their senior officer.

Cezar steps away from Mathias, coming back to where I am standing. I hope he is pleased with Mathias's reply and this is all finished.

*But, I'm not so lucky.*

"Filip, undo Mathias's pants and drop them for me."

Filip snaps to attention, hugging Mathias's body as he wraps his arms around his waist and I hear the belt being unbuckled. He does something, and Mathias grunts painfully.

"Filip, I didn't tell you to play with Mathias. Unless you want what he's got coming, I would get on with it," Cezar scolds, and Mathias's pants and gray trunks are pulled down, exposing taut buttocks, his suit pants a puddle at his feet. "Spread your legs for me." Mathias doesn't hesitate this time. They are as wide as his muscular trapped legs will allow him.

*What the hell does Cezar want me to do to him when he's in this position?*

Filip steps to the side with an evil, knowing smirk as he glares at me. He is as much a creep as Cezar. I return my attention back to Mathias.

"Filip, cut his jacket and shirt up the spine. There's too much in the way," Cezar commands, and Filip reveals a blade he had hidden on himself and tugs on the bottom of Mathias's suit jacket, slicing it clean up the middle of the expensively tailored material. It puts up no fight, letting the pieces separate.

Cezar steps forward, pushing it farther to each side, revealing a large tattoo on Mathias's back. "What is this, Mathias?"

"Norse raven," he replies without turning his head. It is beautifully detailed, the feathers lifelike.

The bird is in flight, ready to snatch up its prey. It covers his muscled, broad back.

"Lucky you aren't receiving your lashings on your back. I would hate to destroy such a wonderful piece of art."

*Lashings?* A fast-paced drumbeat starts up in my head. He said I was going to teach Mathias a lesson. Surely he doesn't expect me to use the cane on the man's body?

Mathias's back muscles ripple as Cezar continues talking. "You are going to have to hold still. I would hate for you to catch a lashing or two over this fine artwork." Cezar turns to me and holds out the cane. I don't make any move to take it from him. "Whiiiisper." I hate the way he draws my name out, his disappointment evident in my lack of enthusiasm. "Do I need to remind you as well about doing as you're told? Hmmm?"

I simply stare at his hand for several seconds, because I'm having trouble reaching for it. I have been beaten, lashed with a belt until my back bled. I can't be involved in hurting somebody like this.

Suddenly, my right hand is yanked out and the cane is thrust into it. I don't want to hold this thing, but I curl my fingers around it, the weight of it foreign in my small hand.

*Am I really expected to administer the lashings?*

I'm standing in disbelief holding a long cane. I

must look horrified. It is thin but strong, and looks like it could do some serious damage.

*I can't.*

I look at Cezar, my eyes pleading with him. I have no pride left.

"Now, my dear, you need to get started. I'm a busy man." He smiles encouragingly at me. He moves me into position behind Mathias's naked body. "You may get your vengeance on Mathias for holding you down, allowing your tongue to be cut. I need you to strike like you mean it." He motions with his hand to start and steps away.

I stand there like a statue, my right arm limp by my side, my left one still encased in a cast I hold against my chest. I can't bring myself to harm another person in this way. I look back at Cezar, wanting him to feel pity for me and let both of us walk away.

He sweeps his hand forward, his eyes crazy-excited, his smile all wicked. "Go your hardest, dear, as he needs to be taught some discipline and reminded that his place as my sentinel is to do and not question."

My mouth is opening and shutting as I look between Mathias and Cezar. My arm still hasn't made a move. I want to speak up, but no words will form. The drumbeat in my head only getting louder and fiercer.

Cezar steps up behind me and wraps an arm around my shoulder, his mouth smashing into my cheek. I want to pull away, but he holds me firm. "Sweetie," he grinds out, "he was only getting six lashings until he questioned me again, so the number has now doubled. That's on him. Keep looking at me like you are and standing there doing nothing," he gives my body a shake, "and three more lashings will be added if you don't start administering a dozen by the time I count to three. This will make it fifteen, and if you choose not to do it, after I have been so patient with you, I will be forced to give you the same treatment and the same number of lashings, and Filip will be the one administering it to both of you.

"Trust me, he won't hesitate, and as you can see, he is one strong man. He will be getting a hard-on hoping you keep standing here fretting about caning Mathias, because he badly wants to be given the opportunity, and he will thoroughly enjoy himself."

My breath has caught in my throat. I want to drop the cane and run.

"One... two—"

"*Stop!* I'll do it," I cry out. I grip the cane tight, reminding myself it is still there, an extension of my arm, ready to inflict grievous bodily harm.

"Fifteen lashings it is then." He claps his hands together.

"What? I said stop." I'm shocked he would add on three more.

"You haven't started. It is about to go up to eighteen, and six is the recommended number for a good disciplining."

*I want to whip Cezar across the face.*

Without thinking about what I am about to do, I hold the cane up and swing it down onto Mathias's firm buttocks, leaving a light red mark.

I can feel Cezar's disappointment before I see him shaking his head slowly. "Oh... come... now. You can do so much better than that." His voice is a drawl filled with boredom. "Let's call that a practice hit, shall we? You've obviously never done this before. Let me help you." He stands behind me and covers my hand with his. "You need to have a good, strong stance. Spread your legs, putting weight onto your back foot." I do as he says for fear of the lashings going up further. "Now let me guide you, because the cane needs to snap on his flesh for a good hit." He positions his body, and then he brings my hand down with powerful force, the air whistling a tune before the cane cracks against bare flesh with a satisfied snap.

Mathias's body barely moves, but he can't contain the low hiss that escapes his lips.

*I can't look at where it hit.*

Cezar nuzzles my ear, his spare hand gripping my

nape. I want to jerk away from him, but I stand strong. "Now don't play coy with me. I've seen your back, so I know you know what a lashing feels like and the power needed to administer a good one."

My face reddens at my shame.

"I want to see some true energy in the caning, or else you will have your palms up against the wall beside Mathias, and Filip won't hold back, I can assure you. So let's say we try again. This is your last warning." His patience is stretched thin. I can see I have nothing to offer to get out of this. Mathias has already received two lashings. "We start counting from now."

*What?* I hold my tongue. *He's already received two.*

"Make sure you count along with me. It will make it more fun." He's so creepily happy about what I'm about to do.

*Seventeen* lashings he will receive, not fifteen. *Fuck!*

I swing the cane and count out loud, and I swing it with as much of a show of my strength as I can. I'm being transported back to the slave cabin where William used the belt on me until I passed out. He never counted out loud. I think the number kept going up. The more I could handle, the more I got, until my mind gave in.

*This time, I am the monster.*

Mathias takes every lashing silently until the tenth one, and that's when the grunts and groans start. His muscled flesh is really getting cut up now. There is no fat on his butt. They are two toned globes. The skin has split in all the places the cane has laid its bite. Mathias's head is hung between his shoulder blades, sheer will keeping him standing in place.

I rein five more lashes onto it, breathing heavily as I speed them up to get this over with, perspiration wetting my hair. I should be happy to get back at him for all his involvement, but I'm not.

I've hit him seventeen times when the cane is tugged from my grasp. "Good girl. You've done better than I expected. You may have a place on my team, after all." I take a really good look at what I have done to Mathias. He won't be sitting down for a long time. His buttocks are now shredded raw, the bloody flesh exposed.

*I did that.*

I know Filip would have done so much more damage than me after five lashings. It offers no comfort that I stopped it from being a lot worse.

"Stand up, Mathias, and turn around."

He pushes off from the wall on a moan and faces us. His hair is wet and sticking to his face. His eyes worship the floor, his arms limp at his sides.

To humiliate Mathias even more, Cezar strips the

remains of the ruined suit from his arms, baring his naked body completely to us. He has a tattoo inked over his heart. It looks like a weird compass.

"Well, well, what is this odd-looking tattoo you bear, Mathias?"

"The Vegvisir compass, it is a Norse protection symbol." Pain is laced through each word.

"I'd be asking for my money back." Cezar shakes his head, grinning.

We both ignore him, our eyes meeting, and then mine travel down south of their own accord. When they reach his long, flaccid penis and my mind acknowledges that I'm staring at it, I quickly look away, anywhere but there. It is too private for me to see him like this. I don't need to share in Mathias's humiliation I know how it feels.

"Whisper, he is rather well-endowed isn't he?"

I don't answer Cezar, I concentrate on the floor. I don't want to play his games. I've done as he's asked, and now I want to be away from here.

I will *not* become a monster for this man's pleasure.

This is how Cezar would have broken down Rose a little bit at a time until she became a robot who does his bidding. I can't allow myself to be broken by this man. I defiantly look at him. He almost looks proud of me.

*Bastard!*

I catch Mathias swaying from the sheer strength of staying upright when in so much pain.

"Filip, stay here and stand sentinel. You can call Rose to attend to Mathias's wounds, and she can make sure there is no infection."

Mathias starts to say something and then stops himself, busying himself with stepping out of his shoes and pants. "What was that, Mathias? Did you want to tell me that Rose needed to rest after what I did to her?"

Mathias's head shoots up. "No, sir!" he shouts in that military way again.

*What did Cezar do to Rose?*

*Was that her blood splattered on the carpet?*

"Mathias, you can escort Whisper back to her room now, and then go wait for Rose in your room."

He nods at Cezar, and I move voluntarily to pick up the remnants of Mathias's suit off the floor, where it has all been discarded.

"No!" Mathias is determined. "I'll get my own things."

I straighten up and head toward the door to wait, watching him bend down on one knee slowly, the flesh on his buttocks tearing a little more, but he doesn't make a sound.

Blood is dripping onto the carpet from the horrible injuries I inflicted. He's holding himself steady with one hand pressed to the floor before he rises, his strong thighs elevating him to stand.

A wave of anxiety hits me. I need to know if Rose is okay. There are far too many monsters in this room. I start breathing deep slowly like I taught myself, to calm myself down. I face the door and wait until Mathias leans around me and opens the door for me, ushering me through it.

"Oh, *Whiiisper*?" Cezar singsongs merrily.

*What does the evil bastard want now?* I stand still, tense, not turning around.

"I hope this serves as a further reminder that I only ask once. Disobey me, and severe punishment awaits you." I hear the door softly close behind me, and then we are both walking.

I badly want to ask about Rose, when he tips sideways into the wall. My immediate reaction is to cup his elbow and tilt him back so he is again balanced. He's completely naked beside me, but it's the farthest thing from my mind. I have spent enough time over the years bared fully to William Dupré. I am desensitized to it.

"Do you need to rest? We can take it slower." I shouldn't be concerned for this man.

"No," he grates out. "Keep walking." The pain must be excruciating.

I make sure I am close enough to help if he starts to fall again, but I can't make eye contact.

I know he is the enemy, but there is something

about him that doesn't ring true. Not like Filip or Cezar. My gut is telling me one thing, but my eyes tell me another. I've only met another four sentinels that are here rotating in the exercise room, and they all feel the same, highly dangerous. Mathias feels different.

I feel very closed in, not having seen daylight in a long time. I start to feel a little overheated. I need fresh, clean air.

I do my best to keep walking, but only find myself getting more lightheaded. I put it down to being so stressed about what just went down in that room. We're not far from my door, but I don't know if I'll make it. I stop walking, reaching out blindly for the wall and taking a moment to steady myself against it. The cold stone is my friend for once, cooling my forehead.

"Whisper?" Mathias is beside me, tilting me up straight. I realize my eyes had closed or I'd lost a few seconds. I open them and see I'm beside room twelve. I've only got a little ways to go. I shrug his hold off.

"I'm fine." But I know I'm not. I'm far from it as panic starts to set in. We reach my door without another incident, and he goes to open it for me. I hold up a trembling hand. "Please, just go and lie down and wait for Rose. I don't need you to take me inside." He doesn't argue; he's got his own problems. I nearly laugh hysterically at the thought of more quiet time. I open the door, enter my room, and shut it, not waiting for a response.

I lean up against it and slide to the floor, putting my head in my hand. My broken wrist is limp by my side. I had my tongue cut, and the pain was awful, but what I just did to Mathias was... barbaric. There will be horrible scars left, and he will be in great pain for a long time, every move sheer agony. Cezar wants to use me to hurt others, like he uses Rose.

*I will not break like Rose.*

I close my eyes.

I *need* Edge.

# MATHIAS

## Brings a Whole New Meaning to Pain in the Ass

I make it into my room, closing the door, and drop my ruined suit on the floor by the bed before collapsing on it. My phone is close enough in the suit pants if I am summoned.

I shut my eyes and just let myself go someplace in my mind other than here for a few minutes.

*The smug fucking bastard is going to pay.*

I wake later to quiet sobs. I must have faded right out. I know it's Rose in my room, because she won't disobey Cezar, and Whisper has been left alone to let it sink in what she was forced to do to me. I don't blame her. Nobody says no to Cezar.

I lie still and take a moment to hear the proof she is actually human underneath all that female terminator she shows everybody, and then I make a small moan to let her know I am coming to. She won't want me to know she has let her guard down, so I don't face her yet.

Her sobs finally quiet. She's probably erasing her tears and erecting her emotional walls of steel. Once I know Rose has her game face back on, the one she wears for all the men down here, I turn my head to face her.

"Hey, Rose." I try to make my voice light and friendly. "I got myself into a spot of trouble after I left you." I give her the best grin I can muster. "How are you feeling?" Stupid question, I know her back would be on fire. At least she's dressed in yoga pants and a tank top, and not that leather catsuit he makes her wear. "You should be resting." An idiotic comment, because Cezar ordered her here. "Don't stand there wondering if this is your fault." She knows you don't question his orders, and she heard me tell Cezar I was finishing up with her back, which was as good as saying no to his command to get Whisper. "This is on me."

She shakes her head, a fierce expression on her face, as her long ponytail swishes back and forth. She's not totally lost inside that head of hers, because she's able to disagree with me. She's no longer a robot in front of me; she is showing emotion.

"Let me guess." I let out a pain-filled breath. "Filip already filled you in on all the grim details, and the *why*? The sadistic bastard."

She nods. She doesn't quite know what to make of my careless words around her.

"Look... I just need a hand getting to the shower so I can clean up the mess my ass appears to have gotten itself into. Can you do that for me?" I'm worried about her. No female should be put through what she has. She's been traumatized enough with however long she's been Cezar's prisoner.

Rose nods her head and becomes all business again. I push up with my palms off the bed, my muscles protesting while cursing that fucker under my breath. Rose tucks her hand under my elbow and braces herself to pull me off the bed until I can stand. "Watch your stitches. You don't want them tearing." She ignores my words and I curse through the pain. My body isn't too pleased to be moving again so soon.

She pays no attention to my nudity and guides me to my bathroom. "I can take it from here," I tell her, but she shakes her head. Her stiff movements tell me how sore she is. I hold onto the doorjamb, taking a few heartbeats to let the dizziness subside that has hit me.

She slides past me, flicking the light switch on in the bathroom, and then I hear the water running in the shower. Gentle hands guide me into the tiled area until I'm underneath the tepid water.

I rest my forehead against the cool tiles, shutting

my eyes, and let the spray clean me up. I want to groan, hiss, and swear out loud, because my ass is one big, out of control, throbbing, stinging pain. This shower is torture, but a necessity to wash away the blood and clean the shredded flesh.

My mask is drenched, and I can't find it in me to care to keep the fucking thing on. I rip it off, letting it fall with a splat to the wet floor.

I know we're not being watched in my quarters. I have carefully searched every inch of my rooms to make sure there are no cameras or bugs invading my privacy since I've been here. There is not much furniture to hide anything in. The surveillance room also showed no signs the sentinel rooms are spied on. Rose's stall is, but not ours.

The other sentinels confirmed our quarters were free of surveillance. We had privacy, but in a way we were as much a prisoner as the females, because we only went up top when we were ordered, and then it was by Cezar's rules to protect his lair. I feel confident none of what is going on in here is being documented or listened in on. That fucker is so sure of himself when it comes to his trusted sentinels' loyalty.

My eyes spring open when I feel the soft touch of Rose's hands as she dabs with a wet cloth over the affected area. It must look a real mess. Blood bruises would be covering my ass, and I can imagine how bad the cane marks look where my skin has split open.

"Rose, you're getting wet. Your back should stay dry." She's half in the shower with me. I feel a tug on my arm and look to the side, water falling down my face, making it hard to keep my eyes open, my beard plastered to my neck.

She's never seen my face, and her eyes widen. She must not have noticed I discarded my mask, because her attention had been solely concentrating on my ass. She looks a little surprised by what she sees.

"What? Not pretty enough for you, Rose?" My smile is forced, but she needs some gentle banter in her life. Her face turns fire engine red, like a switch flips. She's forgotten what it's like to have a man joke with her. Has she ever had that? "Please excuse my humor. It helps to keep my mind off the fact I won't be attempting to sit of my own free will for a few days."

Her hair has been swirled around into a messy bun on top of her head. She reaches into the shower and turns the taps off.

"You figure I've had enough under here and it's time to get my ass patted dry so I can have some fun with the hydrogen peroxide?"

Her eyes soften for only a few seconds before she toughens back up again for me. She's a beautiful woman when she's being human, and I know the female terminator she has to become in order to survive what Cezar dishes out to her takes its toll on her.

When the urge hits, I know Cezar abuses this beautiful woman, because Filip has joked about it enough. At first, I thought she enjoyed it, but I saw the victim inside her when he was cutting her back. Her tears for my flogging have shown me she is still in there somewhere.

Her tongue has been taken, her body abused, her mind conditioned to kill. I wouldn't blame her if she is totally broken mentally and unable to be put back together... but I sense the strength in her.

"I... hep?" The noises she makes when trying to talk aren't attractive. I bet she had a beautiful voice before it was stolen from her. Talking in front of me tells me a great deal. She trusts I won't mock her. She's been paying attention to me, working out who is worth her words.

"Honey, it would seem I need all the help I can get at the moment."

And there goes that soft look in her eyes again, and then she is down to business. I can't let on how much pain I am swimming in, but I need to get dry and horizontal again. If I go down, she won't have the strength to get me up, and she could tear her stitches.

I step out of the wet area and she hands me a

towel to dry my top half, while she gently pats my ass down. I want to hiss in acknowledgement of every place she touches, but it needs to be done.

When she's finished, I target my bed, beeline it, and collapse again. Clothes aren't required at the moment. No doubt, Cezar will order me up and about in a few hours, further punishment to be dressed and on duty. The no clothes policy, I'm going to enjoy for a few more hours.

Rose isn't afraid of me. I feel like we have broken some major ground. Maybe I can work with her. I can earn her trust to learn more.

*"Fuuuck."* My body jerks on the bed. She must have brought the medical supplies with her. The hydrogen peroxide just hit my broken skin. Smart woman gave me no warning. I force myself to relax as best I can as the liquid does its thing, and then she applies the dressing.

Once she's finished, I touch her arm and we make eye contact again. "You better leave and go rest. Thank you. I'm sorry you had to go through being hurt and I couldn't stop it." She hesitates like she wants to say something, because she doesn't know if I can fully be trusted.

We've broken some ground. Is it enough to gain her trust? She's probably wondering if I am playing her. Rose shouldn't trust any man in here.

She gets up and moves toward the door. She

# CONTORTED

releases her bun before opening it, her hair falling back into the neat ponytail. There are cameras watching outside my room. Cezar expects neat and tidy. And then she is gone.

I close my eyes and savor the silence. I know I have some Ibuprofen around here somewhere, but instead, I let myself fade out.

# Whisper

## Flying

I've been trying to color and keep myself busy, because the walls are too silent. It's been hours and hours and hours of nobody coming for me. No food. No water. My stomach is constantly growling.

It's like I've been forgotten.

*No Rose.*

What did Cezar do to her? Did she question him too? Did she say *no* to him?

*How is Mathias?* I shouldn't care, but I do.

My fingers gravitate toward the crayon I haven't used at all since I've been in here. The black one doesn't need to mar my beautiful rainbow pallet, but I can't stop myself. I start scribbling frantically, my breathing heavy as I scrub away the bright and meticulously colorful page, obliterating the beauty and turning it black.

It was pretty, and now it is messed up. Darkness has fallen across the Narnia scene. A black hole has gobbled the characters up, just like I have been. I'm in my very own black hole.

I've been trying not to think about what I did to Mathias, but it keeps playing over and over in my mind. I caned a man until his skin split, and I kept lashing him, because I had no choice.

Every lash threatened to open a box I'd shut tight. I don't want to suffocate under the power of them. I'm alone in this room, fighting to keep them all from springing open, so the bad memories can't drown me in here. Fearful I'll never see Boxer, Lincoln, or Miss Catherine again.

*I will never see Edge.*

My mind is surely playing tricks on me, because he is the last person my heart should want to see, but I do. Captivity has made me desperate.

*Brainwashed me.*

I shake my head, because if it was a snow globe, there would be red instead of white raining down over me, and I need the memories of mistress to stop, the memories of my time with William to go away. But all I can hear is the sticky sound of the blood as the cane continually rained down on Mathias, while I sit alone in this cold unemotional, stone room.

That sharp, wet *thwack* as the cane became more and more coated when it landed on his open skin. The unmistakable cloying, metallic scent getting up in my nose, you could be blindfolded and you would know that scent anywhere.

*Thwack!*

Every lash paved the way for me becoming like all these people, who saw nothing wrong with their job.

Mathias took *everything* I did to him, because he had to.

*Thwack!*

*Thwack!*

THWACK!

I frisbee the coloring book across the room.

My nerves are shot. I can still smell blood in here. I look down at myself and notice the little spots of Mathias's blood polka-dotting my clothes from the cane's air spray.

I start unzipping the hoodie and tear it from my body. Next to go is my top. I need these clothes off my body. They are tainted with another's pain. I check my yoga pants and can see spots of blood. Spitting on my finger, I smudge the blood as I vigorously try to make it disappear, but all I do is make a larger untidy stain. This grates on my last nerve and I spring into action.

Standing beside my bed, I hook my thumbs into the waistband and tear them down, kicking them under the bed, across the room, leaving me now only in my sensible bra and panties.

I stand here, not sure what to do next. My mind is

rambling at me. I can't do anymore fucking coloring. I don't understand these people. Why do they work for such a man like Cezar? I lived my life under a man who took from me every single day of my life. These people don't have any sort of freedom. What is the incentive? Rose has been punished, I've been punished, and Mathias has been caned.

I can feel myself starting to lose it in here. This is the first time I have really begun to feel like the walls are closing in and I have no way out.

My faith in Edge is slipping. He promised me, but so did Boxer. He promised I would be safe... and here I am. I think I know what day it is, but do I really? Is it Saturday, Sunday, or Monday?

All I ever have in here to look at are stone walls for a view. I'm used to Rose's routine with me. I have a schedule. I don't deviate from it. I understand it. I know what is coming in my day.

*I don't know what is coming up next.*

My routine has changed. I need the routine so I'll understand!

I start pacing. I need to calm myself.

The room is too small for pacing. I can only get a few steps in until I have to turn around again, and that isn't good enough.

*None of this is fucking good enough.*

I want to talk to Edge. I want to hear his voice. He said he's coming for me. Where is Boxer? He loves me.

I'm gasping for air.

I need oxygen.

I need out of this room.

I need out of this place.

I need my family.

I'm backed up against the door, banging my head to a slow beat, as I count my inhales and exhales. Then my legs don't want to take the weight that is on my shoulders any more, so I let myself slide down to the floor and keep banging and counting in my head.

My emotions have been constant the whole time I've been held captive here. The whole time I was held by William, because I didn't know any better.

Now, I do.

I know freedom.

The banging is getting louder. I'm no longer gasping for air. Now, I'm mad. The banging keeps a steady beat.

I am so fucking mad.

The banging stops. I open my mouth, and I roar.

*"I am a fucking human being!"*

And then the banging starts up again, getting louder.

Harder.

My vision turns fuzzy. I can no longer focus on this plain, colorless room. I am starting to leave it.

## CONTORTED

My mind is escaping it, and it feels good... until the banging stops and I'm sliding on the floor.
*I'm flying.*

# MATHIAS

## Kuksuger!

I got the call after eight at night to get myself to Whisper's room ASAP.

*What the hell is going on now?*

Anybody else could have been summoned, but I was still paying for my insubordination. Grunting and groaning I get myself dressed, going commando, and swallow a couple Ibuprofen before making my way to stall thirteen. I can hear a loud banging and hasten my pace, the movement irritating my ass until it feels like I'm sitting in a blazing fire pit.

*What the hell is the little rabbit doing in her room to draw attention to herself with all that pounding?*

I reach her door and the banging stops. I turn the handle and expect the door to open freely, but it doesn't. I'm met with resistance, which makes me use muscles I didn't want to use at the moment as I curse. I put my shoulder into pushing the door open and hear a dragging sound, until I can get through it.

"*Dritt!*" I lapse into Norwegian for the word *shit* when I see why the door had to be shoved hard to open. "Whisper?" She is lying in only her underwear at an awkward angle, slumped across the floor, her hair covering her face, and she's not moving.

*Has she been raped?*

I'm going to have to bend down to assess her, and that is going to hurt like a bitch. I take a knee, sweat breaking out on my body from the pain I'm in. I need those pills to kick in, not that they'll do much. "Little rabbit?" I raise my voice, knowing the camera can't pick up sound. Chances are Cezar is dipping his hand into a bowl of popcorn, watching the silent show we're giving him, so I have to still be careful of my actions.

I feel the back of her head, massaging the large egg that has formed, but there's no blood.

*Was she banging her head on her door?*

I brush her hair away from her face. Her skin is ashen and she's out cold. Her chest is rising and falling, and her underwear is intact... thank fuck. I see no evidence of rape and hope I'm right. I touch her shoulder and give her a gentle shake. "Little rabbit?" She doesn't respond.

*Fuck!*

I get to my feet, come around behind her, yank her

up, my hands under her arm pits, and drag her limp body away from the back of the door. Sweat is dripping down my face. She's not heavy. I'm just hitting an eleven on the one-to-ten scale of pain.

I lay her onto her bed and seek out her clothes, which are over by the far wall, picking them up. It looks like she took them off herself, because nothing is torn. There are blood spots, but that would be my blood. I come back over to where she lays just as Cezar strolls through with purpose.

"I saw her having a meltdown in the surveillance room," he states.

*Meltdown? Thank fuck not rape.*

"She faking it?" he inquires.

Yeah, *fitte tryne,* fuckface. *She's faking it.* What she's been through in the past couple weeks alone deserves a meltdown. Not to mention her whole life has been one big fucked-up psychiatrist's wet dream.

He looks at me for an answer.

"I don't believe so." *Asshole.*

"Where's your mask?" he snaps. *Fuck.* I forgot to put one back on. "Here." He pulls one from his suit pocket. He must have grabbed a spare after seeing me in here without one on, but I'm the least of his worries at the moment. "You're lucky she hasn't seen your face." He observes the sweat on my face. He knows I'm hurting. "An allowance is made for your previous punishment. Just don't forget again."

I place the mask on while he bends down close to her face. "Let me inspect her myself." I hold my tongue, because I don't want him anywhere near her while she's in her underwear. He opens her eyes, checking to see if anybody is home.

*Nobody is home.*

He pulls his phone out. "Rose. Come. Stall thirteen now!" He looks at me as he puts his phone away. "This is unfortunate. I saw her banging her head against the back of the door, and then she was roaring something like a crazy person before she appears to have blacked out."

Don't even get me started on who the crazy person is here. *What does he expect?*

He puts his hands behind his back. "Seems she may not be as strong as my Rose, after all. Her previous master had kept her captive for twenty years." He pauses for effect. "I may have, as they say, broken the camel's back." He sniffles a little with exasperation.

Rose arrives, looking like she's just woken up. Her tank top is stuck to her back and there's blood stained on it. She needs her dressings changed. Rose doesn't acknowledge me. She's back in Terminator mode, her defenses strong.

"Rose, as you can see, we have a little problem."

He waves his hand toward Whisper's prone body. "The girl appears to have had a small breakdown. See what you can do for her. If she's decided to become a vegetable, then I'll find a use for her." He sounds too perplexed by the situation to know which way to behave. "I can't be another female down," he mutters to himself. He obviously has never had a girl lose it before—probably because they never had a past like Whisper.

Whisper nearly lost her tongue and had been forced to cane me. She never became a robot after the life she led; she retained her humanity. But Cezar thinks this means she won't be pushed over the edge... but has she?

He keeps all the girls malleable with a workout, three meals a day, and the calming therapy of coloring books. He doesn't rock their boat unless their behavior warrants rocking. That fucking booklet has them brainwashed into thinking they will walk out that door to freedom at the end of his event.

*How can one man have so much power?*

Rose sits on the bed and shakes Whisper like she's a ragdoll. I'm worried about her neck. Rose is back to behaving like a soulless robot, simply following orders.

"Not so rough," Cezar croons. "If she's still in good working order, I don't need her neck broken." Rose stops the shaking and motions she wants a water bottle.

He holds up two fingers. "Go bring two back." She leaves. He turns his attention to me. "Was I wrong to bring you into my fold, Mathias?"

*Shit, where is this going?*

"No, sir. I faltered. It won't happen again." He keeps watching me. I want to look away, but I hold his eyes, determined not to wind up buried somewhere. I have to see this through, for Whisper and Rose.

Rose arrives with two bottles of water, taking a little longer than expected, her back to me. Some more of her bandages are now newly soaked with blood. What did she just do? Her face is flushed, and it looks as though some of her stitches have torn. I see out the corner of my eye Kane walking past the open doorway looking in, smiling.

*Kuksuger!*

What did he just do to her? My eyes flit all over her body, trying to work out what has just gone down, apart from what I can see. She's not letting anything on. Why is he even here? Rose hands a bottle to Cezar, making sure her back is kept out of his eyesight.

"If she wakes up and is coherent, you will both become her friend. I don't care if you color with her or play charades—in fact, that would amuse me to no end—but the both of you are going to spend time with her in shifts every day, babysitting that poor, neglected soul of hers. She will *believe* she has people in here. You will be her frenemies." He grins stupidly at himself. "Whisper is my trophy, and I can't have her losing her mind just two weeks before the event." He twists the top off the bottle and soaks her head with it until the last drop falls, wetting her bed.

Whisper's body starts to respond, so he continues, "Give her the other bottle to drink. We may have neglected her feeding schedule today. Rose, go get her something to eat. Food might recharge her batteries, and then you can return to your stall. Mathias will have first shift." Rose leaves, carefully angling her body away from Cezar.

"Mathias, call me in fifteen minutes reporting her condition, and I'll have worked a time schedule out between you and Rose." He watches Whisper slowly open her eyes. She's staring ahead, unseeing, her big brown eyes very lost. She doesn't see the monster standing before her.

Cezar points to me then makes a chopping motion with both hands. "Aaand... action!" And with that parting smart-ass comment, Cezar leaves.

I go shut the door, allowing me a small amount of privacy to speak with Whisper and gauge her condition. At the same time, I worry about Rose and what happened to her with Kane.

"Whisper?" She doesn't respond to her name. She just keeps staring ahead, a blank look on her face. "Little rabbit, I know you're in there," I speak in hushed tones.

"Don't let this beat you. I'm okay. Rose is okay." I know she can hear me. I need to stay positive, or Cezar could quite possibly execute her before I can save her.

I wave my hand in front of her face and watch her slowly blink. She just needs time to find herself again. She's been overloaded with too much, and her mind is now cocooning her.

"Honey, you've got me in here." I tap her head, careful of the camera, careful of the door opening, careful to keep my voice lowered. I want to tell her I'm on her side. I'm the good guy in wolf's clothing, but I can't.

I pull her forward and slide in behind her so she's nestled against my chest, her body limp and unresponsive. Her eyes open, but nobody home.

My ass is on fire. I swipe the sweat from my face as I angle myself onto my side, grunting through the horrendous pain.

I'll feed her once Rose comes back. I'll be her best frenemy in Cezar's eyes. He just won't know how much I want to play the part. Kane or any of the other sentinels, I wouldn't trust her with. Rose can't talk to her, but she is female, and better Rose than Kane.

Cezar called *Action,* so let the show begin.

# EDGE

## Awkward. Much.

**S**lade rolls us down Miss Catherine's driveway, and I note how cozy the old lady's home looks. This is a place of safety and sanctuary for Whisper. Miss Catherine explained how the girl who arrived on her doorstep that rainy night was so different to the now strong, independent woman she had become. She might only be twenty-one, but Whisper had lived a hard life, setting her worlds apart from other girls her age.

We were two types of opposing souls who had come together that night at the bar. Mine was dark and twisted, and hers was sweet and wild, but hell if I didn't feel something then.

*Fuck the ten-year age difference.*

The Harley rumbles to a stop at the bottom of the old porch steps and we both dismount, removing our helmets just as the front door swings open and a man reveals himself.

*Who the fuck?*

I reach for my gun as he steps out of the shadowed porch toward us, and the man who is gonna hate my guts glares down at us, sporting a matching moon boot. Boxer is in his late forties, and even though he was nearly starved to death, you can tell he's always looked after himself.

His eyes float between me and Slade, coming back to rest on me once he's worked out which one of us he wants to fuck up. We share a look that brooks no misunderstanding.

*Well, there goes our hug-it-out moment.*

Looks like the welcome wagon isn't going to be very welcoming, but I'm glad for Whisper that he is well and up and about.

I assume Miss Catherine's been told to stay put inside her home, when that thought is quickly squashed as she pushes past Boxer, leaving him with a peeved look on his face and a roll of his eyes.

Words I can't quite hear are mumbled under Boxer's breath as he takes a few steps forward to follow her, but she's quicker than him, even in her old age. She simply doesn't want to be stopped in her endeavor to reach me. He gives up, shaking his head, a look of resignation on his face.

Yup! There's that fired-up old lady. Even Boxer can't hold her back. I feel a smile trying to expose itself, but I hold onto it.

"Edge!" She doesn't hide her excitement, and that just pisses Boxer off even more. She's hurrying down the porch steps, dressed in her knitted cardigan, granny dress, and house shoes, looking like the grandma I would've loved in my life... if I had been so lucky. She's such a brave old lady who hasn't judged me like I should have been judged for my past sins. She's only looked at who she sees before her. Yeah, I'm glad she crossed my path. *If things had been different...*

I squash those thoughts, because they aren't.

And then the damn woman surprises the shit out of me by hurling herself at me. I hesitate to hug her back, and then think, *What the hell?* If I get to have one good thing today, it is gonna be this moment.

I haven't been able to *feel* from a peer in too long. I've missed having my mom, the only one who counted, throw her arms around me and give me a hug. I've missed my adopted dad's warm, manly connection we shared so easily. I've missed being free to show my love then have it reciprocated with my adopted parents, and have them remember it, have them know they have a son.

I hang on for a few more seconds, soaking up the genuine warmth I feel from the old lady, trying not to let it be spoiled by the man who would rather her be nowhere near me, and rightly so. "I gather Boxer told you to stay indoor—" Just as my words hit her ear, she cuts off my sentence.

"This be my property, and you bein' my friend means I be able to make my own such judgments. I've got all my faculties last time I be checkin', and I be listenin' to his advisement, but I be choosin' what I be doin' for myself. No man be tellin' me what to do unless I be allowin' it."

I can't help but release that smile I was hanging onto, and then give Miss Catherine a gentle squeeze before I extract myself from her. "Good to see you, Miss C." And I mean it, because my heart has opened up for this old lady, and I can feel how it craves her friendship.

I step to the side, one eye on Boxer, the other on Miss Catherine, gently moving her out of Boxer's line of fire. "Miss C, you've already met my good friend, Slade."

"Yes, I have," she acknowledges him with a smile, and doesn't hesitate to make a move his way and envelop him in a hug. She talks quietly to him, while he nods in return. She really does know how to read a good man with those bones of hers. I won't allow myself to hope she thinks of me the same way. I'm not a good man. There is a great divide of violence and mayhem between Slade's life and my own.

Impatience has prevailed as Boxer thumps his way toward us, like I belong on the bottom of his moon boot. He's none too happy about Miss

Catherine ignoring his order, at least until he knows she'll be safe hugging not only me but also the unknown man I brought with me.

Surprisingly, Boxer makes no move to intervene when he reaches us. He waits, giving the old lady the respect she is due, and that earns him some of my brownie points.

Slade and Miss C break apart. "You boys be comin' on inside. I gots a pot of my special gumbo brewin' on the stove, and the coffee is still hot."

*I think we're all going to need something stronger than coffee.*

"Slade will walk you back in, and I'll be in shortly," I tell her gently. Slade's fully aware of what's about to go down. I'll decide on my terms to get the inevitable over with sooner than later. When she doesn't make a move, I state the obvious. "Boxer and I have to have a guy-chat."

He nods, agreeing with me, his arms folded across his chest, no doubt restraining himself from punching me in front of Miss Catherine. She looks between me and Boxer, her eyes shrewd and all-knowing about exactly what is going to go down.

"Boxer," she crosses her arms across her chest, "remember what I be tellin' you. There be time for all this alpha testosterone-slingin' when Whisper be safe back in our arms. This be the time for alliances." She is such a plucky lady.

"Miss Catherine, you go on inside, and I'll be the judge of what there *is* time for and what I can *make* time for." His eyes don't leave me. "And before you say another word, I know you don't want to be doing as asked, but this is between Edge and myself, and for what my words are worth, we both need you safely inside. I don't need Evelyn out here too."

Doc Evelyn's here too? *Nice.* I'm a fan of the good doc. My face must have shown my interest in her, because Boxer's eyebrows have now shot up to his forehead. Before I can correct him on what he is assuming, Miss Catherine makes a little *harrumph* noise and turns on her heels, heading toward the porch steps.

Slade knows he needs to follow suit. "Sir," he holds his hand out to shake, "name's Slade Malone, former special forces, and I'm here to help the best I can." Boxer nods sharply, giving the offered hand a firm shake. Then he heads on in after Miss Catherine. Boxer's got no grief with Slade, and my boy knows I can handle myself.

I hear a rustle to my left, and Mocha-chocolate, a.k.a. Ghost, has appeared, arms crossed at his chest, standing strong, ready to bear witness to what's about to go down.

I give Ghost a nod, and he looks at Boxer and rolls his eyes in a just-get-it-over-with-because-he's-only-gonna-stand-there-and-take-it way. And yes, I am gonna stand here and take it.

"Boxer." I bob my head. "It's time to get this done so we can move onto getting the fuck to Alaska. You know who I am. I shot Whisper and let those men take her. I fucked up." I don't blame him for the pissed off look waging war on him. He's already been told. I'm just giving him a courtesy reminder, fuelling his contempt for me.

I stand there waiting. He hasn't pulled a gun on me, and I wouldn't blame him if he did. If she were my daughter, I would have shot the fucker who hurt her, without blinking. But she isn't my daughter, she's my sweet and wild, and she's fucking brave.

*And I thank fuck she isn't my child.*

He's not talking, so I keep going. "I'm going to bring her back to you safe. She is under the protection of two motorcycle clubs now, and those men will be meeting us here in the next few hours. They will lay their lives down for her, as I will too. You have my word on that."

Arm pulled back. *Check!*

*Fuck's sake, here we go again.*

Powerful fist clenched. *Check!*

*I'm almost bored by the humdrum of having to allow myself to be fucked with.*

And then my head is snapping to the side as my jaw feels like it's dislocated. I stumble backward, trying to right myself. I take a step forward and wait for the next blow. With a name like Boxer, he knows how to do damage. The pain is intense, and I know he's gone and dislocated it, but I let him have another shot at me.

I stand my ground and wait.

He doesn't raise his fist again, because he knows I'll stand here and get up every time until he's done. All he is doing is wasting his energy and time.

"Your life if it comes down to it?" His only words, and they're deadly serious.

I don't hesitate with my response, riding the pain, as I answer, "You have my word." Which comes out sounding messed up, because I can't shut my mouth properly, but I mean every word.

He watches me a moment longer, his eyes burrowing into me. When he finds what he's looking for, he steps aside, and we both moon boot it up the familiar porch steps, with Ghost disappearing somewhere.

Even if he hadn't given me the nonverbal invitation to go inside Miss Catherine's home, there was nothing stopping me and my men from being in Anchorage tomorrow.

I'm back inside the familiar home, when the doctor approaches me, muttering about men and their macho ways. She takes one look at my jaw and shakes her head.

She directs me to the small kitchen table. "Sit. Jaw

first and then your foot." Her eyes open a little wider when I do as she says. She was expecting me to ignore her. I have respect for the good this woman is trying to do, and I need my fucking jaw to be fixed ASAP so I can be ready to travel.

She sits opposite me, and I hear the growl of a caveman. "So you and Boxer, huh?" She ignores Boxer and shows me a little blush warming her face and her genuine happiness, but busies herself putting on surgical gloves and wrapping her fingers in gauze. Then her fingers are in my mouth and—

*Holy fucking hell!*

I make a god-awful racket, but she fixes my jaw. I hear a satisfied sound coming from Boxer. He's had his moment, and now we can move forward.

She goes for a bandage and I stay her hands. "No thanks, Doc. Don't need to be wrapped up like a mummy." She sighs heavily, but doesn't argue. My jaw hurts, but it wasn't a bad dislocation. I've got a pretty hard head. I'll be black and blue tomorrow, but that ain't unusual these days.

"Foot!" She moves her chair back so I can put my leg up on her lap. I hear another growl from behind me. "Boxer, not now! You know this man only has eyes for Whisper."

I shut my eyes and groan. That was probably the worst thing she could have said.

"What. Did. You. Do. To. Her?" He's in my face like

an angry bulldog, all screwed up, spit flying.

*Thanks, Doc.* She realizes what she said and looks sorry. "Doc, you've just been scrubbed off my Christmas list." I give her a smile that doesn't quite do the job.

"I knew it!" Boxer is about to wig out and go all dragon man on me. Again, I don't blame him for his anger issues.

Miss Catherine stops her fussing over a large pot in the kitchen and raises one eyebrow, a hand on her hip.

*What?* Do they really wanna hear I fucked her and we both enjoyed it?

"Oh... boy," Slade mumbles under his breath, not helping. He's only adding flames to the thoughts no father wants to be thinking, even if Boxer's only seen himself that way for a few months.

"I go away for a few days, and you not only shot her, but you... you... you...."

I wouldn't finish that sentence either.

*Best leave that one alone, big guy.*

I'm actually at a loss for words on what I can say out loud that hasn't already been assumed and thought.

*Well, fuck me. I'm actually speechless.*

"Boxer... she's not a little girl. She be nearly twenty-two and she be an adult. Whatever be happenin' between them be their business." Shit, now Miss Catherine's wading in. Boxer is pacing, and I'm sitting here feeling like I'm in high school.

*Fuck that.*

"Do you *really* want me to spell it out?" I know he doesn't. "What I will tell you is it was consensual."

One finger is pointed in my face, and I can't say I like the proximity of it. "And you didn't tell her you were too old for her? *Christ's sake.* How old are you? Thirty?" he hollers in my face.

Time to do some of my own poking. "Thirty-one, and why would I? Thought she was a woman named Sara and she was around mid-twenties. I didn't know she was twenty-one and Whisper. I knew nothing about her." All I can say is the truth, even though I want to eat those words, because I should have learned something about her.

"I didn't know she had been abused her whole life. I didn't know she needed saving." I'm getting louder and more pissed off. "I didn't know my father died until a few weeks ago. I didn't know the fucker owed a debt and Whisper was the down payment. And I don't know the hell she is going through now. She's been your family for nine months, and she's still your family. So could we get to saving her and sort out the rest when she's *fucking safe?*" My temper has flared, and Doc Evelyn flinches as she works at checking my foot over.

"If I die getting her safely back home, then you

have gotten your payment for what went down between Whisper and me. Hell, I would kill any fucker who did this to my daughter. Do you think I haven't been going slowly mad waiting for a fucking lead?

"We have that now and we need to be jumping on it, getting our asses to Anchorage, and working together, because sitting here yelling at each other isn't gonna fucking bring her back alive." If Doc didn't have my leg in her lap, I would be up and hitting a wall. Punching something feels better than doing nothing. I don't think Miss Catherine would like me redecorating her place, although I still need to get her a new couch.

"Nobody be dyin'," Miss Catherine says optimistically.

A man like Cezar won't let Whisper leave without a showdown, and I aim to give him one. I say a little calmer, "She's had all her rights taken from her, since nearly her birth. Don't fuck it up with her by being overbearing. She needs her freedom now to make her own choices. My father took that away from her, and you need to let her make her own decisions, because a girl like that can't be caged again, and she's too old to be grounded.

"What did or didn't happen between us is our business. Let her have her own mind. Not saying you have to have liked it. Just saying, she needed to do whatever she needed to do. She knows she's not like other girls her age. Maybe she wanted to be." I let all that penetrate his hard head and then watch as the British bulldog in front of me walks away, pacing it out by the fire.

He doesn't have to like me, and I'm good with that, but we need to be able to work together and swap any information not yet shared today.

We need to be on the same team.

••••

Slade and Boxer have been chatting for the past few hours while I play the third wheel. Boxer doesn't have any issues with my man-mountain of a friend. They've had their heads bowed, talking quietly, and I'm not invited. Every now and then, Boxer looks up at me and glares. I glare right fucking back, which isn't getting us anywhere. He doesn't know where to put me, because he wants to hate me. I confuse him, because I didn't fight back.

He wants a reason to hit me again, unlike my father, who had no reason. I had done wrong in my father's eyes, so I took what was given to me, but I was a boy. I've done wrong in Boxer's eyes, so I take it, because I deserve it. But I won't take a repeat performance, because now I am a man, and no fucker is gonna beat down on me unless my conscience says so.

Ghost previously vented on behalf of Boxer and Whisper's friends, but that was all I was allowing, same with Boxer. He had his moment and he took it.

The one person I don't want to hate me has every reason to. Whisper's the only one who counts. She can rain her punches down on me all she wants. She can shoot me where she deems fit. She can stab me in the back. But no man will ever take my power away from me ever again.

Miss Catherine's been keeping one worried eye on me as she busies herself in the kitchen, and it smells real good in there. Doc Evelyn has been helping her. They've given me space, fully aware of the testosterone in the air.

Miss C's cooking up a storm to keep herself active, and because she knows a bunch of hungry bikers will be rolling in soon enough. She keeps looking at me as though she really does care for me, and that just fucks with my mind, because I do want her to care.

I haven't had anybody worrying over me in a long time. Love my adopted parents, but their minds have been long gone from knowing who I am. When I look at Miss Catherine and Boxer, I realize what Whisper has now lost. These two people have known her less than a year and love her like their own blood. They have given her a reason to look to the future. She's been given two roofs over her head.

## CONTORTED

She wasn't caged anymore... until now.

I pull at my hair with both fists. I haven't moved from the kitchen table, my elbows digging into the tabletop. I don't belong here. I belong in Anchorage, and this waiting is pure fucking *agony*.

A small hand clamps down on my shoulder. I look to the side to see Miss Catherine pulling out a chair beside me. A glass of water is placed in front of me. I don't move. She yanks on my hands until I let go of my hair. In this moment, it is just her and me. Nobody else exists.

"What be goin' through that damn head of yours, Edge?" She eyes the bruising along my jaw with silent disapproval.

I play with the glass of water on the table, turning it with my fingers before I answer her, trying to find the right, honest words for her question.

"I'm so glad Whisper stumbled onto your home and she found good people. I'm sorry she was subjected to a life with my father. I feel guilty he took a child because I got my freedom. She's had nothing but shit piled on her, until she found you and Boxer. I should have tracked him down and come back to watch him carefully, to see how he was living his life. I could have saved her years ago."

Miss C stays my hand on the glass, a deep frown etched into the wrinkles on her face. "No! We be livin' in and around Connard, and we not be knowin' what be goin' down in that damn plantation home. He be clever. Not givin' anybody no inklin' to what he be goin' about behind closed doors. She be his carefully closeted secret. He be behavin' like a moral citizen of Connard. Nobody be guessin' he be any different.

"He hardly be comin' into Connard, the town. He be keepin' under everybody's radar. He not be comin' into the bar for a drink, no visitin' the local stores. People paid him no mind. His death came and went without a ripple in Connard," she assures.

"You don't understand, Miss Catherine. I *knew* the type of man he was, because I lived under his roof in another town."

"You were a little boy." She tries to hold my hand, to comfort me, but I let it slip out of her grip.

"I may have been young, but he wouldn't have changed. I *should* have found him when I was older and seen for my own eyes." I lower my voice. "I ran away from my *nightmares*." The last word comes out as a pathetic croak. I'm stronger than this.

"A little boy shouldn't have had to be dealin' with a father like you be havin'."

Past tense, because I got out. I was saved.

I lean in closer to Miss C, trying to get her to hear what I am telling her. What I am owning up to. "I'd been too busy making other people pay for their wrongs that I didn't check on my own fucking breathing flesh, who was a much eviler bastard than those I have sent to hell by my own hand." And there it is, the huge shit pile of guilt that has been fighting to be set free.

"I let this happen." My voice catches. To cover it up, I pound my fist on the table, making the glass jump. "I could have stopped my father. I could have saved Whisper a long time ago. I could have told Hazard, but I didn't. I wanted this kept my disgusting secret."

My. Fucking. Filthy. Secret.

"I walked away with a clean break from the man I knew to be a psychopath. I may have been young, but I knew it wasn't normal how I was treated. I fell into the arms of the most loving couple, who showed me what I had been missing out on. I got a second chance. For whatever reason he wasn't put away at the time, I could have done something about it when I was able to, but I didn't," I growl.

"A town full of people didn't be knowin' what he be doin'. He certainly wouldn't be showin' *you* if you came lookin'. It was all well hidden." She looks so fierce at the moment, wanting me to believe she's right.

"The only thing you be doin' wrong here is shootin' Whisper. Since then, you been wantin' to move mountains to be findin' her. You been takin' a beatin' or two, and you've assisted scum into an early grave. You been honest and been puttin' Whisper first. I be seein' that." She whispers, leaning toward me, "Boxer been seein' that." Then she sits back up again. "These men be takin' many a girl, and they all be no doubt windin' up dead. You gonna be stoppin' that from ever happenin' under this Cezar's rein again, and that be somethin'. You'll be bringin' good through the bad.

"Plenty of wicked in this here world. You can only be cleanin' one thing up at a time. Once your boys get here, I be feedin' them, and you be leavin' for Anchorage soon's you can. You then be close to her whereabouts and the rest will come." She really believes I'm going to save Whisper and bring her back alive.

"You still gots Jenny?" she asks, and I nod my head. "You be sure to be givin' her to Whisper when you be findin' her. Don't be forgettin' in all the action that be goin' down that she will be needin' Jenny." She pats my hands then gets up and walks back to her pots. She has great confidence in me bringing Whisper back to her. She doesn't waver. I didn't realize how much I needed her strength at the moment.

My emotional guard is let down around her. I really believe she sees me for who I am, a lost soul who has been trying to find some ground in this world. I had it for a little over a decade, and then it started to be taken from me, piece by piece. The only two people I could call parents were forgetting their son. I had a biological mother, and my heart hurts for the unknown.

Did *he* kill her?

I take a gulp of the water, because I've got nothing else to do at the moment, and that is hard.

*Real fucking hard.*

Slade slides down in the chair Miss Catherine vacated. "How you holding up?" He's such a grounded man. I'm glad he's here.

I clear my throat. "I'm good. Just need to be getting on out of here as soon as I can."

"Yeah... sitting around is hard." He leans closer to me, his big arms folded on the table in front of him. "Been talking with Boxer. He's a solid guy." He cocks his head to the side. "You get why he's having a hard time warming up to you." It's not a question. It's a state-the-fucking-obvious. I don't need to respond. "What I'm gonna do is hop on that nice Harley of yours, and I'm gonna go and get Phoenix, my badass friend from Cedar Hill, where she is currently having some family time with some of my friends from Ocean Beach. They have taken Joy, the woman who was assaulted under their wings." Thank fuck this Joy chick was saved from what Whisper is going through. I can't think of how Cezar is taking the loss, or who he is taking it out on.

"Edge... you listening?"

"I'm good. Go on."

"While I was riding over here, I thought it would be a good idea having Phoenix on the team, being female, after Whisper's bad run with men." He looks a little sheepish at that last comment.

*And fuck if he ain't right.*

"Boxer and I've been talking, and he thinks the same as me. Whisper will need a female to feel safer around when we extract her. Big, scary-looking biker men might frighten her, and she would have been through a lot of bad stuff." His voice gentles. "Because we're all trying not to think about what is being done to all of those women and what the end game is for this Cezar."

He lets me stew on his words before piping up again. "You've got to understand that no matter your intentions now, no matter what you've talked to her on the phone about... things are gonna get worse before we can get her to safety. If she's a debt, then she will be paying it in a way she won't like."

*Don't fucking remind me.*

"You're gonna make me and Boxer happy knowing there is a professional female on this team going into Anchorage and can be the buffer, *if* need be. Whisper will have been through a lot already, and we don't know how well mentally she is gonna be doing by the time we get to her. Your last face-to-face with her was a showdown, a bullet to her shoulder."

Slade's right. He's thinking what I *should* have been thinking, but I fucking didn't.

He touches my arm. "You hearing me, brother?"

"I fucking know she is gonna be all kinds of fucked up from what a man like Cezar can do to her. I heard her sobs," I say with a quiet restraint that is deadly. "I know how fucked her existence is, Slade. I know what I fucking did to her. That's why I can't fucking sit around doing fucking nothing like I am now." I've grabbed a hold of the glass again without thinking, my knuckles whitening the harder I clench it.

"Edge, release that glass before you shatter it. It won't help. You've allowed yourself enough pain, and that hasn't fixed anything." Pain is something I understand, but I loosen the strangle hold I have on it. "I need to ask you again. You hear what I am saying?"

"Loud and clear, brother." My teeth are clenched. "It's a good idea to have a female on hand for her," I agree with him out loud, because it is true.

I've not wanted to go this deep in my mind with how well Whisper is going to cope mentally. She is brave, but she is alone and reliving my father all over again, maybe worse. Nobody fucking truly knows what my father did to her, other than some fucked-up videos I've been told exist by Miss

Catherine. Fucker kept evidence of his treatment of Whisper.

"I'm going to leave now, and you just keep me up-to-date with the plans for Anchorage." A bowl of Miss C's cooking lands in front of Slade. The old lady's been eavesdropping.

*Surprise.*

"Slade, you be needin' to eat before you be travelin' those hours to get to your lady." She offers Slade a genuine smile. Yeah... she likes him a whole lot.

"Thank you, ma'am." He picks up the spoon that's been placed beside his bowl and gives Miss Catherine a smile that would knock a lot of women off-kilter. "Just for the record, she isn't my lady."

She returns a knowing smile. "Oh, come now. You don't honestly be believin' dem words? You make sure to be bringin' her on by one day. Whisper be needin' a female friend." She gives him a shoulder squeeze and heads back to her pots, and Slade digs into his food.

"Looking forward to meeting her too, Slade," I add, as he keeps right on devouring his bowl of Cajun cooking.

Boxer's phone rings and he snatches it up. "Yeah?" he snaps. He listens, and I want that fucking thing on speaker-phone. Finally, he responds, "Well done, Joel. Put out the feelers. Money's not an issue.

I'll get back to you once I've had the meeting with Edge's men." He disconnects, and I want to know what all the "well done" genius boy has been up to and why "money's not an issue."

Miss Catherine's phone pings and Boxer gives me a look when he sees I've still not given it back, which means return-that-fucking-phone.

**Lethal:** Incoming.

And that's when I hear music to my ears, the roar of a bunch of motorcycles as they near the house.

Boxer is up and headed for the door. He's showing me my place. He's in charge... for now. I get up and walk to the open door. Boxer is down the porch steps, and Ghost has appeared again by his side. The fucker almost glides through the air. I'm getting his name now.

Slade joins me. There are now eight bikes parked in front of Miss C's porch including mine, and seven gruff-looking bikers standing with helmets off, waiting for what comes next.

Boxer announces loudly, "Looks like these men could do with some of Miss Catherine's home cooking." He approaches each man and introduces himself, shaking their hands. "Thank you for coming." Ghost nods at them all, and then Boxer thumps his way back up the porch steps. I move to the side, letting him past me, while Ghost disappears again.

Hazard, my president, all hard man who's aged well in his late thirties, with dark eyes, thick beard, and thick eyebrows, is the first to mount the porch steps. He favors his hair tied back when not wearing his helmet. Could have looked less manly on another biker, but not Hazard. He wore everything about himself well. He makes it to me, clomping up the steps in his heavy boots. We hug it out like two big bears, while I keep my jaw out of the line of his shoulder.

I only asked that none of them wear their cuts from a few towns out. It's bad enough this many bikers roared into a quiet place like Connard, but we don't need any eyes on us. They came in at dusk, which helped, but it would have been better if they came during the night. They're here now, and that's what matters. Sooner we make plans, sooner we're outta here.

"You doing all right?" His voice is as gruff as a bear's. Both thick eyebrows arch when he pulls back, noting the color of my jaw. I must be starting to go all Technicolor. "Taking another fist for the shit you did wrong? Because I *know* you don't let a fucker get the upper hand."

I ignore his second question. "Better, once we get this fucking meeting over with, after everything we know is collectively laid out on the table and plans are in place." He grunts in acknowledgement and understanding and moves past me. Slade's no longer standing by me. He's giving me space to welcome my brothers.

Torque is up next. President to the Lion's Den MC. Messy ash-blond hair to his shoulders, sporting facial scruff and a serious lean look. All of thirty-two years of age.

Lethal follows close behind. The bastard is too pretty to be a biker. He's in his late twenties, clean-shaven, with neat, dark brown, short hair, and eyes that trap women at a glance. He got his handle, because he's good with poisons. If he wants you dead, you are on your way to pay the Ferryman before you can even register what has gone down.

"Glad you're here, Lethal."

He smiles and we man hug with one arm. "Wouldn't miss it for the world, *hermano*."

He gives me a wink, and then Viking swaggers up to me, the Vice President for the Lion's Den MC looking every part his namesake. The guy is blond and built, looking like a Viking warrior with all that long hair, cool blue eyes and a braided beard.

I work my way through a bunch of man hugs from Blueblood and Viper until I get to Drill, who gives me a big smile and claps me hard on the arm. He cocks his head to the side as a finger comes up and touches my jawline. "You been pissing somebody off?"

"Something like that." He might be from the Lion's Den MC, but we're close. I clap him on his other arm. "Good to see you too, brother." His grin broadens.

"Never a doubt, Edge."

"How's Cyn?" I'd told him to make sure she had money and to check in on her and her kid.

"She's good. She was askin' after you." Drill's grass-green eyes are soaking me up. The guy's got a man crush on me, but I ignore it. He knows where I stand with that. We shared Cyn, which is past tense for me now, and we got naked, but *that* line wasn't crossed, no matter how many times we shared her. No matter how bad he wanted some man-on-man action in the mix.

He needs to notice Cyn has eyes for him, and she would gladly find another partner willing to satisfy his sexual needs in a threesome. I'm never gonna be that partner or permanent guy.

Once everybody is inside, I look around at Miss C's home, which seems to have shrunk in size, filled with big, dusty bikers. She's introducing herself and Doc Evelyn, while Boxer is laying his claim on her by sticking by her side, arm around the good doctor's waist until the message is clear.

*Smart man.*

She's a good-looking woman. I saw Hazard running his eyes over her with male appreciation.

space, but your gonna wear a hole in Miss Catherine's floor if you keep this up." I don't look up from his hand. "We get it. We all feel you. We know this chick means more to you than you can even wrap your head around at the moment. We are all gonna get these bastards, and we are gonna enjoy retribution. You feel me?" I keep staring at his hand. "You haven't had the code from the undercover agent, so she's hanging in there, and her family is keeping strong."

I look around the room. Boxer and the two presidents are still in a private meeting. Miss Catherine and the Doc have made themselves scarce, banging away in the kitchen, the smell of food being served up, leaving these men crowding me. Showing me they're supporting me.

"I just need to be doing something instead of nothing. Hear me?" I prompt.

A round of mutterings follows as I sidestep and go prop myself up against the wall, arms crossed. I watch Slade go over to Miss Catherine in the kitchen and give her cheek a peck. I think Miss C actually turns a slight shade darker, if that is possible. "Thank you for your hospitality, ma'am. I'm heading out. The gumbo was delicious."

Miss Catherine touches his arm with affection. "Any time, but you be sure to be watchin' yourself and your lady's back when you be over there in

Alaska seekin' retribution."

Slade belts out a short laugh. "Somehow I don't think Phoenix is gonna like knowing her back is being watched, but I'll make sure." He turns to Boxer and gives him a nod. That nod is full of understanding. Then he's shaking each man's hand. "I'll see you men in Anchorage soon." He jerks his head my way. "Edge will keep me posted." And then he's out the door.

••••

An hour later, with everybody fed and cleaned up, it's time to get down to business. The men have given Miss Catherine and Doc Evelyn a seat at the kitchen table. A show of respect, because this ain't no normal Church.

Boxer stands and surveys the men littered about. "Time to talk about the twenty-one-year-old girl, Whisper, who has been abducted and is the closest I have to a daughter. That makes her precious to me and Miss Catherine." He shoots a look at me as a reminder.

Like I can forget. I refuse to eye roll.

I was going to sit back and let Boxer take the floor, for now. I respect who he is to Whisper, and I respect whose home I am in now, but this was my father's doing in the first place, and these men I've brought in are capable and clever.

Boxer's phone pings, and he looks up from checking it. "Joel, my computer genius I trust explicitly, wants to talk to us all via real time. Miss Catherine, where's Whisper's computer?"

"In her room. I'll get it." She takes her stairs to the next level and comes back down with the laptop. Boxer doesn't treat Miss C with old-person-disease. She is very active, and he treats her as an equal.

He meets her at the bottom of her stairs, always keeping one eye on Doc Evelyn. I appreciate how he looks out for both these women, because we are still alien to him, and I don't doubt Ghost is watching from some hidden advantage, ready to storm the premises if we aren't all behaving like good little boys.

He thanks her and sets it up at the kitchen table, and we all huddle around the screen. Boxer makes sure Miss Catherine and Evelyn are on either side of him while he waits for Joel to call him up. Several minutes go by, and then a good-looking guy with dark, short hair wearing Clark Kent glasses appears on the screen, complete with his own fading bruises.

"Hey, Boxer." He acknowledges Joel with a serious nod, before the younger man continues, "Miss Catherine, Doc, and team." He holds a palm up in welcome. "Good to see y'all are looking well." Then his computer is being moved to include Lincoln, the blond-haired man sitting up against a headboard next to Joel. Although he lost weight, Lincoln is still much broader than Joel, who is lean. His leg is in a cast, since his bones had been shattered with a sledgehammer. "Somebody here should be resting, but he wanted to say hello to you two lovely ladies, so I brought the computer up from my station."

Miss Catherine pipes up first. "Lincoln and Joel, it be so good seein' you two together."

If faces can beam, these two are doing that. They have great affection for the old lady. "Miss Catherine, you are looking well. We haven't had time for a catch-up on all your shenanigans." Lincoln looks almost proud. "Joel filled me in on your adventures while I was keeping Boxer company on a crash diet." The guy is making light of what happened to the two of them. Last time I saw both of them, they were looking like death was only a door-knock away. "I understand you've been up to mischief with Edge and doing some illegal driving. I'm rather impressed."

I'm going to like these two. Miss Catherine turns and makes eye contact with me. Her face is sheepish, because she definitely enjoyed living on the wilder side. Boxer huffs in his seat.

We're all crammed in around the screen. I speak up, "Lincoln, I'm Edge." His eyes hone in on me. "Good to see you looking better than the last time I saw you."

He gives me a good, hard look. "Heard you shot my girl?" *Fuck!* He might bat for the other team, but he's no kitten. "Heard Ghost showed you what we all thought of that." He touches his jaw. "Looks like Boxer also showed you what he thought of that." I don't reply. "Also heard you've been working hard to find her."

"That's what we're all here for." I feel my knee being squeezed. I know it's the old lady.

"Joel lookin' after you, Lincoln?" Miss Catherine can't help but fly the white flag by interrupting. She knows he would be. I can see it in Joel's face the love they share. Fuck society who don't get that love is happiness; don't matter what sex you are. Neither cares there's a bunch of big, gruff men listening in. Nearly dying will do that to ya. It will make you weed out the important things in your life and not give a fuck about what anybody else thinks.

"Yeah." He pats Joel's back, leaving our conversation alone for the time being.

"As you know, Doc only let me out of her sight a few days ago. Sorry we missed our shopping date with you and Whisper. She was looking forward to leaving Connard for the first time and visiting New Orleans for the Black Friday sales." His voice gets softer. "We'll take a rain-check when she comes home." A newfound strength and determination crosses his face.

"I be holdin' you two men to that," she replies with just as much determination.

Then, we get down to the nuts and bolts of this live meeting. We talked about strategy and we laid all our cards on the table. Joel kept listening and punching keys on his computer until we knew more than we had ever known until now.

The bikers sitting with me introduced themselves and exposed their hidden talents and training. We all worked together. A private luxury cabin off the beaten track but close to roads was booked to accommodate us all so we had privacy. Next, tickets were booked for flights to Anchorage.

All the men here were going in on two flights in the morning, with Slade, Phoenix, and a guy named Billy coming on a lunchtime flight. Didn't know what eyes were watching, so we needed to keep Whisper and all the women safe and Adam off the radar. We were all gonna take our time getting to the cabin in small groups, going in quiet. Just a bunch of businessmen on a corporate retreat.

Cezar can't get an inkling a bunch of trained bikers have landed in Anchorage. The man has kept his secrets because he's meticulous. He has people on the payroll. He has eyes keeping him connected.

Several hours later, we were bunking down for the night, spread out all over Miss Catherine's floor and couch, with a fire crackling and a solid initial plan in the air.

There was still much to be done once we knew where this fucking event was gonna be held and when.

One thing that surprised the shit out of me: Boxer isn't coming. The classified information he was able to get came at a cost. He will be forced to stay in Connard and let Adam do his thing and in the timeframe he deemed.

He didn't put up a fight. Boxer knew the high-up suits didn't need to feed him intel, but he called in a pretty powerful fucking marker to be collected. If he broke the agreement, then all intel would be cut off, leaving him out of their loop.

Thing is, Boxer didn't explain there was a whole crew of bikers willing to put their lives on the line for Whisper and the other females, and bring this fucker down and all his minions. He didn't let on about that little tidbit.

No man in this house is willing to wait, because Whisper would be dead by the time the high-up suits deemed the operation ready to be wrapped up. I think Adam knows it's crunch time, because he may have lost his sister to Cezar, but things have changed now. He knows he has back-up with us, because the high-up suits in their safe offices don't know the mental pressure Adam is under.

Don't know a long job like this can break a man and Humpty Dumpty would come tumbling down, but Cezar's men won't put him back together again. Cezar would make sure those pieces are scattered.

*And they don't know Edge is a man on a mission.*

We can rely on Adam to give his contact something, once we've stormed our castle, giving us the time we need.

But one thing I know.

*Things are gonna blow.*

# SLADE

## Firebird and All That Sass

**I rolled up on the Harley at five in the morning** to find Phoenix waiting under a streetlight with a whole bag of sass.

"You're late, Slade."

It's never too early for a bit of 'tude from Firebird.

"Good morning to you, too, Firebird." I throw her a pearly smile for good measure.

I hand her the helmet. Her ash blonde dreads are covered under a colorful bandana she favors as she slips the helmet over them, grabs hold of my shoulders, and throws her leg over, getting comfortable behind me. She's got a nice, thick leather jacket on, keeping her warm from the frosty air.

I don't want to goad her too much at this time in the morning, but hell, she brings it out of me. I've missed her sass.

She slides her hands onto my hips. If my dick could, it would be smiling. I need to get myself another bike; I like having her behind me like this. "You know you can snuggle in a bit more. I can't bite you while I'm riding." With that comment, I bet she's shaking her head and I hear the softest laugh.

We take off, and I switch on the passenger communication so we can talk. I know she's curious about me needing her help. I let the bike have its wings on this quiet stretch of road, my speed increasing as it roars to life in appreciation to be moving again.

"So, Firebird, what do you think about Alaska this time of the year?" *Wait for it...*

"Don't call me Firebird." And there it is, that little bag of sass already opened up. I'm grinning away, because I love it when she gripes about the nickname I gave her. "Slade, you got trouble?"

"Helping a good friend out." I need to explain everything to her, now that I know the first part of the plan Edge and the men sorted out.

"I gather we're not riding all the way to Alaska?"

That's my girl, she doesn't waver when I land her with Alaska. She just wants to know how we're getting there. "Nope. Getting a flight later on. We're heading to Crowley now to Freedom on Two Wheels, a bike repair shop, to meet up with the owner, Billy, who I understand you've already met."

"I have. Nice guy." She holds on a little tighter when I take the corner a little sharply at the last part of her reply.

"Some Lion's Den MC will be waiting for us in Anchorage, along with some Soulless Bastards. I don't know how much you were told about Joy's assault, but the same men who came and helped Billy keep Joy's assault quiet at Coyote Cooter's are gonna be waiting for us in Anchorage. How's Joy?"

"She's a survivor."

"How's Levi?"

"He's on his way to a happily ever after."

I smile at this, because Phoenix sounds a little wistful. I want to tell her I can give her what she needs, but that is for another time. We've got a job to do.

"Also the men who killed the nomads who attacked her are gonna be there too." From the little noise she just made, she didn't know the bit about the nomads getting offed. "Billy may have been... *nice*"—can't help how jealous that one word has made me—"but these are dangerous men. Don't forget that, Firebird." In hindsight, do I really want her around them?

"You need me, because...?"

*I need you for a whole lot of reasons, darlin'.*

"I'll get to that in a minute. Once we get to Billy's workshop, we'll sit tight, have a bite for breakfast, and you'll play hairdresser to Billy." And here comes the punch line. "You know how Joy Parker was nearly taken in Fort Worth?"

"Yes."

"Well, there's more. A twenty-one-year-old named Whisper was successfully abducted a few weeks ago from Connard, Louisiana. She means something to my good friend Edge, one of the Soulless Bastards, and her family needs her back safe and sound.

"Everybody on the team going into Anchorage is getting a makeover. Everybody is either looking like a businessman or hipster. I think hipster is more achievable, with their beards and tattoos. Nobody can be going in looking like a biker. Everybody is prepared to strip out of their cuts and talk the talk, and we have to walk the walk.

"We'll shop at the airport. We need to get rugged up for the cold temperatures in Alaska and dress for the part we are gonna play on the flight. The others are all heading out on two flights later this morning, and we've got a lunchtime flight. You're gonna be the only female among these men."

*Christ, I'm gonna talk myself out of bringing her.*

I proceed to tell her on the short ride to Crowley about what she's in for. And yeah, she snuggled in a little closer when she heard about Whisper. She just didn't realize it.

Retro is gonna try to kick my ass from one side of OB to the other when he finds out I brought his sister in on a mercenary mission with a bunch of men who play by their own rules. But I know she's trained, badass, and can handle what gets thrown at her. Phoenix knows how to pull bodyguard duty if Whisper requires it from Edge. It will take a strong woman to put Edge in his place, if it means protecting Whisper until she is ready.

••••

We've landed in Anchorage, and it didn't go unnoticed the flirting Billy was doing with Phoenix on the flight over. He was thoroughly enjoying himself, but fuck that, she's mine.

I did have a great sense of pride when Phoenix told him all about her PI business, Mack and Cooper Investigations. I think that enamored him even more toward her, knowing she was not only sexy, but she could back it up with a whole lotta badass.

I had a whole nine hours of this in-flight entertainment on top of watching him press the back of his head up against her chest when she was giving him his hipster makeover—hair trimmed and ZZ Top style beard fully tamed. Then she assisted him with his clothing selection. I only have myself to blame. I suggested she cut his hair.

Then I had to put up with him complimenting her with her clothing selections while calling her "doll face" every few minutes.

I was going in as the businessman. Don't have a beard, not full of tats. Only have the one on my chest. I was suited up and I caught the appreciative look in Phoenix's eyes on more than one occasion. And I liked it.

Thankfully, Phoenix is a super quick shopper, and Billy pretty much bought the few extra suggestions she added to his new suitcase before we got on the flight. Airport shopping—you can buy anything.

I left Edge's bike at Freedom on Two Wheels, and we waited out front for the ride he hooked up for us with an old guy named Denver, who's Joy's grandfather, to Dallas Airport.

He looked Billy up and down, grunted something that had Billy smiling out the corner of his mouth when he saw the new less hairy transformation, and didn't say much more. He then helped us lift our backpacks out the back of the truck at the drop off zone. He looked over at Phoenix and me, shook our hands, told us to get the bastards who orchestrated what happened to his granddaughter, and then got back in his truck and drove off.

Odd man, but I liked him.

I herded us inside a cab, making sure Billy was deposited in the front seat, while Phoenix was in back with me.

I'd only met the guy this morning and I liked the man, but I was trying to persuade him with territorial actions—she's *mine*—while she did her best to falsify everything I was putting out in front of him by simply being herself, independent.

I think in the end, we highly amused the guy. Now it's time to sit back and prepare myself for the bunch of bikers I need to somehow prove in front of that she's mine, without Phoenix contradicting me.

Or it would be open season.

# ROSE

## Just Give Me a Reason

**I'm in Whisper's room sitting at the end of her bed**, watching her concentrating on the page of her coloring book. She responds to whatever I put in front of her, but she doesn't acknowledge me. It's like she's on autopilot. She's working on the Venetian Carnival book. These men will be dressed in outrageous Venetian carnival costumes, so I want her broken mind to understand what she will be seeing.

She has decided to stay cocooned inside her mind, not speaking to Mathias or me. I can get her to walk on the treadmill, but not much else. She walks with a blank look on her face. I tried to see if she was faking it, but she appears to be lost inside her head, and Mathias and I aren't even trying to bring her out.

She is safer in there. Cezar isn't interested in traumatizing her any more. If anything, he's grown almost disinterested in her, which can only mean bad things for her after the event is over. I will be putting her to sleep permanently.

With the event only a few days away, everything is running smoothly for Cezar.

I watch Whisper add blood red to the carnival costume. Her fingers are steady as she stays within the lines, separating the golden-orange part of the costume, no crayon stroke marring the other color.

Something has been bothering me with Whisper these past ten days, since she hid inside herself and I've had more contact with her. She's been gone roughly four weeks from family and friends.

Something isn't right about her, apart from the obvious.

I watch the red crayon flow onto the costume, each movement of Whisper's fingers precise, and then it hits me, a light bulb moment.

I spear up off the bed and snatch up her personal toiletries bag, careful of the camera. I rummage through and note her tampon stash hasn't been opened. All the other girls have had their stock replaced, even asked for more, but not Whisper.

*Hell no!*

I gently stay her hand on the crayon and hold up her toilet pack, silently telling her she's due for a bathroom run. Even though she stares right through me, she understands. Mathias and I have had this unspoken agreement, making sure Whisper is well groomed, keeping her useful enough in Cezar's eye. I'm as confused by his behavior as he probably is by mine toward Whisper. We are both doing more than Cezar asked of us.

I take a deep, worried breath and let it out slowly. If what I suspect is true...

*Fuck!*

I'm anxious to know the answer to the rest of my sentence, so I cup her elbow and lead her out the door, making sure she holds her toiletries, a reminder of where we are heading, while we make a quick pit stop at my room along the way.

I've been given a stash of pregnancy tests because of the way Cezar treats me. I haven't used one yet, and don't even want to think of the consequences of being impregnated by such an evil man. I'm kept on the pill, because he never uses a condom with me, but accidents can happen. Nothing is foolproof. I have to let him know when my cycle starts every month, so he knows when he can take me.

I scoop up my toilet pack, a pregnancy test always close by in case it is needed, and we make our way to the bathrooms.

The corridor has fewer sentinels gracing its cold interior, since the event begins in a few days. They are all busy organizing transportation and the many other things needed to keep it a secret from the rest of the world. I've done my part. The girls will be as ready as they can be.

We hit the third cubicle and I enter behind Whisper, the door closing behind me. She is already pulling her yoga pants and panties down. I stop her just before she sits, already having removed the pregnancy test from the box.

I show her the box, pointing to my eyes and then to the box's instructions. I want her to read them, but I am unsure if she is capable of receiving this message. Whisper is staring at the directions, so I push her down onto the seat and spread her legs wide.

She starts to pee, so I put my hands between her long legs and dip the end of the stick into the flow, long enough to be sure I will get a good reading. She doesn't seem to care what I am doing. Everything about the toilet is another autopilot motion for her. She knows the drill and wipes and gets up, pulling her clothes back up while I wait the three minutes needed.

*Three long minutes.*

Finally!

I'm too afraid of the result to look just yet. Taking a deep breath, I summon the courage and look at the two incriminating lines, strong and true.

I fall against the cubical wall, my hand flying to my open mouth, while Whisper is left staring at the back of the cubical door.

*How?*

I am pretty sure nobody has raped her in here.

*But am I one-hundred percent sure?*

I'm not.

I turn to Whisper, shove the test in front of her eyes, and shake her until she blinks enough for me to know she can see what I'm holding up. I thrust the box at her and point to my eyes. "Eeed." Whisper blinks at me, confused at hearing my pathetic attempt at saying '*read.*' She stares at my lips. I raise the test results again. "Oook!" I'm desperate for her to look at those two lines and understand me. She's looking, but is she seeing? Is she understanding?

I place the pregnancy test back in the box, tuck it into my toilet pack, place it under my arm pit, and then I touch her belly with my open palm, moving it around and around in a clockwise motion.

"Baaaby." I hate my voice, the destroyed sound it makes. I need to know if she already knew she was pregnant. How far along she is.

Her hand has slipped to cover my hand, and she's mouthing *baby* to herself over and over.

*Jesus Christ!*

She had no clue.

"What. The. Fuck?"

Startled, we both bump into each in the confined space. If a person could quietly roar, Mathias just did. I didn't even hear the main door open.

Whisper is blinking furiously, like she doesn't know how to process what is happening. I hold my finger to her lips to shush her, while my other hand is gently massaging her belly. I need her to understand she mustn't open her mouth in front of Mathias as the door is being shoved into my shoulder blades.

"You two out here now before another sentinel catches you both in here," Mathias hisses at us, his voice as loud as he dares.

I shuffle Whisper about so I can get the cubical door open, and then I usher her out smack-dab into the man who heard our secret.

Whisper stares ahead, clutching her toiletry bag, while I stand before Mathias, trying to work out what my next move is. I'm fearful Cezar will find out and have her killed.

Mathias drags the both of us by the scruff of our hoodies into the farthest corner of the bathroom, which houses half a dozen toilets, showers, and basins. He puts the shower on full pelt to make some background noise.

He places his hands on his hips and looks directly at me, ignoring the lost girl beside me. "Rose, are you pregnant?"

*What?*

I have a split second to come up with a plan. I need to protect Whisper; she can't take any more bad treatment. I can't trust Mathias with the truth. He is still a sentinel.

His eyes lower to my belly. He knows who the father would be if it were true. *Fuuuuck!* I want to scream, but I hold in place my best poker face and calmly nod once.

He snatches my toiletries bag from me and hunts through it, yanking out the telltale box and sliding the pee stick out. He stares at the two pink condemning lines, his brow wrinkled. He looks up at me, sadness seeping across his features. He actually looks shattered for me.

And then he curses in Norwegian under his breath as he shoves it back in the box and stuffs it inside his suit jacket.

He composes himself and zips the bag up, thrusting it back at me without saying another word. He doesn't even think of the possibility it could be Whisper who is pregnant. This gives me hope nobody has touched her in here, but a deep sadness invades me for the father of her unborn child who will never see them both alive again, who probably doesn't even know she is pregnant. Unless she talks to me and tells me when she last had sex, I don't know for sure how far along she is.

Whisper is getting restless next to me. I don't know what is going on in her head, but she needs to play along if she can understand what I am doing for her. She must keep herself safe. I don't know what Mathias is going to do with this information. Will he keep it a secret?

"Hell, Rose, I came looking for you both, because it's my watch with Whisper. How far along are you?"

*Shit*, I don't know what to say. My face stays neutral as I hold up five fingers.

"Five weeks?"

I nod.

He turns his head, rubbing a hand over his masked face. "That fucking bastard!" he mutters so quietly I can barely hear him. "Does he know?"

I shake my head.

"Of course he doesn't. He sliced your back up. If he had known, he probably would have killed you." He stands there silently, looking at his feet. He's figuring out what he will do next.

"You need to go to your room now, stay out of trouble, and rest. I won't say anything. I'll do what I can for you in here. Go." He gently pushes me toward the door while Whisper walks to the basin and uses it. I haven't even had time to wash my hands, but I don't linger.

Just as I open the door, he whispers, "I'm sorry, Rose." That has my heart accelerating. Does that mean he will tell Cezar? Or is he truly sorry that I could be knocked up by such an evil man?

I swing the door open and leave Whisper with

Mathias, hoping she keeps her mouth shut.

I swipe a tear away as the door closes behind me. *I'm sorry too*, I want to say. For Whisper, because she doesn't know I'm going to be her killer.

I won't be taking just one life. I'll be taking *two,* and I'm the only one who will know.

# Whisper

## It Takes Two ... Baby

I'm curled up on my bed, having eaten my last meal of the day. Mathias has been playing his role of babysitter, not realizing I am the one carrying the baby.

*A baby?*

I must have been shocked right out of the final stages of my comeback, when Rose touched my belly and showed me the two pink lines. My mind may have been slowly returning to me over the past few days, but I didn't let on. It was safer to play a broken little bird than to be made to hurt people.

I turned back into a *Whisper,* and it felt good to not have any expectations laid on me. Mathias and Rose were being nice to me, and Cezar was leaving me alone.

*A baby?*

I hadn't even thought about my period since I had been stolen, but I hadn't had one since before my abduction. This was true.

My body has been through so much. How could a tiny fetus survive? Has it been harmed?

*A baby.*

Edge is the father. He is the only man I have had sex with. I was a virgin before then, and he wore a condom. It must have broken. I wasn't on any contraception, because I hadn't let Dr. Castille that close to me yet. I hadn't planned on having sex with anybody for a long time... until Edge walked into the bar, about four weeks ago.

I don't even know exactly how long it has been since that night I became Sara and let myself feel what a man was capable of doing to my body in a good way.

A soft touch lands on my shoulder. Mathias is making contact with the brainless zombie girl. "I don't know how much you're understanding now, little rabbit, but if you heard Rose is pregnant, you can't say anything to anybody. She will be killed. Nod if you understand."

I don't move.

I get shaken this time and rolled over to face him, his masked face close to mine. "Little rabbit, I know you are frightened. You can see I am okay and you have been looked after. I don't blame you for what happened to me, and I understand you've been through a lot and needed time out."

A tear gives me away as it escapes the corner of my eye. I'm not crying for Mathias; I am crying for my unborn child. Reality is I may not be getting out of here alive. Before, it was just me. Now, there is somebody else to worry about.

*To fight for.*

His thumb smooths the tear away. "I know you can hear me. I've known for a little while now. You are smart keeping yourself safe. We need to keep Rose safe too. Please nod if you will keep her secret."

I slowly nod. I can see some of the tension lift from his body. "Good girl. It's now time for you to go to bed." He gets up and leaves, turning the light off then closing the door. I curl back around, hugging my stomach.

I haven't been able to process this is Edge's baby... or that I'm even pregnant. If I get out of here alive—which I doubt, because the event is so close now and nobody has come to rescue all of us—I can't even think what I am going to tell the man who tried to kill me that I've conceived his child.

*Why should I tell him?*

What I do know is I am going to fight for my child any way I can.

*My child?*

I still can't grasp what Rose showed me.

My. Child.

*My. Baby.*

A fierce protectiveness overwhelms me, and I know I will do anything to save what's mine.

*Anything.*

# EDGE

## It's Not the Clothes That Maketh the Man

**Two weeks spent in the cabin, and Adam was** finally able to get word to Slade about the dress code for Cezar's event. Slade had taken a picture of Adam at the airfield, so everybody was acquainted with who not to kill.

I'm currently test-driving the most ridiculous getup. We had to have Venetian fucking carnival attire, of all fucking getups, and all invitees are required to wear masks at all times.

What. The. Fuck?

Phoenix fusses around me, layering the black and white satin pieces. Over-the-top ruffles surround the neckline, itching the shit out of me, making me wanna tug at it. The mask is snow white, covering only half my face, the eye sockets outlined in black, making it look creepy. She plonks a black velvet hat on my head with several large silver-and-white feathers protruding from it.

I look like an abomination.

I want to roll my eyes at Phoenix and complain about the fucking thing, when she drapes a cape around me with a flourish.

I start fidgeting. "Stay still, Edge," she grumbles, as she fiddles with the ties. I can only grunt my disapproval back.

She stops her fiddling, grabs my jaw, and yanks my face so my eyes meet hers. "You want to save this girl? Honey, this is the meal ticket through those doors. Ignore your friends, who would do exactly the same for their own woman," she says a little louder for their ears, because she knows they are hovering and snickering in the background. She then steps back, admiring her handiwork.

Slade is trying not to smile, and Blueblood is looking on with approval, making me roll my eyes.

*Really?* The fucker looks like one of the three musketeers, with his long, wavy dark hair and moustache and chin scruff. He didn't need any makeover from Doc Evelyn and Miss Catherine, because he already looked part hipster, part movie star when he put his hair in a man-bun.

"You *would* find this fucking concoction agreeable," I grind out to Blueblood. "I mean, who wears a Three Musketeers moustache these days, anyway?"

*All for one and one for all, and all that shit.*

He merely grins at me in response.

Thing is, he can back up his look, because he's a pro at fencing. Just hand him a sword and see how you fair. "I fucking pray this Cezar has a sword lying about, so you can practice on him before I get a hold of him. You can tenderize him for me." I must have thought of every conceivable thing I want to do to that motherfucker over and over.

Phoenix is right. If a bullet train heading for me won't stop me, then one fucked-up meal-ticket-costume certainly won't.

Phoenix takes a step back and eyes my over-the-top flamboyant outfit hiding my identity and tattoos from eyes that may recognize me, looking very impressed with herself.

Dallas "Edge" fucking Masson, blooded son of William Dupré, is ready to make heads roll. Don't matter I gotta wear this shit.

I'm grateful Slade went and collected Phoenix, because there's no way any of this lot could have come up with this creation in record time, and she is a much valued addition to the team. Joel and Lincoln introduced themselves to her via video call, and the two of them worked it all out. Forty-eight hours later, and a FedEx box was at the door.

Phoenix draws my attention back to her. "You've got the golden invite, thanks to Adam. That was half the battle. We now just have to wait for the where and when, and then you are set and we're all here to back you up."

Lethal steps into my personal space and snaps a picture of me. "You fucker," I growl. I'm not mad at him, but he's really pushing it now.

"Just a little keepsake." He winks at me. I ignore him, and he spreads his hands in front of him. "Come on, *hermano*. I'm only forwarding it to Slade so he can contact Adam and show him what you look like tonight. Smart thinking, if you ask me. We all know what he looks like, so we won't accidentally fuck with him. We need him to know you're not one of those sick fuckers there for reals."

"Good thinking. Take a full shot of me, with the cane." The cane is needed as a walking aide due to my moon boot being ditched for the event, because I can't have anybody suspecting who I am. I don't know if Ebony and Ivory got around to telling their little story about meeting William's son and cracking one off in his foot. The story has already been submitted as a bum hip. I will also have the little ragdoll inside my pocket with a tracker sewn inside it. I just have to thump Jenny's head, and it will activate once I am inside, so the teams will know where I am at all times.

I remove the mask from my face, pulling the hat off, dumping them on the couch, and run my fingers through my shorter hair, and then snatch Phoenix up in a hug. "Thanks, babe, for everything." I agree with Billy, she's such a doll, with beauty and brains. Whisper would like her. She wraps her arms around my back and gives me a platonic pat.

I look at Slade's annoyed face, his arms folded across his chest, muscles bulging beneath his long-sleeved Henley. I shake my head in humor, releasing her. I wouldn't want another guy touching my female either, which sobers me right the hell up, because that is what could be happening to Whisper right now.

We both step away from each other, and I look around the large den filled with the men who have my back. They've all had complete makeovers because they're my brothers. They no longer look like their former selves... except maybe Blueblood and Lethal. Everybody else has had their manes chopped and styled, their beards tamed or shaved completely off. All for me. There are beers in hand, but nobody is celebrating.

"Edge," Slade is by my side, his caveman ego intact, "you can rely on me when the time comes to light the fucking place up." He clamps onto my satin-covered shoulder. "Now get out of that fucking ridiculous outfit."

The men who are ready to give their life for my cause are just trying to settle my temper, as I've been hard to live with.

I turn to Slade. "You do know how lucky a man you are, yeah?"

Phoenix has sharp ears and isn't gonna let that comment slip by. She knows how to be around us and blend. She's so effortlessly cool the way she dresses, in her vintage T-shirts and ass-hugging jeans, with her dreads contained under bandanas, but at the same time, she is one of us, without trying to be.

"Oh, there's nothing going on with Slade and me, other than friends who look out for each other."

Could she be any more transparent?

"Well, in that case," Blueblood really does want to play with fire, "Phoenix, I've got room in my bed if you want to—"

MC brother or not, Slade's not gonna let that slide. His chest is hard up against Blueblood's and he's sending a telepathic message to stand down, his fists tight balls at his side. Phoenix is about to step in and rectify the pot she just stirred, when I shake my head at her. She lives in the civilian world, where maybe it's okay for chicks to step in and save their man, but not in our world. No matter how badass and capable she is, she's still got tits.

Slade has to let the boys know she's off limits, regardless of what she thinks about Slade, even though she is walking a fine line. Phoenix is a conundrum, because Slade would fit her well, yet she fights the pull. She must have her reasons, but fuck me if I can think of one against a guy like him.

I whisper into her ear. "Babe, you can't be playing this game in front of bikers." They've all been ogling her ass when she walks past, and they are thinking about getting inside her. Each man is putting up their hand for co-chefing in the kitchen, just to spend time with her.

Her face goes bright red and she starts spluttering. "What game? Just because I don't roll over and spread my legs for Slade, doesn't mean I'm available for anybody else. I'm here to help. And it would be in fucking bad taste, considering what Whisper is going through, don't you think?" Her hands are mimicking Slade's, tight fists by her sides, like she wants to punch somebody but she's holding herself in check. I don't doubt she knows how to fight and win. Slade's told me she knows enough martial arts techniques to take any one of us and lay us out.

"Okay, everybody, let's lighten the fuck up." The tension is lifting as some of the guys disperse into other rooms, while Phoenix, on an eye roll, disappears into the kitchen to start on tonight's dinner. I don't doubt Slade will gravitate toward checking on her soon enough, because Viper, Viking's younger, red-headed brother, who gets his handle because he's a crack shot, with his fresh hipster look is headed straight after her to opt for kitchen duty. After all, she can't feed all these men by herself, and at least one of us always makes it our responsibility to rotate, giving her a helping hand.

I thump my way back with the moon boot to the room I'm sharing with Hazard to start removing this creepy get-up and dress in some real clothes. We've kept to the cabin, only heading to town in small groups for supplies, wearing casual clothes, blending in playing the new part of friends on vacation. Not a fucking care in the world.

Under the cabin's roof, we have been plotting and planning. Joel is a fucking genius. He set this whole thing up and got me the fake gazillionaire perverted life. You can Google the shit out of me now, and all you'd find is I'm a reclusive, obscenely rich, private man, who is very much under the radar and likes it kept that way.

I am the type of person Cezar would be drawn to. I am a phantom, because of my wicked tastes, and Adam made sure I was on the list of attendees.

The upfront cake was a little harder to come by on short notice, but we managed with all my properties hocked to the neck and Boxer added his own cake. I don't give a shit about the money. I can always make more.

Joel seems to believe it is only gonna be used as

flypaper anyway, transferring right back out of Cezar's account once his castle gets overthrown. It is, after all, just sticky paper filling that fucker's account up, according to the man who could make almost anything happen in cyberspace.

*Once a hacker, always a hacker.*

Hell, he could extract every one of those dickwads' attendance fees and donate it to every female in that Pen. Child's play.

I decide to give Miss Catherine a call. She soothes my anxieties. I just don't need anybody else to know I've adopted her as my own.

# Whisper

## The Exorcist has Nothing on Me

**I'm bent over the toilet bowl. My eyes water as** another round of vomit explodes from me. Rose has done everything she can to hide the morning ritual that's been abusing my body.

It first started three days ago, straight after breakfast. I thought it was something I had eaten. Mathias was watching over the poor-insane-girl-who-had-lost-her-marbles. I was keeping up appearances, when I tossed all my cookies over the side of the bed.

It didn't take much convincing for him to believe I had come down with a bad virus. He had it in his head Rose was the one pregnant. I didn't even enter the equation for being knocked up.

I don't know how much longer we can keep up the charade, but I had at least been given a bucket for my room. My saving grace for the whopper of a lie is one of the no-name sentinels is coughing and spluttering around The Pen.

Unfortunately for me, Nicu is now standing behind me, holding my hair while I hug the porcelain bowl, a position I don't want to think about too closely.

Rose has up and disappeared on me, and Mathias is nowhere to be seen either. I can't question Nicu where they are, so I can only play the part of the prisoner with the virus, and I am doing a very good job of it. My face is clammy, my throat raspy from retching.

I feel miserable.

I stand up and swipe the back of my hand over my mouth, leaning against the inside of the cubicle wall. I have to give myself a moment to stop the dizziness swarming me.

I can't even care this man has seen me like this. When I feel I can walk without swaying, I push off and Nicu allows me the room to walk past him so I can reach the sink, resting both hands on either side of it. Our eyes meet in the mirror, and they are all too questioning.

I duck my head and turn the faucet on, wetting my face down and swirl my mouth out with water. "Must have been something I ate, or nerves," I mumble, and stand back up straight, patting my hair down as our eyes meet in the reflection again.

He's not buying it, from the indent in his brow. Next thing I know, I'm swung around and marched to the medical closet, where he rummages until he finds what he needs.

My knees nearly give out on me when I see what he has in his hand before he slides it into his pocket.

He yanks me back around to the bathroom area. "I ain't fucking buying what BS you're trying to sell me. I don't know who and when, but I'm placing a bet on what." He pulls the box out of his pocket, extracting the stick from inside.

"You forgot to pee before. That's why we were coming to the bathroom in the first place. Do it now, and shove that stick where it will get showered on."

I've never seen Nicu mad before, but he sure is at the moment. He's always been a very quiet, calm sentinel. One I knew wouldn't give me any trouble.

"Now!" His voice may be lowered, but he makes me jump, snapping me back to attention.

"I don't have to pee on it. I'm pregnant," I whisper back.

"Humor me." He needs proof for his own eyes.

I do as he says while he discreetly raises his eyes until I'm finished. And then I'm spinning over, clutching the toilet seat as the pee stick is snatched out of my hand. I'm too busy throwing up again, the ammonia smell of my own pee not helping.

When I finally finish, I hear Nicu pacing and

cursing. I feel so vulnerable right now. What is he going to do? I stand up and repeat my previous moves until I am facing Nicu again in the mirror.

"Who touched you in here?" He sounds like he wants to hurt that somebody.

"Nobody." He knows it as truth from the conviction in my voice. "It was from a night best forgotten, by a man who betrayed me." When I say the words out loud, I just want to burst into tears, but I keep myself in check and wait to hear my fate, because there is no way he is keeping this from Cezar.

"Who else knows?"

"Nobody." A boldfaced lie. This man deserves nothing more from me.

"Keep it that way."

*What?*

And then I'm being marched back to my room, both of us silent as the stone walls.

To top it all off, the event is finally here. I know I'll be moved sometime today. I just don't know when and to where. Rose had gone through my performance with me, shown me how to do my makeup, hair, and nails, and what was expected of me.

We arrive at my room, and Nicu disappears, leaving me to curl up on my bed. I'm frightened for the life growing inside of me and what lies ahead.

Truth be known, I'm expecting to be executed.

My door swings open, making me jump. I'm paralyzed with fear, because there is nothing I can do to save myself. I could have run out my room, but to where? There is no escape.

A new bucket is placed on the floor by my bed, and a small container of pills is being pushed under my pillow. "Somebody will come for you soon enough. Take two of these iron tablets." A bottle of water is placed in front of my belly. "Play your part well tonight, and you might just make it out of here alive. Don't try to escape. You will only fail and be killed. Give yourself a fighting chance."

"So the booklet tells me." Sarcasm shoots out of my mouth before I can check it at the door.

"How many weeks?"

I don't pretend ignorance. "I don't know today's date." I can't help being bitchy to him.

"Seventeenth of December."

*Nearly Christmas.* I've never celebrated Christmas. This *was* going to be my first. Miss Catherine was getting a real tree and all, but now....

"How far along are you, Whisper?"

My hand touches my belly. "Around five weeks."

He's doing the calculations in his head. He knows it's the same time I was abducted.

"Who?"

I know what he is asking. What name do I give? I choose an honest answer, because it will mean nothing to this man. "A man named Edge."

His eyes nearly bug out of his head, and then he's covering it up by turning and walking away.

He can't possibly know Edge.

*Can he?*

# EDGE

## Ping! Music to My Ears

My new burner phone has received its second awakening from its slumber on the wooden coffee table in front of me. The first ping was forty-eight hours ago, letting me know to get my ass to Anchorage, Alaska and to have a full Venetian carnival costume to wear.

*Been there, done that, way ahead of them.*

I was told a second message would be left on the 17th of December, today, and to be dressed and ready for a night of wicked debauchery.

Only reason it's now pinging me is because the location and time of that fucker's event is being revealed.

I snatch it up and look at Hazard first.

"We're all ready to do what it takes. We're gonna help you bring her home," he responds to my anxious look.

I survey the room. My brothers and Phoenix are

sitting around on couches or the floor, and I know this to be true. Faces look back at me in loyal support. I have a part to play from here on out.

I check the phone and skip to the location details. "We have coordinates." I immediately forward the text to Joel, who is on standby.

*Ping!*

He's quick.

Joel has the exact details for the pick-up. It's an abandoned stone church on a beach in Juneau. There's a link and map attached.

**Joel:** You got this Edge.

I think I've earned a fan. I silently thank him for his confidence.

Slade's phone then pings. He snatches it off the coffee table and reads his message.

"Who?" My throat ceases up and it comes out all rough. I'm so wound up, my patience a tightrope I'm trying not to fall off. This is the day I get Whisper back.

Slade lifts his eyes to me. "Adam. He says coordinates are for a pick-up only. Final destination will be a private property on a lake in Fairbanks. There's a 9:00 p.m. kickoff. Be armed, and he'll handle the rest. He's revealed a further set of coordinates. I'll forward them to Boxer."

It's gold, this information, and the head start we

need, even if it is only by a few hours. I know Boxer has asked that Slade keep him in the loop. I don't give a shit if he doesn't trust me. I give a shit what our endgame is.

I study the map we've got spread out on the table, and line up the coordinates Slade reads out.

Fucker's chosen a remote place surrounded by frozen land, a lake and trees. Don't know what is there though. Map's not that detailed.

We've already investigated all forms of transportation, and there's no way this lot can be choppered in without giving up the goose. There's no time by ground to get there ahead of me and set up.

That leaves one other way. Tandem skydiving at night, and these guys are crazy enough to pull it off too.

*Ping!*

Joel sends the link for the property with blue prints of the interior. I send back a request for assistance with organizing skydiving transport. I know he and Boxer will make it happen.

I hit the link up, and cyberspace is very accommodating, showing all the photos of the property's interior. It's a luxury home built of solid western red timber with all the bells and whistles.

This is gonna take some more planning. I run my hands roughly through my hair, tugging at the strands in frustration.

Fucker is dead tonight.

There will be no chance for Cezar to use a get-out-of-jail-free card. He's greased enough palms with enough cake; he knows how to work the system. I'm leaving nothing to corrupt lawyers. There's gonna be no OJ-repeat-performance.

Ain't. Gonna. Happen.

This is a man living a fucked-up fantasy under a pseudonym.

The man is an enigma.

But he is flesh and blood. He bleeds like the rest of us.

We are to meet at 7:30 sharp this evening. It's now nearly 4:00, and the sun has shut up shop. We need to get onto the modified plans ASAP.

We all huddle around the computer and talk strategy, which now includes tandem skydiving onto a cleared area and hiking back to the property, so they need to get moving.

We have enough men here who were trained in the military and can work that shit with their eyes closed.

There is a lot of harrumphing and eye-rolling going on between Slade and Phoenix at the mention of who is gonna strap Phoenix to their chest. Slade is mumbling one thing under his breath at Phoenix, and she is grumbling a whole lot of something else, which resembles a lot of sass, while we all try to carry on talking and strategizing.

It ends on a stink-eye from Phoenix, and a deep sigh of resignation from Slade. My take on all of it is Phoenix doesn't do well with heights, but Slade has been there, done that before. Phoenix isn't gonna let the team down no matter what, so she is in, *no matter what,* and she isn't letting some behemoth of a man tell her otherwise. To which Slade replied, "Damn woman."

Discussion over and out.

If this weren't such a serious time, these two would be hilarious. The sexual tension is actually making all of us shuffle in our seats. The babe with the dreads and cool tattoos is giving Slade, the man-mountain, a steep uphill climb for his money.

They should just fuck each other's brains out. I know I'm not the only one thinking it, but for whatever reason, Phoenix is holding out, and that is driving them both cray-cray.

We spend the next half hour on a video call with Boxer and Joel, modifying the plans to match the set-up of this luxury home. We go over everything in detail until we are all comfortable in our roles.

*Ping!*

Slade's got another message from Adam, he's just found out Mathias is another undercover agent he's been working side-by-side with and not known, from his outside contact. The high-up suits deemed it now reasonable Adam should know he's got another team player inside.

This is excellent news, especially for Mathias, because I had that fucker's number on my list after Whisper told me he was a bad guy. All we've got to go on is he's Norwegian so we don't shoot him accidentally. Great.

*Ping!*

Another incoming message for Slade. *Fuckin' A.* more good news, the location of The Pen will be discovered soon when Adam and the sentinels move the women.

I sure want a crack at The Pen, wherever the fuck that place is, but Whisper is the one I need to protect and rescue. She is my priority.

We have our hands full getting as many females as we can out alive, while apprehending as many of the bad guys as possible. Boxer's not breaking any rules the high-up suits put on him because he's kept his ass in Louisiana and we're technically running our own private show at another location, one Adam was deliberately keeping from his contact because we're all on it.

Once Adam reveals the location of The Pen, Cezar's command center in Alaska, this news will keep the high-up suits busy.

S.W.A.T. and all the alphabets like FBI, CIA can all

get patted on the back for their part in helping to bring down this trafficking ring. We only want to save lives and fuck with the bad guys.

It's going to be below zero temperatures and dark, and we have to have an escape plan in place after the raid. Joel is working on it and we will be advised later. We are as ready as we will ever be, allowing for the unexpected.

Boxer seems to think we will have everything we need hidden in the locked basement inside this cabin. Hazard and Torque go and look, using the code given to unlock the door.

A few moments later, we hear "What... the fuck?" in unison, as it filters up the stairs. I automatically look toward the sound over my shoulder, while Billy and everybody else gets up for a looksee.

I gather there is a veritable armory and everything we need magically awaiting our fingertips down below, by the sounds of the *oos* and *ahs*.

Go figure the coinkidink we wound up in a place well armed. I look back to the screen. "Boxer, whose place is this?"

"Ghost's."

*Figures. That man is a mystery to me.*

"Sounds like the fairy godmother of the military waved her wand and provided. You get this place set up the minute you knew Alaska was in the cards?"

He shrugs. "Ghost is a think-ahead-for-an-apocalypse kinda man, but I added a Christmas wish list of my own to cover as many outcomes as possible, and he has a supplier handy he trusts who slipped in and filled my list out before you all arrived. Figured lots of snow, and chances were the area could be remote." He shrugs again. "Made sense to fill the wish list out just in case."

"I gather the basement covers the whole square footage of this cabin?"

"Pretty much."

*Christ.*

"I suppose there's enough skydiving chutes in that there basement?"

Joel is beaming a smile at me.

*Really?*

"Boxer... things that could be used to go boom. Were they on that wish list of yours too?"

"I think you'll find the armory can accommodate just about anything you need to do to get Whisper out alive and to incapacitate a bunch of fucked-up perverts."

The guy loves showing me he is in more control than I want to give him credit for, and seeing me surprised by their ability to keep on surprising me is putting a twinkle in his eye.

I give them an appreciative look that says, *Yeah, yeah. You're the shit, Joel. And Boxer is too.*

We've all just had a moment and released the

tight valve a little that has pressurized our fear of not knowing what Whisper is going through.

An awkward silence hovers between us. Time to cut the chitchat and get ready.

••••

Eight Hummers with dark-tinted windows arranged in a convoy are lining the driveway of the Shrine of some Saint-or-other as my cab pulls up, depositing me in the freezing cold night.

Some old lampposts illuminate the way, as more cabs arrive with men dressed in their finest hoity-toity Venetian carnival costume's spill out of them. They only nod to acknowledge the others.

My cab driver was curious about my outfit. I simply brushed it off as an office Christmas party. I don't think he believed me. I think he was probably now thinking more kink club.

With the use of the cane, I walk toward the seventh Hummer, as two men apiece are ushered toward the previous six SUVs, when the masked, tuxedoed driver waiting by the eighth car catches my eye. He motions to me discreetly with a hand signal I know only too well. We used it in the Special Forces. It was unique only to my team. I should know; I fucking made it up.

*Adam?*

I arrive at his Hummer, leaving the last two men

access to the seventh Hummer. Adam gives me a bow. "Sir, my name is Nicu and I need to pat you down, as per the invitation protocol."

We are all to be known as *Sir* for the duration of the evening. No names revealed. No masks removed. Our lives kept hidden.

This is a game they take seriously.

I spread my arms for him, and whisper under my breath when he steps into me, "Glad you're on the right side, or I would've had to kill you, my friend."

This gets me a little grunt in return as he pats me down, like all the other drivers are doing. He knew the clothing I would be dressed in, aiding him in making sure I got in his vehicle.

Adam, of course, knows I am gonna be packing, and finds the knife hidden in my left calf holster and the small handgun holstered on the inside of my right calf, and breezes over them with a practiced hand. He finds the ragdoll inside another pocket and keeps moving his hands over me.

My OTT outfit is excellent camouflage, with its baggy pant legs and layers of clothing. I'm eager to get in the car, so we can hopefully talk freely. My passenger door is opened and I take a back seat, letting in the night's cold breath.

What I'm not prepared for is the interior light revealing an attractive, athletic female, her face partially turned away from me, in nothing more than her birthday suit, hooker stilettos, and black lace panties, shivering.

I move the tip of my cane under her chin, angling it up slightly. Her eyes are totally void of emotion. I must look a sight in this get up. Her face is beautifully made up, her lush red hair piled high on her head, all sexy Bridget Bardot style.

"Please, allow Rose to entertain you." Adam shuts the passenger door and cranks the heater up.

Anger rises temporarily inside me, because this was the bitch who cut Whisper's tongue. And then I look a little harder.

Familiarity hits me.

My head voluntarily cocks from one side to the other as my eyes try to accept who I think is on the back seat with me.

What the fuck?

Her makeup is a mask in itself. Smokey grays and blacks spread out over her cheekbones, her eyes thick with makeup.

*Ruby?*

I glance at Adam in the mirror, his masked eyes giving nothing away to this woman, but he sees something in my look and cocks his head ever so slightly back at me. He sees recognition in my eyes.

My shock and confusion fight with me, knowing what she had to do to Whisper, but here sits a victim who was stolen under our club's protection. And from the looks of her, she's seriously broken.

*Damaged.*

Whisper had said she was damaged.

Whisper made me promise to save her.

I need to be sure my mind isn't playing tricks on me. I don't know how safe it is to talk now. Are the SUVs being monitored? I decide to err on the side of caution.

"Nicu, does every car have the pleasure of such fine naked tits, or am I the lucky one?" I wasn't born in the South, even though William ended up living there, but I can crack a pretty good accent when I try.

"Yes, every car has a female in attendance as naked as Rose. You are allowed to touch, but no intercourse. You don't want to ruin the night's plans."

*Of course we wouldn't.*

I want to roar at Adam for allowing Whisper to be naked in another car in front of a couple of fucked-up perverts. Why didn't he make sure she was in this car?

"Sir, there is one exception. She will be on display for every man attending tonight when you all arrive at the final destination." Adam makes me wait to hear more. "Her name is Whisper, and she is Cezar's trophy, the one to win."

*To fucking win?*

Knowing she's not naked in one of these Hummers is a relief, but that does not mean she is better off.

I don't pay Ruby any more attention. I want to cover her up and hate knowing she has two men in this car capable of saving her right here, right now, but we deny her that. Instead, she's being driven toward one fucked-up night.

"Rose will now serve you a glass of the finest French champagne."

*Of course she will. Only the best for us damned souls.*

"Sir, Rose is here for you to take advantage of, if she pleases you." Adam knows I won't touch her, but he has to appear as though he is attempting to keep me entertained. This only makes me believe more we are being listened in on.

All I can think about is the motherfucker who has Whisper and what I'm going to see when we arrive. I take the glass, but don't drink what Ruby offers me. I know she expects to be touched. It's what she's used to.

"Sir, a chopper is waiting for us about a half hour away. In the meantime, Cezar has requested I play you some Dean Martin Christmas tracks for the short drive."

*Of course the crazy fucker would think Christmas songs would be appropriate.*

I feel Ruby flinch when "Let It Snow" starts its perky introduction. I look over to see her bury her back against the leather seat, like she is protecting it.

"You don't like this song?" I goad her a little. "You tell Daddy here why you don't like some harmless Dean Martin song."

The look she sends me is defiant, because I am teasing her.

"Sugar, you got me all curious now. I bet you're gonna tell me anything I want to know, simply because I ask. We've already established I'm allowed to touch you. Do you want me to touch you?" I lick my lips and snap my teeth at her, watching the fear in her eyes as I slide right up next to her all cozy-like, pushing the glass of champagne to her lips while grabbing the nape of her neck, forcing her to drink it. "Isn't that right, Nicu? You won't intervene if I start touching this beautiful young lady?"

"No, sir."

I take the glass away from her lips, release the hold I have on her neck, and slide a little away from her.

"I'm only gonna ask one more time, and then I am gonna start touching in places that is gonna hurt you. Why don't you like that song?"

Her mouth opens and shuts, and she looks

terrified to talk.

"Why isn't she talking, Nicu? Cat got her tongue?"

"She has had it cut out, sir."

Those words just screeched to a halt in my head.

My mind does a double take.

*What did he just say?*

Our eyes meet in the rearview mirror again. There's pain buried in his eyes, because he's been helpless to stop what has been going on inside Cezar's walls.

I reach over and use my gloved fingers to pry her mouth open. She doesn't resist. My anger catches up to me.

I.

See.

Red.

I take important seconds to calm the beast within, raging at me to let it free and start fucking people up.

"So she's no good for a blow job?" I release her mouth, acting pompous and unimpressed, and turn my head to stare out the window. "I've seen enough. Daddy is waitin' to get his dick hard, and this one isn't doing it for me. I need a more specific… stimulus. A whore is a whore. I can get a dozen of her served up to me any day of the week, and with a tongue attached. I'm not paying good money for a naked bitch in a back seat." I'm playing the part of a difficult son of a bitch to hide my rage.

"No, sir. I understand."

Ruby twists her body, her only answer she'll give me, until her naked back is revealed.

"Oh... my. You've been branded." I sound perverted and excited.

Inside, I want to punch a motherfucking hole in a wall.

*What the fuck has been going on in that place?*

"Did your master cut you to this song?" I'm even starting to creep me out with this role I'm playing.

She nods, still facing away from me, her head bowed.

I quietly snap a photo of her back. I made sure to put my phone on silent before I left for the Shrine of Saint what's-his-face. She is none the wiser to my actions. These scars are new; they haven't quite finished mending. This was done recently.

"Daddy is gonna love playin' with you." If she could have spat on me, I know she would have turned her pretty head and done so. She's still got fight left in her after what's happened to her, and she's gonna need it to get out in one piece tonight.

"Sugar, show daddy those big eyes of yours." She turns her head and looks over her shoulder. I snap some photos of her. I see the hatred for me underneath her surface. No matter what she's been forced to do to Whisper, she's also a victim.

She loathes me calling her sugar, so I keep doing it. I need Ruby to be angry. Anger will make her stronger to get through tonight.

"Sugar, you concentrate on facin' those titties and that pretty head of yours to the window again. I don't need to see your face no more for a while."

I turn off the interior light, placing us in darkness, and send a couple photos discreetly to Hazard of her face and back while more DM croons away, and then I delete those messages.

There's no time to count Ruby's breathing as a win, because we got a long way to go yet. I've got a promise-list to fulfill for Whisper, and it's gonna get bumpy.

I'm about all Dean Martin'ed out by the time we arrive at the private airfield. Another song starts playing while we sit parked close to two AgustaWestland AW189 choppers waiting.

My impatience to board the chopper and get within touching-distance of Whisper is at war with being the hunter and not the prey.

My screen lights up with a code from Hazard, which equals "we're all in place, just let me know when."

*Hell. Motherfucking. Yeah.*

# Whisper

## Feeling Free and Easy

**I**'m laid out like a human platter down the middle of a wooden table in a big, cozy room. I know this, because there is an antique framed, long mirror attached to the ceiling above me, and I have spent untold minutes thinking about where I am and looking at myself.

In my mind, I'm swiveling my head from side to side like Stevie Wonder, because it feels... floaty. So I keep doing that, because it helps me to think and feels nice, and my hair is very pretty, but when I look at my reflection, I don't seem to be moving.

*Huh?*

Something isn't right with me, and yet I can't seem to be bothered focusing on thinking about what that could possibly be.

I know I'm naked beneath all the pretty flowers and foliage that has been artfully placed on and around me, with fruits and berries and other foods.

I do not understand. I've watched faces coming and going, busily covering me up. They were very serious faces.

Sometimes, I fade in and out. I heard some hammering a little while ago in my head, but my eyes didn't open. I feel even more dreamy than I did when I felt floaty.

More time has passed, and now my reflection is showing me bottles with labels have been placed on the table, and other things I can't quite understand.

My face is now made up like a Day of the Dead person.

Somebody did this to me while I was faded out. I concentrate a little harder on my reflection and notice my lips seem to have been stitched shut, but it doesn't hurt. Pink satin ribbon has been threaded up and down, like my mouth is wearing a corset where a few little rings have been inserted through the top and bottom of my lips.

*Maybe it should hurt.*

As more time ticks by, I keep up with the head swiveling until I realize my reflection is now moving with me. I roll my head from shoulder to shoulder, testing the expanse of my movement.

This pleases me, because now I can see more. I watch people too busy caught up in their duties to notice me, as they bring a decadent ambience to this room with rich colored fabrics and low lighting. It feels almost like a fantasy coming to life around me, and I am a part of this fantasy.

I know I should roll off this table, but my body doesn't have it in me to move. I think I might be restrained, cuffed to the table by my hands and feet, but I can't remember seeing anything, and I can't feel anything. I concentrate on wiggling my toes, because then I will know I have feet. I decide wiggling my fingers might be a good idea too. I work hard at getting with the wiggling program, but it's as though I am paralyzed, but awake.

I give up trying to wiggle things.

*Time keeps ticking on by.*

The last thing I remember is Filip sawing my cast off my arm… then… I try to scrunch my eyes up as I think hard, but they don't seem to move. I don't remember getting here, but here I am.

Flat.

On.

My.

Back.

I start singing a Stevie Wonder song in my head about being lovely and wonderful, when Filip's face appears upside down, hovering over me. I wonder if I was humming it out loud. I can't help a soft giggle bubbling up in my throat.

*I wish I could open my mouth.*

He's cursing under his breath as he slides

something into my neck, but I can't feel anything as I start to fade again, as I fight against the tide that is pulling me out.

I can't swivel my head anymore.

*Go figure.*

My head gets repositioned. Flowers and such are being placed around my head as I fight the blackness, and then Filip disappears.

I liked swiveling.

And then I'm back to singing in my head.

*At least I smell nice.*

And then the black wins.

# EDGE

## Blah ... Blah

**R**uby and the other scantily clad females were choppered out ahead of us, huddled up in long, fur-lined winter coats, with the drivers chaperoning them. Adam remained with the fucked-up perverts as the pilot of our chopper.

A scenic chopper ride later, which was longer than anticipated, has now deposited us onto a private pier complete with helipad. The lake is frozen over, the silver of the moon reflecting brightly over it.

Fairy lights twinkle along the pier as we make the short walk up to the house and climb the many stairs to the ground level. I keep a sharp, discreet eye out for any of my men and Phoenix. I know they are blending into the landscape. Nobody will know they are there until it's time to play ball.

I take in the two casually armed masked men standing on either side of the main entrance, and another two who are keeping watch on the first level balcony. No other minions are in sight, but that doesn't mean they aren't about.

These armed men are mostly for show, because this is just another private high rollers event Cezar has gotten away with. No trouble is expected. Everybody here wants to enjoy themselves, and not to get caught doing it. There's never been a threat to his anonymity... until now.

The main doors are opened for us by Tweedle Dee and Tweedle Dum. We flow through them, following Adam and entering the warmth of the great room.

I don't notice the man at first who has become my shadow, because I'm too busy being distracted by seeking out the delicate-lace-masked women who are statues, posed differently inside what appears to be seven large plastic balls. The kind you can walk on water in. They are spread around the fragrant, dimly lit room. One is on a couch, another on a round table. Some are on the floor, and another on a chair.

No two females have the same hair color. They have skin colors of all nationalities. They appear paralyzed with fear, their eyes unblinking, as though their bodies have been deliberately positioned and then turned to stone. Their hair teased and sprayed to maximum volume wearing fine masks of different colors, lips painted to entice.

Each globe contains fake snow, their naked bodies portraying an erotic pose with their sex on display.

I draw my eyes away from them as I search for Whisper, and then Ruby comes on my radar dressed in a black catsuit and stilettos. The back is scooped low past her crack, allowing every man to see the scarred word PET etched into her skin. An elaborately feathered mask covers half her face, a smug smile frozen on it as she walks past all of us.

The woman who left me an hour ago is not the woman standing here now.

She's different.

Ruby looks over her shoulder and catches the eyes of the men ogling her ass, the catsuit looking as though it is painted on, forming to her every curve, and she waggles her finger at them as if to reprimand them. Her blood red lips pout shamelessly, confidently.

This amuses the men, making them chuckle. Making them trust her and lead them like the Pied Piper deeper into the room.

A man appears as though out of nowhere, with peroxide hair, looking like the devil himself in a horned half mask and a satin suit of white and blood red. His lips are painted to compliment his evil desires for the night in a deep crimson.

"Gentlemen, welcome. I am Cezar Pavel, your host for the evening, and the luscious pet by my side is

Rose."

A low growl starts to work its way up my throat before my wrist is squeezed painfully by the masked fucker standing next to me in a royal blue and gold court jester outfit.

Cezar is blah-blahing away in the background, when the jester leans into me quietly and says one word in a deep voice.

*Ghost.*

Why am I not surprised?

And that's when all hell breaks loose.

# NOBODY

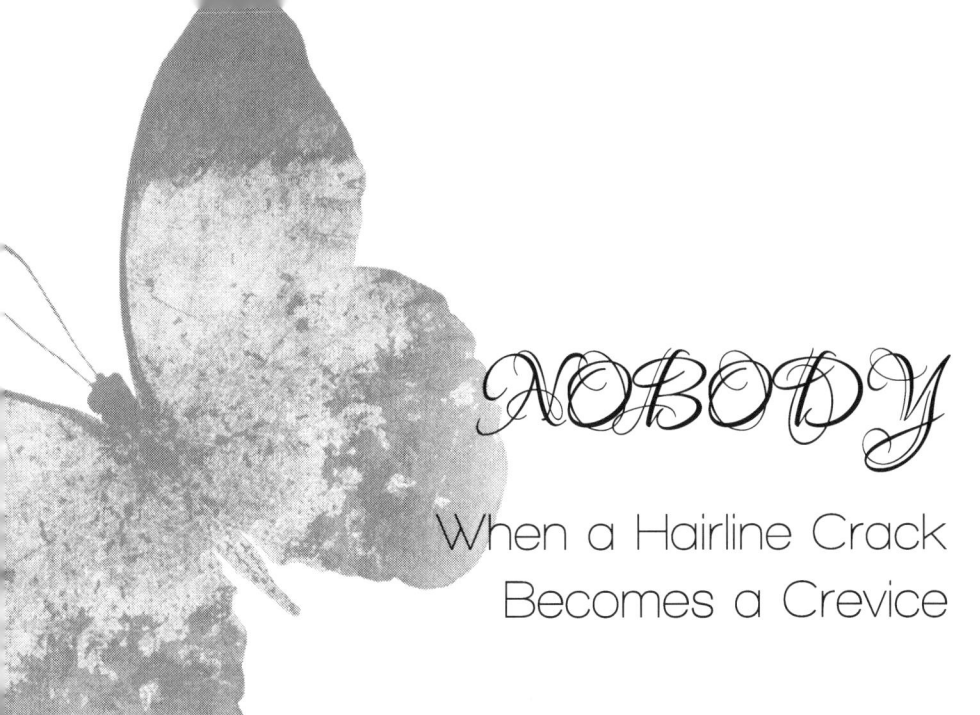

## When a Hairline Crack Becomes a Crevice

Sometime between watching all the girls being drugged, shoved inside a ball, and posed, and knowing how Whisper had been left on that table... a change came over me.

I lost Ruby.

And Rose cracked.

What was left over was a nobody.

Standing there next to Cezar while he *blah, blah, blahed* and knowing all the sick things he was going to allow to happen tonight to paralyzed girls, *Nobody* made a decision.

While these masked men were riveted with Cezar's *blah, blah, blahing*, *Nobody* saw an opportunity, stepped to the side, and picked up the unsheathed Samurai sword, sliding it behind her leg. Some clumsy person had left it leaning against the wall by the large oriental antique vase, forgotten when decorating the great room for tonight. It was not dangerous in its stance, so it had been overlooked.

It was one of those moments where a voice sends you a message, which is telling *Nobody* to pick that fucking sword up and stop all that *blah, blah, blahing.*

So she did.

*Nobody* did something worthy of a *Kill Bill* movie.

In one swift motion, she'd swung that Samurai sword like a warrior, and then there was a spray of red, and a *thunk* that seemed to *thunk* a couple more times until it came to rest.

Total silence.

*No more blah, blah, blahing.*

Then shouts of surprise followed.

*Nobody* had left, and Ruby was back.

I was lying flat on my back, my last breath being stolen from my lungs.

And that is where I lay with a smug smile frozen on my face.

# EDGE

## I Didn't See That Coming ... and Going

**G**host and I look at each other for a split second, and then we're jumping forward, knocking motherfuckers out of the way like bowling pins until we can see what has happened.

Cezar's head has left his shoulders, and Ruby is down. *Jesus H. Christ.* From the hole in her heart, she isn't getting up.

My head turns to see a big, black, masked man lowering his gun, the one used to kill Ruby.

My phone vibrates in my pocket. They would have all heard that single gunshot outside. I position myself toward Ghost, all eyes are on the two dead bodies on the ground and slide it out and check the screen.

Hazard: ?

I risk speaking into the microphone attached to

the inside of my ruffled collar. "Ruby dead. Cezar dead." I clearly mutter.

My phone silently vibrates again.

> **Hazard:** Fuck! Countdown starts. Place gonna blow at 9:22

*And that's how quickly the current can change.*

I show Ghost the message. He's wearing a watch, Boxer would have clued him in. We hit the stopwatch button.

I have no time to acknowledge the ache in my chest for not being able to save Ruby or question why Ghost popped up as an attendee, because I know the answer to that. Boxer needed to be sure Whisper got out.

Ghost nudges me to pay attention.

The fucker is standing over Ruby's body looking down at her. He pays Cezar no mind and then looks up at all of us, surveying the room. "Everybody remain calm. You have nothing to fear. My name's Filip, and I'm now in charge. Unfortunately, your host for the evening won't be able to carry on his duties." This British dick is talking like nothing has happened. "This is very unfortunate and not part of tonight's plans. I apologize you had to all witness his death." No mention of Rose's death.

*Where is Whisper in all this?*

"If you would like to get yourself refreshments

from the table to your right while we clean this up for you, then we will resume tonight's events."

*Is this fucker for real?*

There is nervous shuffling of feet, but they start to head off to the table just as gunfire can be heard coming from outside.

Filip abandons the great room and darts toward the noise, weapon raised. This is a clear indication to the high-rollers that everything isn't under control and they all make a run for it, stampeding all over the place. The pennies have dropped, and they don't want to be caught in the crossfire.

The main doors smash open and shit gets real. The high-rollers are looking for anywhere to escape in their panic. They think this is a police raid and they will be caught up in it.

We trip as many as we can, watching them go down in a tangled heap. Ghost and I start taking them down as a team. He's grabbed one in each hand by the collar, and I whip their masks off before he smashes their heads together like he's a human rock crusher, knocking them out and dropping them.

I've already grabbed two more, rinse and repeat. Four down.

The remaining tangled mess on the floor is making sense of their limbs and scrambling to their feet. My fist is clenched and I take another one down with a throat punch, which has the high-roller wheezing and falling to the floor again. I bend down, flick his mask off, and give him a nighty-night fist to the face, and his lights are out.

Ghost is charging after the last one left fleeing this room. I yell out to him to carry on searching for Whisper, when I see the girl's head on the table. *Fuck!* The five littering the floor are forgotten. My cane has rolled over to one of the snow-globed women, and I scoop it up and keep walking until I get to the table.

Whisper is staring up at the ceiling, her eyes unblinking wearing garish makeup and her fucking lips are sealed together. I hold my breath, unsure if she is even alive.

The gunshots and fighting are now just washed out murmurs to the drums beating in my head.

*Christ! Please be alive.*

Am I too late?

I sweep the food and flowers away from her chest, baring her naked breasts to me, the scar on her left shoulder a reminder. "Whisper. Can you hear me?" I watch her chest and can see slight movement. But are my eyes playing tricks on me? I tear my glove off, remove the blade I'm carrying and gently nick the ribbon until her lips are free. I lick my fingers, and hold them to her parted lips, waiting for the air to hit them. I feel a tingle.

"Whisper, honey, I'm going to lift you off this table and take you somewhere safe." I barely hear the moan in reply from her parted lips. A tear slides down her cheek when she slowly blinks as if it is a real effort.

"Darlin', it's me, Edge." I rip off my mask and hat to show her. "From the bar." All she can respond with is a moan like she's frightened and in great pain. I shuck off the rest of the costume revealing a black suit and white shirt underneath, so I can blend in with the sentinels if I needed to and not wanting to frighten her anymore than she already is. My weapons are now exposed. I quickly conceal them and clip the microphone inside the collar of my business shirt.

"Fuck, babe, what is it?" I talk low into her hair. "It's me. I came to rescue you as promised." I pull out her ragdoll and hold it in front of her face. A tear rolls down her face in recognition, but no movement. "I don't know what…" A bullet whizzes past me cutting off anything I have further to say, imbedding itself in the wall. I duck, pulling out my gun, watching the shooter's next move.

"Step away from the girl motherfucker and put your hands in the air. That's the only warning shot you're getting." He throws some handcuffs at my feet. "Put them on and you'll walk out of here alive." He keeps glancing at the two bodies on the ground near his feet. "What did you fucking do to Rose?" He chokes out in a European accent. Norwegian? Whisper said Mathias was Norwegian and he has a symbol on his right temple.

"Before I answer that, tear of your mask." He does without hesitation and I see he's got a symbol on his right temple. "We're playing for the same team, Mathias." I hold my hands above my head. I can't afford the time for this conversation or risk a stray bullet hitting Whisper. "And I didn't do anything. The female you know as Rose cut Cezar's head clean off in front of everybody with that sword she's still gripping, and then Filip-the-motherfucker shot her dead. All in the blink of an eye. I know who she is and her real name is Ruby Rose. No time to explain anything now."

His eyes keep shooting to Ruby's dead body. "What team would that be?" He's unconvinced and I don't even know if he heard everything I said, he looks lost.

I say Adam's contact's name which registers with him and he goes quiet. "Nicu is in here playing the same game as you." From the look on his face this is news to him. "I gather you two haven't had a chance to chat." He shakes his head. "There's a team of men with me to help get Whisper and the girls out safe. The other fuckers can rot. The gunshots you can hear are my people, and we aren't fucking around.

Now I wanna get Whisper off this table and to safety. If you are gonna stop me doing that, then we have ourselves a problem and I am gonna have to do something about it. I'm Edge and Whisper means a whole lot to me."

I straighten up, my gun still in my hand, but I don't need it. He's holstering his weapon and hurrying to the table. He doesn't seem to recognize my name.

I slide my arms under Whisper and try to lift her off the table. Her body contorts horribly, resisting my efforts, and a deeply wounded animal noise releases.

"She's restrained to the table," Mathias states the obvious.

*Shit.*

I gently lay her back and remove what's covering each hand, expecting ankle and wrist straps. The Norwegian is at the foot of the table, sweeping food and flowers away from her feet. And then we both stare in horror. My eyes fly to her face. Her mouth is open more, and a horrible noise is gurgling up.

Her hands and feet have been nailed to the wooden table with long, narrow bolts, each at angles to enable her limbs to be laid flat. The scented flowers were to combat the metallic smell from her wounds.

*"Jesus Christ!"* we both shout in unison.

"There's no way we can get these bolts out

without hurting her." Mathias looks around helplessly as he talks.

She whimpers in pain.

"What the fuck has he given her? Because it must be wearing off." I am frantic with what we can do.

"She's living inside a paralyzed hell." He curses again under his breath. "Check Cezar's body. He may have more of the drug on him."

I don't want to leave her side, but I get the fuck over there and start going through his costume pockets. There are two syringes.

I take no chances. I find the high-roller on the floor I throat punched and try to wake him up with a shake and a hard slap. When his groggy ass starts to come to, the Norwegian assisting by tipping a bottle of wine on his face to speed up the process. I raise my good foot, stomp down hard on his hand, and hear the snap of bone as he hollers like a baby. I jab the syringe into his neck and pump the juice into his veins.

*One one-thousand.*

*Two one-thousand.*

He's no longer hollering or moving, and his eyes are staring off into some happy place as if his body is paralyzed and no pain is being felt.

*Good enough for me.*

I hurry back over to Whisper. "Honey, I know you don't want this, but it will make you feel nothing until I can get you medical help." Another tear escapes, and she slowly moves her head down and then up a little. I kiss her on the forehead, and as gently as I can, I slide the needle into her neck and release the plunger, waiting for her eyes to stare at nothing. The horrible pained noises have stopped. I tuck Jenny inside my suit jacket.

I take my phone out and message Hazard.

**Me:** Help ASAP. Great room

I hear cursing again from Mathias. "The girls in the balls are starting to twitch, the drug's effects will be starting to weaken. We need to get them all out of here."

I check my watch. "We've got sticky bombs around the exterior of the house, and she's gonna blow in less than five minutes. I'll get the bolts out of Whisper," I tell Mathias.

"I'll get the snow coats and dump them at the main doors for the women." He rushes out the room then comes back with blankets and tosses me two of them. I can see his mind is totally fucked-up seeing Ruby dead.

"You've done enough, take Ruby's body and get out of here. We've got this covered." I tell him as gently as I can. I don't need him losing his shit.

"I'll meet you at the pier." Is all he says in reply and then he wraps Ruby in a blanket, the sword kicked away and scoops her up gently. "Rose was pregnant," he says sadly, and then he's gone.

*Fuck!*

# SLADE

## Taking Out the Trash

We've been sitting, waiting, watching, doing a perimeter check, and there only seems to be four guards lazily doing their job from the two positions. Night-vision goggles give us the eyes we need.

A single gunshot rings out from the house, putting us all on heightened alert and the four guards smarten their act up. When we see Hazard hold his arm up, giving us the all clear... it's on. I've given everybody a sticky bomb. At 9:22... *kaboom*, shit is gonna blow. Our mission, to get every woman out, anybody else is collateral.

I nod to Phoenix, who is dressed in black from head to toe, like we all are, and we head off at a fast-paced jog, our targets the two guards at the main door. Aim is to slap a sticky bomb down either side of the decking at the top of the stairs before taking those two bastards out.

Phoenix has already reached her man and roundhouse kicked him, sending him crashing to the ground before using a stun gun to knock him out, cuffing him and disarming him. All in the time I took to grab my stupid fucker around the neck and sleeper-hold him until his lights went out. Then he got cuffed, disarmed, and for good measure, I toasted him too. I signaled in the air knowing Drill and Billy were ready waiting to take out the trash.

We both look up at the sounds of struggle we can hear going on above us before heading off to the back access.

I check my watch.

# Lethal

## Bang! Bang!

**B**lueblood is a spider monkey the way he can climb things. He's launched himself over the opposite end of the balcony to me, and shot the first guard... *pow*... dead.

The message came in telling us Ruby was dead. He's not fucking around.

The second one takes off at a dash, making me give chase, and just before he tries to slide open the balcony door, he turns and pops one off in my chest, sending me horizontal.

*Bang!*

Lucky for us, we subscribe to Kevlar 101, and I have good reflexes, even as I'm going down.

*Bang!* You're dead motherfucker.

By the time Blueblood got my horizontal ass vertical again, we both knew we had to get moving, because time was a-ticking.

# VIKING

## Joke's on You

**V**iper, my brother from the same mother, has infiltrated the back access by shooting the shit out of the door until there is no resistance, bringing us in on the second level. We cover each other Mr. and Mrs. Smith style, back-to-back.

Tick tock we're on the clock. We need us some enemies as we not so quietly start kicking doors in. This place is bigger than it looks.

Door four reveals three perverts flamboyantly covered head to toe in Venetian carnival costumes. They are decked out in an array of rich fabrics and colors. From poo brown and gold, through to deep purple, silver and black, trying to get out of a bedroom's sliding door. Viper looks at me with an I-guess-this-will-have-to-do shrug.

We grab all three of them, hauling their asses backwards, and knock them onto the floor. Viper has his gun trained on them.

"Fuckers, show me your gloved hands. You're not worth wasting any bullets on." I cuff all three together back-to-back, and then we haul them to their feet.

"You wanted out? Let me show you the door." I slide it way open and we shove all three through until they hit the balcony edge. I knock the masks and feathered hats off their heads, revealing their nationalities on their stunned faces.

"What happens when an Asian, an Indian, and an..." I can't work out where the third fucker is from, "...walk out onto a balcony, handcuffed together?"

Nobody answers me. "Sheesh, rich fuckers normally have an opinion on everything." I wait another couple seconds. "This is what happens." I grab the first guy between the legs, getting a good grip on his balls while he squawks, and start to lift him up. I look at the other two. "I would be getting with the program, or you could lose your shoulder socket. Makes no diff to us." And then I toss pervert number one over, while Viper gives pervert number three a helping hand. Pervert number two just goes with the momentum.

I give Drill and Billy a sharp whistle, it's not like these fuckers don't know by now they're being infiltrated. Two sharp whistles boomerang back. They're also ready to catch any cockroaches who try to scuttle away. We head back inside just as the

lights go out and things go all *Doom* on us.
   Night-vision goggles are a go.

# HAZARD

## Boys and Their Toys

Bullets are peppering the kitchen area as Torque and I try to get to the one with the scar on his face we just chased in here.

Expletives are echoing off the walls as bullets spray the room, and we hunch down on the floor behind an island bar.

My phone vibrates, so I check the message. I keep my voice low. "Torque, get to the great room. Edge needs help. I got this little fuck." He nods and army crawls backward out of the kitchen.

"Heard you broke Whisper's wrist, fucker. Bet word has spread Cezar's dead. Don't look much like you're gonna walk out of here alive tonight," I taunt.

"Fuck. You."

And that's when the lights snuff out.

*Night-vision goggles are the fucking best.*

"Ready or not... here I come," I singsong like a child.

# EDGE

### Let it Blow ...
### Let it Blow ... Let it Blow

**T**orque comes running into the great room just as the power goes out. "I've got my goggles on. What do you need?"

I'm blinded by the darkness.

"Whisper is bolted to the table, Jesus-style. I've got the second bolt out of her hands. She's drugged and can't feel a thing, but we're running out of time."

Torque curses under his breath. "I've got her feet." I hear the sickening noises her flesh makes as he puts his all into pulling each one out. "Mother... fucker." Thank god that fucking drug is cocooning her from the pain. I may not have been able to take my time offing Cezar, but if there is a God, I'm sure Ruby is looking down pretty happy with herself. The bolts clank on the floor. "Done."

"Take the blankets from me, wrap her up carefully, and then head for the safety of the pier.

Keep her warm. We got less than two minutes. I'll be there shortly."

I call Drill and use the torch on the phone to lead the way out the great room. "Seven balls are coming down those steps fast. Get ready." I disconnect.

Feet come running. "Don't shoot us. It's Viper and Viking."

"In the great room, *STAT!* Grab a ball and coat from the main doors and roll that fucker down the stairs to the pier.

More feet come running.

"It's Hazard, Lethal, and Blueblood," Viking announces.

"We all heard. On it!" Hazard shouts.

"One and a half minutes," I call back. "Where's Slade and Phoenix?" And then the power comes back on.

Balls roll down the stairs with brothers chasing after them, trying to keep them under control.

"Less than a minute!" I holler from the rear. I can see Slade and Phoenix are at the bottom, ready to field the balls with Drill and Billy. "Let's hustle."

We make it down to the bottom. Torque is by my side handing me Whisper. I'm breathing heavily, the adrenalin keeping me warm as fresh snow starts falling. She's so small, smaller than when I last saw her in the trunk of Ebony and Ivory's car.

*BOOM!*

*BOOM!*

*BOOM!*

The explosions keep on coming as the sky lights up.

I carry Whisper farther out onto the pier, afraid falling debris will take her from me. That fucker and his home are going up like the Fourth of July. I do a headcount and can't find Adam or Ghost.

Drill and Billy have a combination of minions and perverts lined up on the pier. There are only a baker's dozen in total, all cuffed together in a row, shivering from the cold, while Lethal and the other men are unzipping the balls and pulling out naked, disoriented females and wrapping them in coats.

I sit down a couple feet away from Mathias who is quietly holding Ruby's dead body, staring out at the frozen lake. I'm careful not to jolt Whisper and cradle her in my lap. I can tell mentally he's washed out and he's beating himself up he couldn't have saved Ruby and her unborn child. I can't even begin to process all the emotions and questions I have there.

For now I need to concentrate on Whisper. "Boxer and Miss Catherine can't wait to see you." I dig my hand inside my jacket, pull out Jenny, and hold it over Whisper's unblinking eyes. I hope it will give her comfort as I gently place it inside the blankets close to her heart.

## CONTORTED

I rock Whisper gently, thinking about Ruby. I made a promise to Whisper I couldn't keep, but then that fucking Dean Martin song enters my head.

I quietly start singing, my version of course, as we all watch the fire consume the property.

"Oh, the fuckers inside are frightful
But the ire out here is delightful
And since you assholes have no place to go
Let it blow, let it blow, let it blow

Minions, the smoke won't be stopping
And I've got a front seat for popcorning
These fuckers are ready to roast
Let it blow, let it blow, let it blow

Cezar finally got what was owed
And his sentinels are baking in the glow
While the perverts sit real tight
The chopper will come right on by

My rage I'm still a fighting
And you motherfuckers, we're still goodbye-ing
As long as I hate you so
Let it blow, let it blow, let it blow."

My phone starts vibrating like it's dancing, pulling me out of my stupor.

**Boxer:** Three choppers incoming Ghost requested
He has Adam
Doc Evelyn will be in one if she's needed
How's Whisper?

*Where do I even begin?*

# Whisper

## Cliffhangers Are a Bitch

**I fight so hard to be heard.**
*Ba...by.*

It's all in my head. I work on moving my lips, like I've been trying to do when Edge told me I was safe.

"Ba..by."

It's barely a whisper, but I know I said it.

I try again, but my words are drowned out by Edge.

He's singing.

And then I fade out knowing I am safe.

My baby is safe.

Wow!
Thank you for reading the first three books in the completed series.

This series is a crazy ride. How are you holding up?
You are halfway. Well done!
But there are lots of twists and turns still to come.

**THE NEXT BOOK IS WAITING FOR YOU...**

I will love it if you continue reading on with
**ENTWINED #4**

I would appreciate it if you had time to please rate/review this box set on Goodreads and the other platforms you purchase from because I will LOVE reading your thoughts.

I won't lie; I did have a little cry when I finished this series. These characters, good and bad, consumed me.

I had such a great time writing this completed series you can read today without delay.

Thank you so much for taking a chance on me as a writer, and of course, Edge and Whisper thank you for taking the journey with them.

*Emma*

xxx

If you loved Slade and Phoenix,
be sure to catch up with them in

## The Men of Ocean Beach Series

# ACKNOWLEDGEMENTS

To my family first, nearly a year and we are stronger than ever. Love you all. xxx

It does take a small village of professional services and extra eyes to release a book.

Thank you to Najla Qamber of Najla Qamber Designs for re-covering the Hell's Bastard series. Your creative imagination and design expertise made these covers into something special.

To my lovely editors at Hot Tree Editing, Kayla and Becky, thank you for whipping my manuscript into shape and bringing the shiny. Kayla, I always love your comments.

Thank you, Max Henry for your patience and awesome formatting skills. I love working with you.

Thank you, Tina Louise for reading a small part of an early raw draft and Robyn Corcoran for proofreading the final draft. You ladies rock and I appreciate it greatly.

All the ladies in Emma James's Sisterhood, my closed group, you ladies rock and we have some fun in there. I always have a word-of-the-book for you to ponder with me. FUBAR was our word/abbreviation of Contorted and maybe 'onus'. *wink*

To the readers: Thank you for your patience and

understanding. Contorted took a little longer to release. It was admittedly a struggle concentrating due to the loss of our beloved son, but I won't release a half baked book. I will keep working through my demons until I have something I am proud of and can confidently entertain you. This is the third instalment and there is oh, so much more to reveal.

You can tell from the title things are going to heat up between Edge and Whisper in Entwined. I'm excited.

If you enjoyed any of my books, please consider leaving a review. I appreciate the time spent sharing your thoughts with others.

Until Entwined, I bid you adieu.

*Emma*

xxxx

# ABOUT THE AUTHOR

Hi there,

I'm Emma James. I was born in the Barossa Valley, a beautiful area of South Australia, and I am married with two teenagers and one in heaven. There is never a dull moment in my life and for this, I am truly grateful because life is too short to contemplate the what ifs. You'll never know unless you give it a try.

I certainly wouldn't have thought I could have self-published so many books...but I have. It has been the most amazing experience and a total uphill learning curve, but I fully embraced the challenge for the hard work that it is, and I am rather addicted to writing now.

I'm hoping some familiar faces are reading *Contorted* and also some new readers have joined in along the way. Many more stories are buzzing about in my mind, itching to be set free through my finger tips. I look forward to sharing them all with you.

I appreciate all of my readers and love hearing from you. I hope to bring you an escapism that stays with you and keeps you coming back for more.

# CONTACT

## YOU CAN FIND ME AT:

BookBub
https://bit.ly/2J4THac

Twitter
@emmajamesbooks

Facebook
www.facebook.com/emmajamesauthor

Instagram
www.instagram.com/emmajamesauthor/

Amazon
www.amazon.com/Emma-James/e/B00NH7AVGG

Goodreads
www.goodreads.com/author/show/8415027.Emma_James

Email
authoremmajames@bigpond.com

Emma James' Sisterhood
– Facebook Reader Group
www.facebook.com/groups/763744350386831

Emma's Newsletter
http://goo.gl/27pFQj

Printed in Great Britain
by Amazon